Rose Bud's

By
A.L. Stephens

Rock Creek Press

First Edition. Printed in the United States of America.

Books may be purchased in quantity by contacting:
alstephensbooks@gmail.com or Rock Creek Press at 541-580-4717

PB ISBN: (pbk.) 978-1-946353-13-9
PB ISBN: (EPUB) 978-1-946353-12-2

Books written by the author:

Emma Hart and the Demi-gods

Emma Hart and the Werewolves

Along Came You

Rose's

CONTENTS

CHAPTER 1

"What are you doing here?" I ask. Jason is standing in the middle of my living room.

"What am I doing here?" he snarls out. "What are you doing with him?"

"With who?" I ask, surprised by his question.

"I saw the way his hands were on you," he growls out in slurred speech. He sways a little and I see the bottle of alcohol in his hand.

"Who?" I ask again.

"Dax!" Jason shouts. "I thought it was Kallon I needed to be looking out for, but I should have realized he wouldn't go for you, he's a celebrity. But Dax, he's a no body. I should have known he'd try something with you the moment... the moment there was sign of trouble between us."

"There's nothing going on with Dax and me," I snap out. "He walked me to my door. He hasn't tried anything with me. YOU are the one who cheated, Jason. Not me."

Jason throws the bottle. I duck and flinch away and it hits the wall behind me. I reach into my pocket and grab my phone. I hit the first contact that pops up, I don't even look to see who it is. I put my phone down quickly and step back towards my door.

"You're mine..." Jason says in a menacing tone as he steps towards me with a look in his eyes I've never seen before. I instinctively put my hands out in front of me to stop him from coming closer but all that does is make him grab my wrists and he holds them over my head.

He pushes me back, forcing me to stumble backwards until my back hits my wall. I'm too startled to do anything as he transfers my left wrist into his left hand, to hold both of my wrists. He lifts my hands way above my head, stretching me out. I can smell the whiskey on his breath. His right hand goes around my neck, slowly squeezing until my air starts to get cut off and my eyes start to water. *It hurst so bad.* His lips are at my ear, and he growls out in a whisper, "You hear me... You. Are. Mine."

I can feel the blood pool in my face. I try to pull my arms away, but he holds on tighter. I try to use my legs, but he's got me stretched out so far that I'm on my tippy toes. He squeezes harder and holds it there for too long. I see black dots around my vision. Finally, his hand loosens, and I cough in a ragged breath.

Then his hand is sliding down my chest, pausing a moment to roughly press his palm against my breast. His hand only stays there long enough to cause me to gasp in pain before he moves it slowly to my hip where he grips it tightly. His thumb pressing hard against my hipbone causing me to gasp out in pain again. My shirt has risen just enough for my skin to be exposed.

He pulls my hips towards him while still keeping my

hands pinned to the wall, I can feel how turned on he is. He then slams my butt back, hard, against the wall and pins my hips with his thighs, his erection pressing into my stomach. I feel bile rising up in my throat at his actions, at his reaction to what he's doin got me. He leans his face forward, down to my ear, and growls out, "Mine."

"Jason," I say sternly. I don't yell his name or scream it. I say it loud enough for him to lean back and stare at me. The back of my mind takes note that it hurts my throat to talk. I see a small part of his sanity come back into his eyes, so I say with a little more authority, "Stop."

"No, you're mine!" he bellows, causing me to jump at his volume. He grinds into me harder. He kisses me roughly and his hand on my hip and wrists grip so hard I cry out in pain around his mouth, which makes my throat burn. He slams my hands into the wall, making me cry out again. He reaches with his right hand for the top of my pants, he gets the button undone and pushes them down just a little as he whispers again with that menacing voice, "Miiiine."

The hand he used to undo my pants starts to slide back up, groping and pressing as it moves. His fingers go through my hair and around to the back of my head, while his thumb is pressing into my cheekbone, hard enough to draw another gasp from me. He kisses me roughly and then his hand slides back down until it stops at my throat, he doesn't squeeze as tightly but as he presses his thighs and erection into me harder, his hand tightens. My brain starts to go into panic mode, but I calm myself down. *I have to keep calm if I'm going to get out of this.* I try a different tact with him.

"Jason," I say his name again, without feeling, as loud

as I can get with his hand squeezing my voice box. Ignoring the ache in my throat, my adrenalin takes over as I say slowly, "You're hurting me."

With that, Jason leans away from me and his eyes clear. He looks at his hand pinning my hands above my head and then down at his other hand around my throat. He looks into my eyes with astonishment, like he didn't know he was doing it.

"Abby... I—" he starts to say but I cut him off.

"Let me go," I say, holding my voice at a whisper.

Jason quickly releases me like I've burned him. He takes a couple steps back. He looks at his hands and then back at me.

"Abby—"

I again cut him off and put as much steel in my voice as I can, but it doesn't sound like me, it's hurts so bad to talk, "Get... out... of... my... house."

"Abby... please... I'm sorry, I didn't..." he takes a step towards me.

"Don't," I say putting up my hands defensively, my heart instantly racing. I flinch back even more into the wall. "Leave. Now."

"Please—"

"Leave!" I shout, raising my voice for the first time during this altercation, and I'm rewarded with a pain I've never felt before. It sears down my throat. I'm on the brink of freaking out and I can't let him see me break. The tears can come once I know I'm safe.

"I'm sorry," he says taking steps away from me. He walks backwards with his hands raised in a defensive way, like I'M the one that was just attacking him. When he gets to my front door he says, "I'll call you later… I'm sorry, Abby."

I don't say anything for fear that if I do, I'll burst out crying. I wait to hear my lock in the door click into place before I slip down the wall. The tears fall freely from my eyes, but I press my hands over my mouth to keep the wail that's about to rip from my throat, muffled. I can't stop it from coming, even with how painful it is to my throat. I scream into my hand as I slide down the wall, and lean over to the floor, curling into myself, into the fetal position.

I let the fear I kept at bay flood me. The fear of what Jason was doing, what he could have done. He could have forced me to... He could have killed me. Those two thoughts bring another shuddering scream out into my hands. Jason… my Jason for the last 9 years hurt me. He's never hurt me before. He's never acted like this before. I curl more into myself and let the tears flow. I cry so hard that I can feel myself starting to hyperventilate.

I've never had a panic attack before but if I had to guess, this is what it feels like. I'm shaking uncontrollably. I can't catch my breath long enough to pull more air in and my heart is racing. It doesn't help I can't stop crying. I faintly hear a door open, running footsteps. My panic flailing, thinking that somehow Jason has returned, but before I can open my eyes or move to protect myself, my panic attack pulls me into nothingness.

◆ ◆ ◆

"Abby?" I hear my name being called from a female

voice, but it sounds far away. "Abby. Please, wake up!"

Darkness pulls me welcomingly into its grip again.

◆ ◆ ◆

"Abby," a female voice says my name again, pleading.

I again hear the faint sound of a door opening and closing and heavy running footsteps. I'm not close enough to consciousness to say anything. I'm only able to hear from what feels like a long ways away.

"She won't wake up," the same female voice from a second ago says with panic.

"What happened?" a man's voice says. I mentally shrink away from it and let my mind protect me from what he might do to me. Nothingness pulls me down again.

◆ ◆ ◆

My ears start to work again, but it seems like my brain has to fiddle with my mental dials to make it make sense. Like one would do with a radio to make a channel come in clearer.

A female voice, the same as before, pleads, "Abby, please wake up."

The same male voice from earlier, says, "Yes, that's right. A twenty-five-year-old female, unconscious. She's starting to show signs of—" the man takes a ragged breath to calm himself down "—showing signs of bruising around her neck and wrists. She was found about fifteen minutes ago. —" he pauses

"—Yes, there's signs of a struggle. Papers scattered across the room and a broken lamp. I checked the apartment for the intruder, but I didn't find anyone. —" another pause "—No, no signs of that, she's still dressed. Listen, how far out is an ambulance? —" the shortest of pauses "—Forget it, I'll drive her in myself."

He stops talking and as the nothingness starts to pull me back, I realize it's Dax and Betty talking. It has only been fifteen minutes since I first heard Betty's voice? It feels so much longer than that. But then darkness pulls me under once again.

◆ ◆ ◆

When I become aware again, I feel more awake. Not only can I hear clearer, but I can feel and smell this time too. I hear a steady beeping sound, along with a distant murmuring of voices from further away. I can feel that I'm lying in a bed, a blanket tucked around my body in a tight way that's comforting. I feel my left hand is wrapped in a way I know without trying, that I won't be able to move it. My right wrist aches but it's not wrapped the same way. I move my head to the side, not opening my eyes but the movement shoots pain down my neck. I moan out in pain but that just makes it hurt worse. The only thing I can compare it to is the one time I had strep throat, only this hurts ten times worse. I breathe through my nose deeply, trying to calm myself and I smell the scent that only a hospital has. I hear the beeping sound picking up speed and add that with the smell, I come to realize that I am in a hospital room.

I slowly open my eyes and blink until the room comes into focus. Moving my head slower than I opened my eyes, to keep my neck from protesting in pain again, I look around the room. The blinds on the window are opened and I can see it's dark outside. I look the other direction and see the door is open enough for someone to slip inside. The murmuring I heard is coming from just outside my door.

I hear hurried footsteps and then a strained voice from in the hall says, "What's wrong?"

The door gets pushed open even more and Kallon steps in, followed closely by a nurse and then Betty, and then Dax. Another nurse is right behind those two, she hurriedly steps around and comes to stand in front of Kallon, her hand on his chest.

"Let us check her," she says to Kallon calmly. She hasn't seen that I'm awake.

"Abby?" Kallon says in a strangled voice as he looks at me, ignoring the nurse.

"I'm—" I wince. Fire… so much burning in my throat. Not just the burning but it feels tight like Jason's hand is still squeezing it. I raise my less injured right hand and put my fingers to my throat.

"Mr. Keller, let us check her out and get her more comfortable," the nurse that's standing to my left says as she pulls her stethoscope from around her neck.

"Abby?" Betty says as she walks up beside Kallon. One hand going to his arm and the other on her chest. She looks as if she's been crying.

"Bet—" I start to say but can't get a word out without my throat protesting.

"Please don't make me call for help to escort you three out," the nurse standing in front of Kallon says sternly. "I can see you guys care for her, but you aren't helping her by making her feel like she needs to talk, it clearly is hurting her to do so. Please, step outside."

"Come on, Betty," Dax says as he gently grabs her hand that's on her chest. His other hand touching Kallon's shoulder. He looks at me like it's tearing him up to leave. He says in a strained voice, "Mr. Keller, sir, let's step out in the hall so they can help Miss Rose. We should call the Rose's back and tell them she's awake."

Kallon looks at Dax, who nods down at the nurse standing in front of them, and Kallon looks at her like he's just now realizing someone was right in front of him. He looks back at me and then at the nurse beside me, then back to me.

"We'll be just outside the door, okay? We aren't leaving you," Kallon says with so much emotion in his words, my eyes start to tear up even more, this time not from the physical pain I'm in.

The nurse waits for Kallon, the last of the three, to step out into the hall. She shuts the door and then picks up the phone next to the door and only has to wait a couple of seconds before she says into the receiver, "Hey Dave, it's Stacy, can you come stand in front of Miss Rose's room? She's awake and her friends are eager to see her.—" pause "—Thanks."

She comes over to my right side, taking my hand, as the other nurse keeps checking my vitals.

"Miss Rose, my name is Stacy," she says with a warm smile. She nods to the nurse across from her and adds, "This is Cara. You're in Presbyterian Hospital. You've been here for about three hours, it's now 10:11pm. You're safe."

I go to say something but wince at just the thought of the pain talking will cause me.

"Don't talk," Cara says, patting my shoulder gently. I slowly look over at her. "You have some damage to your vocal cords as well as severe swelling and bruising."

My eyes go wide, I look back at Stacy, and her hold on my hand tightens a little.

"You're going to be okay," she says gently. "It'll take some time, but you'll be okay."

I look down at my hands and see my left hand heavily bandaged. I raise it and look at them with a questioning look.

"Quite a few of your small bones in your wrist have hairline fractures. Had the pressure been any harder or had your hand been slammed into something, it would have completely fractured them," Cara states calmly.

I raise my right hand that's bandaged lightly but has an ice pack lying next to it.

"Your right hand is just bruised but again, any more pressure and it would be in the same state as your left hand," Cara answers my silently asked question. She puts her stethoscope back around her neck and doesn't wait for me to quietly ask for any other injuries when she says, "You have deep bruising to your right hip, wrapping around to your buttocks. No other physical injuries were found."

I gently push my right elbow down into my hip and I'm rewarded with a throbbing pain. I close my eyes and calm myself. *How could Jason have done this to me?* When I open my eyes, I feel tears running down the side of my face.

"Oh, Miss Rose, you're going to be okay," Stacy says, as

she gently rubs my shoulder.

There's a knock at the door and a male nurse sticks his head in, "Cara, Stacy, the policemen and detective are back and would like to talk to Miss Rose now that she's awake."

"Dave, she can't talk," Cara says protectively.

"I'll let them know," the male nurse, Dave, says. He looks down at me and gives me a kind smile and adds, "Good to see you awake, Miss Rose."

I look at Cara questioningly again and she says, "The police came about an hour after you were admitted. We have to call them when we get patients who have been abused or attacked with or without a witness to tell us what happened. I'm guessing the detective is about to clock off for the night and wants to get at least a statement from you before he goes home."

"He's one of the good guys," Stacy adds. She fiddles with something next to my IV and asks. "Do you want your next dose of Percocet that the doctor approved?"

I gently shake my head no and make a gesture for something to write with. My hand aches at the gesture. Cara picks up the tablet she had put down when she came in and taps on it a second and then my TV turns on to a blank white screen. She hands the tablet to me.

"Type on this and we can see it on the screen," she says kindly.

I type:

Tylenol or Ibuprofen, please.

Stacy looks from the TV to me and asks, "Are you sure?"

I type:

Percocet makes me feel loopy and too tired.

"You need rest," Cara says gently.

I know and I will. I just don't want to feel loopy.

"Okay," Stacy says patting my shoulder. "We'll get you started with Tylenol and Ibuprofen. You'll need both."

Thank you.

"You're welcome," Stacy says with a smile.

There's a knock on the door and Dave pokes his head in again, "Hey, so a couple of things. The detective is insisting on coming to talk to her and her friends are asking when they can come in."

I type:

Please let my friends in.

"Are you sure you're up for it?" Cara asks.

I nod gently.

"Okay," Cara says. She turns to Dave and says, "Let them in."

Dave doesn't have to say anything, Kallon must have been eavesdropping at the door because he pushes the door open and side steps around Dave and comes to my side where Cara is standing. She smiles up at him and steps out of the way.

Betty is right behind him and comes to stand on my other side, Stacy steps away as well. Dax walks to her side. I see him put a supportive hand on her lower back, she leans into him slightly.

Cara says from the door, "We'll go get orders for your meds. Push the call button if you need us."

I nod once, carefully, at her to let her know I will.

"How are you feeling?" Kallon asks.

I point to the TV screen and write:

I'm ok. Throat, wrists, and hip hurt but I'll be fine.

"Is anything broken?" Betty asks with a hitch in her voice.

I raise my left hand and write:

Hairline fractures.

"Can you tell us what happened?" Dax asks in a strained voice.

"I'd like to know that answer," comes a male voice from the doorway. I look over and see a dark-haired man that's graying around the side by his ears and is wearing black slacks and a white button-down shirt. He has a badge hanging around his neck. He steps up to the foot of the bed and says, "I'm Detective Jones, Miss Rose. I have a few questions of my own if you don't mind answering them for me?"

I look at Kallon and then slowly look over at Dax and Betty. They nod at me, and gesture for me to go ahead. Knowing they're here and aren't going anywhere, I feel supported and safe.

I ever so lightly nod my head yes to Detective Jones.

"Is it true you are having trouble talking due to your injuries?" he asks as he pulls out a phone and grabs the digital pen from the side of it. He taps around on his phone and then looks up at me.

I nod and point at my throat. Betty, Dax, and Kallon all gasp. I look at Kallon and see he's clenching his jaw. His hands are in fists by his side. I don't look over at Dax and Betty but return my eyes to the detective.

"You're able to use the tablet to answer questions that need more than a yes or no answer?" he asks.

I nod again.

"Okay. Before I start my questions into what happened, at any time this becomes too much, you just let me know, okay?" he states kindly.

I nod.

"My first question is, do you remember what happened to you?" Detective Jones asks as he writes something down on his notepad.

I nod yes.

"Do you know who did this to you?" he asks, pausing his writing to look at me.

I write:

Yes.

I feel my eyes filling with tears. Betty squeezes my hand. I see Kallon's fists getting tighter at his side and I glance at him. I've never seen him so upset. The vein in his forehead is starting to pop out.

"Miss Rose?" Detective Jones calls my attention back to

him. My eyes fly to him. I must look startled because he looks at Kallon and narrows his eyes at him and then back at me. "Do I need to ask these men to leave the room?"

"What?" Kallon and Dax ask in shock, turning towards him.

I hurriedly type:

No! No! It wasn't either of them. They'd never. It was

I take a breath and look down at my shaking hand. Even after Jason did this to me, how can I still want to protect him?

"Abby please, tell us who did this?" Kallon asks with pain coating his tone.

Jason

Betty let's out a gasp and a cry and puts her hand over her mouth. She looks up at Dax and I see tears starting to run down her cheeks. He pulls her into a tight hug and holds her.

"Who is Jason?" Detective Jones asks and writes without looking.

Jason Phillips, my ex boyfriend.

"Has Mr. Phillips ever been violent with you before this incident?"

Never.

"This next question might make you uncomfortable

with current company. If you'd like, they can wait out in the hall until you've answered?" Detective Jones asks, looking at Kallon and Dax.

I see both men stiffen and act like they aren't going anywhere. I can't think of a type of question about my attack that would make me feel uncomfortable around them, so I type:

It's okay. They can stay.

"Okay," he says. He clears his throat and continues with his question, "There were no signs of sexual assault, but I have to ask. Did Mr. Phillips attempt to force you into any sexual acts that you did not want to participate in?"

Oh, that type of question, I think to myself, feeling my face redden for some reason. I see Kallon stiffen beside me and I see he's starting to shake a little.

I take a minute to think. *Had I not stopped him, would Jason have forced me to have sex with him? Would he have taken it that far?*

I type my internal answer on the screen for them to read:

I don't think so.

"What do you mean by that, Miss Rose?" Detective Jones asks after he's done looking at the TV.

I stopped him before he did anything.

"Do you feel like he would have?" Kallon asks. Detective Jones is about to say something to Kallon, but he sees me typing so he stops, and he makes a note on his phone.

I don't know. But it doesn't matter what I feel, because I stopped him from doing anything else than this.

I raise my wrists, point to my neck, and move my hospital gown over to the side just enough to show them my bruised hip. Kallon leans over to see and then he hisses and closes his eyes tight.

"How did you stop Mr. Phillips?" Detective Jones asks.

I got his attention by calling his name and told him to stop. That only made him angrier. He

I stop for a second and look at Kallon and Dax. I take a deep breath and then continue typing:

unbuttoned my pants and pulled them down a little and then ground into me harder. His grip got extremely painful. He didn't budge when I cried out. I got his attention again by calling his name and told him he was hurting me. He pulled away instantly and stepped back once he realized what he was doing.

"If you're willing and able, can you start from the beginning. If you can remember what time it started?" he asks as he taps on his phone.

"Is that necessary?" Kallon asks. "She'll have to relive it all over again so soon and not only that, type it all out."

"The sooner I get the full details of what happened, the better. And the more information she'll remember. The mind does funny things to unpleasant experiences, details might start to slip," Detective Jones had started off looking and answering Kallon but by the end, he is looking kindly to me.

I don't need to tell the detective that what happened will forever be burned into my memory. But I don't tell him that, I just type:

I don't mind but my hand might get tired.

I look up and see that they've all seen the TV. I look at the detective and he nods for me to go on. So, I clear off the screen and start typing as fast as I can with one hand, about what had happened the moment I walked into my apartment and found Jason standing in my living room.

◆ ◆ ◆

When I finish typing, I put my hand down on the icepack still lying by my thigh and let the coolness sweep through the wrapping. I squeeze my hand gently into a fist. It's really starting to hurt now. It wasn't just an ache anymore. The detective is writing furiously so I look at Kallon. I can see he's done reading but he's staring at the TV like he wished he could rip it from the wall. I look away from his upset face and look at Dax, only his face mirrors Kallon's. I look down at Betty and see she's not looking at the TV but crying into her hands.

I gently reach out to get their attention by hitting the railing of my bed with my fingernail. They all look at me and I look at Betty, raise my eyebrows and mouth, 'What's wrong?' to her.

"This is all my fault," she wails. She almost falls to the floor, but Dax catches her. Detective Jones grabs a chair nearby and brings it over to her to sit down on. I go to type but my hand protests. Thankfully, Kallon asks the question I was about to write.

"How is this your fault?" Kallon asks coming over to squat down next to her, Dax does the same thing to her right side.

"I... I came back to the shop to make sure everything was ready for the morning. Jason came to the side door, around 5 o'clock. He had flowers and candy. He asked if I'd talked to Abby after work. I told him no. He asked where you were. I reminded him it was family dinner night. He smiled and said he wanted to surprise you. He went through the kitchen and used the back stairs to go up. I called you but you didn't answer. I left a voicemail and a text. Just to give you a heads up he was here. I never heard back. And then when I got your call, and heard what was happening," she starts to cry harder. Then she adds through her ragged breathing, "I must... have missed you... because I wasn't... very far... away when I got... your call... I kept you on my phone... and I used... Maggie's phone... and called Dax... I figured he had... just dropped... you off... and was close by... as well... I got to you first... and then Dax showed up... a couple minutes later... He drove us here."

"This is not your fault," Kallon says.

"Not at all," Dax says rubbing her back, while rubbing

his hand over her knee.

I pull the tablet closer and type through the pain.

This is all Jason, Betty. No one is at fault except for him.

Dax pats Betty's shoulder and motions for her to look at the TV. It just makes her cry even harder. Dax looks at Kallon for help. Kallon shrugs and starts to rub her back.

"Did Mr. Phillips make it a habit to enter your apartment using the back entrance?" Detective Jones asks.

I gently shake my head no. Kallon stands and comes to stand next to me on my right side.

"Did he have access to your apartment? As in, does he have a key?" Detective Jones asks.

I again shake my head no.

Detective Jones makes a note and then asks, "Did he try to contact you before you arrived home?"

I wince as I type:

He called me a couple hours before, but I told him I didn't want to talk to him. He called back but I let it go to voicemail. I turned my ringer off. That's why I didn't get Betty's call or text.

"You two had broken up prior to this incident?" Detective Jones asks.

I nod. I look at Kallon and nod at him. He understands my gesture and turns to the detective.

"They broke up this afternoon. Just a couple hours

before…” Kallon trails off. He then adds, “She caught him with another woman.”

“Were you there, Mr.?” Detective Jones looks at Kallon. We all know he knows who he is but apparently he needs Kallon to say it.

“My name is Kallon Keller. And yes, I was there. We went to the Farmer’s Market and ran into Jason and his—” he looks at me “—his girlfriend. He didn’t try to explain what was going on, just that they were friends. He didn’t deny when the girl said they’d been together for about two years. We saw him kiss her and grope her ass. Abby told Jason they were over and she walked away. He grabbed her and I stepped up and told him to take his hands off of her. He did and we left.”

Kallon looks at me and I type:

That’s all correct.

“Okay. I think I have everything. Just one more question, Miss Rose. Do you want to press charges?” Detective Jones asks, pen at the ready

I close my eyes and let my brain fight with itself for a moment.

The side that still loves him says: *It’s Jason. He didn’t mean it. The look in his eyes when he realized what he was doing proves he didn’t mean to. He just got so upset. It was the whiskey’s fault. We know how he gets when he drinks that stuff.*

The side that is done protecting Jason says: *It doesn’t matter, he still did it. He’s proven he’s capable of hurting us. He came close to god knows what today. We can’t trust him.*

Love side: *We can’t just throw him to the wolves. Think of how that will make him feel.*

Done side: *He wouldn't have stopped whatever he was thinking of doing if we hadn't stopped him. He doesn't deserve us to consider his feelings.*

"Miss Rose?" Detective Jones calls me out of my internal debate. I open my eyes and tears are once again running down my face. He repeats his question but with more kindness, "Do you want to press charges?"

"There needs to be a paper trail," Dax states from beside Betty, who's still sitting in the chair looking just as upset. "If he does this again to someone else, it'll show that it's not his first time assaulting someone."

I know Dax is right. I close my eyes and take a steadying breath before I open my eyes and nod at Detective Jones.

"You want to press charges?" he asks to clarify.

I type out the three letters:

Yes

"Okay, I'll finalize my report and get the chargers drawn up," Detective Jones states.

"Will there be a trial?" Kallon asks, he already has his phone out.

"That will all depend on Mr. Phillips, his lawyer, and the judge. It depends on how he pleads as well. Also, if the judge comes down hard on him and Mr. Phillips feels like it's not a fair decision, they could appeal and go to trial," Detective Jones says matter-of-factly.

I just nod. Kallon rubs my shoulder while he absentmindedly texts someone.

"Just a heads up, the nurses will take pictures of your injuries to have as evidence," Detective Jones says as kindly as he can.

I just lean my head back, close my eyes, and nod.

"I think that's enough for today, don't you Detective?" Cara's voice comes from the doorway. I look up just as the detective is stepping to the side and I see Cara leaning against the door frame, holding a tray. I'm not sure how long she's been standing there.

"Yes, I think I have everything," he says. "Mr. Keller, would you mind coming out into the hall with me for a second?"

"Sure," Kallon says. I look at him and then at Dax. Dax watches for Kallon to signal if he wants Dax nearby but Kallon just walks out of the room, so Dax relaxes into his stance.

I tap my railing again to get Dax and Betty's attention but only Dax looks at me. I point at Betty.

"Betty, hon? Miss Rose wants you," Dax says sweetly to Betty. I'm going to have to ask him, the next time I can actually talk, if he's sure he's not interested in Betty.

Betty jumps up and comes to me, "Yes, Abby?"

I open my mouth and try to whisper, instead of talk, "It's... not... your fault. Please, stop... blaming... yourself."

I wince and lean my head back.

"Okay, okay, just don't talk anymore, you'll only hurt yourself more," Betty says, pushing my hair down on my head.

Cara walks over with the tray and says, "We got your Tylenol and Ibuprofen approved but we're going to give it to you through your IV so you don't have to swallow the pill. I'll bring in some warm broth and warm Jell-O for you to drink.

We'll test out some thicker foods slowly, just to see what you can tolerate. Stacy was grabbing another ice pack for your neck, it's time to ice it again. How's the ice for our wrist?"

I poke it with my pointer finger and fill that it's still full of ice. I hold up my thumb. Cara smiles and after she administers my medicine into my IV, she gently picks up my left arm and hand and checks it over.

"Can you wiggle your fingers for me?" she asks.

I try and I no sooner get my pinky and ring finger to move and my hand aches with extreme pain. I wince and pull it to my chest, out of her hand.

"Okay, okay, we won't test that again. I'm sorry," Cara says, patting my leg. "How does your hip feel?"

I shrug. I honestly forgot about it. I'm sure once I'm wearing pants, it'll remind me constantly that it's here too.

"I'll be right back with your broth and Jell-O," Cara says.

Kallon walks in a couple minutes later as he's hanging up with someone.

"Yeah, sounds good. Thanks," he says. He puts his phone in his pocket and comes to my right side again. "Everything going okay in here?"

I nod. Dax and Betty both say, "Yeah," at the same time.

I try to tilt my head to the side and look at him questioningly. He looks at me confused, so I grab the tablet and type out:

`What did the detective want?`

"Oh, he just wanted to take down my personal information. He asked for your phone number, I hope it's okay that I gave it to him?" he asks.

I raise my right hand and hold up my thumb.

Cara comes in shortly after and I tentatively take a drink of the broth. It hurts but more in the muscles having to work to get it down my throat type of a way rather than how it felt when I had strep all those years ago. I drink it down quickly and everyone chuckles at me greediness. I reach for the Jell-O and drink it down. I'm not sure what to expect with it being warm but it's not bad at all.

"I'll have the kitchen bring up some macaroni and cheese for dinner and see how that does going down, sound good?" Cara asks. Just then, there's a knock at the door and Stacy steps inside.

"Hi," she says. "I brought you another ice pack for your neck. And unfortunately, Detective Jones asked me to take pictures for their report."

I nod slightly and lean my head back, so they can get a better look at my neck. I hear my friends hiss and I wonder what it looks like.

"If you gentlemen could step outside, we're going to have to take a picture of her hip and we don't want anything to accidently be shown when we move her gown," Stacy says, waving her hands at Dax and Kallon, shooing them out the door.

Betty holds my hand as Cara moves my gown around so Stacy can get the best angle for a picture. After she's done taking what feels like one hundred pictures, Cara brings over the ice pack for my neck and carefully wraps it around me. I have to fight the urge to throw it off of me, but I remind myself it'll help the swelling go down. I lean my head back and close my eyes.

"Try to get some rest, we'll be back in about an hour with dinner. Push the call button if you need us," Stacy says. I peak through my eyelashes and watch the two nurses leave the room. Kallon and Dax walk in and shut the door behind them.

"Rest, Abby, we'll be here when you wake up," Kallon says from beside me. He reaches down and holds my hand. I squeeze back gently, hopefully he takes it as me appreciating him being here.

CHAPTER 2

I wake up in a panic, Jason is back, strangling me. I thrash my arms at him, they aren't being restrained this time.

"Miss Rose, it's me," a female voice says. A second later a light turns on and I see Stacy, the nurse, standing next to me.

"Oh," I squeak out and then grab my throat. I mouth out, *Sorry.*

"I should have woken you up before I removed your ice pack from around your neck. I'm so sorry for scaring you. Are you alright?" she asks.

I nod or try to, but my neck is extremely stiff. I wince in pain and reach my hand behind my neck and rub. My muscles are so sore.

She finishes taking the ice pack off, that I now realize is just warm water. She takes out her little flashlight and checks my eyes and takes my blood pressure.

"Can I check your neck?" she asks, pointing at me.

I nod slightly. I hold still as she touches and examines around my throat.

"The swelling has gone down a little but not much, and your muscles feel very tight. You'll be sore for a while, hon," she says with tenderness in her tone.

I make a motion to write and she grabs the tablet off the rolling table where my food from earlier had been sitting. She turns it on and makes sure the TV is on and then hands it to me. I look at the time on the tablet and see it's, a little after 4am.

I type out:

It feels stiffer this morning than last night.

"That could be from you straining during the altercation. The soreness shows up a while later, kind of like whiplash," she says.

Will I be jumpy whenever someone gets close to my neck forever now?

"Oh, hon, you've been through something traumatic. It'll take some time to work through it," Stacy says kindly.

Where are my friends and family?

"Your friends were sent home. Visiting hours were well over by the time you woke up. We let them stay long enough to see you wake up. They sure put up a fight when we told them they needed to go home. Your parents argued about who was staying with you, but we finally convinced them to both go home and get some rest. We assured them we'd call if anything changed. We also reassured them you'd be fine. They left and promised to come back first thing in the morning," she says.

She looks at her watch and adds, “Visiting hours will be in about four hours. I’ll be gone but the next nurses will be here.”

I nod and put the tablet down.

“Do you need anything else?”

I gently shake my head no.

“Okay, I’ll make a note on your chart to let everyone know they need to wake you up before they check your neck, okay?” she asks as she walks towards the door.

I nod slightly and then lie back down. She hits a button that turns the light off above me and I’m back in darkness, except for the light in the bathroom. I close my eyes and fall back to sleep.

◆ ◆ ◆

I get woken up by the smell of amazing coffee. I open my eyes and see Kallon and Dax taking seats in chairs in the room. I tap my fingers on the railings and wave at them.

“Sorry, did we wake you?” Kallon asks from the chair next to me. He scoots it so he’s even closer to me.

I nod my head a little and point at his coffee.

He chuckles and says, “Maggie sent one for you too.”

Dax stands and brings a cup from the table next to where he’s sitting.

“Don’t ask me what she called it, but she promised you’d like it,” he chuckles as he hands it to me. “You look better this morning.”

I roll my eyes and take a sip. The warmth is a welcome feeling to my throat and the taste… my eyes go wide.

"Good?" Kallon asks.

I look around and point to the tablet, someone had moved it. He grabs it from the table and hands it to me.

This girl better never leave me. She's twelve and can already make amazing coffee concoctions.

"She's learned from the best," Kallon says with a nod in my direction.

I slightly shake my head and take another sip.

"Does it still hurt to talk?" Kallon asks.

I nod. I happen to glance at the clock and see it's barely after 8am. Realization hits me.

I type quickly:

The movie set! The bakery!

"Don't worry," Kallon says, patting my hand. "Dax and I took the catering food over and got it set up. Stephanie said not to worry about having someone there, she'd keep an eye on it. Dax and I will go back to get it cleaned up at 10. Betty and Maggie are holding down the fort at the bakery. Your dad called Royce and told him what had happened. Royce and Bridget are taking care of Rose's tonight."

You aren't working today?

"No, it was a day I wasn't needed very much. I was able to take the day off," Kallon says looking at me and then he looks down at his cup.

You can't miss work just to sit in the hospital with me.

"Yes, I can," he says sternly. "And I am. Your parents will be here shortly."

Was Mom still crying when you talked to my dad?

"She wasn't happy," Kallon says.

I remember Mom and Dad coming into my room not long after I'd fallen asleep after Detective Jones had left. I was awake long enough for them to tell me they left Patty at home. She would have been a mess seeing me in the hospital. Mom was a lot like Betty, she couldn't stop crying. Mom and Dad couldn't believe Jason had done this to me.

I lean my head back and adjust the ice pack under my wrist, realizing it's a new pack. Someone must have brought it in while I slept. I turn my hand over and let the coolness work its magic on the top part. I look up and see the guys staring at me. I mouth out: *What?*

"How do your wrists feel today?" Kallon asks.

I shrug. My right wrist doesn't feel great, but I can at least move it. Which is more than I can say for my left. Just the slightest move of my fingers sends it into agony.

"Not great?" Kallon guesses.

I smile and give a little nod. I type:

I hate not being able to talk.

"I know but you have to give—" he takes a breath "—your vocal cords a chance to heal. He... hurt you pretty bad," Kallon says. I can see he's holding his cup tightly in his hands.

Do you know where my phone is?

"Your mom brought it after she went to your house to grab a couple things for you," Dax says, as he holds up a bag that's sitting on the floor next to him. "She also said she cleaned up."

Kallon and Dax share a look and then they look at me.

What?

"He did a number on your living room," Kallon says. He gulps, I can see his Adam's apple bob up and down. "I'm honestly surprised he didn't hurt you worse or..."

I didn't notice anything when I walked in. All I saw was him and that he was mad, really mad. How bad was it?

"There were papers all over the room. The broken bottle of whiskey. A lamp had been knocked over and broken. And an end table was on its side," Dax says.

The bottle I knew about but the rest I didn't.

"He must have done the rest before you got there," Dax says.

Any word on if the police have talked to him?

"Not yet, but Detective Jones said he'd let us know when they did," Kallon says as he pats my hand.

There's a knock at the door and Kallon looks at me. I nod at him, and he says, "Come in."

The nurse for the morning shift, Sue, comes in and smiles sweetly. She reminds me of my grandma.

"Good morning sweety," she says as she looks around the room. "Looks like you have a couple good looking visitors this morning."

I nod and smile at my friends.

"How are you feeling?" she asks. "I know I was just in here a couple of hours ago, bothering you, but alas, it is my job."

I'm okay. I think I need to use the bathroom though.

"Well then, let's get you up and give it a go," she says with a chuckle.

I sit up gingerly, and she helps me slide my feet to the side of the bed. I haven't realized how sore my entire body is until now. Sue reaches behind me and makes sure my gown is coving my backside.

"Don't need to give these boys a show," she chuckles again.

I look over at Kallon and see he's quietly laughing but his cheeks have turned a little pink. He's no doubt thinking of the folder of pictures he accidently picked up the other day. I shake my head at him and wince at the pain.

We make it to the bathroom and Sue gets me situated.

She leaves me to do my business, which thankfully I can do on my own. Once I'm finished, I wrap my gown around me and open the door. Sue makes sure it's still covering me and helps me back to my bed.

I grab the tablet and type:

`When will I be able to go home?`

"As soon as you can take pain meds orally, dear," she says as she covers me back up with a blanket, patting my hand.

`Can I try it now or whenever my next dose is due?`

"If you'd like to, but there's no rush," Sue says patting my hand again.

`I'd just feel better being at home.`

"I understand. I'll get the pills ready for your next dose which will be—" she looks at my chart "—in about an hour."

`Thank you, Sue.`

"Oh, no worries, deary," she says as she walks to the door. "Can I get you anything? Any of you?"

The guys tell her no thank you and I just shake my head. She nods and leaves the room.

"Are you sure you want to go home? Another day here wouldn't hurt anything," Kallon suggests.

It'll hurt my sanity. I don't like feeling cooped up and they come in every two hours to check on me. I'm tired and want to sleep in my bed. Plus, I'm not really hurt to where I NEED to be in here. I'm only hooked up to the IV because my throat hurts.

"Mmmm your throat is a little bit more than just 'hurt'—" Kallon uses air quotes "—You haven't looked at yourself in a mirror, have you?"

I shake my head no. He stands and looks around the room. He steps into the bathroom and comes out with a little mirror in his hand. He holds it out for me and I take it. When I look into it, I watch my mouth fall open. I touch my neck and run my fingers over what looks like a handprint from someone who had paint on their hand. Only, I know it's not paint, it's a big bruise. A dark purple bruise. I look at my eyes and see a little bruise on my left cheekbone and I touch it.

I look down at the tablet and type:

I don't remember this happening. He didn't hit me.

I take a minute to think. He never did hit me, but he had his thumb there when he was holding my head. I put my thumb up to it and type out my question:

Could it be from his thumb?

I look at Kallon and his eyes are shut, he takes a deep breath before he says through his teeth, "It's possible."

Are you okay?

I tap my rail to get Kallon's attention and then point to the TV screen.

"No, I'm not okay. You're hurt. Someone who was supposed to love, cherish, and protect you, hurt you," he says rubbing the back of his head with his hand. "I'm having a hard time not sending Trevor and Dax out after for him."

Kallon. I'll be fine. Yes he hurt me, but I'll be fine in a week or two.

"Abby," Kallon groans out as he closes his eyes. He opens them and leans forward. "He could have hurt you far worse than he did. He could have hit you. He could beat you to a pulp. He could have forced… He could have… killed you. He choked you so hard that he left the mark of his hand around your throat. He held your face so hard his thumb left a bruise on your cheek. The bruises on your hip…"

Kallon, we can sit here and talk about what he could have done, for hours. But the fact is, he didn't do any of the things we can think of. Yes, he hurt me, but he stopped. I'll take the little injuries that I have and be thankful it's not worse.

Kallon exhales but doesn't say anything else. He sips his coffee and looks down at his hands angrily. I look at Dax, but he has the same expression as Kallon. One that says, if Jason were to walk through the door right now, he wouldn't be leaving this hospital. I'm not going to make excuses for Jason, but I don't want the guys to be this angry.

I'm about to say something but I'm startled by a knock at the door. Surely it can't be Jason? Kallon looks at me and I nod again, a little more reluctantly this time after thinking about Jason walking through the door.

"Come in," Kallon says.

The door opens slowly and my mom's head peaks around. Her eyes find me and she beams at me.

"Good morning," she says as she walks in. Kallon and Dax jump from their seats and nod in her direction.

I type:

Morning, Mom.

"How are you feeling today?" she asks.

I'm ok. If I can take my meds orally, I'll get to go home.

"That's good news," she says as she takes the chair that Kallon is now offering her. Once she's sitting down, she looks at the tablet on my lap. "Still unable to talk?"

Yeah, that's still pretty painful.

Mom's eyes start to well up with tears and she sniffs out a, "I'm so sorry, Abbigail. I still can't believe this happened to you. How could Jason put his hands on you?"

By the time she asks her question, she's crying into her hands.

Mom, please stop crying. I'm going to be ok.

I tap my bedrail with my hand, but she doesn't look up from her hands. I look at Kallon and then nod my head at the TV and then at Mom.

"Mrs. Rose, Abby says, Mom, please stop crying. I'm going to be ok," Kallon relays what I wrote and puts his hand on my mom's shoulder. He looks at me and then at Dax and adds, "We won't let anything happen to her again."

Dax nods and walks over to the door and stands at attention. Taking on the role of a stationed guard.

Nothing else is going to happen to me. Jason will face his consequences for this and hopefully get the help he needs for his drinking.

I tap my rail again and this time Mom looks up at me. I point to the screen and they all look up at it.

Mom takes a calming breath and says, "You're right, he won't hurt you again because he won't come around you ever again."

I nod and put the tablet down. I situate my wrist on the icepack and let it rest for a minute. There's another knock at the door, but instead of asking, Dax opens it and looks out into the hall. He nods at someone and opens the door wider. My dad walks in carrying a drink carrier and a brown bag of something.

"Good morning," he says as he walks in and places the drink carrier and bag on the table.

I lift my hand up and give a small wave as Kallon and Dax

greet Dad with a good morning of their own.

"Did you find a parking spot okay?" Mom asks him.

"I did," Dad answers with a smile. He comes over to my bed and gently grabs my hand. "How ya doin', Buds?"

I smile at him and type out:

I'm ok. Should be going home soon.

"That's great news," Dad says. "We told Patty this morning what happened. That way if people at Rose's talk about it or ask her questions, she won't be blindsided."

Good idea. Is she ok?

"She was upset but calmed down after a bit," Mom says. "We dropped her off at Rose Bud's to hang out with Betty and Maggie."

"Speaking of Rose Bud's," Dad says as he reaches for the drink carrier. "I brought some coffees and pastries. Betty said that the guys stopped by on their way over already but, I told her one can never have too much coffee."

Thank goodness for that or I wouldn't have a business.

They laugh and nod in agreement. Dad hands the guys their cups and when he gets to me, he sets it down on the little table that's now sitting over the bed, above my lap.

Thank you.

"No problem, sweety," he says with a smile. "Maggie said she made all new drinks and hopes you like them."

I smile and type:

I'm sure I will. I liked the one Kallon and Dax brought in. How did Rose Bud's look when you were in there? How's Betty?

"It was busy but not overly so," Dad says thinking thoughtfully. "Betty was handling everything the way she always does, just like you. Maggie is quite the little barista."

I smile.

She sure is!

I take another sip from the coffee Kallon and Dax brought. I close my eyes and savor the taste. It tastes like a warm pumpkin muffin. Rose Bud's isn't like the other coffee shops, we have pumpkin flavored drinks year-round. I've had new customers become regulars just from their year-round love of pumpkin flavored coffee.

I hear a buzzing and open my eyes to see Kallon reaching into his pocket and pulling out his phone.

"Excuse me for a second," Kallon says. He walks to the door and steps out into the hall. Dax shuts the door after Kallon has taken some steps out of sight.

"Abbigail, honey, why don't you come home with us once your discharged?" Mom asks with a little trimmer in her voice.

I appreciate that Mom, but I want to be at home in my bed.

"You'll feel safe being back there? After all this?" she asks, waving her hand at me.

I'm not going to give power to Jason by being too scared to go home. I won't let myself become terrified of my home just because of one bad thing. It's my home.

"But Abbigail—" Mom starts to say but my dad cuts her off.

"Viki, if she wants to go to her home, she'll go home. I think she's right. She can't let this totally take over her life. If she doesn't go and face it, she may never want to," Dad says, going to stand beside my mom, placing his hand comfortingly on her shoulder.

"I just want her to be safe," Mom says with a sniff.

I am safe.

"Jason hurt you," she says, sounding both appalled and anguished.

I know that. And he won't be allowed into my home again.

As I finish typing, Dax says with regret in his tone, "No one will ever enter Miss Rose's home without my knowledge."

I hurriedly type:

Dax, it's not your fault. It's no one's fault except for

Jason's.

Dax just nods and goes back to being the ever-vigilant guard. I smile at him and slightly shake my head. I take another sip of my first coffee and find it's gone. I reach for the coffee my parents brought and take a drink.

Holy crap! It's delicious! My eyes go wide, and I look over at my parents and then over to Dax.

"Good?" Dad asks with a chuckle.

I nod slowly.

It tastes like a gingerbread cookie. How does she do it?

"Sounds like she's getting some holiday mixtures perfected," Mom says with a small laugh. She just doesn't sound genuine in her laughter at the moment.

There's a knock at the door and before Dax can open it, it opens, and Kallon walks back into my room.

"Good news and bad news," he says coming to stand at the foot of my bed. "That was Detective Jones. Good news, they found Jason this morning and took him in for questioning. They were going to charge him with 1st or 2nd degree assault… Aggravated Assault, but his attorney got it dropped to 3rd degree assault, which is the bad news. The detectives agreed, but only if Jason told them the truth and the whole story. They didn't really have to ask him any questions, he fessed up to everything. Even though he said he blacked out for parts of it, he still could remember being there and having his hands around your throat."

Well, that's something.

"It should have been more," Kallon says through his clenched teeth. "But part of his plea agreement is that he stays away from you, goes to rehab and must attend AA meetings for a year after rehab. If he misses one or comes near you, the plea goes out the window and he automatically gets charged with Aggravated Assault."

I lean my head back and relax. Jason is going to get the help he needs. Hopefully he'll get some counseling while he's in rehab too.

He must feel awful for what he did, to confess to it all.

"He better feel more than just awful," Kallon says again through his clenched teeth. He takes a breath and says, "What he did to you should eat at him for the rest of his life."

I don't write anything. I know Kallon is expressing his frustration and if I tell him to calm down, it won't do any good.

"You don't plan to talk to him, do you Buds?" my dad asks, pulling my attention away from Kallon.

If he reaches out, I'll hear what he as to say. Isn't part of rehab making amends? I won't forgive him for his benefit, I'll forgive him for me. So, I can fully move on from this.

"I guess you're right," Dad says when sigh. "I don't want you meeting him alone."

"I second that," Kallon says.

"She won't," Dax says with a nod at me.

`Overprotective`, I type with a smile. I don't get a smile from any of the men in the room.

Before anyone can say anything, there's a knock at the door. Dax opens it and steps to the side and Sue walks in with a cup in one hand, a bottle of water in the other, and a smile on her face.

"Medicine time. Shall we give the pills a go?" she asks walking up to the side of my bed. My mom gets up and Dad pulls the chair away, clearing the area for Sue.

I nod. Sue hands me the cup with my Tylenol and Ibuprofen and then opens the bottle of water and dumps it into my cup that has a straw.

"Take one pill at a time, just to make it easier to swallow, dear," Sue says patting my hand.

I nod and pop one of the pills in my mouth. I grab my water and take a bunch of water into my mouth. When I swallow, I about gag on the water because of the pain from the pressure of all that liquid trying to make its way down my throat. Water sprays out of my mouth and nose, and I cough which hurts, but I'm able to swallow the pill down, nonetheless.

"You okay?" Sue asks, handing me a napkin.

I nod and pop another pill, but I take less water. This time it goes more smoothly. I repeat the action two more times and beam at her once I have succeeded in taking all four pills without too much problem.

"How did that feel?" Sue asks.

Fine, once I figured out the amount of water I should use.

"I'll call the doctor and let him know you were able to successfully take your pain meds orally. He'll have your discharge papers to us shortly after that," she says, patting my hand and then checking my vitals one more time.

Thank you.

She winks at me and then leaves the room, patting Dax on the arm as she passes him at the door. He smiles down at her like a boy would smile at his grandmother. I look over at Kallon and see him staring at me. He has a look on his face like he's contemplating something.

What?

I type and point to the screen.

"Nothing, just thinking," he says and then puts a smile on his face that doesn't fully reach his eyes.

I look at him and squint my eyes at him, letting him know I don't believe him. He laughs and leans back against the wall. He crosses his arms across his chest and his biceps bulge. My heart races at the sight of his posture and embarrassingly, my heart monitor picks up on the chaos happening inside me. I look away quickly and reach for my coffee.

"What's the matter?" my mom asks, looking at my heart monitor and then at me. Kallon pushes off the wall and walks over to the other side of my bed, concern filling his face. He looks at my monitor and then down at me. I look at him and then my mom, and then at the monitor.

Must be all the coffee finally kicking in. I'm just sitting here, all the caffein isn't being used like it usually does while I'm working.

"Are you sure?" Mom asks, touching my arm. I just nod. None of them will ever know the real reason. *How embarrassing.*

I lean my head back, resting it on my pillow. All of sudden, I'm overwhelmed with the feeling of exhaustion.

"We'll let you rest, sweety," Mom says. "We'll go to your place and get things set up for you."

Not having the energy to ask her what things she's talking about, I just nod. She bends down and gives me a hug. Dad comes up next and squeezes me gently. They turn and head towards the door.

"Keep an eye on our girl," Dad says to Kallon. He looks at Dax as he walks by him, "Make sure she's watched over."

"We will," Dax and Kallon say at the same time.

My eyes are starting to close as I see Dad nod to both of them and then follows my mom out the door. I hear the scrape of chairs on the floor, and the sound of people taking a seat, but my eyelids feel too heavy to lift. Someone, probably Kallon, pulls the blanket up and covers me to my shoulders. A small smile spreads across my lips and then I'm drifting into the sweet blankness of sleep.

CHAPTER 3

I don't feel like I've been sleeping long when I feel a soft touch on my arm.

"Miss Rose, honey, I need to take your blood pressure one last time," I hear Sue's sweet voice say next to me. I pry my eyes open and look over at her. "I've got your discharge papers for you as well. Unless you've changed your mind and would like to stay another day."

I shake my head slightly and try to push myself up into a sitting position. Someone, probably Kallon, had lowered me down so I was sleeping on my back. Sue reaches for the controls to my bed and eases me back into the position I was trying unsuccessfully to achieve. I look around the room and see that Kallon and Dax aren't here.

What medication was I given earlier? I suddenly felt overly exhausted. I thought I was just taking Tylenol and Ibuprofen. And where did my friends go?

"Your chart said to give you your last dose of Percocet in pill form before discharge, just to help with the pain of moving around outside of the hospital. Once you get home, you should be able to stay on top of your pain with Tylenol and Ibuprofen," Sue says looking at my chart again. "Your friends said they were pulling the car around and getting lunch to take back to your place."

I see. I didn't know I was going to be given Percocet. What time is it?

Sue looks at her watch and says, "It's a little after 11 o'clock, dear."

I nod and let her get to her final assessment of me. She takes her time, checking my blood pressure, my oxygen levels, and flashes her little flashlight into my eyes. She asks to check my neck and I nod. She's very gentle and only touches where she needs to. Next she checks my wrists.

"You'll have to make an appointment with your physician to get another Xray done once the swelling has gone down on your wrists," she says as she lays my wrapped left hand down.

I nod and make a mental note to call my doctor this afternoon. She pulls the little rolling table back over to me that has the tablet sitting on it and puts my discharge papers on it and hands me a pen.

"Just sign the best you can, hon," she says sweetly.

I grab the pen awkwardly and sign my name, my wrist protesting at having to grip something. I set the pen down and smile up at Sue.

"I'll get everything in order for when your friends come back. They sure are good looking gentlemen and I can tell they care deeply for you," Sue says. She smiles and then adds, "Cara and Stacy asked me to get Mr. Keller's autograph for them, do you think he'll mind?"

I smile and shake my head. I grab the tablet and type:

I'm sure he'd be happy too. And if he protests, I'll get him to do it anyway. You all have taken such good care of me. Thank you.

"You are most welcome," she says as she walks towards the door. She waves and leaves.

I don't have to wait long for Kallon to return. He walks through the door, finally smiling.

"You've been discharged!" he says excitedly. "I bet you can't wait to get out of here."

I give him a thumbs up.

"Dax has the car parked close to the entrance, I'll call him on our way out and he'll meet us at the doors. You want to go now?"

I nod and go to get out of bed, but I realize I'm still in my gown. I pull at the front of it and look up at Kallon.

"Oh... probably don't want to go home in that," he chuckles. He walks over to the bag my mom had brought and brings it over to my bed. He helps me slide my feet to the floor and stands close by as I stand. I'm still pretty sore but I'm hopeful the more moving around I do, the better I'll feel.

I open the bag and find my comfy clothes. A pair of old sweats and a baggy hoodie, socks, and a pair of underwear and sports bra. I look up at Kallon, my face flush with embarrassment.

"Umm, I'll go get Sue," he says with his own

embarrassed sounding laugh. I nod and he leaves the room.

I dig in my bag and find my phone. I look and see it's dead. I'll have to plug it in when I get home. Kallon walks in a second later, closes the door, and his face looks concerned. As he walks to me, I tilt my head to the side just a little, in a gesture to ask what's up.

"So, there aren't any nurses at the nurse's station," he pauses for a second, looks at the door and then looks back at me. He adds, "I can help you change, or we can wait until someone comes back?"

My face goes red and I shake my head.

"I won't look, I can help you get dressed without seeing anything," Kallon says as he holds his hands up. He then laughs and says, "Although, I've already seen everything anyways."

I elbow him but I can't help but laugh also. He has seen everything, well, everything he'd see if he helped me get dressed. But this feels different than accidently finding pictures of me.

"But seriously, Abby, I won't look. I know how much you're wanting to get out of here. Me helping you will make it that much quicker," he says sincerely. He puts his right hand over his heart and says, "I promise."

I close my eyes and then nod. I open my eyes back up and mouth, *okay*, to him.

He nods and lets me choose what I'm putting on first. I decide to do my underwear first and then my bra. I'm pretty sure I can get those on while still wearing the gown, and it'll be just that much more coverage, so he doesn't accidently see anything, again.

I turn towards Kallon and I hold out my undies. I see

him visibly gulp as he takes them from me. He bends down and I place my right hand on his shoulder as I lift my right leg up so he can put my foot through the hole. We repeat for my left leg. Kallon starts to pull my undies up, his eyes shutting as he gets closer to my mid-section. His fingers graze the side of my legs ever so softly, I feel goosebumps spread across my legs. When my undies are pulled into place, I let the gown down. My right hand is now on his chest, instead of his shoulder. He's just so tall. I move my hand away and mouth a 'thank you' to him. He nods and takes a small step away.

Next, my bra. I turn and grab it, inwardly groaning at how embarrassing this is for both of us. I turn back and hold it up and shrug my shoulders.

"Umm," Kallon says and thinks for a minute. He finally suggests, "Why don't we put your sweats on first and then you can turn away from me, we take the gown off, and I can help slip this over your head, you can adjust the front, I can help in the back?"

I nod and put the bra back down on the bed. I turn to grab my sweats and wince. The movement was too quick and my neck protests.

"You okay?" Kallon asks, instantly at my side, his big hand on my right elbow.

I nod and grab my sweats, slower this time. I turn and hand them to Kallon. We put them on the same way we put on my underwear. Once we're done with the sweats, I grab my bra and hand it to Kallon, not looking at him. I turn so my back is facing him.

"Don't worry, Abby, you're safe with me, I won't look," he says reassuringly.

I nod and reach for the neckline of my gown with my right hand and pull it off. My breasts free for the world to see, my face heats with embarrassment. *I can't believe I'm standing in the same room as Kallon Keller with my boobs out.*

"Arms up," Kallon instructs kindly.

I raise my hands up and feel Kallon slide the material of my bra over my hands. He's being so careful not to jostle my wrists. He puts it over my head but it's a tight fight, it pulls my head in a bad direction, and I'm gifted with my sore muscles screaming in pain.

"Uggh," I moan out.

"What? What?" Kallon says as he stills himself.

I shake my head and whisper, "Just... get... it... on."

"Shit, Abby, I'm sorry," he says in a strained tone.

He slowly lowers my bra and as I try to adjust it up front with one hand, he fixes it in the back. I'm not as situated as I would like to be but at least my boobs aren't out anymore.

"Are you okay?" Kallon asks. He hasn't moved from his spot behind me. I nod and reach for my hoodie. His hand comes out and touches mine, stopping my movement. He grabs my hoodie and pulls it towards him. I see it coming over my head and once my head is free, I lift my hands slowly and put them through the arm holes.

"Better?" Kallon asks, turning me to face him finally.

I nod. Kallon runs his hands down my hair, laying all my crazy fly aways down, I'm sure. I mouth, thank you.

"No problem," he says as he walks over to where my shoes are sitting on the floor. "I'm sorry I hurt you."

I grab the tablet and type:

You didn't.

"I could tell something hurt you," he says as he kneels down to help me put my shoes on, my right hand going to his shoulder again.

It wasn't from you. Thank you for helping me.

"My pleasure," he says.

I softly smack him on the shoulder and try not to laugh, as it hurts if I do.

"I didn't mean it like that," he says. His face turning pink. "I… never mind."

I pat him, and when he looks up I raise an eyebrow, and tilt my head at him.

"Nothing," he says with a chuckle. He finishes with my right shoe and starts on my left.

"What?" I whisper out and try to hide the grimace from the pain.

"Nothing, I'll tell you another time," he says. He pats my left calf when he's finished with my shoe. "All done."

I type out:

Where's all the stuff I was wearing when I got brough in?

"Your mom took them home," Kallon says, picking up my bag. I put my phone in it and reach for it. Kallon pulls it away and says, "Nope, I've got this."

I look at him, about to argue but he throws it over his

shoulder and then offers his opposite arm to me. He smiles his infectious grin that makes me smile back, without meaning to.

"You don't play fair," I whisper out and wince.

"Shhh, don't talk," Kallon says with concern and a hint of humor in his tone, like he's taking a little bit of advantage of the fact I can't talk. I give him a fake glare and then take his outstretched arm. "Let's take it easy going down."

Just as we reach the door, there's a knock and it opens. Kallon and I stop walking and in comes Sue with a wheelchair.

"Oh no, no," she says with a tsk. She then chuckles and says, "You get chauffeured out of here, my dear."

My mouth pops open and I feel Kallon's body shake. I look up and see him trying not to laugh. He's staring at me. I shoot him a look that's supposed to say it's not funny, but it only makes him laugh out loud.

"I forget that it's hospital policy to be wheeled out," Kallon says, trying to be serious.

Sue pats the wheelchair and says, "Have a seat, deary."

I glare at Kallon as he walks me over to the chair and turn my attention to Sue but change my expression to a kinder one. I sit down and let her put my feet onto the footplates. She stands and pats me on the shoulder.

"Thank you," I whisper. The slight vibration in my voice box leaves me wincing.

"No thanks necessary, dear," she says with a smile. She looks up at Kallon and nods at him.

"It was nice meeting you, Ms. Sue," Kallon says. "Tell Cara and Stacy it was nice meeting them as well. If those papers I autographed for them, and you, aren't up to their liking, I can bring something else by."

"Oh no, Mr. Keller, what we have is more than enough. Thank you for taking pictures with us before they left," she says, touching his arm with a soft pat.

He smiles and nods at her and starts to push me out of the room. I look behind me and see that Sue is already back to work, stripping my bed and clearing off the tables. Nurses really don't get the credit they deserve for what they do for not only their patients but every patient in their department.

When we get to the elevator, Kallon pushes the button to take us down. I honestly don't even know what floor I'm on or where in the hospital I've been for the last day.

As we wait for the elevator, I hear Kallon from behind me tapping on what I think is his phone. I then hear him say, "Yeah, we're at the elevator. We'll be down in a couple of minutes.—" there's a pause "—Okay, thanks."

He hangs up just as the door opens. Kallon wheels me in and situates me so that I'm facing the doors again and he's standing behind me. The door closes and just as we start to make our way down, his hand brushes my shoulder. And an electric current runs through me and I try not to shiver. I hear Kallon inhale sharply and his hand hesitates for a second before he moves it away.

When we finally come to a stop and the doors open, I let out the breath I was holding. I hear Kallon do the same.

He whispers, "What is it about elevators?"

He said it so quietly, I'm not sure if he meant for me to hear and he asked it rhetorically, so I don't answer him. And honestly, I don't have an answer. Most elevator rides don't bother me, but this one, it was different. It no doubt is because of who I was in the elevator with alone.

Kallon pushes me forward and we head down more hallways. I finally see the signs that show us which way to go. It doesn't take that much longer before we enter a huge foyer and I see the main doors. I also see Dax standing just on the other side of the doors.

Kallon hurriedly pushes me through the doors and Dax takes the bag from him.

"Good afternoon, Miss Rose," Dax says to me. "You look like you're feeling a little better."

I wave and smile at him. I shrug my shoulders and gently tilt my hands side to side in the, 'meh' gesture. He smiles a kind smile and opens the back passenger door for me. Kallon comes around and offers me his hand. I take it and feel that same electric buzz like always.

"Miss Rose!" I hear someone call from behind us just as Kallon is about to help me into the car. I turn slowly, remembering how I hurt when I turn fast. I see Sue hurrying up to us. "I meant to give this bag to you."

She hurries over to me and hands me a bag that has the hospitals emblem on it. I look inside and see a couple ice packs for my neck and a couple for my wrists, as well as two wrist braces.

I look up at her and mouth, 'Thank you.'

"You shouldn't need the brace for your right hand but if it gets too sore because you over do it, it's good to have it for support. Icing procedure is in your discharge papers but be sure to ice your neck and wrists every night. Although, you should ice your neck every chance you get," Sue says as she walks backwards towards the doors.

I nod at her and again mouth, 'Thank you.'

Dax asks, “Can I take that and put it in the car for you?”

I nod and hand him my bag. I look up at Kallon and he smiles down at me.

“Ready to go home?” he asks.

I nod and smile back. He helps me into the car and then goes around to get in on his side so he’s sitting beside me. I go to reach for my bag, but I’m once again rewarded with pain. It shoots from my neck down my back. I lean back with a groan.

“What hurts?” Kallon asks worry coating his tone. I point to the back of my neck and down my back. He swivels in his seat and puts his hand on my back, that buzz shoots from his hand touching the middle of my back, down to my toes. He says gently, “Lean forward.”

I do as he asks and close my eyes. He starts to rub my muscles lining my spine from the middle of my shoulders down to my lower back. He takes his time, working each area for a good amount of time. He reverses his movements and starts to work his way back up. It hurts but in a good way. When he reaches the middle of my shoulders he pauses there and rubs in small circles.

“I’m going to rub your neck, unless it’s too soon for anyone to touch you there. If it’s too much, tap my hand, and I’ll stop, okay?” he says with kindness in his voice.

I nod slowly.

His hand works up to the base of my neck. When he gets to my neck, he works his way up half an inch, by half an inch. He’s taking his time, letting me get used to his hands being on me. Letting me understand I’m not in danger. I can feel my panic mode starting to activate but I take deep calming breaths, telling myself he’s not going to hurt me.

And then the other feeling takes over. It overrides the feeling of panic as soon as I acknowledge it. The electric buzz. It not only starts where his hand is massaging my neck, but in my stomach. It truly feels like butterflies are fluttering around, but they're electrified. My blood feels like it's a constant current of electricity.

Kallon gets to a spot on my neck that is especially sore. His skilled fingers work their magic, and a moan escapes me, I wince inwardly from the burn in my throat.

"That's the spot," Kallon says in a whisper, his mouth closer to my ear than I realized. An involuntary shiver runs through me. "I can feel a knot there."

I give a small nod.

"Sir," Dax says from the front, pulling me out of my daze. "We've arrived at Miss Rose's."

Kallon clears his throat and says, "Thank you, Dax."

Kallon slides his hands down my neck, to the middle of my back, and rubs one more time before he pulls his hand away. I'm left feeling cold and missing something. I lean back and unbuckle my seatbelt. When I go to reach for my bag again, slowly this time, I see that it's already gone. I look over just as Kallon is getting out of the car and see he's got it in his hands again, along with my bag from the hospital.

Dax is already at my door and opening it for me. He offers me his hand and I gingerly get out. By the time I'm standing on the sidewalk, Kallon is beside me. He wraps his right arm around my shoulders and puts his big hand on my right shoulder. He offers me his left hand and I take it in my left.

"Take it slow, walking will be a little stiff until your

muscles relax," Kallon says quietly.

"Sir," Dax says from behind us. We turn slowly and see he's putting a finger to his ear. "The area is clear."

"Thank you, Dax," Kallon says. "Tell Trevor and the others to take up posts. We're going to take her up."

"Yes, sir,"

I tap him on the hand and he looks down at me. I raise an eyebrow at him, a gesture I can do without any pain.

Kallon takes a deep breath before he says, "I hired a couple extra guys to make sure your safe."

My eyes go big, and I mouth out, 'What'. My eyebrows about to disappear into my hairline.

"It's Trevor, who would have been here anyways, and Mike and Paul. They are Dax's and Trevor's fill-ins if they're ever sick or need a day off or two," Kallon explains as we make our slow pace around my building.

I stop and look up at him incredulously.

"I know, hard to believe they get sick or need a day off, huh," Kallon says jokingly.

I glare for a second and then tilt my head, hopefully indicating that is not what I meant.

He understands because he says, "I'm sorry. I just want to make sure Jason doesn't try to come back, if he gets released on bail. He's shown we can't be too careful."

I look around, wondering now if Jason would really come back to hurt me again. I'm instantly hit with the feeling that he wouldn't. This incident was a one-time thing. The part of my brain that is done making excuses for Jason, screams that one time is one too many times. It's also saying that we don't know what Jason is capable of after he did what he did.

My internal voice sounds mocking at the last part and imagine myself rolling my eyes as I say it. *Maybe I'm going insane. I'm having a conversation with myself, imagining what facial gestures I'd do while talking to myself.* I shake my head, gently, and then continue our walking.

"You aren't going to argue with me about this?" Kallon asks skeptically. I look up at him with a glare and point to my throat. "You can't really argue right now, can you?"

I touch my nose and point to him. He understands and laughs a little. We reach my door where Dax is holding the door open for me. Three large men are standing next to him, I recognize Trevor.

"Miss Rose," Trevor says, looking at me. I know when he sees the bruise on my face, his expression darkens. *I'm glad he can't see my neck or hip*, I think to myself. I nod at him and give a small smile.

"She can't... talk still," Dax says to Trevor. He turns to me and says, "This is Mike Dawson and Paul Anderson. They'll be hanging around for a while."

I glare up at Dax and then turn my glare to Kallon. They're being overprotective. I turn my attention back to Mike and Paul and change my expression to a smile. I see them chuckle and look at each other before they look at Dax and then Kallon.

"It's nice to meet you, Miss Rose," Mike says. He's built a lot like Dax and Trevor. In fact, all four of the bodyguards look like they were made from a cookie cutter big man making factory. They're all about the same height and size. The only noticeable difference is their coloring. Mike is dark skinned with short black hair and dark brown eyes.

Paul, who nods and smiles at me but doesn't say anything, has very fair skin and red hair. His hair is the longer of the four but still cut short. His eyes are a pretty green.

"Let's get you up to bed so you can rest," Kallon says, gently pushing me towards my door.

As I walk by Dax, I touch his arm that's holding my door, and mouth out, 'Thank you.' Dax just nods. As we walk through, I turn and watch the door shut. I see Dax say something to the other three and they split up and walk away, Trevor going with Paul towards the main road, Mike going back towards where the alley is behind my building. Dax just turns his back and stands in front of the door.

I point it out to Kallon with my right hand and turn my hand over in a 'what's up' gesture.

"Dax's post is this door. Trevor's is the front door to Rose Bud's and the other two will take turns walking the perimeter and being stationed in the back at the loading door."

I whisper, "Not... all... day?"

"Shhh, don't talk. But yes, all day. I'm going to call Detective Jones and get an update. I want to know where Jason is at all times," Kallon says in a tone that tells me this isn't up for debate.

I shake my head and start to walk up the stairs, slowly. If he thinks I'm going to let this drop, he has another thing coming. As soon as my phone is charged and I can text, he'll get an ear full... well eye full because he'll have to read it, but he'll get my point, nonetheless.

We make it up to my door and I'm about to put in my code, but Kallon reaches forward and enters the code for me. I look at him with shock on my face.

"You told it to us when we brought you home, remember?" he says. He adds sincerely, "I'd never use it without your permission or without you present."

"Dax?" I whisper out painfully.

"Yes, he knows it too," Kallon says. "But like me, he'd never use it without your permission or in an emergency like yesterday."

My parents and Betty are the only ones I thought knew the code. I'm surprised Kallon and Dax paid attention enough to remember it, the handful of times they've come here with me. I've lost count how many times I've brought Jason here, but he never let on if he knew the code or not. Guessing he had to resort to using the bakery to enter my home, I'm going to venture a guess that he doesn't know it. That says a lot about his attention when we were together.

"Are you mad?" Kallon says as we walk into my place. I stop for second and look around. My heart jumping into my throat. It looks like my place. Everything is where it should be, the mess has been cleaned up. Even a new lamp was bought to replace the one Jason broke. I feel my breathing starting to come in in short bursts, my heart now racing. Kallon steps in front of me, bends down, and looks me in the eyes. "Abby, you're okay. You're safe here."

I give a little nod and take a calming breath and step further inside. With Kallon by my side, I walk over to my couch and sit down. Kallon sits beside me.

"Are you mad that Dax and I know your code?" Kallon asks again.

I shake my head no. Kallon is still holding my bag, so I put my hand out and point to it. He hands it over and I reach into it and grab my phone. My phone charger is still plugged in where I left it in the living room, so I lean over and plug in my phone. I try to lean back but can't, my muscles are screaming at me.

I whimper out a pathetic sound and grit my teeth. *I can do this.* I go to lean again but my muscles don't budge. I whimper again.

"Here, let me help you," Kallon says. He stands and kneels in front of me. He gently pushes my shoulders back so that I'm not leaning over, I'm now leaning back against the couch. He asks, "Better?"

I nod. A tear falls down my cheek.

"Oh Abby, don't cry, please," Kallon says, hurrying to sit beside me. He pulls out his phone and opens a note taking app and hands me his phone to me. "What's wrong?"

I type as fast as I can with my one hand and tell him:

I'm just frustrated. I can't seem to do anything by myself, and I don't want to be scared to be here, but I can't help reacting like I just did while thinking about yesterday.

"That's just it, Abby, it happened yesterday. It's fresh in your mind. It'll take some time to reassure yourself that this is your safe place. That what happened yesterday was a fluke and will never happen again," Kallon says. He gently pulls me into his side and wraps his big arm around me. I fight the urge to sigh into him. I fight the urge to let the electric buzz consume me.

I type out:

Thank you.

"Can I get you anything?"

No.

"Your next pain medication isn't due for another couple of hours, do you want to take a nap until then?"

Yes.

I go to hand him his phone back but then I realize something. I hurry and type out:

Weren't my parents going to meet us here?

"I think they were going to run by the grocery store and get a few things for you since you don't seem to have food in the refrigerator," he chuckles. "They said they left a big bottle of Tylenol and Ibuprofen on the kitchen counter."

I nod at him and go to stand. I turn and type on his phone:

I'm going to go lie down in my bed. Will you wake me in about three hours for my next dose?

"I can do that," he says. I hand him his phone and head to my room, ever so slowly. Kallon says from behind me, "Do you want help?"

I turn and see him standing, making to step towards

me. I put my hand up and wave him off. After my mini melt down about doing things on my own, he doesn't argue with me. He just takes a deep breath and sits back down.

"I'll be right here if you need me," he says, patting the couch cushion beside him. "Bang on something if you need me."

I smile and give him a small nod. I continue on to my room. It takes me a minute to sit down and get into a comfortable position. I carefully and slowly, move my pillows into a nest type shape and crawl into it. I lie down on my side so that I'm cradling two pillows, one in my arms and one between my legs. I don't have the flexibility right now to reach down and pull my blanket up to cover me without being shocked with a jolt of pain, so I opt for no blanket. I close my eyes and let myself fall to sleep.

CHAPTER 4

"What is he doing here?" I hear Jason yell. I open my eyes and see him standing over me.

"Who?" I ask, frantically sitting up in my bed.

"Kallon!" Jason bellows. "I knew it! I knew something was going on with you two. I didn't want to believe it but he's out on your couch, sleeping. What, he couldn't bother coming in here to sleep with you? To fuck you?"

"Jason, stop it!" I yell. "There is nothing going on between Kallon and me. We're just friends. I don't know why he's sleeping on the couch. I... I must have fallen asleep in here."

"Bullshit!" Jason screams. He rushes me and back hands me. I fall back on my bed and he's on top of me. I scream and I feel the pins and needles sensation in my throat.

"Jason, stop!" I scream again. This time it feels like my throat is on fire. Jason starts hitting me. In my face, in my stomach. His hand goes around my throat and he squeezes. I can't breathe. *He's going to kill me just because a friend is sleeping on the couch.*

"You. Are. Mine. No one else will ever have you," he

whispers menacingly in my ear. He then bellows, "ABBY!"

I thrash against him, trying to get him off me. I pull on his hand, but he just slaps me with his other hand. I pull and pull, trying to get him to let go.

"Abby!" Jason yells again, only this time it's Kallon's voice. I stop fighting and look at Jason. How is this possible? It's Jason but it's Kallon's voice, as he yells again, "Abby!"

I close my eyes and scream. I feel the fire in my throat and my muscles instantly lock up in pain. I feel tears rolling down my cheeks but now, his hand is gone from my throat. I can breathe. His weight is off me, only his hands are gripping my shoulders.

I stop screaming and take ragged breaths in, trying to catch my breath. I'm waiting for him to hit me or put his hand around my throat again.

"Abby?" Kallon's voice asks, full of concern. "Can you hear me? Wake up. Abby?"

Wake up? I think to myself. *I am awake, aren't I?* I open my eyes and see Kallon leaning over me with his hands on my shoulders. He's holding me securely but also in a gentle way.

I sit up, too fast. I cry out in pain. Kallon pulls his hands back and stands. He puts his hands out in front of him, defensively.

"I'm not going to hurt you," he says. "You were having a nightmare."

I look around my room, looking for Jason. I start crying from the pain in my neck, my muscles, and the remnants of my nightmare. I cover my face with my less injured hand and try to slow the hysterical crying that's about to rip through me.

"Abby," Kallon says choking on my name. I look up and

see him wanting to come to me. I reach out to him and he's instantly on my bed and gingerly pulling me into him. He pushes pillows away and arranges me so I'm cradled under his arm protectively. "I've got you. You're safe. No one is going to hurt you. He is never going to hurt you again."

I'm exhausted from my nightmare and the fight I had in my mind, so I drift back to sleep immediately.

◆◆◆

"Abby?" I hear my name being called softly by Kallon. "Abby?"

"Mmm," I moan out and then wince. *Shit, when is this pain in my throat going to go away?* I think to myself quickly.

"It's time for some medicine," Kallon says gently. He then asks, "Do you want me to go get it and bring it in here?"

I shake my head a little and try to push away from him to sit up but my muscles protest. I must have been thrashing in my sleep during my nightmare, my whole entire body aches. I let out a whimper and fall back against Kallon.

"If you'll let me, I'll carry you out to the living room," Kallon says.

I don't really have any other choice. I don't want to be left alone, I want to be in Kallon's, well anyone's, presence at the moment, so I nod against his chest. He carefully eases from me and stands. He then effortlessly reaches down and picks me up. The surge of electrification that ricochets around inside me almost makes me gasp. He holds me tightly against his chest and walks out of my room, down the hall, and into the living room.

He's so gentle with me that I don't feel a thing when he lays me down on the couch. He walks quickly into my kitchen, and I hear my fridge door open and close, and then a rattle of bottles as he walks back to me.

He sets the two bottles of over-the-counter pain killers on the table in front of me and a bottle of water. He also has a cup of pudding in his hand. He sits and opens the pudding and holds it out to me.

"Your parents stopped by while you were sleeping, before your nightmare," he clarifies before I can panic that they were here during or after. "They brought in a lot of soft foods and soups for you. I think you should eat something before you take your pills. Even with them being over the counter, it looks as if they got you the long-lasting kind. So good news, you'll get some decent sleep before your next dose is needed."

I smile at him. I take a small, tentative bite of the pudding and swallow. It slides down easily enough. I take another bite. I hadn't realized how hungry I am. Before I know it, the pudding cup is gone.

"Do you want me to heat up some soup?" Kallon asks, taking the cup from me and putting it on the coffee table. I shake my head no and point to the bottles of pain relief. He sighs and grabs the bottle of water he brought out and opens it. He hands it to me and then opens the two bottles of pills and dumps out two of each into his hand. "It's a little after 1 in the afternoon. If you don't wake up until around 7, I'm afraid I'm going to have to play nurse and wake you up so you can eat something. Getting rest is important, but so is eating and drinking lots of fluids. Getting dehydrated will only make the healing take longer."

I nod at him as I take the first pill. It doesn't take too long before I've gotten all four down. I take another sip of water, to show him I don't want to get dehydrated either. I hand it to him and he puts it on the table.

"Do you want me to take you back into your room?"

I shake my head no and lie down on the couch, my head on the cushion. Kallon runs from the room and returns a very short time later with pillows from my bedroom. He lifts my head and puts one under it. I smile up at him in thanks. I lift my left hand and he takes the hint and puts one underneath it. He looks lost as to what to do with the last one and looks at me. I shrug, so he puts it on the chair next to the couch. He pulls the blanket off the back of the couch and puts it over me. He then sits down by my feet. He pulls my feet into his lap and starts rubbing them one at a time.

"Do you want to watch something on TV?" he asks as he picks up the remote. I shake my head no and close my eyes. I just want to sleep. He says, "Okay, I'll just put something on for background noise."

I don't hear what he chooses, I'm asleep before the TV has time to turn on.

◆ ◆ ◆

I wake up to the amazing smell of fettuccini alfredo. I take a deep breath in, savoring the smell. I open my eyes and see Kallon sitting where he was when I'd fallen asleep. I try to look over my shoulder into the kitchen, but I can't move without the pain returning.

"Royce brought over your favorite for dinner," Kallon says with a smile.

I sit up carefully and stretch my neck and back. I stand slowly and walk over to my phone and as I grab it, my screen lights up, telling me it's charged. I have so many messages and voicemails, I don't even know where to start.

I head into the kitchen. Kallon stands and follows behind me. I open my text messages and see I have a message from just about everyone I know. I click on the first one, it's from Kayla, and read her texts, from her most recent down to the first worried one she sent yesterday.

Kayla: I talked to Momma Viki. She calmed my nerves… a little. If I don't hear from you soon, Peter will have to tie me down to keep me from driving to see you.

Kayla: Oh, my gosh! If it weren't for Peter stopping me, I was about to get in my car and drive up to New York and have a word with Jason! How could he do this to you! Are you okay?

Kayla: Just got off the phone with Momma Viki.

Kayla: CALL ME! Please!

Kayla: Are you ok? Momma Viki called as she and Papa Stephen were on their way to the hospital, she didn't tell me what was wrong. Just that you were hurt. She's going to call me back once she finds out what's happened.

I send a response.

Me: Hey… I'm home. I want to say I'm fine but I'm not. I'm hurt pretty bad. Not just physically. I think I'm still in shock because I still can't believe Jason would be capable of this. I can't talk, my voice box is damaged but the doctor and nurses all said I should recover, it'll just take time. Kayla, my neck is bruised so bad. It looks like someone dipped their hand in red paint and then grabbed me. :-(

I hit send and then go on to the next message. It's from Stacie, not the nurse, this one is a bartender at Rose's.

Stacie: Hey! I heard what happened! I hope you're ok.

I send out a quick text to her, letting her know I'm okay and that I'm home resting now. I read through most of the other texts and they are similar to Stacie's. So, I do something I don't usually do, I copy and paste the same response to all the other texts. I don't think I've ever had so many texts to reply too. I appreciate all their thoughts and concern, but I don't know how to phrase, 'I'm okay. I'm home now and resting' any other way. I save the other text's for later and decide to send Betty a more in-depth text.

Me: Hey, I'm home. You probably already know that. My phone was dead and I took a nap while it charged. How did things go today? Thank you for all your help! I truly, TRULY appreciate you!

I open mine and Royce's text history and respond to his differently as well.

Me: Hey Royce, thanks for the food! How are things going there?

I look up to start scooping some fettuccini on to my plate, but I see that Kallon has already done it. He's putting water in my electric teapot and then goes and gets a bottle of water out of the fridge and walks back over to me. He looks up and smiles, I can't help but smile back.

"You're fingers and hand are going to get tired with all the texting you're doing," he says with a chuckle. He then becomes serious and says, "You had a lot of people worried about you."

Me: My hand and fingers better toughen up, who knows how long I'll be using my phone to communicate.

Kallon reads the text and laughs, then says, "That's true, but I think you'll be talking sooner than you think."

Me: What's with the teapot?

After a quick look at his phone, Kallon answers, "You should drink as much warm liquids as possible. Warm water isn't the best tasting, but it'll help your vocal cords. I could make you some broth or warm Jell-o, your mom picked up both at the store."

Me: Oh, that's a good idea. Warm water is fine. I actually prefer it to be a little warm, instead of ice cold.

"I remember," Kallon says with a smile.

Me: Don't get me wrong, a nice cold glass of water taste good on a hot day or after a long day working in the hot kitchen but ninety-five percent of the time, I like it to be at least room temperature.

"I've never known anyone else who likes warm water over cold," Kallon says with a small laugh and a shake of his head. I point to him with my eyebrows raised. "Yeah, I prefer warm water too. I can drink more at once."

I smile and nod my head. The teapot beeps that it's ready so Kallon pours me a cup of hot water.

"Do you want to go sit down and eat?" Kallon asks as he tries to pick up both plates of food with the mug of water and the bottled water.

I put my phone in my sweats pocket and step forward and grab the plates of food. When he looks down at me, I smile and nod my head towards the dining room. It looks like Kallon is going to say something, probably argue with me about picking up the oh so heavy plates, so I start walking, not giving him a chance to say whatever it is he's wanting to say. Even though my hurt wrist protests a little, it's not painful enough for me to hand the plate over to him. I hear him huff out a breath but then I hear him walking behind me.

I get to the table and put our plates down. Kallon puts our drinks down and sits. I take one noodle into my mouth and it instantly salivates at the flavor. I chew it slowly, turning it to mush. I brace myself as I swallow but it doesn't hurt. I smile over at Kallon and take another bite.

"Not bad?" Kallon asks as he twirls his fork in the noodles and proceeds to put a huge bite into his mouth. I unintentionally glare at him. I catch myself and laugh inwardly.

I shake my head no and put another bite, much smaller than Kallon's, into my mouth. It tastes so good! After having hospital food, which wasn't bad by any means, but this, I've said it before and I'll say it again, over and over, Royce makes the best fettuccini alfredo!

We sit in silence for a while, both enjoying the delicious food. I take a sip of my hot water, glad to see it's cooled down a little. It really does make my throat feel better, it's very soothing. I feel my phone vibrate in my pocket, so I fish it out.

I see Kayla is calling and just as I'm about to answer, she hangs up. I look up at Kallon and shrug my shoulders. I go to our text to see what was up, but I see the three little dots, signifying she's typing out a message. Her first text has me smiling.

Kayla: Shit! Sorry, you can't talk! I'm texting you what I was going to say when I called you.

Me: Lol it's ok.

While I wait for her text to come through, I eat more of my food. I feel the table vibrate from my phone.

Kayla: First off, I'm sorry this happened to you. Second, I'd love a chance to throat punch Jason, and see how he likes not being able to speak, swallow, or anything like that. Third, what happened that he freaked out like that? Alcohol? I know you said that had been steadily getting worse.

I feel tears welling up in my eyes.

Me: Yeah, I believe it was mostly the alcohol because he was drinking, but also because he was so angry and feeling guilty. Yesterday was the worst day ever. I had asked Jason if he wanted to hang out, but he said he had a meeting. So, I decided to go with Kallon and Dax to the Farmer's Market. We ran into Jason and HIS GIRLFRIEND while we were there. The girl told me they'd been dating for about two years. I told Jason we were through. We left. I went to my parents for Monday night dinner and when I got home, Jason was there waiting for me. He showed up while I was at dinner, Betty didn't know about us breaking up. She said she tried to call and text me, but my ringer was off. Apparently, Jason had trashed my condo while he waited for me to get home. I only remember him and what followed. I didn't have time to look around the house before he was on me. He had a bottle of alcohol and threw it against the wall behind me. When he was close, it's all I could smell. I'm pretty sure it was on his clothes, but his breath smelled of nothing but alcohol.

Kayla: GIRLFRIEND!? What the actual hell?!

Kayla: Girl, how freaking scary! I can't even imagine how that was for you. I'm so sorry!

Kayla: I'm sorry he cheated on you. I'm sorry you found out the way you did but I'm the sorriest he hurt you, in more ways than one. At least you know now and can start a new, different life without him.

Me: How do I stop loving him? Even after everything, I still feel like I love him.

Kayla: It'll take time. Your heart will catch up to your brain. Because you do see how unhealthy he is for you, right?

Me: I do, I just wish my heart would hurry up and see it too.

I take a sip of my water while I wipe away a tear. I have to get my heart and brain on the same page.

"What's the matter?" Kallon asks. I jump a little, I'd gotten used to the quiet. I type him a message, he's already got his phone on the table.

Me: Just talking to Kayla.

Kallon looks up from his phone and his eyebrows are crunched together. He asks, "Is everything okay?"

I send another text.

Me: We're talking about Jason and what I'm going to do about him.

Kallon's hand squeezes his phone momentarily but when he looks at me, he looks totally at ease.

"What you're going to do about him?" he asks. I look down at my hands, seeing the left one wrapped and the right one slightly puffy. He clears his throat and says, "You don't have to talk to me about it if you don't want to."

I realize he'd taken my silence the wrong way.

Me: Oh, no, no! I don't mind talking to you. I actually enjoy it. :-) Umm… Kayla just mentioned that my heart needs to catch up to my brain on the understanding that Jason isn't healthy for me.

"Your heart… meaning you still love him?" Kallon asks with disbelieve in his tone. "You'd let him back into your life after what he's done?"

Me: Yes, I still feel like I love him. Part of me is debating on giving him another chance if he goes through all the steps he's supposed to with his plea agreement. Rehab, AA. The other part of me is screaming at myself to let him go, that part is my brain.

"We can love things that aren't right for us," Kallon says softly.

Me: I know. It's so hard for me to be strong when it looks like he's taking steps in the right direction. In a healthy direction. He'll be sincere when he apologizes. He always says the right things and I believe him. If he's willing to change…

"I haven't known you for very long, but I know that you feel that way because you have the biggest, kindest, most loving, and forgiving heart out of everyone I know. I hope you can be strong if he does try to weasel his way back in because Abby, guys like Jason don't change, he's set in his ways. He only keeps you on the hook because he knows how great you are, but he also has his side piece or pieces because he doesn't know how to love someone like you and he's selfish. You are his rock when he messes up, at work, with you, with life in general. He knows how much you love him, he knows you're forgiving, which is why he's always sincere when he apologizes. He means it in the moment, but he doesn't mean it deep down. But just know if he does work his way back into your life as your boyfriend, or whatever he is, I'll be here for you."

I want to argue with him. I want to tell him that Jason isn't like that, but I take a quick minute to think and come to the conclusion that Kallon is right. He's known us for a short amount of time, but he can see the real Jason. He's not blinded by years of forgiveness and skin-deep apologies. I lean over and lay my head on his shoulder and hug his arm. I pick up my phone and send a message.

Me: Thank you. You are quickly becoming a good friend.

"I feel the same," Kallon says into my hair.

I sit up and start eating again. It doesn't take long for my food to vanish. I was starving. I drink the rest of my, now lukewarm, water and stand to take my stuff into the kitchen.

"Nope, you go rest," Kallon says. "I've got this."

Me: You know how to do dishes?

Kallon shoots me a disbelieving look and says, "Of course I do. I might have a housekeeper for every place I own but I still know how to do things for myself. My mother would be appalled if I didn't."

I quietly laugh and relinquish the dishes to him. His answering smile leaves me speechless, even more than I already am. I head to the living room and snuggle into the couch with the blanket and pillows. I pull out my phone and go through the rest of the texts. The last person is Jason. My heart rate picks up speed, I sit up out of my relaxed pose and swipe up to the first text he sent yesterday and read from there.

Jason: Please let me explain.

Jason: Abby, answer your fucking phone!

Jason: Talk to me please! It's not what you think.

Jason: ABBY!

Jason: She's just a friend. Yes we've slept together but it didn't mean anything. She said what she said to piss you off.

Jason: I'm coming over.

Jason: Where are you!?

Jason: Are you still with HIM?

Jason: I'm at your place waiting for you. Where are you?

Jason: ABBY!

Jason: Anser ur fking phon!!!!!!!!!!!!

Jason: Pleas Abbsy, I just wanna tlk.

Jason: I'm so sorry!

Jason: Please Abby, forgive me for what I did. I didn't...

Jason: I didn't mean to. It was the booze. I'm sober now. What I did early, I... It sobered me up quick and made me really look at myself. I'll never be able to take it back but please forgive me. I didn't know what I was doing. I'm so sorry,

Abby. I love you.

Jason: I just talked to a Detective Jones. I'm meeting him at the police station with my lawyer. I'll do whatever they tell me. I'll prove to you that I'm sorry and that I'm going to change. Please don't give up on me, I love you.

Jason: I made a plea bargain but before I signed it, I asked the detective how you were. He went into detail. I am so unbelievably sorry. Sorry doesn't even begin to express how sorry I am. I broke your wrists? You can't speak? The bruises around your neck... I... I don't even know what to say except it was the alcohol. You know how I get when I drink. I'm done with it. I'm never touching the stuff again. I'm not going to see Deven and Shane from work, they are bad influences, and they won't understand why I'm sober. They won't be supportive. You will be, though, right? I know I have a lot of making up to do and I'll do it all. I'll do anything and everything you want. Please, Abby. I love you.

I can tell by his spelling mistakes when he was the drunkest. I click out of the texts and go to voicemails. I'm both on the verge of crying but also ready to throw my phone across the room. *Holy shit!* I have twelve voicemails from Jason. I shake my head and listen.

ANSWER YOUR PHONE!

Don't fucking hang-up on me! You know how that pisses me off! I'm calling back, answer the call.

ANSWER YOUR PHONE!

Fine, if you don't want to talk, I'll talk. Val is just a friend. She said we've been together for two years to get a rise out of you. Yes, I've slept with her, but it was an accident. It won't happen again. We can work through this.

You haven't answered any of my text or called me back so I'm coming to your place so we can talk in person.

Where are you? Betty was in the bakery. Where are you? Still with that dickhead Kallon?

*Abbbbbbbbby wheres are you? I have a bottle of good booze here waiting for you to sample it. We can have some shots and talk this out. *hiccup* I'm a couple shots ahead of you *laughs drunkenly* but you can catch up.*

It's undeniable how drunk he is, I continue with his voicemails.

*Abby! Abby! Abby! Calllllllllll meeeeee. *laughs drunkenly**

*Ares you fuckinging him right now to get back at me? *hiccup* All it's doing is pissing me off thinking of him *hiccup* with his hands on you. Call me so I know you aren't *hiccup* sucking him *hiccup* off.*

*I just tried you again but *hiccup* you're still not answering me.... Abbbby... plllease... Oh, wait I see you walking around the corner.... *hiccup* What the fuck! *hiccup* That big ass bastard Dax has his *hiccup* hands all over you. I thought it was Kallon... but nooo... Dax. *hiccup* What the actual FUCK ABBY!*

Hey, Abby... it's me, Jason. I am so sorry about earlier. I don't know what happened. I blacked out or something. One second I'm watching you being walked to the door by Dax and then you were in your apartment and then nothing, nothing until I snapped out of it and saw my hands around your... your... neck. I had you pinned. I don't remember any of it. I'm so sorry. Please forgive me. I love you.

I just sent you a text, but I wanted to call you as well. You aren't wanting to talk to me and that's fine. I wouldn't want to talk to me either. I just want you to know that I made a plea bargain and I'm going to follow it to a T. I want to prove to you that I'm the man you fell in love with all those years ago. I want to show you that I'm still me. I'm never drinking again. I'm going to do better. I'm sorry. I love you, please don't give up on me... on us.

I take a deep breath and decide to keep all of his voicemails as a reminder of how quickly things went bad. I go on to the voicemails from my mom.

"Hey, honey, it was good seeing you tonight. Don't worry about Jason, things will work out the way they are supposed to."

"We just got the call from Betty. Forget that last voicemail, Jason is dead to us. How dare he lay his hands on you! I have half a mind to call his mother. In fact, I'm going to do that right now. We're on our way to the hospital. Hang in there, honey, we love you!"

I laugh inwardly at my mom's last voicemail. A small piece of me hopes she called Jason's mom, but a bigger part of me knows it won't do any good. The other voicemails are a lot like the texts I received. All of them concerned and sending me well wishes, and asking what they can do to help.

I let out a big breath just as Kallon is walking into the living room.

"You okay?" he asks. "Pain killers wearing off already?"

I shake my head no and then decide to show him Jason's texts. I open them back up and hand my phone to Kallon. He's quiet for a minute. I watch his facial expressions turn from outrage to resigned.

He hands my phone back, pulls his out of his pocket, and says, "You haven't responded."

Me: I don't have a response.

"Hmmm," Kallon says as he reclines back into the couch, he puts my feet back on his lap so that I'm stretched out.

Me: What?

"Nothing," he says. I push his leg with my foot and raise an eyebrow at him. "Okay.... Can I tell you what I got from those messages?"

I nod.

"To me, I don't see any apologies. I see excuses. I don't see him actually taking responsibility for what he did. He shucks off the girlfriend and cheating like it doesn't matter. He puts the blame on her but when she told you how long they've been together, I saw sincerity in her eyes. She looked regretful and scared that they got caught but she didn't look like she was saying it to make you mad. He doesn't apologize for what he did and leave it at that, he continues to blame it on the alcohol."

Me: You don't think he'll learn to take responsibility once he's in rehab and AA? The 12-step program will help him see what he's done is wrong.

"I think he'll learn how to apologize better but taking responsibility for one's actions and truly making amends... I don't know. If he doesn't already know how to take responsibility, he'd have to change a hell of a lot for me to believe he's capable of that. You sound like you've already forgiven him? Without him doing any of the work."

I look at him and grit my teeth. I type out angerly:

Me: I have NOT forgiven him. I can't help but hope that he changes, even if we don't get back together. I still want the best for him. I want him to, someday, find a girl that makes him want to settle down, even if it's not me. I want him to be in a better place so that she doesn't have to go through what I've gone through. I want to forgive him for myself but I'm not there it.

I take a breath to calm myself. I'm not really mad with Kallon. I'm just upset that he can see through Jason so easily.

Me: I do see you're point. He's always apologized like that. An apology wrapped up to look nice but it's just crap. Like I said before, he knows what to say to sound like he's sincere. I'm glad you can see through him, I'm a little envious of it.

"I'm here to help," Kallon says jokingly.

Me: I'm going to need your help standing my ground, so I don't let him in so easily.

"I'm here for you," Kallon says, putting his hand on my foot and giving it a gentle squeeze. I smile at him and then a yawn escapes me. He asks, "Are you tired?"

I nod and hold up my right hand and tilt it side to side in a gesture to mean, 'a little'.

"Close your eyes and rest. I'll wake you when it's time for more medicine," Kallon says, adjusting the blanket so it's covering more of me.

I do as he says as I lean my head back and close my eyes. Before I know it, sleep over comes me.

CHAPTER 5

The next couple of days go by in what feels like one big mushed up day. Sleeping was my number one activity which is why it probably feels like one long day has passed. I would stay awake long enough to shower, eat something, drink some warm water, take my medicine, and then fall back to sleep.

Kallon, Dax, Betty, and my parents have taken turns being here with me. Kallon and Dax ended up staying the night, every night since I was brought home. I finally talked them into sleeping in my guest rooms after they had awkwardly slept on my sectional couch the first night.

I secretly wanted someone to stay in my room with me, I was terrified of having another nightmare, but I had told myself I needed to get over it and suck it up. I couldn't have someone in the room with me forever, so learning to deal with it was the only way. I luckily haven't had a nightmare since the first night.

My parents would come sit with me during the day while Dax maintained his post by my front door, until nighttime then he'd come inside. Kallon had hired a nighttime watch crew so that the daytime guys could get some rest. It took me getting fierce with my texts with Dax for him to relax at night.

Betty would relieve my parents of their babysitting duties after she was done down in the bakery. She relayed well wishes from my customers and they even sent get well cards, balloons, and flowers. The second day, Maggie took a whole hour of comforting to reassure her I was going to be okay. She never left my side, every time I woke up, she was sitting in the oversized chair next to my head where I slept on the couch.

Stephanie was checking in with me daily, reassuring me that the movie set was just fine the way things were being worked out and told me not to stress about it. That, I must thank Betty for as well. Not only was she holding my bakery together, but she was making sure the baked goods for the movie set were ready for Trevor and Randy. They would take them if Kallon wasn't ready. Kallon was usually picked up as soon as Trevor got back from taking Randy over to the studio. Kallon insisted he wasn't needed on set until mid-morning, but I have a feeling he'd made them rearrange some things so that he was assured that I was okay in the mornings before he left.

When Kallon would get back from filming, Betty and Maggie would go home. The second day I tried to tell them to head out at 5. I told them that with Dax at the door and the guys at their posts around the building, I was safe. Betty told me it wasn't about me being safe. She knew Dax and the guys had that covered, but it was about having someone here if I needed anything. Having someone so I didn't feel alone. I tried to argue with her but there's only so much arguing that can be conveyed through text. There was a moment when she wouldn't even look at her phone. I had glared at her and just as I was about to try to talk again, she shook her head and read my text.

My bruises haven't gotten any better, if anything they've gotten worse. The one on my cheekbone is a dark purple and sensitive to touch. But if someone thought that one was bad, they better keep their eyes from traveling down to my throat. That bruising has turned from angry red to a dark purple, blue color. My muscles are still sore around it, but my voice is slowly coming back. I can whisper without too much pain. I think it's because I haven't been forcing myself to talk the first couple of days and have been drinking warm liquids like crazy. I've been gently testing my vocal cords a couple times a day but still text when I need to talk to someone.

I step out of the shower and I look at myself in the mirror while I brush my hair. My bruise around my hip is still the same as my throat, purple and blue. As with the other bruises, this one is sensitive to the touch. I've been living in sweatpants and high waisted leggings so that my pants don't put much pressure on it. I wrap myself in a towel and walk into my bedroom, then into my closet. I grab a pair of underwear and a bra, and another pair of sweats and a long sleeve shirt and head to my room.

As I'm getting dressed I hear Betty holler down the hallway, "Kallon's here!"

I finish getting dressed and head out of my room to the living room. When I get there, Betty and Maggie are putting on their shoes and Kallon is answering a question Betty must have asked.

"Yes, I promise. Steph says everything is great. You don't

have to worry so much about it," Kallon says with a smile.

"What's wrong?" I whisper as I get close enough that I know they'll hear me.

They turn to me with surprised looks.

"You can talk?" Betty says excitedly.

"Sorta," I whisper.

"How does it feel?" Kallon asks as he walks towards me. I see that he still has his film makeup and hair do in place. He must have come straight here from the set. He's been going home and showering and then coming here. He has a black duffle bag sitting by his feet.

"Okay," I say. I elaborate with, "Exhausting."

"It's taking all your energy just to say single words?" Betty guesses.

I nod.

"Why don't we save your voice a little longer," Kallon suggests. "Texting us has been working fairly well, don't you think?"

I nod my head yes and then bob it side to side in a, 'I guess', kind of way. I pull my phone out and text him my question that no one has answered yet.

Me: So... what's wrong?

Kallon grabs his phone out of his pocket and reads quickly and then says, "Nothing is wrong. Betty has just been worrying about the set. She was asking if Steph was wanting someone to be on set or if us taking the food has been working out well enough. I told her Steph isn't concerned at all about someone being there, she just wants you to get better."

Me: I'll be back next week.

"Has your doctor cleared you for that?" Kallon asks, looking pointedly at my wrapped hand. I shoot him a glare. "I didn't think so. Don't you have a checkup appointment on Tuesday?"

I glare at him again before I type out a response.

Me: Yes... my appointment is on Tuesday. And..... no, I haven't technically been cleared to go back to work yet....

"Well, then, you won't be going back until he gives you the all clear," Betty says with finality in her voice. I look at her with a shocked look of betrayal on my face. "Don't look at me like that. If you come back to work too soon, you could ruin any type of progress you've made. We've got it under control. You just worry about getting yourself completely healed."

Me: I'm so bored though. I've slept so much I think I'll be good on sleep for the next year.

Betty looks at her phone and laughs. "Well, you can catch up on reading and TV shows."

I look at her with a disbelieving look.

She laughs and gives me a hug while she says, "I better get Maggie and myself home. Please text me if you need anything."

I nod when she steps away from me.

"Bye Kallon," Betty says with a wave as she walks to the

door.

"Bye," Kallon says with a smile.

Maggie gives me a hug and then walks to her mom. Maggie looks upset about something. As they walk through my front door, I send a text to Betty asking what's up with her.

"How was your day?" Kallon asks, pulling my attention from my phone.

"Good. Slept," I whisper.

Kallon points to my phone and says with an exasperated laugh, "Text me. Don't waste your precious progress on me."

I roll my eyes and type out a response.

Me: My day was like yesterday. A lot of sleeping. How was your day? Why are you still in your makeup and hair?

After reading the text quickly, Kallon says, "My day was good. Got through quite a bit of filming, so that's nice. I'm still in makeup and hair because I wanted to work as late as possible today and I didn't want Betty to have to wait for me to go home and shower. So, I thought maybe I could borrow the guest shower tonight?"

I try not to picture Kallon Keller naked in one of my showers as I text a response. I can feel my face heating just enough it would be noticeable if I looked up at him.

Me: It's all yours.

Not sure my face has cooled yet, I keep looking at my phone. Which is when I see a message alert from Betty.

Betty: Maggie is just worried about you. She's afraid something is going to happen to you while we're gone. I can't blame her, I'm worried too.

Me: I'll be fine. Nothing is going to happen.

Betty: Just please, let us know if you need something.

Me: I will. :-)

"Everything okay?" Kallon asks. I look up and see concern on his face. The good thing about Betty's texts, it was enough to take my mind of him in my shower.

Me: I asked Betty what was wrong with Maggie. She said she's just worried about me, they both are. I told them I'm fine, which I am. I promised to let them know if I need anything.

"She's a good friend," Kallon states.

I nod. There's a knock at my door. Kallon looks at me and I nod again.

"Come in," he says. He's not worried about who it might be with Dax and the guys outside. No one, meaning Jason, could get past them and then knock at the door if it was someone meant to harm me.

Dax opens the door and walks in. He's got his arms full of paper bags. I raise an eyebrow at him when our eyes meet.

"Mr. Keller thought Chinese food would be a good change of pace tonight," Dax answers my silent question.

I look over at Kallon with both my brows raised now.

He smiles and says, "I thought you might like a change in food. Soup and pasta can start to taste the same."

I smile and nod. I have started to get tired of it all. The soft foods were nice at first, but my throat is starting to feel almost back to normal. I just needed to rest my vocal cords a little bit more.

Dax walks over to my dining room table. Kallon and I follow. We each unload a bag and open the containers. My eyes bulge at the amount of food now sitting out. I look at Kallon and wave my hand at it all.

"I wasn't sure what you could handle so I got a little bit over everything. Dax and I can eat whatever doesn't feel good to your... throat," he says. He still clenches his teeth anytime he mentions my throat.

I grab my phone from my pocket and reply.

Me: Thank you for this but you don't have to over buy just to make sure I have more than enough to eat. I can always chew something into mush before I swallow.

"I know," is all Kallon says. Before I can argue, he hands me a paper plate that came in one of the bags and says, "Dish up."

I stare up at him, but he just smiles at me. I don't take the plate and he puts it down on the table.

"Okay, yes I shouldn't over buy but I just wanted to make sure you have options. You've been stuck eating soup, pudding, Jell-O, and pasta for the last couple of days. I wanted to make sure you could try an assortment of things tonight," Kallon says as he offers me my plate again.

I shake my head and take it from him.

"Too. Much," I whisper.

I hear Kallon chuckle, but I also hear Dax's sharp intake of breath of surprise.

"Yeah, she's testing herself," Kallon says as he looks at Dax and then back down to me. "I've told her to text, so she doesn't ruin her progress."

I roll my eyes at Kallon but then smile over at Dax.

"It's good to hear your voice, even if it's in a whisper," Dax says with a smile. He then adds, "But Mr. Keller is right, you should save every last bit of progress you have until you are completely healed."

That earns Dax his own eye roll, which makes him chuckle. We dish up and then find a seat around the table away from the containers of food. We don't say much as we dig into our plates. I find that eating the Lo Mein goes down smoothly but I have to chew the veggies and meat a little extra. But the flavors? Oh man, they're just what I needed!

I close my eyes and let a small moan escape and I'm happy to find it doesn't hurt, too bad.

I open my eyes and look up and see that Kallon has his fork halfway from his plate to his mouth and he's staring at me. I'm reminded of all the other times he's looked like this while I've been eating. I put my hand that's holding my fork to my mouth and raise an eyebrow and try not to laugh. He's still staring, so I raise both my eyebrows.

He slowly puts his fork full of food in his mouth and looks down at his plate, shaking his head. I put my fork down and shoot him a text.

Me: What?

Kallon looks at his phone that's to the side of his plate and shakes his head, but I see his face turn a little pink under his tanned skin.

Me: I know it's not polite to eat with my mouth open, but I'm pretty sure I had it closed. Do I have food on my face?

I take a napkin from the pile, also from the same bag the plates were in, and wipe my mouth.

Kallon laughs out loud and says, "No, you were perfectly polite."

Dax looks up from his food and he looks from Kallon to me and then back to Kallon. He shakes his own head and goes back to eating.

Me: Then why were you staring at me?

"I'm just happy you're enjoying your food again," Kallon says with a lopsided smile that makes my heart stutter. I'm about to ask him what he means but his phone starts to ring. He looks down at it and then picks it up and says, "Excuse me a minute."

I nod and he stands and walks out and down the short hallway towards the guest rooms. After a minute of staring at the empty doorway, I go back to eating my food.

Dax's phone chimes and he looks down at it and a small smile crosses his face. I don't feel comfortable enough to ask who it is. I never know what is socially acceptable when it comes to someone getting a text or call and asking who it's from. I turn my attention back to my food and eat as much as I can. Out of my peripheral vision, I see as Dax picks up his phone and types away.

I've finished my first helping of food and I'm scooping more noodles on to my plate when Kallon walks back in. He sits down, puts his phone by his plate, and starts eating, but I notice he has a worried look on his face.

Me: Is everything ok?

He glances at his phone and a smile instantly clears his worried expression. He looks at me and says, "Yes, everything is fine. Why?"

Me: You just looked worried.

"Oh, just some business things. Change of plans that I don't know how they'll be received. I'm hoping well enough but, I never know," he says with a smile. He clears his throat and then looks at my plate. His smile deepens and he asks, "Everything go down okay?"

I laugh as loud as my throat will allow at the question, not sure why I find it so funny, but I nod to answer him.

"What so funny?" Kallon asks. He no doubt can't find anything funny about his question either.

I shrug and start eating my noodles. Kallon puts his fork down and clasps his hands in front of him and looks at me pointedly. With his smile that makes my stomach flip, he says, "Tell me what you're thinking, what made you laugh so loud."

Me: I honestly don't know why I laughed at your question. Maybe just the thought of being asked that, it's not something I thought I'd be asked, I guess.

Kallon laughs a little and says, "Yeah, I can see how that could make you laugh. I never thought I'd have to ask that question, outside of it being written in a script."

I laugh a little at that too. We sit in silence as we finish our meals. As the guys finish, I stand and grab their plates.

"Nope, I got this, remember?" Kallon says as he stands. I grab my phone and quickly send him a text.

Me: No, I'll do this. You go shower. I haven't done anything but sleep for the last couple of days, please, let me do this so I don't go crazy with boredom or laziness.

Kallon stares at his phone and then stares at me, debating something in his head. He finally hands me his and Dax's plates and sighs.

"Fine," he says. He then leans into my space, his hands on the table to my left and my chair to my right, which makes him less than a foot from my face, and adds, "But just so you know, resting isn't being lazy, it's how you heal, remember?"

I watch as Kallon looks down at my mouth for a fleeting second and then his gaze is back on mine. As I try not to visibly gulp and force myself to not look at his lips that have gotten closer as he talked, I nod. He steps away and smiles.

"Alright, I'll go shower. Leave the food cleanup for me. You shouldn't clean up my overspending problem," he says as he walks from the room.

I put the plates down as I shake my head and close the containers and start to put them into the bags. I see Dax stand

and he starts to help with the containers. I swipe his hand away and wag my pointer finger at him in a 'no-no' gesture.

"We can argue about this all night but either way, I'm helping you put this food away," Dax says with a stubborn look. "So, just let me or we can have this staring contest until Mr. Keller gets back out here and you know he won't let you touch the containers or the plates if you try to be stubborn about it."

My mouth falls open in shock. I pick up my phone and type out a furious text.

Me: Me stubborn? You two have been the stubborn ones. I'm not an invalid, I can clear the table after meals.

Dax grabs his phone off the table when he hears the ding from my text. He looks at it quickly and grimaces.

"I'm sorry we've made you feel that way. We don't think you're an invalid. We just want you to rest and heal. The best way to do that is to take away the worry of household chores or anything else that requires physical exertion."

Me: I'm thankful for the rest, I wouldn't be as healed up as I am but clearing the table of some paper plates and food containers can hardly be described as physical exertion.

"Maybe now but the first couple of days, it was all you could do to stay awake," Dax says in his, and everyone else's, defense. "You are getting your strength back, which means you're healing. But if you wouldn't have let us help, you'd still be back at day one."

I don't send a text in reply, I just nod. I put my phone

down on the table and we start to cleanup, both silent.

I know Dax is right. I know that me resting the last few days and probably for days to come are the only way I'll get better but it's so hard for me to do nothing. I've been working since I was old enough to help at Rose's. If I wasn't working there, I was in our kitchen at home making my own recipes for desserts and other things. I cleaned up my own messes. I went to school and worked. When I was overseas, if I wasn't at school or at work with the chef or baker I was mentoring with, I was still in my kitchen working on my food. I've never had anyone wait on me like my friends and parents have these last few days. Not that they've never tried, I just never felt like they should have to, that I should always pull my own weight.

When I walk into the kitchen to throw the paper plates away, I see my kitchen counter has fresh hand towels sitting on them. When Dax walks in, I point to them.

"Betty must have done a load of towels," he states.

I walk back out to the dining room and see Dax has cleared the table. *I wonder if the guest rooms has towels?* I ask myself. I never did check before I offered the guest rooms to Dax and Kallon. I walk toward the hall leading to the guest rooms and bathrooms, I stop at the laundry room and look inside to see a stack of folded towels. I grab the stack and walk them to the guest bathrooms. Kallon must be in the one on the right, since the door is shut and as I stop and listen, I can hear the shower running. My face turns red as I picture him in there.

STOP IT, ABBY! I shout to myself. *Do not think of him like that. He's your friend and business partner. Don't go there.*

But who can help their thoughts when they know that Kallon Keller, multiple magazine's voted number one hottest man, is currently naked in their shower? Of course images are going to pop up without intentionally thinking about him... naked... in the shower... with water running down his chest to his stomach to his...

STOP IT! I shake my head and move away from the door, suddenly feeling like a peeping Tom. I walk over to the other bathroom and put half the stack of towels in the cupboard and just as I'm walking out into the hall, the door of the bathroom across from me opens. There stands Kallon with just a towel wrapped around his waist. I freeze. I can't help the perusal my eyes do.

First on his hair that looks like he just ran the towel over it, it's sticking up in all directions. Down to his face, where he's looking at me in surprise. My eyes slide down to his neck, where his Adam's apple bobs as he swallows. Then down to his glistening chest where the little bit of chest hair is still damp, like he didn't take the time to completely dry himself off. My eyes still continue down, down to his abs. *How fit can one man be?* My eyes trail a water droplet as it runs from his peck, down over his rippling abs, down to where the towel sits low on his hips. I can see the sexy lines of his V. What's the name of those muscles? If my memory from my only human anatomy class in high school serves me correctly, it's Transversus Abdominis. Again, my mind is whirling with the sight of him, I'm stunned silent and frozen. My eyes having a mind of their own, look down and see a little bit of a... Realizing what I'm looking at, my eyes dart up to Kallon's face. He has a smile on his lips but the look he's giving me tells me he knows I was just checking him out.

My face goes red, I hand him the stack of towels, and

bee line it down the hall. At the end, I take a left and go to my room where I shut my door, hurry to my bed, and fall on to my stomach.

How humiliating was that?

"Good job, Abby," I say to myself, not even caring about the slight pain from saying it. How long was I standing there staring at him? It didn't feel like that long but now that I'm thinking about it, it was definitely too long. And if he noticed, it was absolutely too long. I groan out loud and roll over on to my back, throwing my arm over my face. I can't go back out there. I can't look him in the eye. I'm so embarrassed.

I've only been lying on my bed for a couple of minutes when I hear a soft knock on my door. I sit up and freeze. A couple of heart beats later, another knock, but it's a little louder. I close my eyes and hold my breath.

"Abby, I know you're in there," Kallon's voice comes from the other side. He sounds like he's holding back a laugh. I fall back onto my bed and squeeze my eyes shut even harder. "If you don't come to the door to shoo me away, or text me to tell me to go the hell away, I'm coming in."

I open my eyes, sit up quickly, and scan my bed, looking for my phone. I pat myself down quickly and can't find it. *Where did I leave it? On the table but I didn't see it when I walked through. Did Dax put it somewhere for me?* I don't have time to think about it more because the door is opening and Kallon is stepping into my room.

When he finds me sitting on my bed, a huge smile spreads across his face. I burry my face into my hands and lean down on to my lap, shaking my head slightly.

"Abby," Kallon says, I can hear he's still smiling but he

has comfort in his tone. I hear him walking over to me. I feel the heat of him when he gets in front of me and soon his hands are on the side of my knees, he must have squatted down. His voice comes directly in front of me when he says, "Abby."

I just shake my head.

"Look at me, please," he says gently. I again shake my head. "You don't have to be embarrassed."

I move my hands quickly and look at him in shock. I find him staring at me with that smile again. I fall to my back and squeeze my eyes shut.

I hear Kallon chuckle but then I feel his hands leave my legs but they're instantly on my arms. He gently pulls on me so I'm sitting up again.

"Look at me," he says again. I shake my head no again. "Please."

Oh my gosh! The way he says please makes me feel like he could ask me anything in the world and I'd do it for him. I grudgingly open my eyes. He still has his stomach flipping smile on his stupidly handsome face that is mere inches from mine. I can't help my eyes dipping down to his lips and I can't help when I bite my bottom lip. His eyes flash to me biting myself and I see his pupils expand and then he's looking back into my eyes.

Kallon has to clear his throat before he says, "Don't be embarrassed. Did I notice you checking me out? Yes."

I go to fall back to the bed, my face flaming red hot now. Kallon's chuckle comes from down deep in his throat, but he doesn't let me fall to the bed.

"Hold on, let me finish," he says, pulling me back up. "The way I see it, we're even. I saw those pictures of you in that folder and did it seem like I was in a hurry to shut it?"

My face goes even redder, I didn't think my embarrassment could get worse. I was wrong. I close my eyes.

"Answer me, Abs?" Kallon says. My eyes fly open. It's the first time he's called me that and damn me if I don't like the sound of it. "Did I look like I was in a hurry to shut the folder?"

I glare at him and shrug.

"No, I wasn't," Kallon says. He raises one eyebrow in the sexiest way and smiles at me. "I'll admit I took some time perusing what I saw, what man wouldn't?"

I watch as his eyes travel over my face, down my upper body, to his hands holding mine, and then back up again. He smiles shamelessly.

"Out of respect for you, I shut it once I realized what they were, but it took a hot minute for my cognitive thoughts to catchup to my... well, to my man thoughts," he laughs. "Please don't be embarrassed about your woman thoughts running away with you before your own cognitive ones could catch up."

"Not. The. Same," I whisper.

"Where's your phone?" Kallon asks. I point out the door. He turns towards the door and then back at me. "We'll finish this out there, come on."

He stands but doesn't let go of my hands, so he pulls me up into a standing position. I pull back and shake my head.

"Abby, I'll carry you out there if I have to. We're going to talk about this until you aren't embarrassed about it. I'm not embarrassed about it," he says matter-of-factly.

I glare at him and when I start to walk towards the door, he lets go of my hands, almost reluctantly it feels like at first.

I push that thought out of my head and stalk out of my room, down the hallway to the living room where I see Dax sitting with a book. He looks up with a confused look on his face.

I point to my chest and then do a gesture of a phone to my ear.

"Oh, I put your phone over there," he points to where I've been napping on the couch these last few days.

I nod in thanks and walk over to it and sit down. Kallon comes and sits right next to me, not giving me any space. I look up at him in frustration and glare. He holds up his phone and nods his head down at mine sitting on the armrest.

I pick it up and text him.

Me: You weren't embarrassed by me looking at you because you are you. But it doesn't matter because I'm not embarrassed anymore so we don't need to talk about it.

Kallon chuckles as he reads my text and I see him typing his own out. I try to get a peak, but he pulls his phone away.

"No more peaking," he says and then winks at me. My face heats. *I'm never going to hear the end of this embarrassing disaster.*

Kallon: You are too. But why? And why do you say I wasn't embarrassed because I am me?

Me: I'm not. And you are you… meaning… You've done movies where you've been more naked than that. You showed your ass once. You would have to be very "ok" with people looking at you to do that.

Kallon: I guess that's true. But you're still embarrassed, your face is red.

I reach up and put my unbandaged hand to my face and

feel that it's still warm. I look up and glare at Kallon, again.

Me: Fine, but I don't want to talk about it.

Kallon: Why?

Me: Because it'll make me more embarrassed. I honestly didn't mean to check you out. You caught me by surprise.

Kallon: So, you admit to checking me out? :-D ;-)

Me: You are insufferable.

Kallon takes an overdramatic intake of breath and puts the hand closest to me to his heart.

"I am not," he says with fake outrage. I hold up my phone at him and look over at Dax. He's reading his book, but he looks like he's fighting a smile.

Kallon: Tell me why you're embarrassed so we can move past this. Like I said, I wasn't embarrassed when I saw your folder.

Me: You weren't? Not even a little bit? Because I was. I still can't believe I left that thing lying around.

With my peripheral vision, I see Kallon look down at me, so I look over at him. He's got the left side of his lips pulled up into his cheek and he's squinting at me. Like he's trying to decide something. His cheeks turn pink and his lips slide into a smile. He looks down at his phone and starts typing away. I look away and watch the three little dots until his message comes through.

Kallon: Alright, yes I was a little embarrassed, only because I wasn't expecting to see pictures like that and then for them to turn out to be you. I was also a little embarrassed by how long it took me to register I should shut the book and give it back to you. :-D

Me: That's why I'm embarrassed. I wasn't expecting to find you standing there naked with a towel around your waist. AND it took me WAY too long to look away.

Kallon: So, we're even.

Me: Sure.

Kallon: You don't sound so sure.

Me: How long are you going to tease me about it?

Kallon: I won't.

I look up and glare at him until he looks at me. He laughs and shakes his head.

"I won't!" he declares loudly.

Me: Yes you will.

Kallon: I won't tease you about it, promise.

I again look up at him and take a deep breath before replying.

Me: Ok, I believe you.

I smile up at him. He smiles at me and then picks up the remote and turns on the TV.

"Do you want to watch something?" he asks.

I nod and snuggle down into the couch and wait for Kallon to pick something for us to watch.

CHAPTER 6

"Heads up!" I hear a man shout and I open my eyes quickly. I see a football coming my way. It hits the ground and bounces to my feet.

"Sorry about that," the guy says as he jogs over to me. He's in shorts and no shirt. I can't help but admire the way he looks.

I pull my eyes away from his abs, look him in the eyes, and clear my throat before I say, "It's okay."

"I've seen you here before," he says with a smile. He's got a great smile. All straight and white teeth.

"Have you?" I ask.

"Not in a stocker type of way," he says as he holds his hands up. "My buddies and I play football over there—" he points over to his friends who are all standing there and then wave him back over when they see us looking their way. He holds up one hand. "—Anyways, I've just seen you at this tree sometimes, but always reading."

"Oh," I mumble unsure what to really say. So, I add, "It's my favorite place to come to relax and read."

"That's cool," he says with a smile.

"Billy, lets go!" a guy from his group hollers.

"I'm Billy," he says as he reaches down to shake my hand.

"Abby," I say, shaking his hand back.

"It's nice to meet you," he says. "If you're still here after our game, maybe I can take you to get a coffee or something. There's a great place across the street there."

He points out Rose Bud's. I smile and laugh. I don't think I've ever seen him in my bakery before but, maybe I have but was too busy to pay attention.

"That would be nice, but I'm waiting for someone," I say with a crinkled nose.

"Of course you are," he says with a little laugh. "Someone as beautiful as you wouldn't be single."

"Ha!" I laugh out. I don't need to tell him that I'm single and have been for a year now. And the person I'm meeting has no interest in being anything but a friend.

"Okay, well I'll see you around," he says and then picks up his football and runs back to his friends.

"Bye," I say, but he's already too far away to hear me.

I lean my head back and think about Kallon. And how this time last year I was recovering from Jason's attack. I still haven't seen Jason in person. He's been emailing me and writing me letters from his treatment facility. He's been there for almost a year now. I think he realized how bad his addiction was once he got there. He confessed to me that he was doing drugs as well, not just drinking. I haven't replied much to him, I'm trying to keep my distance.

My life has been better without him in it. I don't feel like I've walked on eggshells around anyone, which has been nice.

Today is the first time I've looked at another man in a way other than to notice he's a man.

Kayla has tried to get me to look at Kallon in a different way, but I've been forcing those feelings into a box and tucked it away in my head. I am not going there and she can't make me. He's not interested in me like that, or at least he's never made any moves or suggestions that he does.

"Abby!" I hear someone shout. I look up and see Kallon jogging over to me. He's in jeans, a black t-shirt, and a ball cap. I stand and wave. He comes up to me and hugs me. "Sorry, I'm late. Work ran over. I got here as soon as I could."

"No worries," I say, ignoring the racing of my heart.

"Have you been waiting long?" he asks.

"About an hour or so, but I've been reading," I say, holding up my book.

"Aww, Abby, I'm sorry," he says, running his hand through his hair. "I should have texted or called you."

"It's really okay," I say. "I haven't had a chance to come and read, so it was nice."

"Happy birthday," he says as he hands me a cupcake he was holding behind his back.

I tilt my head to the side and laugh.

"Thank you," I say. "You didn't have to do that."

"I did it last year. It's going to be a tradition. I'll meet you here for our birthday's and we'll split a cupcake."

"What? I don't even get my own cupcake?" I ask in mock shock.

"Nope," he laughs. He's gotten to know me well this last year that he knows when I'm being serious or just joking. "So, how are you doing?"

"I'm fine," I say.

"Liar," he says as we sit down. I take my seat with my back against the tree while he lays down beside me. He takes his hat off and leans on his right side and props up on his arm.

I laugh and say, "I'm really fine. I was actually just thinking about last year before I was interrupted."

"Sorry, I didn't mean to interrupt you," he laughs.

"You didn't."

"Who did?"

I nod my head over to the guys behind his back. He turns and sees the guys. Billy is caught looking our way and turns quickly.

"That guy?" Kallon asks and turns back to me. He's got a weird expression on his face for just a second but then it's gone.

"Yeah?"

"You can do better," he says with a laugh.

I shake my head and laugh again, and say, "I don't know, he was pretty hot."

"You need someone with more substance than looks, Abby," he says as he picks up the book I'm reading. "Along Came You? Again?"

"I started thinking about this time last year and how I was catering the set for that movie. Don't get me wrong, I love that we're still catering for the movies you're in but that one will always hold a special place in my heart. So, yes, I'm reading the book again."

"You know, my premier is next weekend," he says, suddenly looking shy. He picks a piece of grass and rolls it in his fingers.

"Yeah, I remember," I say nudging him with my leg. "Has Tiffany picked out her fabulous dress yet?"

"Did I not tell you?" Kallon looks up quickly. I shrug and shake my head no. "We broke up a couple weeks ago. I could have sworn I told you."

"No!" I exclaim. "You didn't! What happened this time?"

"Why do you say it like that?"

"Because, in the year we've known each other—"

He interrupts me by saying, "It's been over a year."

"Okay, in the more than a year that we've known each other, you've had more girlfriends than I can keep track of," I say with a laugh. I see his hurt expression, so I add, "I'm not judging. I'm actually really curious what happened this time so I can maybe help you find your long-term person soon."

"Honest answer?" he asks.

"Obviously! When have I ever wanted you to lie to me?" I ask, laughing.

"She didn't like my relationship with you. She told me I had to choose between you or her," he says, picking another blade of grass.

"What did you say?" I ask, actually shocked now.

"We fought," he states.

"And?" I ask. *Is he here to break off our friendship?* We'd still have to be business partners but...

"I'm here aren't I?" he says with the smile that makes my heart stutter. "I've seen you every night since the fight. I told her I wasn't going to be with someone who would try to make me choose. She told me we were over and stormed out. I haven't seen her since."

"Oh, Kallon," I say, putting my hand on his head. *His hair is so soft!* "I'm sorry."

"It's okay," he says, reaching up and pulling my hand down to his and holding it for a minute. "It wasn't meant to be."

"You deserve someone with more substance than what she had to offer anyways," I say with a laugh, mimicking his earlier statement about Billy.

"Thanks, Abby," he says jokingly.

I go to take a bite of my cupcake, but he lets go of my hand and uses it to stop me.

"Hold on," he says. He pulls out a candle and a lighter. "You have to make a wish."

"Ugh, Kallon..." I whine. "I just want to eat my cupcake. I promise to share it with you."

"Oh, you'll share it with me. I bought it from my favorite bakery," he says and looks up at me with a wink. He puts the candle in the middle of the cupcake and then lights it.

"Thanks," I say with a small giggle.

"Happy birthday, Abby," he says with a deep voice. He then leans up and kisses my cheek. We freeze.

It's the first time we've been this close, other than to give a quick hello or goodbye hug. But it's the first time he's kissed me in any way. My head turns towards him, without me telling it to. I look him in the eyes, and I watch as his eyes search mine and then they glance down to my lips. I involuntarily swipe my tongue out and across my bottom lip, pulling my lip in as my tongue goes back into my mouth.

"Abby..." Kallon breaths. I can feel his breath against my lips.

"Yeah," I say breathlessly.

"Abby, I want to kiss you," he says.

I'm not thinking straight but I say, "Okay."

His eyes fly to mine, searching for the truth in my word. He looks back down at my lips and as he closes the distance, my eyes shut. As our lips meet, flame that has been forced to be dormant erupts in my chest... in my stomach... everywhere.

Our kiss starts off sweet and soft, just our lips pressed against each other. I think when he realizes I'm not pulling away, his starts to move towards me, pulling me to him as well. His lips open slightly and pulls in my upper lip. So, I pull in his lower lip. I've been dreaming of this kiss for over a year. I was poorly mistaken on what it would feel like. My heart is racing and I can hardly breath. My stomach is doing flips and I. Want. More!

I feel Kallon's tongue touch my lip, so I open more for him. Our tongues touch and there's another eruption. Electricity this time. I put my free hand to his chest, grab his shirt, and pull him to me. His hand goes to the small of my back and pulls me closer. He's leaning up fully on his hand now, holding his weight while he pulls me to him.

I lift my other hand, but I forgot I had the cupcake in it. I'm wearing shorts today, so I feel something hit my leg. I jump away from Kallon and look down. I had tipped the cupcake and the wax fell on to me.

"Ouch," I say, wiping it away, causing frosting to smear in its place. I look up at Kallon feeling embarrassed.

He leans away and smiles. He asks as he wipes the frosting off my thigh, "Are you okay?"

I watch as he puts his finger in his mouth and sucks the frosting off.

Holy mother above! I involuntarily lick my lip again. His eyes fly to it. He leans in like he's going to kiss me again. I put my hand out to his chest and stop him, my sanity back in full force.

"Wait," I say. He stops and looks at me concerned.

"Abby?" he asks. I can feel his heart pounding in his chest.

I take a deep, calming breath, and say, "We... I... Should we have done that?"

"Kiss?" Kallon asks, slightly hurt.

"Yeah," I say.

"Did you not want to?"

"It's not that," I say. "I did."

His heart stopping smile spreads across his face, and he leans in, "So, what's the matter?"

My mind starts to get fuzzy again as he gets closer. My eyes can't look away from his lips. My mind can't forget how it felt for those lips to be on mine.

I clear my throat and tear my eyes away and force them up to his eyes.

"You just broke up with Tiffany a couple weeks ago," I say, looking down at my hands.

"Yeah," he says, as he puts his finger under my chin and lifts my face up to meet his.

"I just think maybe we should take it slow," I say.

He leans away and nods. His face still looks relaxed, but I can see a different emotion in his eyes. "Okay, if that's what you want."

"Kallon, I—" I start to say but stop. I take a breath and finish. "—I don't want to be a rebound."

He pulls back like I slapped him.

"Do you think that's how I feel about you? That I would use you as a rebound?" he asks, sitting up.

"No... I don't know..." I answer truthfully.

"Well, I wouldn't," he says as he stands up.

"Hey, wait," I say standing up too. "Where are you going?"

"I don't know," he says. I drop my cupcake and put my hands on his arm and stop him.

"Please don't be mad," I say in a small voice.

He spins and looks at me and says, "I'm not mad Abby. I could never be mad at you. I'm embarrassed that you would think I'd use you as a rebound."

"I don't think you would but..." I start to say. I look over his shoulder and see Billy and his friends watching us. "Can we go back to my place and talk about this please? You're still planning on taking me to the airport, right?"

He relaxes and steps back to me, taking one of my hands in his, "Of course I am."

"Okay, then can we talk about this where people can't get entertainment out of it?"

"Yeah, alright," he says, looking around. I look around too and see more people looking our way than I originally realized. I bend down, grab my book, cupcake, and his ballcap and put it back on his head. He grabs the book out of my hand and then uses his free hand to hold my now empty hand and starts to walk us out of the park. I see Dax and Trevor not too far away. "We have to stop for another cupcake, you didn't get to eat that one."

"It's fine," I say as Dax and Trevor fall into step behind us.

"We can get one later."

He looks down at me and then looks ahead of himself. We make it to the street and wait for the light to turn to the little walking man. When it turns, we hurry across and onto the sidewalk. The walk to the bakery is quick. Kallon turns like he's going to go inside but I pull him towards the end of the building.

"I'd rather not go in there. Betty is forcing me to take the day off, since it's my birthday. But if I go in there, I'll want to stay and work," I say.

"Right... Umm, Dax, will you go get Abby another cupcake please. Betty knows which one is her favorite," Kallon says with a smile. He looks down at me, and then looks back up at him, and adds, "Take your time too while you're at it."

I see him wink at Dax, which makes Dax shake his head. He and Betty have been seeing each other officially for the last seven months. I was so excited when she told me. I laugh and shake my head. We make it to my door and he punches in the passcode. We walk up the stairs but this time I enter the code and open the door.

I'm thankful I was able to get over the initial shock and trauma from Jason's attack. I love my home and it would have killed me to not be able to live here. I only had a couple nightmares after that first one but after I sat in the place where he hurt me, I was able to face the fear of it happening again and reassured myself it never would. It also helped that Kallon and Dax stayed with me for a whole month.

I put my bag on my little table and walk into the living room. I sit down and Kallon comes to sit next to me, not giving me any space. I laugh and turn away from him, putting my legs under me, and pointing my knees towards him. He takes off his hat and tosses it and my book on the coffee table and then he looks at my knees with a questioning look.

"I need room to think," I say.

"Meaning you can't think when I'm close to you?" he asks with a smirk.

"Can you?" I ask in return.

"Hardly ever," he says leaning closer to me.

I laugh and put my hand out, stopping him again. Even though at his words, my butterflies in my stomach erupt into fluttery chaos.

"As much as I want to kiss you again—"

He takes a sharp breath in and says, "Do you?"

"Yes," I say in a shaky voice, but I keep my hand on his chest, keeping him at my arm's length away. "But, Kallon, I'm leaving for the weekend. I don't want to do anything that'll confuse the hell out of me while I'm gone."

He leans back and looks at me with concern. He asks gently, "What do you mean? Explain that to me, please."

"I mean, I'll get in my head the moment I leave. I'll believe whatever you tell me but as soon as I'm away, my doubt will creep in. Can we put this—" I wave between him and me "—whatever this is, on pause? Just until I get back from Kayla's wedding?"

He puts his head back and takes a deep breath. I pull my hand away, so that I'm not touching him anymore. Touching him isn't helping my resolve.

"Yes, we can," he says. He takes another breath.

"Are you mad?" I ask quietly.

"No," he says as his head snaps up. "Of course not."

"Then what's wrong?" I ask.

"I'm trying to calm myself down..." he says in an embarrassed tone.

"Calm yourself?" I ask. "So, you are upset?"

He laughs and I see his face turn red. *Kallon Keller is embarrassed?*

"No..." he says. He looks down at himself pointedly and then back up at me and then back down at himself. I look down and my eyes see what he's saying. He's got an erection pushing up his pants. I pull my lips into my mouth into a hard line and my eyes go wide. I look up at Kallon and he's looking at me. "Yeah... I'm trying to calm down."

I try not to laugh and put my hand on his shoulder, "I'm sorry."

"Touching me, doesn't help," he says but he reaches up and grabs my hand anyways.

"That's just from... kissing? Or did you think we were gonna..." I ask, leaving the question open.

"It's from you," he says, his face going even more red. His eyes go wide as do mine and he says, "Should I have said that?"

I clear my throat and ask, "Well, it depends on what you mean."

"I mean, this is what you do to me. No matter what we're doing," he says quietly. "I can usually hide it better, though. That kiss... sent me over the edge. Almost too far."

I watch as his cheeks darken even more.

"Do I do something I should stop?" I say as I look down at my hands. For some reason, I feel awkward and embarrassed now.

"You aren't hearing me, Abby. It doesn't matter what

you're doing... It's... you," he says 'you' in a whisper. I look up from my hands and see him staring at me. The amount of desire in this man's eyes makes my mind go blank and then all thoughts of waiting are out the window.

"Oh, fuck it," I say and jump at him.

CHAPTER 7

My lips are on his before I can stop myself. His hands slide from around my waist and up my back, pulling me into him. I'm sitting awkward so I slide my leg over his lap so I'm straddling him. I can't help when my hips rock down and into him and I almost jump in surprise as his erection pushes into me. Desire flares inside me.

"Mmmm," Kallon groans into my mouth as he feels me rock into him again. "Abby..."

"Sorry," I say, I sit up off him, so I'm not tempted to rock again. Because believe me, the temptation is there.

"It's okay, I don't mind," he says into my mouth before he's kissing me passionately again.

I pull my mouth away, but he pulls me back and kisses my jaw, down to my neck.

"It's... not nice," I breath.

"Oh, it's very nice," he growls into my neck. He then lifts his hips and grinds into me.

"Mmmm, Kallon," I moan. "We can't."

"I know," he says. "We won't."

Part of my brain is believing him, but the other is

thinking he's full of shit. He pulls my face down to his, his hands going to the back of my head, making my messy bun even messier. Our kissing deepens. His hands stay in my hair, but mine travel from his chest to his shoulders, up his neck and then into his hair too. I pull him closer to me and he, of course, responds instantly.

A part of my brain registers a door opening somewhere but the other part doesn't care. The same part that heard the door, notices footsteps coming up stairs. My other part starts to care a little more but not enough to stop the kissing. But when both parts hear the sound of the keypad being pushed on my lock at my door, I pull away from Kallon and just as the door is opening, I slide off of him and try to sit the way I had been before we started kissing.

I look at the door and see Dax walking in. He's not looking up but looking at a cupcake in his hand. He must have lit it when he got to the top door. I hurry and pat my hair down and adjust my shirt, it had started to ride up. I glance at Kallon and he's trying to hide a laugh, but he also looks annoyed that we got interrupted.

"Happy birthd—" Dax starts to say as he finally looks up into the room. He looks at Kallon, sees his messy hair. I want to kick him for not fixing it. Then Dax looks at me. I try to smile at him with ease, but I can feel it looks forced. "—ay Miss Rose."

"Thanks, Dax," I say as I get up and walk towards him. I look back at Kallon and say, "And Kallon."

"Ummm, I'll leave this here with you. I need to go check in with Trevor," Dax says and gives me the cupcake and then leaves quickly. The door didn't even have time to shut all the way before he's pulling it open and walking back out.

"Liar," I say, and I hear him laughing as he's going down the stairs. I turn to Kallon with my cupcake and hold it out. "I don't need another one."

"You didn't get to make a wish," Kallon says as he stands. He stops and hunches over a little for a second. He looks like he's in pain.

"What's wrong?" I ask, walking towards him, concerned.

"Just give me a second," he says. He reaches down and pulls the legs of his jeans down and then grabs his crotch and adjusts himself. My eyes go momentarily wide as I see the handful he has, but before he can catch me staring, I force my eyes up to his face.

"Does it hurt that bad?" I ask.

"Yes," he says with a laugh and looks up at me.

"I'm sorry, I feel like that was my fault this time," I say with a crinkled nose and slight grimace.

"It's definitely your fault," he says with a laugh. He groans as he goes to take a step.

"Can I help?" I regret the question as soon as I say.

His eyes fly up to mine and that desire is back. He takes a breath and says, "Not this time."

He takes another tentative step and winces.

"Kallon," I say walking to him. I blow out the candle and put the cupcake down on the coffee table and touch his arm. Then pull it back when I see him close his yes. "Sorry. I just… I don't like seeing you in pain."

"It's not really pain," he says with a laugh. He adds, "Well, it is but it's not… it's just really uncomfortable."

"What else other than… that… helps?" I ask.

"A cold shower?" he says it as a question.

"Go use mine," I say. He looks up at me with wide eyes. "I mean the guest bathroom."

"You wouldn't mind?" he says with a hint of embarrassment.

"If it'll help you feel better, I don't mind at all," I say. I'm trying not to picture him in there with a hard on, but I can't help it. A smile crosses my face and my cheeks warm. He looks at me and is about to say something, but I step up to him and turn him and gently push him out of the living room. "Go shower."

"Will you text Trevor or Dax to bring my bag up. I brought one so I could change into sweats while we waited to take you to the airport," Kallon says as he wobbles towards the bathroom.

"Sure," I say with a laugh.

"Don't laugh, or you'll be taking a shower with me," he says, turning towards me. I stop laughing and pull my lips into my mouth. I put my hands up in surrender and step away. He laughs and turns back towards the hallway.

I walk to the intercom and push the button.

"Dax are you there?"

"Yes, Miss Rose," he says with a hint of humor in his voice.

"Could you or Trevor grab Kallon's bag out of his car?"

"Sure thing, Miss Rose," Dax says.

"Thank you," I say, not sure if he's still standing there.

I walk into the kitchen and get a drink of water. I wet a paper towel and wipe my face and neck. *I need to calm down!* I wasn't lying when I told him I didn't want to do anything before I leave. Kissing is one thing, but I don't know if I would have stopped us again if Dax wouldn't have interrupted us.

There's a knock on the door and I go to it and open it. Dax is standing there with Kallon's bag.

"You didn't have to knock," I say, stepping back to let him inside, he doesn't move.

"I felt it was necessary," he states with a smile.

"You've never knocked before," I say.

"I've never interrupted anything before," he says with a full-on laugh.

"Shut up," I say and hit his arm. He doesn't step in but hands me the bag. "Come in here."

I reach out and pull him inside. He looks around and turns to me.

"Where is Mr. Keller?" he asks in a whisper.

"Taking a shower," I say. "He just wanted to change into different clothes since you guys are hanging out until it's time to go to the airport."

Over the last year, I've given up trying to drive myself anywhere. I've accepted that Dax is my driver and bodyguard or as I like to fondly call him, my big brother, for as long as Kallon and I are business partners. And now that we are... whatever this is, I'm sure it'll be even more important to Kallon that I have Dax around.

"I'll be outside," Dax says, turning to go back out.

I step in front of him and say, "No! You have to stay in here."

"Why?"

"Because... I need my big brother," I say with a sigh.

"Meaning?"

"Guh," I groan out and throw my hands in the air. "Because I can't do anything with him right before I leave. If you're here, I won't."

"Mr. Keller won't like me interrupting," Dax says matter-of-factly.

"Mr. Keller—" I enunciate his name "—knows I don't want to do anything before I leave, so he'll probably welcome the babysitter too."

I look at him pointedly.

"Alright," he says and walks into the living room and sits in what has become his chair. He pulls a book off the side table and opens it. I've left the book there for him because I've noticed he's been reading it when he's here.

I sit on the couch and turn on the TV for background noise. I grab my book off the coffee table and try to read but all I can think about is the make-out session Kallon and I just had. The thought brings the fire and the new, all consuming, feeling of need into the pit of my stomach. I bite my lip and try to focus.

I've been focusing on my book and getting into the story so when Kallon walks into the room and comes and sits right next to me, again, not giving me any space, I look up at him in frustration and glare. I turn so my knees are between us once again. *Like they did any good last time!* I shout at myself.

Kallon interrupts my internal shouting and asks, "Are you watching this?"

I look up and see it's on a baking show.

"No, I didn't even look to see what was on when I turned on the TV," I say with a laugh.

"Do you want to watch something else with me?" he

asks, pointing the remote at the TV.

I look at the clock on my phone and see it's 7:22pm, *I need to start packing.* I shake my head no, put my book down on the table, and I say, "I should go pack and take a little nap."

"Oh, okay. Yeah, you probably should. We'll take you to the airport. We should probably get your there around 12:30, so we'll leave around midnight?"

"You guys don't have to take me, I can drive myself," I say even though I know it won't matter.

Kallon looks down at me, and says, "I thought we were past you feeling like an inconvenience. Dax and I will take you, and then I'll go home and sleep until I'm needed on set."

"Dax isn't coming with me to Kansas," I say, sternly.

Dax smiles and shakes his head. He looks over at Kallon and says, "Mr. Keller, I told you she'd say that."

Kallon shakes his head at Dax and looks at me, "Dax should go with you. He can help you with anything you need."

"I've traveled to my best friend's house many times and have never had a problem. Plus, Peter is picking me up from the airport and we're picking up breakfast on our way to their house. Kayla and I will gather all of her things, my dress and shoes included, and we'll head to the hotel. We have a whole day of pampering planned. Dax, you'll be bored out of your mind. PLEASE, stay home and enjoy some Abby free time," I plead.

Dax smiles before he says, "I really don't mind—" I interrupt him with a glare, so he adds "—but if you wish for me to stay in New York, I will. But only if you promise to text me when you get to the airport in Kansas when it's time to fly home, so I can pick you up from the airport."

I grin at him and say, “I promise.”

I see Kallon looking at Dax and smiles. When he looks at me, his smile is even bigger.

“Alright, fine. Dax stays here. But we’re still taking you to the airport,” Kallon says with humored resignation in his voice.

“Deal,” I say.

“What hotel are you staying at while you’re there?” Kallon asks nonchalantly as he watches the show he put on TV.

I stand and say, “Air Suite Hotel.”

“Oh nice,” he says as he pushes the channel on the remote.

“Yeah, I’ve stayed there before, it’s really nice,” I say as I step away. I feel weird leaving them to go pack and nap.

Kallon must be able to read my mind, or my thoughts are written across my face, because he says with a true laugh this time, “Go pack and take a nap. We’ll be fine and we aren’t going anywhere, so when you’re up and ready to go, we’ll be ready too.”

“Thank you,” I say and then smile.

I walk out of the room. When I get to my bedroom, I plug my phone in and then start to pack for my weekend away. I can’t wait for Kayla’s wedding, but I can’t wait to get back home either.

CHAPTER 8

My alarm goes off sooner than I like but I roll over and turn it off. I glance at the time, even though I know what time it is. 10:45pm. *Ugh.* I'd finished packing around 8 and when my head hit the pillow, I was out. It'll be nice to get to Kayla's and hopefully find some energy there. I know with her wedding less than 48 hours away, I'm sure we'll be busy getting things finalized. I just hope when we're getting our manicures and pedicures, and our full body massage at the hotel, Kayla will be able to relax.

I roll out of bed and even though I showered a few hours ago, I take another quick one. I put on the clothes I had laid out while I was packing; my favorite jogger sweats, a tank top, and put on a hoodie for the little bit of chill that's still in the air. I braid my hair into a French braid. I don't normally do it like this because it'll fall out and while cooking and baking, that's not ideal. But for traveling, it's a nice loose hairdo so by the end of my travel, I don't have a headache from the tighter braid I usually do.

I'm taking a smaller suitcase so that I don't have to check a bag and honestly, I'm not taking a lot of clothes. Just a couple pairs of comfy clothes and that's it. I throw my phone charger in the inside pocket of the suitcase and check my nightstand for anything else I want to take. I see my small iPad I use for my Kindle and put it into my travel purse, which is a midsize messenger bag. I put my phone in my back pocket.

I grab my neck pillow and wrap it around the handle of my suitcase and head to the door. When I open it, I can hear quiet murmuring out in the living room. When I walk out, Dax and Kallon look my way.

"Have a nice nap?" Kallon asks with a smile, making my heart race.

As I put my things down by the front door, I say, "I should feel rested but for whatever reason, it definitely wasn't long enough. I'll rest on the plane, and I'll be to Kansas shortly after that, and in the morning we'll finish up whatever Kayla needs done for the wedding. Then the afternoon is dedicated to relaxing and having fun before the craziness of Saturday begins."

"Did you say you're getting pampered at the hotel?" Kallon asks as he does something on his phone. He looks up as I nod. "Sounds like a nice hotel to offer those types of services. What all are you ladies getting done?"

"Mani's and Pedi's, and then massages. We'll spend the rest of the day in Kayla's hotel room relaxing. We'll have room service for dinner, so we don't have to go out. Neither one of us are super into partying," I say with a smile. I can't find myself to really look at Kallon in the eyes. *He seems preoccupied when he's not looking up at me when I answer his questions. Does he regret our kissing already?* The question jumps into my mind, but I push it away.

Kallon smiles up at me and asks, "When we first met, didn't you come back from her getting engaged?"

"Yes but did you notice it was a year before her wedding? And it wasn't your typical engagement party. We sat around watching movies and playing games. We drank but not to get wild and crazy drunk. We finalized some of her wedding things, she's a planner, and then just had a good, fun weekend. We went out to dinner at a nice restaurant but that was the craziest we got," I say thinking back to that weekend.

Kayla was so gung-ho about getting everything figured out right away. We really did spend all the time calling vendors and photographers, everyone. She wanted everything done with plenty of time before the wedding, so she wasn't a nervous wreck leading up to it. I can't blame her, it makes sense. And she's always known what she'd want, so it was just a matter of finding the right people to give it to her.

Kallon laughs and says, "Sounds like a good weekend to me."

Dax stands and says, "If you're ready, I'll go get the car."

I look at my watch and see that it's 11:45pm. I nod my head at Dax, and he walks to the door and leaves.

"I really can drive myself," I say at the door and turn towards Kallon. I see him stand and he walks towards me.

"And pay to park your car? Dax or Trevor would have to take me home anyways," Kallon says. "And I wouldn't be able to do this."

He puts his hands on my shoulders and pulls me to him and kisses me softly, gently. His hands slide down my arms and then wrap around my waist. I drop my travel bag and put my hands to his chest.

I pull away and ask, "Why?"

"Why what?" Kallon asks and then he kisses my forehead. My heart leaps in my throat. In all the years that Jason and I dated, he never kissed me so tenderly.

"Why would one of them have to take you home?"

Kallon laughs and says, "I'm not going to stay here when you aren't around."

My mouth drops open in an 'oh' gesture. I hadn't even thought about that. As I laugh quietly, I say, "Good point but I wouldn't mind if you guys did. I've gotten used to you guys being here."

Kallon smiles down at me and says, "We've enjoyed keeping you company."

Before I can reply, I hear footsteps on my stairs. I look at Kallon and he raises an eyebrow at me. I'm waiting to see what he does, but he just keeps holding me. *Alright, if he's not embarrassed for Dax to see us, neither am I.* A couple seconds later, Dax is walking through the door.

"If we leave now, we'll get you to the airport with plenty of time," Dax says with a smile as he walks over to my suitcase and picks it up like it's a small little bag. He doesn't even hint that Kallon holding me in his arms is anything unusual.

I nod and walk over to the table next to the door and pull my wallet out of my bag I use for everyday life. I check to make sure I have everything and then I turn to grab my travel bag off the floor, but I see Kallon holding it. I put what I took from my bag, into my travel purse.

Kallon steps away and grabs his bag from the chair next to the couch. He slings it over his shoulder and when he looks up, he's got that stomach flipping smile on his face. I take a deep breath and push the butterflies and the flip, back down where they belong.

"Shall we?" he asks as he gets to the door, Dax is holding it open now.

"Sure," I say and sling my bag over my shoulder and head out the door. I pause and grab a large envelope off the table and put it in my travel back. It's the gag orders for Kayla and Peter to sign. The walk down is quiet, so I hear my automatic lock slide into place.

I'll send a message to Betty in the morning to let her know that Maggie can hang-out in my apartment if she wants to. Ever since last year, she's been choosing to help down in the bakery.

We get outside and I take a deep breath in and let it out slowly. Kallon steps up beside me and offers me his arm. I look up at him and he's just looking out in front of him, smiling. I take it and we start walking towards the front, where the car is waiting no doubt.

When we get out front, I see that Trevor is standing at the front of Kallon's car where he can keep an eye on Dax's car, which is parked directly in front of Kallon's. Trevor steps up onto the sidewalk and reaches for Kallon's bag. Kallon hands it to him and I watch as Trevor puts it into his car.

Kallon opens the back door of Dax's car, which I guess is mine but it's still weird to call it mine. I step down and as I turn, I say, "Thanks for everything. I'll let you know when I get back home."

I had thought Kallon was going to ride to the airport with us, but I guess he's having Trevor take him home now. I don't blame him. It's late, he should go home and get some good sleep.

"We're not saying goodbye yet," Kallon says with the smile still on his face looking at me. "I'm riding with you to the airport."

"Oh. But... you don't have to. I understand if you want to get home, you need your rest too," I stammer out.

"Abby, I want to ride to the airport with you," Kallon says with a chuckle. He steps to me and pulls me close to him and kisses me sweetly. He pulls back too quickly, and says, "Trevor is taking my stuff home and then Dax will take me home once we drop you off."

"Oookay," I whisper, he turns me and gently pushes me towards the car.

I get in, slide over and Kallon climbs in beside me. After Dax shuts the door, he hurries around the front of the rig and gets in and buckles his seat belt. I buckle myself and look up to see Kallon watching me.

"What?" I ask looking around me.

"Nothing," he says with a small laugh.

He reaches out and pushes a stray hair behind my ear. There's a zap of electricity that runs from his fingers to my ear where he touches, down my neck, and it settles in my stomach. I keep the gasp from escaping my lips by biting down on my bottom lip, to help keep them shut. Kallon's hans freezes for only a second, but I notice. He leans in and kisses me.

This one is gentle and sweet too. He pulls back and then tucks me under his arm. I lean my head against his chest, listening to his heartbeat pound away, and breath in slowly, loving his cologne. I'm feeling exhausted again, I yawn, and that annoys me.

"Close your eyes and rest, I'll wake you when we get to the airport," Kallon says softly.

I nod and let my eyes close. Sleep finds me quickly.

◆ ◆ ◆

"Abby," I hear Kallon's voice close to me. "Abby, we're at the airport hon."

I open my eyes and find that I'm leaning against Kallon still. I sit up and give him a sheepish smile.

"Sorry," I say. "I didn't mean to sleep all the way."

"It's okay," he says softly. "I don't mind at all."

I stretch my neck side to side and then unbuckle my seatbelt.

Dax gets out and goes around to the side of the car and opens the door for Kallon and me. After Kallon puts his hat on, he gets out. I slide across the seat, holding my bag on my lap as I go. Once I get out, I see that Dax has gotten my suitcase out of the trunk, and Kallon is reaching for it.

"I'll be back in 5 minutes, Dax," Kallon says as he reaches for my hand and pulls me onto the sidewalk.

"Yes, Sir," Dax says to Kallon. He turns to me and says, "Let me know when you get to the Wichita airport to come home and I'll be sure to be here to pick you up. Have a fun and safe trip, Miss Rose."

"Thank you," I say.

Dax nods and moves to the front of the car and is opening the driver's door when Kallon starts to pull me towards the main entrance doors and is rolling my suitcase along with us. When we step inside, Kallon stops.

"Please let me know when you get to Wichita," Kallon pleads as he turns to me. His hand goes to my cheek.

I just nod. I don't think I have words right now. The only people to ever come to the airport for me were my parents. Jason never dropped me off or picked me up. I don't know what to make of this, of Kallon being here to say goodbye.

He rolls my suitcase over to my side and steps into my space a little more.

"Can I give you a kiss goodbye?" he asks.

I nod. He steps to me quickly and pulls me to him. His other hand lets go of my suitcase and is on my other cheek. He bends and our lips touch. I swear if there isn't an actual flare of electricity or flame from that small touch, I'd be surprised. The warmth I feel from it leaves me feeling giddy.

Kallon reluctantly pulls away and with a smile on his face, he says, "Enjoy your flight, I'll see you soon."

"Thanks," I say, breathless. I smile up at him and step away pulling my suitcase with me.

He stays by the door as I walk away, towards the check-in line. Once I'm in line, I turn and wave goodbye. He smiles and waves and then turns and hurries out the door. I turn back around and wait my turn.

The line moves quickly but it's still a good 20-minute wait before it's my turn. The man at the computer calls for the next person and when I step up to the counter, he smiles warmly at me.

"Good evening, Miss, my name is Chuck Bringham. Can I get your name, please?" he asks.

"Hi Chuck," I say, returning his smile. I pull my wallet out of my bag and dig my ID out of the pocket and as I hand it to him, I say, "My name is Abbigail Rose. Flying to Wichita, Kansas, on the 3 am flight."

Chuck smiles and takes my ID. He starts typing away on his computer and his facial expression drops and his eyes fly up to meet mine. He looks startled and then he goes back to looking at his computer screen.

"Is there a problem?" I ask. I open my phone and bring up my email with my confirmation number and show it to him.

"No, no problem," he says with a little too much politeness. "Just wait here, please."

Before I can say anything, Chuck turns and goes through the door behind him. I look to my right and see a woman looking over at me with concern. I look at the woman helping her, and she glances at the screen Chuck had been using, and she smiles at me with the fakest smile I've ever seen.

What the heck is going on? I think to myself.

I look through my emails, trying to find something from the airline that might explain what's going on. I don't see anything from them saying my reservation had been cancelled due to overbooking or anything. I go back to my confirmation email and can't find anything wrong in that one either.

I wait another 5 minutes and then the door opens and Chuck steps out with a big burley man. He looks scarily similar to Dax and Trevor, only he's wearing official TSA apparel.

"Miss Rose, this is Seth, if you wouldn't mind following him," Chuck says as he waves a hand towards the big man to his right. He hands me my ID back.

"What's... going on?" I ask.

"If you'd just come with me, I'll explain when we get there," Seth says. He reaches for my suitcase and pulls it up into his arms and then takes a step away from the counter.

"Am I... in trouble for something?" I ask. My heart is pounding so hard, I feel like it's going to burst through my chest.

"No, Miss Rose, just please follow me. I'll explain when we get there," Seth says again and then comes to me and gently grabs my elbow and we start walking away from the check-in counter. I put my phone in my pocket and keep my eyes down as we pass all the people. I don't want to see their curious looks but worse, their accusatory looks, even though they have no idea what's going on. I don't even know what's going on.

I look up once we've passed most of the people and Seth has let go of my elbow. I see we're walking towards the security gates. Seth bypasses the line and takes us around. We go through some doors and then we stop at the last one. He holds up his phone and the TSA agent on the other side of the door, looks through the window and nods at whatever he sees on Seth's phone. The lock on the door clicks and Seth pushes it open, ushering me through first. We walk through security and past a couple terminals and make our way down a hall I've never been down before.

"What's going on?" I ask, my voice shaking.

"Just about there," Seth says.

Another 5 minutes of walking and we come to a door where Seth punches in a code and we hear it unlock. He opens the door and steps back, gesturing for me to go ahead of him. I tentatively walk through the door and I'm surprised to see a lounge looking room.

"What is this?" I ask.

Seth leads me over to a smaller counter where a woman

is standing. He shows her his phone and she smiles up at him. When she looks at me, she beams.

"Hello, Miss Rose, we've been expecting you," she says. She looks down at her computer before looking back up at me and adds, "My name is Marjory, I'll be checking you in and taking care of you until your flight."

"I'm ss..ssorry," I stammer out. "I don't know what's going on. Why am I here?"

"I'm sorry for the theatrics but we had strict instructions not to tell you until you were in the lounge," Seth says with a sheepish smile.

"Instructions from who? I still have no idea what's going on or where I am," I say a little annoyance creeping into my tone.

"My apologies," Marjory says. "This is the lounge for privet jet owners."

"I am not a private jet owner," I state. And then it hits me. Kallon. My mouth falls open and before Marjory or Seth can say anything. I ask, "Who gave you instructions?"

"Mr. Kallon Keller," he answers. He continues with, "He owns a couple jets and he instructed us to change your flight plan today. Marjory will make sure you are refunded your plane tickets before you get to your destination, so that there are no hold ups in that area. We'll print off your return flight instructions so that you don't go through this again in Wichita."

I stare at him dumbfounded. My thoughts come back to me, and I say, "People can't just change other people's flight plans, can they? I mean, what if he wanted to kidnap me and send me to Timbuktu."

"People can't change your destination, only upgrade your flight. If you truly are upset about this, we can take you back to check-in and you can go through that process and be on your way, on your original plan. I've only just started the process of refunding your tickets, Miss Rose. I can stop right now," Marjory says, putting her hands on the top of the counter, away from her computer. "I don't think Mr. Keller was meaning to do anything ill intended or evil in nature."

I take a deep breath and calm myself. I KNOW he wasn't doing it to be anything except kind, but it feels like too much. After all he's done for me this last year. After everything with Jason. This just feels like too much.

"No, that's okay. I'll take the upgrade. But Mr. Keller will be hearing from me," I say the last part a little quieter.

"Very well, Miss Rose, if you'd like to take a seat, I'll bring some refreshments out for you shortly. Make yourself at home, your flight leaves in two hours," Marjory says with a smile and then she goes back to her work on her computer.

Seth walks with me as I pick a seat and leaves my suitcase with me and then goes and stands by the door. I have a suspicion he's going to be there until I leave. I pull up my message history with Kallon and send him a text.

Me: Made it to my gate.

I don't have to wait long and the three dots popup, like he'd been waiting for me to text him.

Kallon: You did?

Me: Yup.

Kallon: .... You did?

Me: Yeah, why?

Kallon: What gate are you at?

I click out of messages and go to my email and see that it shows I should be at gate 28.

Me: 28. Why?

Not even a minute goes by and the phone next to Marjory starts ringing. *No way did he call her?!* I pretend to be on my phone and listen to her.

"Hello, Private Lounge One, this is Marjory, how can I help you?" she says into the receiver. She pauses for a minute and out of the corner of my eye I see her look over at me. I double down on pretending to be on my phone, all I'm doing is mindlessly scrolling up and down on mine and Kallon's text history. She continues, "No sir, she's here—" pause "—I'm not sure, but she's sitting right in front of me sir—" longer pause "—Yes, sir, have a good day."

I see the dots appear at the bottom of the screen. This should be good.

Kallon: Very funny.

Me: What?

Kallon: You aren't at gate 28.

Me: Then where am I?

Kallon: .... Are you mad?

Me: Not really. More confused than anything. This is too much, Kallon.

Kallon: Can I explain?

Me: I have two hours to kill, go ahead.

Kallon: Along Came You made me do it.

Me: What?

Kallon: The book? The one you're reading again. Do you remember the scene from the airport?

Me: Yeah....

Realization hits me and it makes me laugh out loud. I can see Marjory looking over at me, but I ignore her. I knew this felt familiar, but I couldn't figure out from where.

Kallon: You re-reading it gave me the idea and you gave me the opportunity. You've had a rough year, I wanted to take some stress off your flight. You can relax and enjoy your flight. Happy birthday!

Me: You should have told me. I thought I was in big trouble when the customer service agent left me at the counter and then this big man, Seth, who looks like Dax and Trevor came out and had me follow him. He didn't say anything to me until we got to the lounge. I was freaking out.

Kallon: If I would have told you ahead of time, would you have gone to the lounge check-in?

Me: No, I would have told you I'm perfectly fine traveling commercial. Which I am, but I don't want to cause a fuss with Marjory or Seth. And I don't want to walk back through the airport, stand in line for another 20-30 minutes and then go through security. I'd probably end up being late for my original flight.

Kallon: That's why I didn't tell you. I knew what you'd say and I wanted to do this for you. I know you have a hard time letting people help you, let alone do nice things for you. Please don't be mad at me.

Me: Promise you won't do this again and I won't be mad.

Kallon: Promise me you'll let me do things for you without it turning into an argument and I'll promise to never surprise you with changing your flight plan again.

Me: That's not... You don't have to... Kallon! Why do you feel the need to do these things for me? It can't be just because we're business partners or that we just kissed.... today. I'm a good kisser but not that good. ;-)

I hold my breath. I'm not sure I should have asked that.

Kallon: I do these things for you because I like you, a lot. But also, yes, you are my business partner, but you're also my friend. You're fast becoming one of my closest friends, realest friend. I also like you, a lot. I know I said that already, but I feel like I need to say it twice. And you ARE good at kissing but that's not the reason for this. ;-) I want to do these things for you because I can. What's the point of having all that I have if I can't share it with my friends and family?

His answer is what I was thinking he was going to say and then some.

Me: You're becoming one of my closest friends too. I like you, a lot, too. But I just feel like it's a little one sided on the giving side of things. I have hardly anything to give in return.

Kallon: You being real with me and not putting up with my shit is all that I need, Abby. :-) And maybe some more of your kisses.

Me: See, that doesn't seem fair. :-D

Kallon: It does to me.

Me: We'll agree to disagree on this.

Kallon: I can live with that. :-D So, are you mad at me still?

Me: No... :-) And... thank you. This is really nice of you.

Kallon: Now, was that so hard?

Me: Yes... :-P No... I'm sorry I made a fuss.

Kallon: It's ok, I expected it. Dax even told me how you'd react.

Me: Dax knew?

Kallon: Yes... But in his defense he told me it wouldn't go over well.

Me: He knows me well.

Kallon: Big brothers usually do.

Me: HAHAHA

Kallon: Get some rest, Marjory will wake you when your plane is ready.

Me: YOU need to get some rest.

Kallon: I'm on my way home, Abby. You are the one in an airport.

Me: Is your bed comfy?

Kallon: Eh, it's alright. I feel like it's going to be missing something.

Me: What's that?

Kallon: You.

Me: Hahaha I've never slept in your bed. How can it be missing something if it's never been there?

Kallon: I've held you while you've slept multiple times, that's what I'll be missing.

Me: It's been a year since the last time you held me while I slept.

Kallon: Are you forgetting the multiple times you've woken up on my shoulder or on my lap while we've hung out and watched movies over said year?

Me: No but that doesn't count. We weren't in a bed.

Kallon: You were still in my arms. I'm glad I got to hold you on the way to the airport. My arms won't feel so lonely tonight.

Me: Oh… my… gosh…. Smh…

Kallon: hahaha What?

Me: You're being dramatic, Mr. Keller.

Kallon: I'm speaking the truth, Miss Rose.

Me: Whatever. :-)

Kallon: Get some rest and I'll talk to you tomorrow.

Me: Ok… Night, Kallon.

Kallon: Goodnight, Abby.

I put my phone down and I can feel that I have the stupidest grin on my face. *How is this happening?* I pick my phone up and set an alarm to go off at 2:30 and pull the lever on my chair to recline back. *I don't want to admit it, but this is nice.* Only a couple seconds go by before I feel someone tap my arm. I open my eyes and see Marjory standing beside me. She's holding a blanket and a pillow.

"Would you like these, Miss Rose?" she asks.

"Yes please," I say. I lean up and she puts the pillow

behind my head and then drapes the blanket over me.

"Would you like anything to drink or eat?"

"No, thanks," I say as I get comfy.

"Very well," she says. "I'll be right over there if you need me."

"Thank you."

I close my eyes and listen to the sound of the music Marjory has softly playing over the sound system and I fall to sleep.

CHAPTER 9

"Miss Rose," I hear a soft voice say from beside my head. I open my eyes and see Marjory standing there. I rub my eyes and sit up and smile at her. "They're pulling your jet around, if you'd like something to drink or eat while you wait, I can grab something for you. You can then take it onboard with you."

"Water, please?" I ask.

"Yes, Miss Rose," Marjory says and walks away.

I sit up and pull my phone out of my pocket. It's 2:35am. *Hmm... I don't remember my alarm going off.* I open my alarm app and see I had set the alarm for PM, not AM. It's a good thing Marjory was here or I would have missed my flight.

I stand and fold the blanket and put it on top of the pillow that I laid on the seat of the chair. I stretch and then sit in one of the less comfy chairs. When Marjory comes out, she's got a fancy looking bottle of water, I was expecting just a glass of water.

"Thank you," I say after she hands me my drink.

"You're welcome. You'll be able to board in 10 minutes. Your flight attendant is Louie Warrington and your pilot is Captain Sterling. Louie will come and get you when you can board and then you'll meet Captain Sterling on the jet."

"Thanks," I say and then take a drink of the water. I realize it's room temperature and ask, "Did Mr. Keller tell you I like warm water?"

She smiles and says, "He did."

I shake my head but can't help the smile on my face, "Thank you."

"My pleasure. Let me know if you need anything else, Miss Rose."

"I will... thank you."

It doesn't take long for a different door in the lounge room to open and another man steps out. He walks over to Marjory and they talk for a couple of seconds before he comes over to me.

"Miss Rose, I am Louie Warrington. I am one of Mr. Keller's personal flight attendants which means I am your personal flight attendant for this trip and your return flight on Sunday. If you're ready to board, I can show you the way," Louie says as he extends a hand to me.

"It's nice to meet you, Mr. Warrington," I say as I shake his hand.

"Please, call me Louie," he says with a smile.

"Only if you call me, Abby," I smile back.

"I'm sorry, I cannot. But I insist on you calling me Louie," he says with a chuckle.

I don't have the energy to argue with him. If he wants to be formal with me but have me be casual with him, fine. It's too early, or late, however you want to look at it, for me to insist on anything. I nod and reach for my suitcase and bag.

"I've got these, Miss Rose. If you'll follow me right this

way."

I let him take my suitcase and bag and I follow him as he leads me to the door he had come in through. Seth walks over and opens the door for us.

"Thank you," I say to him. I then turn to Marjory and say to her, "Thank you, too."

"Our pleasure, have a safe flight," Marjory says. Seth just nods in reply.

I follow Louie through the door, and we walk down a little hallway, and then we come to another door. When he opens it, I see we're heading outside and there's stairs to go down. I step out and go down the stairs but wait at the bottom for Louie. He points forward and I see a sleek, fast, badass jet in front of us. My jaw falls open.

We walk over to it and there's a man dressed in pilot attire standing next to the stairs. When we get close, he smiles at me.

"Miss Rose, it's a pleasure to meet you. I'm Captain Sterling, I'll be your pilot this evening," he says and then smiles even bigger.

"Thank you," I say.

"If you'd like to go up the stairs, Miss Rose, you can pick anywhere to sit that you'd like," Louie says from behind me.

I again nod and make my way up the stairs. When I get inside, I'm stunned into place. It's the nicest plane I've ever been on. I've never been on a privately owned jet before, but I've seen them in movies and TV shows. They didn't do them justice.

There are couches to lay down on and the chairs all look like they recline themselves. They also look like they swivel.

There's also four of the recliners situated around a table with a glass top. I look further down and see another recliner, but it's got a little table in front of it, maybe for one person to get some work done.

"Is everything okay, Miss Rose?" I hear from behind me. I look and see Louie at the top of stairs waiting for me to continue and Captain Sterling is right behind him.

"Sorry," I say and step further inside.

"You are absolutely fine," Louie says.

"Anywhere?" I ask, pointing around to all the options.

"We ask that you sit in a chair at take-off so that you can be buckled in, and then once we're at cruising altitude, you can sit wherever you like," Louie says with a kind smile.

"Okay," I say. I pick a chair midway down the jet and take a seat.

Louie hands me my bag but keeps my suitcase and says, "I'll put this away until we land. Is there anything you'd like out of it?"

"Oh, my neck pillow from the top, please," I say. He reaches down and takes it off the handle and hands it to me. I grab my ear-pods out of my bag and put it and my neck pillow on the seat next to me. "Thank you."

As Louie walks away with my suitcase, I look over and see Captain Sterling standing by the cockpit. When he notices me looking at him, he beams at me. I can't help but smile back.

Louie comes back and asks, "I know it's late, but can I get you anything to eat or drink?"

"No thank you," I say. I hold up my water and add, "This is good for now."

"Sounds good, Miss Rose."

He walks over to Captain Sterling and says something to him. Captain Sterling nods and Louie walks behind a little partition wall and disappears from view. The Captain walks over to me.

"We're all set in here. I'm going to go take my seat and when I get the all clear to take off, I'll let you know. Please stay seated and buckled until I announce it's safe to walk around."

"Thank you," I say with a smile and then buckle my seatbelt. A thought comes to mind. "Oh, when should we be landing in Wichita? My friends are picking me up."

"We should be getting in only a half hour earlier than your original flight, Miss Rose."

"Thank you."

He nods and walks away towards his cockpit. I see him sit and put his headset on. He starts pushing things on the dash and I hear the engine turn on.

Before we take off, I pull my phone out to send some texts out. First, I text Kayla and Peter.

Me: Hey! I'm on the plane. I'm not on my original flight, so don't watch for it. I'll text when I land. I should be getting in around 6am.

I click out of their group text and open the one with Dax and Kallon.

Me: I'm on the plane. Thanks again. This thing is amazing. I'll let you know when I land.

Now I click onto my parents group text.

Me: I'm on the plane. I'll text when I land. Love you guys!

And finally, I click on Betty's name.

Me: I'm on the plane. Thank you so much for all you do! I'll let you know when I land.

I close out of my messages and click on Spotify. I find my brown noise play list and turn it on. I put one of my ear-pods in my right ear and listen to the sounds. I turn my phone onto Airplane mode, and I put it in the little cupholder, the one that's not holding my water bottle. I grab my neck pillow and put it around my neck. I close my eyes and prepare for take-off. Take-offs have never been my favorite.

After a few minutes, when I'm about to doze off, I hear over the speaker, "Miss Rose, we are clear for take-off. I'm going to taxi us out onto the runway and then we'll be on our way. Sit tight and enjoy the flight."

With my eyes still closed, I hold up my hand and give him a thumbs up. I put my other ear-pod in and focus on the sounds. I take calming breaths and will myself to relax. I think about my spot at the park, where I go to think or read. I imagine listening to the birds chirping, the kids laughing, and the sound of the trees swaying in the breeze.

Before I know it, we're over the bumpy part of take-off and we're into the smooth ascent into the sky. I relax more into my seat and drift off to sleep.

◆ ◆ ◆

I feel a tap on my arm and I jolt awake. It takes me a minute to remember where I am. I look around and see a man standing next to me. *Oh, right, Louie.*

I pull my ear-pods out of my ears and smile sheepishly up at him.

"I'm sorry for startling you, Miss Rose," he says apologetically with his own sheepish grin.

"That's okay," I say tiredly. I yawn and stretch.

"We've arrived in Wichita," he says with an easier smile.

"We have?" I ask in surprise. I look out the window next me. And sure enough, I see we're taxing down a runway. "Already?"

"Yes, Miss Rose," he says with concern in his voice again. "I tried to wake you once to see if you needed anything, but you were out. I put a blanket on you and decided to not try again, just to let you sleep. I figured you'd wake up when you were ready. But as we are here, I thought it best to wake you."

I look down at my body and see a super soft blanket spread over the top of me.

"Thank you," I say with a laugh. "I was exhausted."

I slept for 3 hours? I pull my phone from the cupholder and see that it's 5:05am. I forgot about the time change. But I still slept for 3 hours. I turn off Airplane mode and get the notifications of texts from everyone I messaged before take-off.

Peter: Kayla is sleeping but she's excited to see you. I'll be at the airport by

5, just in case you get in early. See you soon, Abby!

Dad: Sounds good Buds. Have a great time. Mom wanted me to make sure to tell you to please send Peter and Kayla our love.

Betty: Don't even worry about it. Have a great time!

Kallon: There are worst ways to fly. :-D haha Have a safe flight.

Dax: Glad to hear it. Safe flight.

I send them all the same reply. That I've landed and taxing to our designated area. My first response is from Peter.

Peter: I'll meet you at baggage claim.

Me: I don't have any checked baggage, I'll meet you at the front doors.

Peter: Don't be ridiculous, I'll meet you at the arrival gate.

Me: Peter you don't have to do that.

Peter: Yes I do.

Me: Smh...... Okay, see you soon.

Kallon is the next to reply.

Kallon: Glad to hear it. How was your flight?

Me: Great apparently. I slept through it all. :-D

Kallon: Good! I'm glad you were able to sleep.

Me: Are you on set?

Kallon: Yes. Should be a quick day.

Me: Good deal.

Kallon: They're calling me back. Talk to you soon.

Me: Sounds good. Have a good day.

I'm just putting my phone down when it notifies me that I have another text. This one is from my mom.

Mom: Hi Abbigail, I'm so glad you made it safely. As your dad said, please give Kayla and Peter our love. Enjoy your weekend away. Rest as much as you can. Love you honey!

Me: I'll pass the message along. Today should be a fairly relaxing day. Love you, too!

I put my phone in my bag and take my neck pillow off and put it on my lap. Louie walks up and hands me a glass of orange juice and a blueberry muffin.

"Thank you," I say with a smile. He nods and walks to the back of the jet. He walks back out a few minutes later with my suitcase.

"Would you like to put your pillow back on here?" he asks, pointing to the handle.

"Oh, yes please," I say, grabbing my pillow and going to put it on the suitcase.

"I can take care of that, Miss Rose. You go ahead and enjoy your snack. We should be parked in about 5 minutes," Louie says as he gently takes my pillow from my hands.

I'm fighting the urge to recoil from all the help Louie is offering me but it's his job, I need to let him do it. I'm not sure when I started to have an adverse reaction to people helping or being kind. Unless it was from family, but even then, I tend to not ask for help, or decline when it's offered.

If I'm truthful with myself, I know exactly when and why it all started. Jason. It started once I moved back from being abroad and opened up Rose Bud's. Any time I'd ask him for help, he'd make me feel bad for not considering how busy he already was with his own stuff. Or if he did help, there were always strings attached. On the flip side, I was always expected to help him, which I did. I help anyone who needs it.

"Miss Rose?" Louie says again, he's standing next to me. I jump, not realizing he's there. "Sorry for startling you again, but we're ready to de-plane, if you'd like to follow me?"

I look around and see that we are in fact stopped. I must have been so preoccupied with my thoughts I hadn't realized we'd parked.

"Yes, thank you, Louie," I say earnestly. I unbuckle myself and stand, grabbing my bag as I go. I reach for my water bottle and cup of juice. I ate my muffin while I was lost in thought.

"Leave the glass and muffin wrapper, I'll clean that up," Louie says kindly.

"Oh," I say a little reluctantly. "Okay. Thanks."

I put my bottle of water into my bag and sling it over my shoulder. I don't even attempt to grab my suitcase from Louie's hand, I know he'll just insist on taking it for me. I follow him to the door, Captain Sterling nowhere to be seen. Louie steps to the side and motions for me to go first.

I step out into the sunlight and look down, finding where Captain Sterling had gone to. He's waiting at the bottom of the stairs for me. He smiles up at me, I return the smile.

"Thank you for flying with me today," he says in a lighthearted way.

"Thanks for flying so well," I say with a soft laugh.

"Have a great day Miss Rose, I look forward to seeing you Sunday," Captain Sterling says as he reaches for my hand and bows his head.

I smile up at him and shake his hand back. After he's let go of my hand, I step back and turn to Louie.

"Which way?" I ask him.

"Right this way, Miss Rose," he says as he gestures with his hand towards the left.

"Bye," I say to Captain Sterling and follow Louie. The Captain tips his hat at me and then climbs the stairs back up to the jet.

I follow Louie over to a door on the lower level of the airport. We walk into another lounge, only through the sitting area and through the lobby, there's a door that leads to outside.

"Are we not at Wichita Airport?" I ask with a little panic in my voice.

"We are," Louie says as he comes to a stop by a comfy looking recliner in the lobby. "This is the departure and arrival lounge for all private jet owners. This is where you'll come when you leave on Sunday."

"Oh," I say. I need to text Peter, he's waiting at the arrival gate for no reason. "Where exactly is this compared to the airport? My friend who is picking me up, is waiting for me at the arrival gate."

"This is a high security, gated area, so your friend won't be able to come in here unless they've been cleared to do so. There's a car that can take you to meet them at the entrance of the airport," Louie says with a smile.

"Okay, thank you," I say as I pull my phone from my pocket.

A big man, with a short military haircut, wearing black slacks, a white button up, and black jacket to match his pants, walks from a door to my left and Louie nods at him. He resembles Dax and Trevor just like Seth did, only he seems to be 10-15 years younger, with a head of hair.

"Miss Rose, this is Freddy. He'll be with you from here

on out. Have a good rest of your day," Louie says as he hands Freddy my suitcase. And without waiting for my reply, Louie hurries from the lobby and sitting area, back outside.

"What..." I start to say but Louis is already gone. I turn to Freddy and ask, "What does he mean you'll be with me from here on out?"

"I'm your driver, Miss Rose," Freddy says. He reaches his hand out and I extend mine. His grip is firm but gentle. His smile shows his white, straight teeth. He has beautiful hazel eyes. "My name is Fredrick Paulson, but you can call me Freddy, everyone does."

"It's nice to meet you Freddy but I'm still confused. I didn't hire a..." I put my head back and breath in a sigh. *Kallon.* I look up at Freddy, he has a humorous smile on his face, like he was expecting this reaction. "Did Mr. Keller hire you?"

His smile widens, "Yes, Miss Rose. I am one of his many bodyguards and drivers."

"How many does he have?" I ask, sidetracked. "Were you on the plane with me?"

"I believe, there are five of us under contract, Miss. And yes, I was in the back."

"You were? I didn't see you get off. Why does he need five?"

"I moved up to the front while you were sleeping. You were zoned out when we parked. I came inside to make sure your car was here. And it can get pretty dangerous for Mr. Keller when he travels," Freddy says. "He tends to have two of us as bodyguards and a third for a driver, to always have the car ready."

"How dangerous?" I ask, no longer annoyed at Kallon

but concerned.

"Fans and the paparazzi can get pretty crazy, especially when a movie is premiering."

"I can see that," I say. "But why does he have you here with me?"

"As far as what I was told, you need a driver," he smiles.

"I told him my friend was picking me up. And once I get to their house, we're going to the hotel we'll be staying at. She has a car, she can drive us."

"I was told to drive you and Miss Smith around wherever you would like to go," Freddy says. He motions for me to go to the doors.

"Hold on," I say as I pull my phone out. I click on Kallon's name to call him.

It rings twice before someone picks up.

"Hello," it's not Kallon but it's a man's voice. I look at the caller ID and see that I did call Kallon.

"Hello? Who's this?"

"This is Randy, Miss Rose. Mr. Keller is in the middle of a shoot. He told me to respond to any texts that you send him. I wasn't expecting you to call."

"Oh, hi Randy," I say. "I just have a quick question."

"I probably have the answer but if I don't, I will relay it to Mr. Keller when he has a break and I'm certain he'll get back to you right away."

"Did Kallon send Freddy here to be my driver?" There's a pause and the sound of Randy trying to hide a laugh. "Randy?"

"I'm sorry, Miss Rose, yes, he did," Randy says with a snicker. *"I don't mean to laugh, but I just knew you'd have something to say about it. I even warned Mr. Keller about it when*

he instructed me to call and have the agency send Freddy. He told me he'd handle it."

"Handle me, you mean," I say seething. I take a breath to calm myself. I can't take my irritation out on Randy, it's not his fault. "Why is it that everyone knows how I'll react except for Kallon?"

"Oh, you're mistaken, Miss Rose. Mr. Keller knows you very well and knows how you'd react."

"So why does he insist on doing these things?"

There's a pause and I hear Randy's snickering stop immediately, his tone changes to sincere but also serious when he says, *"Because he cares about you, Miss Rose."*

My annoyance disappears.

"Okay, thank you for answering my questions, Randy. Please tell Kallon to call me when he has a free moment," I say, trying to sound more kind than I had started out.

"I will, Miss Rose, have a nice day," Randy says and then the call ends.

"Alright, Freddy... let's go," I say exasperatedly.

"Yes, Miss. Rose," he says.

Realizing I still haven't told Peter what's going on, I stop and type a text to him quickly.

Me: I am so sorry. I'm not going to be coming from the arrival gate. Meet me at the airport entrance and I'll explain when I see you.

Peter must have been waiting for a text because the three dots appear shortly before his response pops up.

Peter: Is everything ok?

Me: Yes, just meet me at the main entrance, I'll explain.

Peter: Ok.

I put my phone in my pocket and look up at Freddy who is staring at me with concern.

"Sorry, I was telling my friend who was waiting for me at the arrival gate, that I wasn't going to be coming from there. He's going to meet us at the main entrance so I can explain why he didn't have to drive all the way here," I say, annoyed.

"Ahhh, I can see how not being told about me could cause a problem there," he says apologetically.

"It's not your fault," I say. I start to walk towards the door and once we get outside, I see the same car that Dax drives me around back in New York, sitting in front of the doors. *No way...* I stop walking and watch as Freddy walks to the back of the car and puts my suitcase into the trunk. Under my breath, I say, "Unbelievable."

"What was that?" Freddy asks as he steps up to the back door and opens it for me.

"Nothing," I say. I get inside and buckle myself in. Once Freddy is seated and buckled, I ask, "Do you normally drive this type of rig?"

He looks in the rearview mirror and I see him smiling, "No, Miss Rose. I was instructed to get this one specifically."

"Got it," I say as I pull my phone out of my pocket. I text Kallon.

Me: Kallon. You seriously don't have to do all of this. A private jet? A driver? The same car as back home? I would have been happy with anything. I would have been fine with flying commercial. I would have been fine riding with Peter and Kayla.

I close my phone and watch as Freddy drives us around the airport. Before we pull up to the main entrance I say, "Peter doesn't know about Kallon being Charles Webb and I haven't had the chance to get him and my best friend, his fiancé, to sign the gag order. So, I'm going to call Kallon, Mr. Webb, okay?"

"Sounds good, Miss Rose," Freddy says as he pulls up to the main entrance.

We don't have to wait long before I see Peter walking out. He starts looking around, his eyes sliding over the rig, not expecting me to be inside, and then pulls out is phone. Before he can call or text me, I open the door. I hear Freddy curse under his breath but before he can get out, I'm already stepping out of the car. Freddy hurries around and holds the door for me.

"Abby?" Peter asks, shocked.

"Yeah, it's a long story," I say as I step up to him and give him a big hug.

"It's so good to see you," he says, hugging me tight.

"It's good to see you too," I say as I squeeze him back. I turn towards Freddy and say, "I'm going to ride with him, so I can explain all of this. Do you mind just following us?"

"Whatever you'd like, Miss Rose," Freddy says. "But I'd like to take you guys to your friend's car. Instead of you walking through this huge parking structure, the temporary parking is clear on the other side."

The tone in his request suggests it's not a request at all.

"All right, fine," I say. "And this is Peter Jacobs. Peter, this is Freddy."

"Nice to meet you, man," Peter says, extending his hand

out to Freddy.

"Nice to meet you as well," Freddy says as he shakes Peter's hand. After they're done shaking, Freddy steps to the car and motions for us to get in. "I'll take you to your car."

Peter looks at me with eyebrows raised and nods his head at me to get in first. I slide in and Peter follows behind me.

"Miss Rose?" Peter says as we watch Freddy walk around the car.

"Oh, shut up," I say to him, elbowing him in the side. I buckle my seatbelt and I add, "I can't get them to call me Abby. Well except Dax and that's only when it's just us."

"Dax? What is this all about?" Peter asks but his voice drops to a whisper when Freddy gets inside. Peter hurries to buckle his own seatbelt.

"My new business partner, Mr. Webb, is very kind," I say. "Do you mind if I wait to tell you and Kayla at the same time."

"Sure, Abby, whatever you need," Peter says putting his arm around me. "How are you feeling?"

"Right now, hot," I say, pulling on my hoodie. "I didn't think it'd be this hot so early."

"Well, it is 78 degrees outside," Peter says with a laugh.

"It was chilly when I left for the airport back home," I say nudging him again with my elbow.

"And what was chilly?" Peter laughs.

"58 degrees, I think," I say. I start to pull my sleeves out but reach my arm over to Peter and say, "Here, pull, please."

He laughs and pulls the end of my sleeve as I pull my arm inside. I had planned for this, knowing Wichita is warmer than home, my tank-top will come in handy. I pull my hoodie off and sigh in relief.

"How was your flight?" Peter asks.

"It was good. I slept the entire time," I say. I point to Freddy and say, "I didn't even know he was on the plane with me."

"How?" Peter laughs.

"I slept the entire time and he snuck off before I woke up," I say. Freddy looks in the rearview mirror, smiling.

"So how are you feeling?" Peter asks. He makes me look up and he checks my neck. He then asks for my hands. "You look like you're completely healed."

I see Freddy's eyebrows come together.

"What does he mean by that?" Freddy asks.

"This time last year... I was pretty banged up," I say.

"Meaning?" Freddy asks with a growl this time. For someone who I just meant, he seems pretty protective already.

"My ex hurt me," I say. A horn behind us blares, we all look behind us and then in front of us. The light has turned green.

"No wonder Mr. Webb wanted someone with you," Freddy says as he starts to drive.

"Jason won't be coming to the wedding," Peter says through gritted teeth. He's seething.

"Peter, I'm so sorry. I didn't want this to mess up your wedding party... the groomsmen," I say, squeezing his hand.

"Didn't Jason tell you when you guys were still together?" Peter asks, now more shocked than angry for a moment. "Jason declined to be a groomsman. He told me he wasn't sure if he'd be able to make it to the wedding at all, so he didn't want to commit to being one."

"What?" I ask. "When did he tell you that?"

"The day after I proposed, when I called him to ask him to be my best-man. He declined that first. So, then I asked if he'd be a groomsman, that's when he told me about how he might not be able to make it," Peter says matter-of-factly.

"How could he possibly know he wouldn't be able to make it a year in advance?" I shout.

"Easy, Abby," Peter says. He moves the hand I'm holding, to my back and rubs soft circles. "But yeah, that was over a year ago, around the time the dickhead hurt you. I know he's in rehab, so he wasn't really lying. He's been emailing me, I haven't responded, but I did email him and told him not to come and to stay the fuck away."

"Peter, I'm so sorry," I say, leaning into him. "I know you two were really close."

"Were being the operative word there. He's changed so much Abby, I don't even recognize him anymore. It used to make me upset, that my best friend had no interest in me, but I don't give a shit anymore. After what he did to you, the sweetest person in the entire world, he's not welcome near Kayla or me anymore."

"I doubt he'd show his face at the wedding," I say.

"I told him not to come, so he better not," Peter says sternly.

"Sorry to interrupt but we're getting into the temporary parking lot, where did you park, sir?" Freddy asks.

"Ha!" Peter barks out a laugh. "I'm not a sir, Freddy, call me Peter. And I'm parked in the back corner, it's a black Toyota 4Runner."

Freddy nods and maneuvers his car around the parking lot.

"That one right there," Peter says, leaning forward and pointing to the SUV he's had since he turned 16.

Freddy pulls up and gets out, opening my door for me.

"Thanks," I say.

"I'll follow you," Freddy says over to Peter who is out of the car and walking around to me.

"Yup," Peter says. He puts his arm around me and walks me to his car.

"I'm not going to fall over or pass out," I say, nudging him with my shoulder, again.

"I know," he says with a sigh. "I just hate that Jason did that to you and I want to protect you."

"I know, I hate it too, but it's been a year. I'm okay."

We get to his car and he opens the door for me. Once I'm in, he shuts the door gently and runs around to the other side. *These guys need to stop acting like I'm breakable, I'm fine.*

He jumps inside and buckles, and says, "I had breakfast delivered to the house, so we can go straight there."

"Delivered? Fancy," I say with a laugh.

"It's handy," he laughs too. "Plus, Kayla can't wait to see you."

"Oh, I'm excited to see her!" I say, bouncing a little in my seat. I know the drive from the airport to their house will take about 30 minutes, so I settle down in my seat.

CHAPTER 10

The drive to Kayla and Peter's house went quickly. I asked Peter if he was excited for tomorrow. He said he was excited to marry his best friend but was ready for the stress of planning the wedding to be over. Even with Kayla being a planner and had everything figured out within the first month, she was still stressing. He asked me how work was going and he was happy to hear the movie set gig was still going so well.

We've been quiet for the last 10 minutes of the drive when we pull onto their street, and I see their house come into view. I sit up and a big grin spreads across my face. I see Kayla sitting on the steps, waiting for us. She jumps up when she sees Peter's rig and starts to jump up and down, clapping her hands together.

Peter doesn't have the car in park before I have my seatbelt off, the door open, and I'm running to hug my friend. We collide, falling to the ground, with Kayla on top. We're giggling like little girls who haven't seen each other in years, or in this instant, over a year.

"How are you?" she screeches into my ear. "Happy

birthday by the way!"

"Thanks! And good now," I say back. "I've missed you!"

"I've missed you!" she squeals. She pulls back and says, "But really, how are you?"

She sits up off me and pulls me up to stand.

"I'm good," I say with a smile.

She does the same thing Peter did, she looks at my neck, and then my wrists.

"I still can't believe he hurt you as bad as he did," Kayla says with a snarl.

"Me either," I say. "But can we not talk about Jason? I know it's hard not to but, I'm moving on from him and that means no dwelling on what he did, or what he could have done. It's been a year."

I see Kayla wanting to say something. She bites her lip and then says, "Deal but can I ask one thing before we have a Jason free weekend?"

I laugh and say, "Yes, go ahead."

"Don't get mad at me but, are you really moving on from him? For real this time, I mean," she asks timidly.

"After what he did to me?" I ask. I sigh and add, "I know I've taken him back too many times. I know I've given him too many second chances but the moment he put his hands on me and hurt me, there are no more chances after that. At first, I was at war with two different parts of myself. The part that still loved him because he was my first love and the part that was more rational. But I've had plenty of time to think this last year and I've come to the conclusion that I was in love with a man that didn't exist anymore. I was in love with Jason from high school. He hadn't been that man for a few years, even before the incident. So, yes, I'm moving on from him. I won't ever be able to trust him again and I hope I don't have residual trust issues because of him. I don't even think I'll be able to be friends with him. The more I distance myself from him, the more I see how awful he was to me. The last time I saw him was that night. He's emailed and tried calling but I haven't answered or responded other than to tell him to stop."

"I'm so glad to hear that, Abs," Kayla says as she hugs me. When she lets go, she looks over my head. Her eyes go wide, and I watch as her eyes go up and down in slow motion, "Umm who is that?"

I turn and see Freddy leaning up with his arms crossed over his chest, against my car... his car... the car he's supposed to drive me around in. He does look awfully good standing there like that. He's taken off his jacket so his muscles strain against the sleeves of his shirt.

Someone near us clears his throat, we jump and turn towards Peter.

"Hi, remember me, your husband to be? Eyes on me, Kay," Peter says pulling Kayla into him. He kisses her softly and she pulls away laughing.

"Hmm I'm having memory loss, who are you, strange handsome man?" she asks while laughing.

"Ha, ha, very funny," he says pulling her in again.

"My eyes might wander but you have my heart, Love," she says sweetly. My heart aches at the need it wants to have what they have. And it breaks a little more at the realization that Jason and I never, ever had that. No matter how much I thought or hoped it would be like that. At the same time it breaks, it starts to beat strong and fast at the thought of the possibilities that Kallon has brought into my life in less than 24 hours.

I clear my throat and say, "Freddy, this is my very best friend, Kayla. Kayla, this is Freddy, he's my... driver."

Kayla's head turns to me so fast, I'm surprised she didn't pull a muscle. She turns in Peter's arms, so that she's standing with her back against his front.

"You have a driver here?" she asks in shock.

"Let's go inside and I'll explain," I say. "Freddy, would you mind grabbing the large envelope out of my bag?"

"Sure will," he says, jumping away from the car. He smiles at Kayla and says, "It's nice to meet you, Miss Smith."

"Damn," she says quietly, but both Peter and I hear her.

"I heard that," he states with a laugh.

"I'm sorry babe, but you do see him, right?" she asks, looking up at her soon to be husband.

"I do, and he's a very handsome man," he chuckles.

I laugh and shake my head at them. They've always had this relationship where they both can admire someone else's beauty or handsomeness without the other getting jealous. I guess when you are one-hundred percent certain of the one you're with, all jealousy goes out the window. Another stark difference between mine and Jason's relationship and theirs. I couldn't so much as look at another man without him thinking I was wanting the guy or cheating on him. Now I realize it was just him projecting his guilty conscious on to me. He had said he hadn't cheated on me for very long, but I never believed that. He'd probably been cheating on me since I was abroad for school. He still hasn't sent the 'atone for all of my mistakes' email yet, to ask for forgiveness for all the wrong he's put me though.

Stop thinking of Jason and the crappy relationship you've already realized you had. This is supposed to be a fun weekend. We've had plenty of time to think about Jason and everything that comes with him, we don't need to waste anymore brain power on him. Think of Kallon and what could be with him. My little pep talk has me taking a breath and putting a smile on my face.

Freddy walks up to me with my envelope and hands it to me.

"Thanks," I say. "Do you want to come in with us?"

"No, Miss Rose. I'll stay out here. Just let me know when you're ready to leave," Freddy says with a dip of his head and then he nods to Peter and Kayla too.

"If you change your mind, just come on in, man," Peter says.

"Thank you," Freddy says but he turns and walks back to his car.

"Guess that ends that conversation," Kayla says with a laugh.

"They do that a lot," I say.

"And you'll explain who 'they' are inside?" Kayla asks.

"Yes," I answer with a laugh.

We turn and walk towards their house. When we get inside, I smell cinnamon and coffee. My stomach grumbles.

"Hungry?" Kayla asks.

"Starving," I say. The muffin I had as we were taxing on the tarmac feels like it was hours ago. I pull my phone out of my pocket and see it's just a little after 6am. The muffin was an hour or so ago.

Peter leads us into their dining room where some To-

Go boxes are sitting. He opens one and shows me cinnamon rolls and then he opens another to show me bacon. My mouth waters. Kayla turns and hands me a cup from our favorite coffee shop in town and I take a sip.

"You remembered?" I ask in awe. The last time we went, we got chai teas and I fell in love with them.

"Of course, I did," she says, and her tone implies 'silly' at the end.

They sit and start to hand out plates, I sit too but instead of dishing up, I say, "Before we eat, I need to explain something real fast."

Peter and Kayla look up at me with confused looks on their faces. I hold up the large envelope and explain.

"In here are gag orders. You read it over and if you sign it, I can explain everything that's been going on since I left here last year," I say, pulling the contracts out.

"And if we don't sign?" Peter asks sounding really concerned.

At the same time, Kayla says, "Last year?"

"Yes, last year. If you don't sign, then I can only explain certain things, but not everything," I say truthfully.

Kayla reaches over and grabs a contract and then pulls a pin from the cup behind her, that's sitting on the counter of her kitchen. She's about to sign but I stop her, "You need to read it."

She stops and stares at me for a second then shrugs. Then she and Peter read over their copies of the contract. It doesn't take long before they're both signing their papers.

"You guys are sure?" I ask. "If you let slip, it's ten-thousand dollars. Jason slipped and had to pay."

"We understand," Peter says. He seems nervous but he reaches over and grabs Kayla's hand. "Whatever it is, we won't tell anyone."

Kayla nods.

"Okay, you know how I said we had a new buyer for Rose's?—" they nod "—And I told you Kallon Keller got me a gig at his movie set and I still have that gig but for a different movie?—" they nod again. "—Well, he's the same person. He bought out my parents' shares, he's my new business partner. Only, he goes by Charles Webb when it comes to business. So, if we're talking about anything business related with me and my business partner or Rose's, he's to be called Charles or Mr. Webb. We can refer to him as Kallon when it comes to my friend and Rose Bud's and my catering."

Kayla and Peter are silent for a long time. They're barely blinking. Then Kayla shrieks and claps her hands.

"Are you freaking kidding me?" she asks.

I laugh and answer, "No."

"Kallon Keller is not only your friend and got you the catering job for his movies but he's your business partner now?" she asks in disbelief.

"Yes, he's all of the above," I state.

"I'm calling it, again, you two are going to fall in love with each other and live happily ever after," she says. She looks at Peter, "Remember me saying this at their wedding. Remind me when I'm writing my matron-of-honor speech."

Peter laughs but nods.

"Umm, no! Guys, we're friends," I say, it's not really a lie, we are friends.

"Maybe for now," Kayla says.

"Can we add this to the subjects to not talk about this weekend?" I ask.

"Absolutely not!" Kayla shouts. "I want to hear everything about him."

I look at Peter for support, but he holds his hands up in defeat, "You know how she gets. She's going to want all the details before she's satisfied. I know when to pick my battles and this is not one of them. You're one your own, Abs."

"You are no help," I glare.

"Not when it comes to my Kayla. I try to give her everything her little heart desires," he says leaning over and kissing her head.

I pretend to puke but then smile warmly at them.

"Let's eat and then get going on our girl's day," Kayla says dumping food on to her plate. "We have so much to talk about."

"Great," I grumble.

Peter and Kayla laugh as we all dig into our food.

"I love you," Kayla says, giving Peter another long kiss, pulling him close to her.

"Mmm, I love you too," he says into her mouth.

"I'll see you at the alter tomorrow," she says pulling back but keeping her arms around his neck.

"I can't wait," he says, kissing her nose. Really, they're too sweet. I turn away, feeling the tears well in my eyes. *STOP IT!* I take a breath and walk towards the door.

"I'll grab my keys and we can go," I turn and see Kayla

wheeling her huge suitcase towards the door. I grab the bags with our dresses but stop her before she can get to her keys.

"Leave your car here, we'll have Freddy drive us around. That way, you and Peter will only have one rig at the hotel Sunday morning," I suggest.

"Ooh, that's a great idea!" she says excitedly.

Peter hurries and opens the door for us.

"Behave tonight," Peter says before he kisses Kayla one more time.

"You do realize you're about to marry the least wild person ever?" Kayla asks him.

"Second least wild," I correct her. I point to myself and say, "I hold the number one spot for that category."

They both laugh and Kayla amends, "Okay, the second least wild person."

"You never know, you two might get a wild hair tonight," Peter says laughing as he lets go of his soon to be wife and pushes the door wider for us.

"The wildest we might get is staying up late on your wedding eve night," I say and poke him in the shoulder as I walk past him.

"See, behave!" he says sarcastically. "No seriously though, girls, have fun tonight."

"We will, Love," Kayla says as she finally steps away from him. "See you tomorrow."

"See you tomorrow," he says from the door.

When we get halfway down the walk, Freddy runs forward and grabs the bags from my hand and then takes Kayla's suitcase from her. He turns and walks back to the rig, opens the back and puts our things inside.

He beats us to the door and opens it for us.

"Thanks, Freddy," I say giving him a smile. He just nods.

"Yes, thank you Freddy," Kayla says doing her best not to giggle.

I get in and slide over to the left side and buckle up. Kayla gets in and buckles her seat belt.

"Where to?" Freddy asks as he gets in and situated.

"Air Suite Hotel, please," I answer.

He nods, pulls up the hotel and it's address on his GPS, and pulls away from the curb and starts to drive. Kayla turns and waves at Peter. He's standing at his door, waving, and grinning like the lovesick man that he is.

"Okay, tell me how this started?" Kayla asks as she waves her hand around at the car and Freddy.

So, I tell her about when I met Kallon and his insistence on me using Dax and the car at home. Which turned into here with Freddy.

Kayla turns towards me and grins, "I've never had a driver before."

"It's actually really nice, but it was hard for me to get used to," I say with a laugh.

"Of course, it was," she says as she nudges my side.

"What's that supposed to mean?"

"Just that I'm not surprised it took you time to get used to it. You aren't one to take people up on an offer of help. So, having someone give you a driver and car? Yeah, of course you wouldn't necessarily like it."

"It's not that I don't like it, or didn't like it, it just feels like... too much."

"I can see how it could feel that way."

"But..." I prompt because I know there's a 'but' coming.

"But... maybe it's time to let someone help you. Help take care of you," she says, reaching over and taking my hand. "You do so much for so many and you don't even realize it. How many of your elderly customers do you charge half price for their meals at Rose Bud's? How many meals or drinks have you comped at Rose's for people celebrating an anniversary or a birthday or just someone who was eating alone? How often are you eager to jump at the chance to answer the call from someone when they need help?"

"I want to be the one helping, I don't want people to start thinking I need help," I say quietly.

"We all need help sometimes, Abs," she says, squeezing my hand. "And sometimes, the help that we need, isn't the normal help someone would think to offer."

"Like what?" I ask, genuinely curious.

"Like someone giving someone a car and driver so that she doesn't have to wait for a cab. Also, that she doesn't have to drive her catering van and can get some stollen minutes of sleep between her jobs," she smiles.

My grin widens, I haven't told her about the most recent things.

"Or maybe like how someone would secretly change my tickets from a commercial flight to his private jet because he knew I could use the privacy to rest," I smile at her. "Something like that."

"Umm exactly like that!" she squeals. Freddy looks at us in the rearview mirror, I smile up at him. "Excuse me!? When were you going to share that little tid-bit of information? Are you kidding me?"

"I'm not kidding. And I was pretty angry at first," I say.

"Why?"

"Because Kayla, it's too much."

"No, it's not."

"Yes it is," I say. My voice getting quiet. "I have nothing to offer him in return. I told him that."

"And what did he say?"

"He said that my friendship and my honesty are all he wants," I leave out the kissing part. I'm not ready to share that because I don't even know what it means.

"Oh... my gosh... is he for real?" she asks and then pretends to faint. "He sounds absolutely perfect."

"Kayla, it doesn't feel right, to accept all this."

"Why? All he's asking is for you to be his friend, which you are and you're a damn good friend."

"It's not enough, for all he's doing for me."

"Hold on," Kayla says and turns towards me. She pulls both of my hands into her own. "I think I understand what you're saying now. Am I understanding you correctly, that you don't think YOU are enough to receive someone like Kallon, who wants to help you, to care for you?"

"My friendship is nothing compared to everything he's done for me. The flight today and the return flight, will cost him thousands of dollars. My drivers and the cars, thousands of dollars. Everything costs him so much more than I could ever repay."

"Oh, my sweet Abby, Jason has really done a number on you, hasn't he?" Kayla asks sadly.

"What? Jason? What does he have to do with this?" I ask completely caught off guard by her bringing Jason into the conversation. "I told you I haven't seen him in over a year."

"He's beaten it into you that the only value in life is the amount of money someone has and the amount of money something costs will tell the value of a gift," Kayla says with a snarl. She takes a calming breath and says a little more gently, "Your friendship is worth more than any amount of money. YOU—" she points to me "—my dear friend, YOU are worth more than all the money in the world. Kallon sees that. He values your friendship and honesty over money. Money can be remade. Another movie, another business deal, another job... poof money made. But you... you are one of a kind. You are a rarity."

"Kayla..." I say in my 'I'm about to argue' tone, but she cuts me off.

"No, Abby. There is no argument here. Fuck Jason for making you feel lesser than money. Fuck him for making you feel like you didn't deserve more. Fuck him for making you feel like you weren't good enough for someone to WANT to do nice things for you. Fuck him for not taking care of you," Kayla is breathing hard and is so angry. "I know I said we wouldn't talk about Jason, and we won't, not after this. But if I ever see him, I'm donkey kicking his balls into his throat for how he treated you, not just when he assaulted you, but all the years before that, too."

"I don't think I've ever heard you say 'fuck' so many times at once," I say with a laugh. I'm a little taken aback actually. I understand what she's saying but I can't wrap my head around it being true.

She laughs and says a little embarrassed, "Well, I got mad. I'm sorry."

"It's okay," I say. "But next time, tell me how you really feel."

Kayla bursts out laughing and I join her. I look up and see Freddy smiling, trying to hold in his laughter.

The conversation we have for the rest of the ride to the hotel is us figuring out what else needs to be done for the wedding tomorrow. There's not much. Freddy pulls up to the lobby of the hotel and hops out and opens my door.

"Thanks, Freddy," I say as I get out.

"You're most welcome, Miss Rose," he says with a nod.

"Please call me Abby," I plead.

"No, Miss, I can't do that," he says as we walk to the other side of the car. He opens the door for Kayla, but she's still getting her bag picked up from the floor.

"Come on! If I can get Dax to call me Abby, you can too," I say.

"Dax calls you Abby?" Freddy asks.

"Only when Kallon isn't around," I laugh.

"Okay, I can make the same deal. Just don't tell Mr. Keller," he says in a whisper.

"I won't unless he asks but why would he?" I counter ask as I laugh.

Kayla steps out and we head to the back of the car.

"Why don't you girls go and start getting checked-in? I'll bring your luggage inside," Freddy suggests but he hands me my messenger bag.

"Thank you, Freddy," Kayla says. She loops her arm through mine and pulls me towards the door. She feels me being reluctant and I know she guesses why because she says, "Let the man do his job."

"Guhhh..." I grumble. "Kayla, why can't I help him?"

"You need to learn how to let people help you without feeling like you have to do something in return," Kayla says sternly. "We have Jason to thank for that as well, no doubt."

I don't say anything because, I don't have an argument for it. She's absolutely correct. I do feel like anytime someone does something for me, I have to return the favor. I know some people say to pay it forward, which I do, but I also am programmed to pay it back. Apparently too often.

We walk through the doors and into the hotel. It's gorgeous. The floor is a white marble and the walls are a darker wood. The couches around the lobby are a dark leather that match the walls well. The counter where the hotel clerks are standing, looks like it's made from the same wood from the walls.

"Hello," the girl behind the counter says to us as we walk up. "My name is Milly, how can I help you today?"

"Hi Milly," Kayla says. "I'm Makayla Smith, checking-in."

"Aww yes, Miss Smith," Milly says as she types her name in. "I see you had arranged for an early check-in which is absolutely fantastic. I also see you're getting married tomorrow, congratulations! Oh, wait, what's this? I have a note I need to read, just a moment, please."

Milly reads something on her screen and then she smiles. She then types away on her computer. Kayla looks at me and I shrug.

"Is there a problem?" I ask.

"No, no problem, Miss?" Milly looks up and asks.

"Abbigail Rose," I say. "I have a room, but I'll be staying with Kayla tonight and then checking-in to mine tomorrow."

Milly just smiles at me and continues to click away on her keyboard. After another minute of awkward silence except for the sound of her nails on her keyboard, Milly looks up and smiles at Kayla.

"You and your wedding party—" Milly says with an even bigger smile "—have been upgraded to a presidential suite. Tomorrow, you will be transferred to the honeymoon suite. Your weekend stay has been comped and you have an open tab for the bar, room service, and any other services you'd like to have while you are staying here at Air Suites Hotel."

"What?" Kayla and I say at the same time. Her gaping mouth mirrors mine.

"Yes you heard me correctly, Miss Rose, Miss Smith. Now if you follow the hall to the right—" she smiles and points to our right "—there is an elevator that will take you up to your level. Your floor number is 14, you push that number in the elevator. When the elevator stops, you put your card in the slot and then the doors will open. There is a small lobby once you step out of the elevator. You put your card in the slot on the door and you may enter your suite. You are one of two suites on that floor, so you don't have to worry about anyone coming and going, except for who you wish to use the room."

She hands us each a keycard and just as we're stepping away from the counter, Freddy walks into the lobby. He has a huge rolling cart with our suitcases on the bottom and our dress bags hanging from the bar that goes across the top.

"Ready girls?" he asks.

"I guess," Kayla says still dumbfounded.

"Lead the way," Freddy says as he rolls the cart. But then he stops and says to the clerk, "I'll be back to move my car in a few minutes."

"No worries. See you in a few," Milly says with a big smile. *Freddy has a fan,* I laugh to myself.

We walk to the elevator and only wait a minute. We put the cart in first and then we maneuver ourselves around it. Kayla pushes the number 14 and we wait patiently as the elevator takes us up. When the elevator stops, Kayla puts the card into the slot and the door opens. The lobby isn't as small as I was expecting. Four of the luggage carts could fit in here easily with room for people. Kayla puts her card in the slot and once the little light turns green, she opens the door.

"Hoooollllyyyyy crap," she says in awe.

I step inside and I can see what she means.

Right inside the door are two closets and then immediately further in, is a guest bathroom. Kayla is frozen to the floor, so I walk in further. French doors open into the main room, which is the dining room and kitchen, and a large living room. I turn to the left and find a small hall. To my immediate left there's a closet and then a little further in, a bathroom with a separate room for the toilet and a separate room for the huge bath and shower. I turn and see the door to the bedroom. I can see two large beds. I think they're queen sizes. I walk in and find one of the biggest flatscreen TVs I've ever seen in a hotel, on the wall. There are two large recliners at the foot of each bed. I walk to the left of the room where there's a sliding glass door and open it. It leads to a balcony that has a view of Little Arkansas River and Oak Park.

I turn and see Freddy and Kayla standing in the room. I hadn't heard them following me.

"This is unbelievable," I say smiling at her. I ask, "Did

you check out the other side of the living room?"

She shakes her head no. I take her hand and walk us back through the suite, glancing over my shoulder to see Freddy following us. The living room looks like something from my dream. It has over sized chairs that look like I could fall into and sleep, they look so comfy. The couch looks very similar in comfiness. There's a fireplace that has small flames burning as we speak. I see another set of sliding glass doors, but I keep walking forward until I come to a door. I open it and see a huge walk-in closet to my right. I continue walking us forward and a huge bathroom is to the right also. To the left, it opens into the master bedroom. On its wall is another equally huge TV as the one in the other bedroom. Across the room is another sliding glass door and I pull Kayla to it. It opens to a bigger balcony and I see the sliding glass doors that lead to the living room. I turn and see it has a private hot tub.

"Holy..." I say. I turn to Kayla and see she has a startled look on her face. I walk back to her and pull her inside. I sit her on the bed and ask, "Are you okay?"

"I don't understand. How is this possible?" she replies.

She looks at me. I put my hands up and say, "Don't look at me. I can't afford this."

"Then who?" she asks.

I start to laugh when I realize once again who could have done this.

"Kallon," I say through my laugh.

"What?" she looks taken aback.

"Kallon did this," I say. I pull my phone out and see that it's almost noon. He won't be done with filming yet. So, I send him a text.

Me: Will you call me when you have a second, please? I promise not to yell… too much. :-D

"But why?" she asks as I put my phone away.

"Because it's what he does," I say.

"This is amazing," she says breathless.

"Should we change and get ready for our manicures and pedicures, they start at noon, right?" I ask.

She just nods.

"Okay, let's get changed and we'll head downstairs. This is your room," I say.

"Oh, heck no it's not," she says standing up. "You take this one."

"It's your wedding eve night, you take the master room. Bree and I will share the other room," I say. Her sister-in-law is the other bridesmaid.

"Bree doesn't get to come today or tonight, it's just us," Kayla says. "Her baby has decided he no longer wants to take bottles from my brother and he isn't sleeping through the night. So, she doesn't want to leave him, and she doesn't want to bring him here on the chance he'll keep me up. I told her I was fine with them coming but she still refuses. She's still coming to get ready with us in the morning and will ride over with us. She just needs to make sure the baby sleeps well tonight and hopefully she can get him to take a bottle again."

"Awww, poor Bree," I say feeling bad for her. She was looking forward to our wedding eve sleepover.

"I know," Kayla says sadly.

"Well, no matter, this is still your room," I say with a

smile. Then I turn to Freddy and say, "Could you bring Kayla's luggage in here please? You can leave the dress bags out there, for now. I'll go get changed and meet you in the living room, Kay."

"Yes, Miss Rose," Freddy says. He turns and leaves the room quickly.

"Abby—" she starts to say but I cut her off.

"We aren't arguing about this. It's your wedding eve night, you get this room," I say and then I leave the room, not giving her a chance to argue.

I meet Freddy at the clothes rack and smile at him when he looks up.

"After I give Miss Smith her suitcase, I should go move the car," he says as he lifts her suitcase off the cart and puts it down on its wheels beside him.

"Sounds good," I say. "I don't think we'll need to go anywhere."

"Call me if you need anything," Freddy says as he hands me my suitcase.

I nod at him and head towards what is now my room. I can't wait for our girl's day to really get started.

CHAPTER 11

"What color would you like, Miss Rose?" Sally, the nail technician, asks.

"Umm, let's do a light pink, please," I say. "One that's as natural looking as my fingers?"

"Okay, I've got just the one," she says as she leads me to her booth.

I sit down next to Kayla. She was brought over a few minutes before me.

"Are you sure you don't want to get acrylics or anything?" Kayla asks.

"No. I don't like my nails too long," I say as I smile over at her.

Kayla shrugs and goes back to telling her nail tech, Kristine, about her wedding prep tomorrow.

Sally turns to them and gets involved in the discussion. It doesn't take long for her to finish trimming and filing my fingernails. Then she's finished painting them too.

"They look great," I say, showing them to Kayla.

"Oooh, I like that color," she says, holding her hand out to me. I put my right hand into hers and she pulls it closer to her face. "It's got little flecks of gold in it!"

I hold my hands to my face and look at my nails closer.

"I didn't notice that before," I exclaim. "It's so pretty!"

"I thought you'd like that one," Sally says with a smile. She stands and asks, "Do you want to move over to the pedicure chair to start your pedicure or would you rather wait for Miss Smith?"

"I'll wait," I say. And then I ask, "If that's okay?"

"Totally fine," Sally answers. "I'll just get this cleaned up and get your pedicure chairs and water ready."

"Thanks, Sal," Kristine says as she starts painting Kayla's nails.

"What else do you girls have planned for today?" Sally asks as she puts the polish away and wipes down her table.

"We've got full body massages at 2," Kayla says with a dreamy sigh.

"Oh, that'll be nice," Sally says.

My phone vibrates in my pocket. I pull it out and see I have a text from a number I don't recognize.

+1(878)555-2665: Hey, this is Freddy. If you need anything, please let me know.

Me: Hey, Freddy! Will do. But, umm.. how did you get my number?

+1(878)555-2665: Mr. Keller gave it to me.

Me: Did he?

+1(878)555-2665: Yes, Miss Rose. I hope that's ok. I had forgotten to swap numbers with you before your appts started, so I called Mr. Keller and Randy asked Mr. Keller if he could give me your number.

Me: Oh, ok, yeah that's totally fine. I'll add you to my phone now.

I quickly add Freddy's number to my contacts and scroll

down my text history. I still haven't heard from Kallon myself. *It's barely after noon, he's still working.* I say to myself to calm my nerves. *Why am I nervous about talking to him or him not talking to me?*

I shake myself and turn my attention back to Kayla talking to the girls.

"You're wedding isn't going to be big?" Sally asks in shock.

"No, my fiancé and I wanted to keep it small. Just our immediate family and our closest friends. We still have over one-hundred people coming but if we invited everyone that we wanted to, or thought we should, it would have been well over five-hundred people invited. The food was one of the most expensive things," Kayla answers with a shake of her head.

"You should have still invited them!" Kristine says with fake exasperation in her tone. "They probably wouldn't have all come but at least they would have sent you a gift or money."

Kayla laughs and says, "We aren't getting married for any of that, but I see your point."

Sally turns to me and asks, "So, do you have a date for the wedding?"

"Umm, no," I answer and then thinking of what Kayla just said, I freeze. *Jason's plate!* I put my hand to my face and say, "Oh, shoot, Kayla! I'll pay you for Jason's plate. I didn't even think about it being an inconvenience to the catering side of your wedding."

"No, don't even worry about that!" Kayla says hurriedly. She reaches over with her right hand, which is finished and squeezes my hand.

"No, I will, please. It's my fault he's not here," I say with a shake of my head.

"The HELL it is!" she exclaims so loud, I jump. "Don't you ever say that! You don't take responsibility for that ass-hats actions anymore!"

I look at Sally and Kristine, they are professional enough to not look at us. They are acting like their jobs of finishing Kayla's left hand and cleaning up the other table is their top priority. But I can tell their listening, who wouldn't be?

"Kayla, I'm not taking responsibility for what he did. Or how he's treated me through the years, I'm not making excuses. What I meant is that had I realized our relationship wasn't going anywhere, I would have ended it a long time ago."

"Okay, well that, yes, I can see as your fault," she says with a laugh and then squeezes my hand again. Her smile softens when she adds, "Abby, you loved him. It's natural to hold out hope that he'd pull his head out of his butt sooner rather than later."

"Yeah, well, I've learned my lesson," I say squeezing her hand. "I just wish I had someone at the wedding, you know. I had it in my head from the moment Peter proposed that I'd finally get to be in a wedding and have a date. I'll just make sure my maid-of-honor duties are fulfilled to a T."

"You've already done that just by being here," she squeezes my hand again. And then she gets a look in her eye and lets go of my hand and grabs her phone. I'm about to ask her what her look means but Kristine interrupts me.

"All done my dear," Kristine says. Kayla puts her phone down and then looks at her nails.

"Perfect!" she exclaims happily.

"I'll have you ladies follow me to the pedicure chairs and I'll get your feet soaking," Sally says as she stands and gestures towards the line of chairs sitting on the other side of the room. She has two chairs ready for us, the tubs for our feet full of color changing water from the lights inside.

We sit and take our sandals off and turn at the same time and put in our feet. It feels glorious!

"Oh, I could get used to this!" Kayla says with a moan.

"In the little pocket to the right of the chair, you'll find a remote to control the massage chair. It won't feel nearly as good as your massage you have scheduled for this afternoon, but it'll feel good enough," Kristine says from across the room as she cleans her station up.

"Your pedicure comes with a scent option," Sally says as she rolls another cart over to us. One is already in front of Kayla. On the cart, is all the tools they'll need for our pedicures plus small totes with packets of things.

"What does that mean?" I ask. "I've never gotten a pedicure before."

"You choose a scent and we dump the scented salts into the water to soak your feet. Then, we have a mask and lotion to go on later. It all smells like the scent you've chosen," Sally says as she hands me something that looks like a menu.

I look down and see the list of scents they offer.

"Okay," I say as I look down the list. "I'll do cucumber, please."

"Oh, me too!" Kayla says from beside me. I look over and see she's got a menu in her hands as well.

"Perfect," Sally says as she grabs a packet from the cart in front of me. She opens it and dumps the little crystal salts into the water. I instantly smell cucumber. I close my eyes and put my head back.

"That smells amazing," I say.

I hear Sally rip open the packet for Kayla and then she's pouring it into the water. She asks, "Would you girls like a warm towel to put over your eyes to help you relax even more?"

"That would be amazing," Kayla says with a sigh.

"Yes, please," I say almost dreamily.

"Can we get you something to drink, now that your hands are free?" Kristine asks from close by. I peek out from under my eyelashes and see her standing between mine and Kayla's chairs.

"Sure, what do you have?" Kayla asks.

"An assortment of wine, champagne, juice, soda, water, and I could even get a beer or mixed drink brought in from the bar downstairs," Kristine answers.

"Champagne sounds good to me," Kayla says. Then she asks me, "Abby?"

"Yeah, why not. We're celebrating! I'll have a glass too," I say, keeping my eyes shut but smiling all the same.

"Sounds good, I'll be right back with those drinks and then we'll start your pedicures," Kristine says as I hear her walk away.

"Miss Rose, I don't want to startle you but I'm going to put a warm towel over your eyes okay?" Sally says from beside me.

I jump and open my eyes, and say, "Sorry, I didn't hear you walk up."

"My apologies," she says with humor in her voice.

Before she puts the towel on me, I glance over at Kayla, and see she's on her phone.

"Kay, we're supposed to be relaxing, what are you doing? Didn't we confirm everything already?" I ask her.

"Not everything but I'm just about done," she answers with a smile.

"What else is there?" I ask her.

"Don't worry about it, it's a last-minute thing, I've got it. You relax," she says with a bigger smile.

"Kay?" I sit up and look at her.

"I promise, if it was something you could help me with I'd let you deal with it," she says with a laugh. I glare at her until she puts her phone down. She sighs and says, "There, I'm done."

"Okay," I say with a relieved smile. Sally smiles at me and holds out the towel. I lean my head back and she places it over my eyes. I sigh again and say, "Thank you, Sally."

A few minutes later, I hear Kristine walking back into the room. I know it's her because Sally is way too quiet and there wasn't anyone else here.

"I'm going to set your drinks on the table between you two," Kristine says.

"Thank you," Kayla and I say at the same time.

I peek out from the towel and see where the drinks are placed. Kayla has her towel in her hands and sees me looking at her. She reaches out and hands me one of the glasses. Once I've taken it, she takes the other.

"To a fun and relaxing day with my best friend," she offers her glass towards me.

"Cheers to that," I say, clinking my glass to hers.

I take a sip and find the champagne to be the best I've ever had. I take another sip, a little bit bigger one this time.

"Wow, this is really good," I say. "Could I get the name of this before we leave?"

"Absolutely," Kristine says, I can hear the smile in her voice.

I relax back into my chair and let Sally do her thing with my feet and legs. When she's finished with trimming and what not with my first foot, she moves on and puts it into a bag with something hot in it. It's not unpleasant but feels weird. I peek under the towel and see it's a type of liquid.

"It's a warm wax, Miss Rose, it'll make your skin extra soft," Sally says when she sees me looking.

I just smile and put the towel back over my eyes. I'm surprised it has stayed this warm for this long.

"So, Abby," Kayla says, pulling me out of my zoning out moment.

"Yeah?" I say prompting her to go on.

"Tell me more about Kallon," she says, and I can definitely hear the smile in her voice.

"What do you want to know?" I ask, on guard for wherever this conversation is going.

"Do you like him?"

"There's not a lot to dislike," I say with a laugh.

She laughs too, "From what I've seen and what you've told me, I can see that. But I'm asking if YOU like him."

"We're friends," I say.

"Abby," she says, sounding a little exasperated. "Do... you... like him?"

"I'm not going there with him," I state matter-of-factly.

"Why not?"

"We work together," I state again.

"So," Kayla says it in a 'what does that matter' tone.

"It hardly ever works out between two people who work together. It could become extremely awkward and hard to work with him. Plus, he's... Kallon."

"Okay, I'll come back to that last part. But the first part, Abby? Your parents were married and worked really well together."

"That's because Mom was the manager side of the restaurant and Dad was the kitchen side. They balanced each other out really well and were good at communicating."

"Seems to me, you and Kallon could be similar," she suggests.

I think for a minute and then peek out from my towel and look at her. She's sitting with her towel in her lap.

"It doesn't matter, Kay, it'd never work," I say, sounding sadder about it than I mean to.

Her eyes light up at my tone, and she asks, "Why?"

"He's Kallon."

"Okay, now on to that. What do you mean by that?"

"You know what I mean," I say, I look pointedly at the girls doing our pedicures. I don't want to tell them it's Kallon Keller. I don't want to be bombarded with questions about how I know him.

"He's still just a man," Kayla says pointedly.

"I know that," I say in my defense. "He's a great man, he really is. He's kind and thoughtful and funny. He's intelligent and fun to be around. But I could never live up to his standards. Or what the public thinks should be his standards."

"Good lord, Abby," she says as she closes her eyes and pinches the bridge of her nose. "I could see Jason chipping away at your self-confidence, but I didn't think it had gotten this bad."

"What? I'm confident in myself," I say defensively again.

"No, you aren't," she says with kindness. She looks at me with a stern look, which doesn't match her tone. "Maybe in your work but when it comes to you, as a woman, you're not confident at all. If you were, you'd see that it's Kallon that needs to step it up himself to be what you deserve."

"Oh my gosh," I say with a laugh. "You haven't even met him, Kayla. If... no when you do, because you need to come visit me in New York, but when you come up there, I'll introduce you to him and you'll see just what I mean. With everything he has... Who he is as a person, is the most impressive thing to me. He's chivalrous and genuinely kind. He doesn't like to showboat anything he has and he's a hard worker, so I can see how he doesn't want to be taken advantage of when he's worked so hard to build his business and everything. He's sweet and thoughtful. He didn't have to stay with me while I was healing, but he did, because he didn't want me to be alone. He got me a lawyer to deal with any legal things that might have come up with Jason, so I didn't have to do any of it. He took care of everything with the catering—" I'm about to say the gig at the movie set but again, I don't want to have this conversation turn into something with the girls. They're nice and all but it'd be too much. "—gig. Not to mention the extra security around the bakery just to make sure Jason didn't show up. The flight here... Freddy... the hotel room, even though I haven't confirmed that it was him, but I know it is.

Kayla, he deserves someone so much better than me."

"There is no one better than you," Kayla says sternly.

"Well, it doesn't matter. Even if I did like him that way, he isn't interested in me like that. I am so not his type," I say with a laugh. Thinking about all the women he's been with, makes my heart hurt. I am nothing like those women. I don't know what I was thinking kissing him.

"What's his type?" she asks defensively for some reason.

"The opposite of me."

"Ugly?" Sally asks from down at my feet. I quickly look at her and my mouth is open. "I'm sorry to push my two cents in on your conversation but honestly, Miss Rose, you are beautiful. You both are."

"See!" Kayla exclaims. "They agree with me."

I shake my head and laugh, "It doesn't matter, I'm not saying anything to him. It'll make things awkward between us."

"Say what to him?" Kayla asks excitedly. "That you like him?"

"Again, Kay, someone would be utterly stupid to not like him," I say with a small laugh, it's fake but I'm good at faking it. I add, "Plus, even though Jason and I broke up over a year ago. I'd feel silly jumping into something, or someone, right now."

"First, it wouldn't be silly at all, especially if it was Kallon. Second, it's been a year. But I can see you aren't going to fully admit it, are you?"

"I don't know what you're talking about," I say with a small smile as I grab for my glass and take a drink.

"Give me one reason why you won't admit it?"

"Because I don't want to risk losing our friendship,

Kayla," I say. I can feel myself getting a little upset now. "He even said he values my friendship over anything. Why would I risk that just to hear what I already know?"

"You know for certain he doesn't think of you as more than someone he works with or just a friend?"

"Yes...," *LIAR* my inner thoughts scream at me.

"If you ask me—"

I cut her off, "I'm not, I'm not asking you. I know you want me to be happy and find someone that'll treat me better than Jason did, and I love you for that. But Kay, it's not Kallon. I promise you that."

"Don't promise something you aren't one-hundred percent certain of," she says with a tilt to her head and a smile.

"Ugh, can we change the subject please because this is going to have to be put in the box of 'things we'll just have to agree to disagree on', there's not a lot in it but this is definitely going in there."

"Abby—"

"Please, Kayla..." I beg. My voice cracks and I can feel tears starting to well up in my eyes, so I shut them and lean my head back. Honestly, the thought of Kallon telling me that us kissing was a mistake hurts more than it should. *We... are... just... friends.*

"Okay, okay," she says, I feel her grab my hand. "I'm sorry. I don't want to upset you."

"Let's change the subject then, please," I say.

"Okay," she says in a small voice. I look at her and see her back on her phone.

Now I feel bad.

"Kay," I say sitting up to look at her. "Please don't be

mad. It's just... I..."

"What?" she asks.

I can admit it to Kayla, can't I? It won't hurt anything if I do? Maybe if I get it out of my head, it won't fester.

"Okay, yes I do like him, alright. But it doesn't change a thing. All it does is make me feel worse because I know it'll go nowhere. These feelings will sit here and go nowhere. I feel like a shitty person because Jason was right," I say with a break in my voice. "He could see that I liked Kallon, but I told him I didn't. I've been fighting these feelings since the first time I saw him. I know it's not entirely my fault what happened with Jason, him attacking me, but had I been honest with myself, how I felt... feel about Kallon, I would have broken up with Jason. Because I would have admitted I didn't have those feelings for him anymore."

"Abby, it's not your fault—"

"It kind of is though. I didn't make Jason drink or at least I didn't put the bottle in his hand. But maybe I did make him feel like there was something there between Kallon and me. Even if I was denying it and hiding my feelings, to myself, Jason could still feel it, and see it. Even though I was trying everything I could to stay connected with Jason, he could still feel me pulling away."

"He pulled away a long time before you did," Kayla says in my defense.

"I know, and it happened well before Kallon came into the picture but if I had been more honest with myself, I would have broken up with Jason a long time ago. But I kept hanging on."

"And like I said before, that's normal when you've been

in love... been in a relationship with someone for as long as you guys had been together. Couples go through ups and down, hard times and good times. It's normal to think that it was just a hard time," she says squeezing my hand.

"For two years? A hard time for years?" I ask in a small voice. Kayla looks at me shocked. "Yeah, it hadn't been recently. It's been two years. When he broke my trust, when he told his work about our little scare a couple years ago. I could feel myself changing how I felt about him. I started to pull away then, to guard myself."

"That's understandable. He broke your trust, he needed to earn it back. He's done the opposite with all the cheating and lying. You just tried to make it work. To work through while guarding your heart, that's natural," Kayla says.

I look down and watch Sally massaging my calf and then down to my foot.

"Abby?" Kayla asks, drawing my attention back to her. "Can you see what I mean?"

"Yes," I say. "But it doesn't change how I feel."

"I can't argue with that, we'll just need to help you feel differently," she says with a laugh. I can't help but laugh a little too.

"Can we forget all this talk and just relax and enjoy today?" I ask. "It's your wedding eve, remember? It's supposed to be fun."

"I am having fun," Kayla says with a louder laugh.

"Of course you are, Nosey Nelly," I tease her.

"I'm not being a Nosey Nelly if I'm looking out for my best friend," she says. I can tell she's about to go on another tangent, so I cut her off.

"Okay, you're right. Now let's enjoy what's left of our pedicure. I'm sure we've entertained these girls enough with this conversation," I say smiling at Sally and Kristine.

"Oh, you are fine," Sally says with a sweet smile. "Your conversation isn't the worst we've heard."

"Good," I say with a laugh and put my head back.

We spend the rest of our pedicure resting and relaxing.

CHAPTER 12

We're making our way back to our room after the best massage I've ever received. I guess it's the only professional massage I've ever had, Jason's half ass massages don't really count. Kallon's foot massages were pretty decent though.

We were surprised when we went to pay for our pedicures and manicures to find that the bill was already covered. We didn't want to expect it after our massages but, again, no bill was due.

I keep checking my phone to hear back from Kallon but still nothing. It's now after 4, so he should be getting off work soon, seeing as it's after 5 back home.

"What do we want to do for dinner?" I ask Kayla. We didn't have lunch but we've sure been enjoying the champagne.

"What do you want?" she counter asks and then hiccups. She laughs and says, "Maybe we should order room service and stay in tonight. I'm already feeling tipsy. That champagne went down too smoothly."

"Agreed!" I say a little too enthusiastically. "Let's get to our room and look over the menu."

We make it to the elevator and take it up to our floor. When the door dings open, we step out and as Kayla tries to put the key in the slot, we start laughing hysterically. The door across the little hall opens and we spin. We didn't know someone had gotten the other suite.

"Miss Rose, Miss Smith, having trouble with the door?" Freddy asks from the doorway of the other suite.

"You're staying there?" I ask, surprised.

"Yes, so I can be close if you need anything," he says. He steps up to us, with his hand out. I smell his cologne.

"You smell good," I say without thinking. I put my hand to my mouth and start to laugh. "Sorry."

He looks down at me and then at Kayla who's laughing too. He smiles and asks, "Have you two been drinking?"

"Yup," Kayla says and pops the 'P'.

"Wonderful," he says with a laugh.

"What's the matter with that?" I ask. I put my hand on his arm. "You've got big muscles."

"Miss Rose let's get you inside. Have you eaten today?" Freddy asks.

"Just the breakfast we had at Kayla's," I say, still laughing. *Pull it together!* I chastise myself internally. I stop laughing and stand straight.

"What's wrong?" he asks quickly. My sudden change of demeanor must have surprised him, "Are you going to puke?"

I laugh again, "No!"

"What was that then?" he asks as Kayla finally decides she's not getting the key in the slot and hands it to him. He slides it in effortlessly.

"You're good at finding the hole, aren't you?" Kayla asks.

He looks down at her and she winks and laughs.

"Oh... my gosh," Freddy says with his own laugh.

"He's not arguing with you," I say to Kayla. I pat his arm again and add, "With these arms, I'm sure he could find any hole he wanted."

"Oookay," he says as he puts his hands to the small of our backs and ushers us inside. He's trying not to laugh. "That'll be enough about me and holes."

"Are you single?" Kayla asks.

He looks down at her with big eyes.

"Yes," he answers reluctantly.

"So is Abby," she says and then wiggles her eyebrows at me and then at him. I burst out laughing again.

I look up at Freddy and his eyes have gone wide. He looks down at me and I can see him fumbling for words.

"Awwww, you've got him all flustered, Kayla," I say, patting his arm again. I can't seem to keep my hands off his biceps.

"Don't you think she's beautiful?" Kayla asks.

I stop and look at her, I shake my head and say, "Kayla, no."

"I just asked a question," she says with another tipsy laugh. I push her away from Freddy and I mouth 'sorry' to him.

"She is beautiful," Freddy says and then clears his throat. Kayla stops in her tracks, keeping me from pushing her further into the living room. She spins around to look at him. I turn my head towards him too. "You are beautiful, Miss Rose. But—" he clears his throat again "—I'm here to protect you."

"You can protect her really well from the comfort of her bed," Kayla says. "I'm sure you could help her with something.

She was just saying the other day how it's been a long time since she's or—"

I turn bright red and whirl towards my so-called best friend. I put my hand over her mouth and shout over her as she mumbles the last of that word, "THANKS FREDDY! I'll call you if we need anything else."

I push with all my might and Kayla finally starts to move while laughing hysterically.

"Yes, Miss Rose," I hear Freddy say and then I hear him walking back to the door.

"What?" Kayla finally asks once I've got her on the couch.

"Why would you—" I say too loudly and then lower my voice "—say that to him?"

"Say what?"

"That I haven't… that it's been a long time since I had an orgasm!" I snarl.

"When?" she asks confused.

"Just now," I growl.

"Did I?" she asks now feigning confusion.

I laugh and say, "You're a bitch."

"You love me though," she says with another laugh. "I bet sleeping with Freddy would be amazing."

"Kayla!"

"What? You know I'm perfectly happy with Peter, more than happy. I am utterly satisfied every time with him. I mean it would be amazing for you, to sleep with Freddy."

"Kayla!" I exclaim again. I walk towards the door. I didn't hear it shut. Thankfully he's nowhere to be seen. I walk back to her and sit beside her. "You can't say things like that."

"Why not?" she says with a pout. "It's the truth. He looks like he would know what he's doing."

"Oh... my gosh!" I laugh. "You can't tell that just by looking at someone."

"Sure, you can," she says as she leans back onto the couch and wiggles her eyebrows again.

"Why are you trying so hard to get me laid?" I laugh.

"Because you need it," she says laughing. "And what kind of best friend would I be if wasn't a good wingman... wingwoman."

"Trying to get our driver, bodyguard, whatever he is, to sleep with me is not the way to go about getting me laid," I say. I sigh and add, "I need to take a break from guys anyways. Get my head on straight and focus on work."

"It's been a yearlong break. You focus on work too much as it is," she says as she sits up and leans towards me. "If you ask me, you need to focus more on getting that orgasm you so desperately need."

"What?" I exclaim. "I do not."

"Oh, Abs, you so do!" she says laughing harder. "Your stress level will be so much lower if you had a good pounding."

"KAYLA!" I say and then start to laugh hysterically. "No more drinking for you, you're getting ridiculous."

"One more bottle," she pleads. "We'll stop drinking at 8 o'clock and start hydrating."

"Deal," I say excitedly, conceding quickly. The champagne really is too good to not have any more. *And it's just us in the suite, what trouble could we get into? Now if Freddy comes back in here?* I stop that thought in its tracks. *Nope, there's no if Freddy comes back in here.*

As I pull my phone out, I tell Kayla, "Find the room service menu. If we're ordering another bottle, we need some food first."

I send Freddy a text.

Me: Hey, so no matter what we call or text you from here on out, ignore everything, please. Unless you hear us scream like we're being attacked, do not come in here.

I don't have to wait long for his response. He must be so bored sitting in that suite all by himself. *Maybe we should invite him back over?* My thoughts go to how good he smells and his biceps. My stomach flips. *Nope! Definitely not inviting him back over. Not that he'd do anything, but I'd act like a fool trying. NO! No, I won't.. wouldn't.*

Freddy: And why is that, Miss Rose?

Me: Just promise me you won't come back over here.

Freddy: If this is because I told you, you were beautiful, I won't take it back, but I can act professionally.

Me: It's not because of that, thank you though. I just have a feeling Kayla might get carried away. We're getting one more bottle of champagne.

Freddy: Oh man... yeah copy that. Just let me know if you need anything.

Kayla looks up from the menu and says, "I can't decide. Should we get a little of everything?"

"Maybe not everything, but maybe a couple things?" I say. I then suggest, "Why don't you order a few things that sound good. It's your wedding eve, I'll eat whatever."

She smiles and jumps from the couch and sways.

"Wow, too fast," she says as she steadies herself. She laughs and then as she walks away, she says, "I'll go order!"

My phone vibrates in my hand, I look down, expecting a text from Freddy but I see it's from Kallon. My stomach feels like it's on a rollercoaster. *It's just a text!*

Kallon: Hey, just got home. So, how mad at me are you?

I shake my head and smile.

Me: I'm not mad.

Kallon: Are you sure?

Me: I was just upset. I'm not going to be able to repay you for any of this. ANY of it. Ever.

Kallon: I don't want you to.

Me: You made Kayla's day. Is this one of your hotels?

Kallon: I don't know what you mean. :-D

Me: Kallon…

Kallon: Ok, yes it is. I couldn't resist surprising you girls with the upgrade. You two deserve the best tonight. It's your best friend's wedding weekend.

Me: How can I ever repay you for this?

Kallon: I can think of a way.

Me: Like how?

Kallon: I'll tell you later.

Me: Hmmm… that makes me nervous.

Kallon: Hahaha So, how's your day been?

Me: Beyond good. We've been spoiled the moment we got here. Thanks to you!

Kallon: Is Freddy working out alright?

Me: Yeah, except Kayla just tried to get him to sleep with me.

Shit! Why did I just tell him that? His response is quick.

Kallon: She did what?!

Me: She has no filter when she gets tipsy.

Kallon: What did she say and what was his response?

Me: hahaha It's not a big deal. I'm not sleeping with him.

Kallon: Why won't you tell me?

Me: Because it's embarrassing.

Kallon: Why?

Me: Because she let something slip and it's embarrassing to me.

Kallon: You can tell me, I won't make it worse.

Me: Oh, the heck you won't!

Kallon: Now I really need to know.

Me: No, you don't.

Kallon: Either you tell me or I'll call Freddy and ask him.

Me: NO!

Me: Please don't.

Kallon: Come on, it can't be that bad.

Me: It is.

Kallon: Please tell me, the suspense of not knowing is killing me.

Me: Really, it's no big deal.

Kallon: Ok, then I'll be right back after I call Freddy.

Me: NO! Fine, I'll tell you. Lordy, you're annoying!

Kallon: :-D

Me: She asked him if he thought I was beautiful. I tried to get her to get into the suite to get away from him, so she'd stop blurting stuff out. He said yes, he thought I was beautiful. He then said, 'but I'm here to protect you.' She said he could protect me from my bed. She then continued on with 'I'm sure you could help her with something. She was just saying the other day how it's been a long time since she's...' and I covered her mouth and told Freddy thank you and he could go. The end.

Kallon: That's not the end. What did she say that you don't want to tell me?

Me: Kallon, it's really embarrassing, please don't make me say it.

Kallon: Have I ever made you feel like you couldn't tell me anything? Have I made fun of you for anything? Maybe I can help you.

My eyes go wide as I read the last sentence and burst out laughing. I look over and see that Kayla isn't in the kitchen anymore. I don't remember seeing her go by.

"Kayla?" I holler.

"In my room!" she hollers back.

"Okay, just checking on you," I holler in return. I go back to my texting with Kallon. I feel brave, probably from this liquid courage coursing through my veins!

Me: You might but no. LOL

Kallon: What does that mean?

Me: Nothing. I shouldn't have said that, I'm tipsy.

Kallon: We're going to talk about this. You say I might be able to help you. Tell me, please. I want to help you any way I can.

"Bahahaha," I can't help laughing out loud. I cover my mouth and hold my breath. Hoping Kayla didn't hear me again. She doesn't come running in, so I'm guessing she didn't.

Me: You're going to feel ridiculous having said that once I tell you what she said or tried to say.

Kallon: I'll be the judge of that. :-D

Me: Orgasm.

The three little dots appear and then disappear twice before his reply comes through.

Kallon: I'm sorry, what?

Me: You read that correctly.

Kallon: She told Freddy it's been a while since you've had an orgasm?

Now it's my turn to decide what to say. There's a knock at the door, which makes me jump. I walk over to it as there's another knock and from the other side I hear a woman's voice.

"Room service," she says.

I open the door and see a woman standing with a tray in her hands. It has two bottles of champagne in a bucket and two glasses. *Kayla!* I scream at her in my head. *I didn't agree to a bottle each.*

"Thank you," I say to the woman. "I'll take it."

"We'll have the food up shortly," she says with a smile.

"Thank you," I say. She turns without hesitation and goes to the elevator and gets on right way, the doors opening the second she hit the down button.

I close the door and walk to the kitchen putting the bucket and glasses down on the counter. My phone buzzes in my hand.

Kallon: Abby?

If I'm having this conversation with him, I need another drink. So maybe the two bottles are divine intervention. I pop the lid off one and grab a glass, filling it halfway and downing it. I fill it up to the top and drink it halfway again and then top it off. I walk back to the couch and send Kallon my reply.

Me: Yes, she told him that.

Kallon: Oh...

Me: Yup.

Kallon: Follow up question...

I laugh and take a sip of my champagne. *Liquid courage don't fail me now!*

Me: Okaaaay........

Kallon: Was she lying?

Me: Oh my gosh! Kallon....

Kallon: What? :-D

Me: Why do you want to know that?

Kallon: Just curious.

Me: No, she wasn't lying.

Kallon: Hmmm.... You haven't mentioned being with anyone since Jason.

Me: Okay?

Kallon: Has there been anyone?

Me: No...

Kallon: So, it's been a REALLY long time.

Me: KALLON!

Kallon: haha sorry but I'm actually being serious. Didn't we have a conversation about how he was super selfish when it came to that kind of stuff?

Me: Yes.

I'm still awed at the fact that he remembers the conversations we've had, even if it's been over a year.

Kallon: So how long exactly has it been?

Me: How long has it been for you?

Kallon: Do you really want to know?

Me: No, not really.

Kallon: I didn't think so. My answer might surprise you though.

Me: Really? I'm guessing Tiffany?

Kallon: No...

Me: When?

Kallon: When I got home last night. Now you answer.

Me: Who was with you?

Kallon: No one.

Me: Oooh…

Kallon: That cold shower didn't really help much after saying goodbye to you at the airport.

Me: hahaha I'm sorry.

Kallon: I'm sure you are. :-D Now, your turn.

Me: I honestly don't know.

Kallon: You can't remember.

Me: No, like I think… never?

His three dots are there and then disappear like last time.

Kallon: Okay then. That's definitely 'a while'.

Me: Yup.

Kallon: Are you embarrassed for telling me?

Me: I have liquid courage on board. I'll be more embarrassed in the morning.

Kallon: What have you girls been drinking?

Me: Champagne. Which is absolutely delicious! We need to get it for Rose's.

Kallon: If you think it'd sell, I'm game.

Me: It definitely would.

Kallon: So, did you tell Kayla about us?

Me: Us?

Kallon: The kissing, making out, waiting until after the weekend?

Me: Oh… ummm… no.

Kallon: Why not?

Me: I don't know.

Kallon: Yes you do. Use that liquid courage.

Me: Alright… I didn't know if you'd… still… want to… me… after there was some space and time between us. I didn't want to bring it up to her and then come to find out you regretted it and then have to explain to her it was nothing. I started to compare myself to all the women you've dated and I couldn't figure out why you'd want to be with me. I'm nothing like them.

I watch as the three dots blink at me. I sip my drink and wait for his reply. I have a feeling he doesn't like my response.

Kallon: I guess I didn't do a good enough job making you believe my feelings for you while you were here. I do not regret anything and I can't wait for the next time I get to see you. Our kissing, make-out session, was the best time I've ever had with any woman, and that's not a lie. I will never lie to you, Abby. Which is why I'm going to tell you I do agree with you on your last statement.

Kallon: You are nothing like the women I've dated in the past because you are so much better! You can't see yourself through anyone else's eyes but your own, and you don't see yourself clearly. You are kind, thoughtful, sweet, funny, strong, brave (even without liquid courage), smart, and beautiful. You are so much more than those women ever thought they could be.

My heart stutters and then speeds up double time at his words.

Me: You don't have to say all of that.

Kallon: I'm not saying it because I have to, I'm saying it because it's the truth.

Me: Well, thank you. :-)

Kallon: Do you believe me?

Me: Yes.

Kallon: No, you don't. :-D But I'll get you to believe me.

Me: hahaha ooookay.

Me: So other than trying to convince me you like me, how was your day?

Kallon: hahaha see, you're funny.

Kallon: My day was good. We finished up on a scene that was proving to be a pain in the ass. So, it's nice to have it done.

Me: What are you up to now?

Kallon: Getting ready to take a shower.

Me: Another cold one?

Kallon: I'm at home, I don't have to take a cold one. ;-)

Me: Oh, my goodness.. :-D Smh.

"Kayla!" I shout.

"Yeah," she answers.

"What are you doing?"

"Talking to Peter!"

"Oh, okay. Champagne is here. Food should be here shortly."

"Okay!"

Kallon: Hahaha I'm kidding. I'm not to that point yet.

Me: Yet?

Kallon: If we start talking about you not having an orgasm for 'a while' again, it will push me over the edge, thinking of what I can do to rectify that.

Me: Well, we don't want that. :-D

Kallon: Which part? Talking about it or pushing me over the edge.

Me: Both?

Kallon: You sure? :-P

Me: Do you enjoy… self-care?

Kallon: If it's you I'm talking with, then self-care is very enjoyable.

Me: You are ridiculous.

Kallon: :-D :-P

Another knock at the door makes me jump.

Me: Someone is here, I think it's our food.

Kallon: Okay, you go eat and enjoy your girls evening. I'll go take a shower, a normal one. :-)

Me: Smh. Behave.

Kallon: I'm trying!

Me: Go shower!

Kallon: You go eat!

I get up off the couch and walk towards the door. There's another knock and it sounds like the same voice from earlier that says, "Room service."

"Kayla! Foods here," I say as I'm about to the door.

Me: I'm about to!

I open the door and sure enough, the same woman is standing there. I move out of the way and let her come in. She wheels the cart into the kitchen and stands up.

"Let us know if we can do anything else for you," she says with a smile and a nod and then she heads towards the door.

"Thank you," I say. And then a thought hits me, "Oh, I need to tip you."

"No, Miss Rose, it's all been taken care of," she says over her shoulder. "Have a great evening."

She's out the door before I can get to her. I shake my head and turn back towards the kitchen. I look at my phone and when a response from Kallon doesn't come, I put my phone down and take the lids off the plates of food to see what Kayla ordered.

"Kayla!" I holler. It looks as if she ordered something from every option. There's steak, pasta, sea food, a burger and fries, nachos, and some chicken wings.

"What's up?" she asks, skipping into the kitchen.

"We aren't going to be able to eat all of this," I stammer out.

"Speak for yourself, I'm starving," she says as she grabs a

fry and pops it in her mouth. She looks at the clock on the stove and says, "We've got hours before we have to go to bed. We can eat and sip our champagne and catch up. Tomorrow is going to be crazy, I won't get time to talk with you. And then you leave the next day."

"And you leave for your honeymoon," I say grabbing a fry and tap it to the one she picks up.

"Seriously, Peter and I cannot wait to be on that plane," she says with a sigh. "Even with all the preplanning I had done last year, it's still been pretty stressful these last few months. Like making sure it was all finalized and everything would be here on time. I should have gotten a wedding planner."

"You had everything planned our senior year of high school, you knew you were going to marry Peter someday," I laugh as I eat another fry.

"I really did," she says around a mouth full of burger.

I pick up a fork and stab a shrimp and pop it in my mouth. It's soaked in butter and it taste delicious.

"Kay, you have to try the shrimp," I say as I push the plate towards her but before it's too far away, I poke my fork into some crab and eat it too. "Oooh my gosh, the crab too!"

We sit in silence and just eat. Everything tastes so good. I can't help but eat a little of it all, okay, a lot of it. The fettuccini alfredo is good but not as good as Royce's.

"Did you get this for me?" I ask as I twirl the fettuccini around my fork for another bite.

"I did, I know it's your favorite."

"Thank you."

"I'm getting full," Kayla says as she leans back away from the cart. She grabs her bottle of champagne and drinks from the bottle, ignoring her glass all together.

"Me too. Let's go to the coach and talk, I..." I take a breath and decide right now I'll tell her about Kallon. I smile at her and say, "I have something to tell you."

"What?!" she exclaims.

"Just come on," I say as I grab my bottle and head towards the living room.

"Have you been holding out on me?"

"I'll explain, just come on."

Kayla runs by me and then jumps onto the couch. She pulls a blanket from the pile on the ottoman and puts it over herself, getting comfy.

I shake my head and walk around the couch, grab a blanket for myself and sit down.

"Spill it!" she exclaims.

"Okay but don't be mad that I didn't tell you before. I don't want this to turn into something to take away from your night."

She looks at me with a serious look, and says, "You're scaring me."

I laugh and say, "It's nothing bad, I promise."

"Okaaay."

I take a breath, close my eyes, and say, "Kallon and I kissed."

I'm holding my breath, waiting for her to react. When she doesn't, I open my eyes slowly and look at her. She has the most shocked expression on her face. I burst out laughing so hard, I spit a little drink out of my mouth.

"Excuse me?" Kayla asks. I nod and grin so wide, my face actually hurts. "When?"

"Yesterday," I say sheepishly with a grin.

"Tell me everything!" she squeals.

CHAPTER 13

****BEEP**BEEP**--**BEEP**BEEP**--**BEEP**BEEP****

I roll over in bed and hit my phone, my alarm's going off. It has to be wrong, there's no way it's time to get up already. I open my eyes and see that it is in fact 9am. Normally sleeping until 9 would feel like sleeping in but after drinking until 9 last night, it took that long to finish the champagne and then we stayed up until 2am drinking water and Gatorade to ward off any hangovers today. Both Kayla and I were practically crawling to bed, we were so tired.

I roll out of bed and head through the suite. I get to Kayla's bedroom door and peer inside. She's still sleeping.

I'll get us some coffee and breakfast ordered and let her sleep another twenty or so minutes, I think to myself. I can't believe my best friend is getting married today.

I walk back into the kitchen and find the menu. I decide on ordering us a traditional meal of eggs, bacon, pancakes, hashbrowns, toast, and a bowl of fruit. All the things to help soak up any last remnants of alcohol and protein to get us through the morning. I pick up the phone and put in our order.

I see my phone sitting on the counter, so I pick it up. I don't remember putting it on the charger. I see I have some missed texts from Kallon.

Kallon: How was dinner?

Kallon: You girls must be enjoying your evening. Have fun and be safe. Hope to hear from you in the morning.

Kallon: Good morning, Abby. I'll be away from my phone for most of the day. Have a great day, talk to you soon.

His lasts text came in at 7:15 this morning. I decide to send him a message anyways, even if he doesn't get it until later.

Me: Dinner was great. Kayla ordered too much food, but it helped with all the champagne we drank. I told her about us kissing. She squealed with excitement. We stayed up until 2 watching movies and catching up, but also so we could hydrate. Neither one of us wanted to have a hangover today. We seriously need to order that champagne for Rose's. I hope you have a good day and you aren't super busy with whatever it is you're up to. Hope to talk to you later. :-)

I put my phone down and walk back to Kayla's room.

"Kay?" I ask quietly. She doesn't move. I step in and sit on her bed. I touch her shoulder and try again, a little louder. "Kayla?"

"Mmmm," she says sleepily.

"I just wanted to give you a heads up, it's barely after 9. I've got breakfast and caffeine coming."

"I'm getting married today," she says still sleepily, as she rolls to her back and stretches.

"Yes you are," I say happily.

She sits up fast and says, "Holy shit, I'm getting married today!"

Her quick movement surprises me so much I fall to the floor on to my butt. I start laughing and say, "Yes, you are."

I see her peer over the side of her bed with big eyes. One second she looks shocked and then she's laughing hysterically. I get up and jump on the other side of her on the bed.

I exclaim excitedly, "You're getting married today!"

Kayla gets on her feet and starts jumping up and down, so I join her. We fall onto our butts and giggle like the little girls we're acting like. Suddenly, we hear a knock on what I guess is the front door.

"That'll be breakfast," I say rolling off the bed.

"I'm starving," Kayla says as she gets off the bed too.

"How are you feeling?" I ask as we walk into the living room.

"Surprisingly good. I think all that hydrating helped, good call on the Gatorade."

Another knock at the door has us walking a little faster. I wait to hear a voice telling us it's room service, but it doesn't come. I pause at the door at the next knock and look at Kayla. She shrugs and looks through the peep hole.

"It's Freddy," she says as she opens the door.

Freddy is standing in front of us dressed in black dress slacks, a white button up shirt, a thin black tie, and a black suit jacket to match his pants.

"Good morning, girls. I see you didn't need me to check to make sure you were awake," he says. When he sees our confused looks he adds, "You texted me last night to come over a little after 9 to make sure you two were up."

"I did?" I ask.

Freddy pulls his phone out of his pocket and shows me the text.

"That was me," Kayla says. "I couldn't find my phone after you went to bed, so I thought I'd better have someone who hadn't been drinking all night make sure we woke up just in case we over did it."

"Good thinking," I say. I step back and say to Freddy, "We have breakfast coming, would you like to join us?"

"No thank Miss Rose—" he sees me raise an eyebrow at him, so he amends with "—Miss Abby. I had breakfast earlier. I need to go check on the car. Are you guys needing to go anywhere this morning?"

"No, our hair and makeup will be coming to us. We do have someone that would probably love to get picked up if you wouldn't mind going and getting her," Kayla says.

"Would that be alright?" I ask. "Bree is the other bridesmaid."

"You tell me when and where to go, and I'll go pick her up," Freddy says with a smile. "Just let her know I'll be coming to get her. I don't want her freaked out when I pull up."

I laugh and say, "We'll tell her. I'll text you her address."

"Sounds good. See you later, girls," he says with a nod. He turns and walks back to his suite.

"I'll text Bree if you want to send Freddy her address," Kayla says as we shut the door and walk into the kitchen.

"Can do," I say. She tells me Bree's address, so I send it in a text to Freddy. She finds her phone in the couch cushions and types something out on her phone, I'm assuming to Bree to give her a heads up that Freddy will be picking her up.

"I should tell Kimi and Sandy our room number and let the front desk know that we have some more people that'll be coming so they can get access to the elevator. Kimi and Sandy will be here around noon to start our hair and makeup. My mom and Vivienne will be here around 11. Do you think four hours is enough time to get the five of us done?"

Vivienne is Peter's mom and she's just as sweet and kind as her son.

"Yeah, I think so. I'm not getting a lot done. You're still good with me getting the side braid with some curls?"

"Whatever you want to do. I think my hair will take the longest."

"As it should," I say with a laugh. "My makeup will be minimal so, yeah I think four hours will be plenty. We're supposed to be in the car and heading over at 4, right?"

"Yeah, we should get there by 4:30, or a little earlier. I want some 'no look' pictures and the bridal party will do some quick pictures before the wedding. Bridesmaids with Peter, and groomsmen with me. Me with the party, and then Peter with the party. He won't see me until I'm walking down the aisle and then we'll do all of us after the ceremony. I'm hoping getting some of the pictures done before will make the pictures after the ceremony go quicker so we can join the reception sooner rather than later."

"I like that plan," I say as I put some alarms on my phone. I still don't have a response from Kallon. *Stop worrying about it. He said he'd be busy today.*

"What are you doing?" Kayla asks.

"I'm putting some alarms on my phone so we can stay

on schedule. The sooner we can get to the venue, the sooner we can get pictures taken. Do all the guys know they're supposed to be there by 4:30?"

"I told them 4:15, at the latest," Kayla says with a smile. "Peter said he'd make sure they were there by 4."

"He's such a good man."

"Yes, yes he is."

****KNOCK**KNOCK****

"Room service," we hear from the door.

"I'll get it," I say as we both go to walk over. Kayla sits back down and lets me get the door.

I open it and see a young man standing with a cart of food.

"Good morning," he says with a smile. His name tag is 'Ted' on it.

"Morning, Ted," I say back with a smile. He looks at me confused so I point to his name tag. He looks down and nods his head in understanding. I chuckle and say, "You can put that in the kitchen, if you'd like, or I can take it."

"I've got it Miss Rose," he says, his smile growing.

"Thank you."

I open the door wider and let him in. After I shut the door, I follow behind him. I see that some orange juice was added to the tray and some flowers. Sunflowers, my favorite, and daisies, Kayla's favorite. *How did they know?*

"Here you go Miss Rose, Miss Smith, enjoy your morning and let us know if there's anything else we can send up," Ted says with a nod as he grabs the cart with the plates and whatnot from dinner last night.

"Who told you our favorite flowers?" I ask, curiosity getting the better of me, even though I already have an idea who told.

"I'm not sure Miss, the tray was prepared for me to bring up. I can ask once I get back down there and let you know," Ted says looking confused.

"Oh, no that's okay," I say hurriedly. "There's no reason for that, I have an idea on who told the staff."

"If you're sure? I don't mind," he says, his smile is back on his face.

"No, thank you. It's alright," I say as I reach for my messenger bag for my wallet. I'm dead set on tipping today. As I pull out some cash, Ted's eyes go big. He backs away with one of his hands raised, the other still on the cart.

"That's not necessary," he stumbles backwards, in a hurry now. "Have a great morning."

"Wait, please, let us tip you," I say going after him.

"No Miss Rose, really it was already taken care of," he says as he gets to the door.

"Did Mr. Webb tell the staff to not take our money?" I ask as he opens the door and freezes at 'Mr. Webb'.

Ted turns slowly and looks at me, "So you do know him?"

"Yes," I say coming to stand in front of him. "Answer my question. Please."

"Yes, he did," he says as he looks out into the lobby like he's going to be overheard.

"Did he tell the staff not to tell us?" I ask, guessing at his unease. He nods. I put the money in his hand, but he tries to give it back. “Please take it.”

“Miss Rose, I promise we’ve been tipped well,” he says as he puts the money back into my hand.

He steps away and hits the button for the elevator. The doors open immediately and he steps inside. He smiles at me as he pushes the button and the doors close.

“Ridiculous,” I mumble under my breath as I go back inside. I walk to the kitchen and see that Kayla has put our plates on the counter this time, instead of us eating off the cart. “Kallon has told the staff to not take our tips and has apparently tipped them himself.”

“Oh, damn him,” she responds sarcastically.

“Doesn’t it feel like too much?” I ask her. “He’s comped this amazing suite, everything yesterday, and all the food and drinks we could ask for. The least we should be able to do is tip for room service.”

“It is too much but will making the room service people feel awkward for not taking our money make it better? No. Will getting upset at Kallon for being so kind be a weird thing to get upset about? Yes. Maybe have a chat with him about limits. If he’s going to do things like this, to limit when he does them,” Kayla says before she takes a sip of her coffee. “Holy crap, this is good.”

“I’ll definitely be talking about boundaries and limits with him,” I say as I pour a cup for myself.

“That doesn’t surprise me,” Kayla says with a chuckle as she takes another sip.

“Wouldn’t you?”

She shrugs and says, “If a guy is so hell bent on taking care of things, I’d let him. Especially if he knows how much you don't expect it or need it. Which is why he wants to do it for you. He WANTS to do these things for you, not because he feels he has to but because he wants to, Abs. You just have to get used to it."

"I will never get used to it," I say as I take a sip of the coffee. *Oh... my... goodness!* Kayla wasn't lying. "This is so good!"

"It's almost as good as yours," she says with a smile.

"Almost," I smile back.

We sit in silence for a minute while we eat, Kayla scrolling her phone.

"Shit," she whispers under her breath.

"What?" I ask, looking up from my plate.

Kayla closes her eyes and says, "Veronica is coming to the wedding, I forgot to tell you."

"I figured she would be, she's Peter's cousin."

"You'll be okay with seeing her?"

"Yes, I'll be fine. We've never gotten along but I've always been civil with her."

"Vivienne just asked if Veronica could come get her hair and makeup done with us this morning," Kayla growls. She types furiously as she says, "No, sorry she can't. The time slot for our hair and makeup was prearranged and it's for bridal party only."

"I'm going to go shower," I say as I slide off my seat.

"I'm going to shower too, maybe a bath first," she says as she downs the rest of her coffee.

"See you in a bit, Mrs. Jacobs," I say with a laugh.

She turns and beams at me, "I love the sound of that!"

She skips happily away, overjoyed to be marrying her

best friend today.

As I walk to my room, I send a text to Freddy.

Me: Hi Freddy. We'll need to be leaving by 4 for the venue, just a heads up.

His response is quick.

Freddy: Sounds good, Miss Abby. I'll have the car out front and ready for you.

Me: Thank you.

I get to my room and toss my phone to my bed. I decide I like Kayla's idea and decide on a bath before my shower. The next hour is spent soaking and relaxing.

Once I get out of the shower, I walk into my room and find a box sitting on my bed. I open it and see a silk robe and a note. I open the note and read it.

Abby, my bestest best friend, thank you so much for all that you've done for me over the years. For helping me when I fell and skinned my knee in Kindergarten, that's the day I decided you were going to be my best friend. And helping me find the courage to try out for cheer squad and being there when I became captain. I know cheer wasn't your favorite, but I have always been grateful that you went to all of our competitions to support me. And most importantly, thank you for encouraging Peter to ask me out, you knew I liked him, but he needed a little push to take that step. I can't believe I get to marry him today and I am so grateful that you are going to be standing with me. You and Peter are the two most important people in my life. Thank `you for being such an amazing friend and the sister I never had. I love you, Abs!`

I pull the light pink robe out and see that 'Abby' is written in black cursive letters on the back. I slip my towel off and put my new bra and undies on and then put the robe on. It feels divine against my skin. It's long enough that it hits me mid-thigh, so I don't have to worry about my butt hanging out while I wait to get my hair and makeup done.

I grab my phone off my bed and see that it's almost 11. I head back out to the main room and see Bree sitting at the island, drinking some coffee.

"Bree!" I say excitedly.

"Abby!" she jumps and puts her cup down, then runs to me. She gives me a big hug and says, "I'm so happy to see you!"

"I'm happy to see you too! How are you?"

"I'm good," she says but then yawns. "I'll be better once the baby is sleeping through the night again."

"Kayla told me about that, I'm sorry. That must be tough?"

"Makes for long nights and days but we'll figure it out," she says with a laugh.

I hear soft footsteps coming from the other side of the suite, so we turn and see Kayla walking towards us holding a box in her hands. She's got her own robe on, only it's white. She turns and it says, 'Mrs. Jacobs', on the back in the same black cursive writing.

"Thank you for my robe," I say, giving her a big hug. "I love you and it."

"You are most welcome," she says hugging me back. She

steps out of the embrace and hands the box to Bree. "This is for you."

"Awww thank you," she says as she opens it. She pulls out the note and as she reads it, I see tears fill her eyes. When she's finished she gives Kayla a hug, and says, "I love you too."

Her robe is the same color light pink as mine and says 'Bree' on the back. There's a knock at the door. I go and answer it and Vivienne and Kayla's mom, Brenda, are standing there smiling at me.

"Happy wedding day!" I say to them, hugging them both.

"Oh, sweet Abby," Brenda says. "It's so good to see you!"

"It's so good to see you too," I say, stepping back. "Both of you."

"I'm happy to see you've healed completely," Vivienne says, bending her head so she can get a better look at me. "I know it's been a year, but from what Peter told me, Jason did a number on you."

I nod and say with a small smile, "Yes, well, thankfully it's been a year and I'm alright."

They loop their arms through mine and we walk into the suite as Brenda shuts the door behind us.

"We still can't believe he was capable of that," Vivienne says. "You know he was like a second son to us. He spent more time at our house than his."

"I know and I think he did so well in high school because of you and Leonard. I don't want to think how he would have turned out had he not had you two to guide him, even if he's changed so much since," I say sadly.

"His parents were no help to him," Brenda adds.

"No, they were not," Vivienne says harshly.

I feel Brenda shake herself and she squeezes my arm gently, "Let's not dwell on what happened but celebrate today."

"Here, here!" I cheer. "Today is all about Peter and Kayla and their love."

The moms stop and pull me back to them.

"This place is amazing," Brenda says.

"Yes, it is," Vivienne says in awe.

"Kay said a friend of yours did this?" Brenda asks, turning towards me.

"He did," I say with a smile. "He's very generous."

She eyes me and then says, "Yes, yes he is."

"Mom!" Kayla says as we walk into the kitchen. "I'm getting married today!"

"Yes, you are my darling," she says as she hugs her daughter.

Kayla turns to Vivienne and pulls her into a hug as she says, "Today I get my husband and officially get a second set of parents."

"Sweet Kayla, we've always considered you our daughter," Vivienne says hugging Kayla back tightly. "Today is just for the paperwork."

They laugh and pull away. There's another knock at the door and I head to answer it as Brenda and Vivienne say hello to Bree and pour themselves some coffee.

I get to the door and see two women standing here holding two big bags each.

"Kimi and Sandy?" I ask.

"That's us," the one with dark hair says, extending her hand out to me. "I'm Sandy."

"It's nice to meet you, Sandy," I say putting my hand out to shake hers.

"I'm Kimi," the curly red head says.

"Nice to meet you Kimi," I say, shaking her hand as well. "Come on in, we're all in the kitchen."

Kimi and Sandy get introduced to everyone in the kitchen and then they get to work on us.

CHAPTER 14

"I know I've said it about ten times already, but you look so beautiful, Kay," I say to Kayla as we're riding the elevator down to the lobby.

Her dress is form fitting and then flares down at her feet. It's open in the back and dips down to her sternum in the front. It's covered in millions of shimmering diamond simulants that have been sown into a thin piece of see through fabric that covers her just off-white dress. There's a hidden button in the back where she can hike the train up after the ceremony, so it doesn't drag all over the floor during the reception. She's absolutely breath taking.

The photographer was here, taking pictures but she took off to get to the venue by 4 o'clock. It was pretty fun watching her move around the room, getting the best angles for Kayla. There were a lot of pretend shots. Like we got Kayla in her dress and then Brenda and I pretended to help fix her dress or her hair. I think she got a lot of great shots.

"Thank you, Abs," she says, squeezing my hand. She whispers for only me to hear, "Why do I feel so nervous?"

"Because it's a big day, no matter if you've been dreaming

of it since high school," I whisper back. Her mom and Vivienne are chatting away with Bree behind Kimi and Sandy, who are standing just behind Kayla and me.

Kayla takes a deep breath and says, "It's like when I'd go to a competition for cheer. I knew we would do well, but I was always so nervous."

"You'll be fine once you see Peter at the altar," I say, squeezing her hand gently as the doors to the elevator opens.

We step out and the people in the lobby literally stop what they're doing and turn towards us.

As we walk by an older couple standing at the check-in desk, the lady says, "Wow, you look beautiful dear."

"Thank you," Kayla says sweetly.

We make it out front and find Freddy standing in front of a limo. Kayla and I stop walking at the same time.

"What in the heck?" we say simultaneously.

"Another gift from Mr. Keller," Freddy says with a smile as he opens the back door. Kayla walks forward speechless and as she gets in, Freddy says, "You look beautiful, Miss Smith."

"Thank you Freddy," she says, her cheeks turning pink.

I step to the side and let Bree go ahead of me, she's giggling like a little girl. Brenda and Vivienne are chattering away about how amazing this is. I step up to Freddy and touch his arm.

"If you talk to Kallon today, will you please have him call me?" I say as I feel my little clutch purse, that matches my dress perfectly, one last time to make sure my phone and our room key is still in it. Which it is, I've checked a handful of times.

"Yes, Miss Rose," he says. He takes my hand from his arm and helps me towards the car. He pauses before he lets go and says, "You are stunning."

"Thank you," I say, my cheeks heating just as Kayla's did.

My dress is a dark wine color. It has one shoulder and gives enough cleavage that my girls are seen but not so much that I'm afraid they'll fall out if I decide to dance. It's floor length and the best part, it has pockets. My hair is braided from my right temple down and around the back of my head to below my left ear, with a couple strands pulled out to curl around my face. I'm wearing a pair of dangly earrings and a single diamond necklace that Brenda got us three girls. The diamond sits at the top of my cleavage. My shoes have just enough heel that my dress doesn't drag on the floor but it's long enough that my feet don't show.

I slide into the limo and sit next to Kayla, who is beaming.

"I can't believe Kallon did this," she says leaning forward and grabbing the bottle of champagne from the ice bucket to the left of her. She shrieks and says, "It's the good stuff!"

My alarm on my phone goes off so I reach into my clutch and turn it off. It's 4 o'clock. As I look up, I see that Kayla is taking a sip directly from the bottle. It had already been opened so we don't have to worry about it spraying all over us and the car. I grab five glasses and Kayla pours a little into each one. I hand one to Brenda, then Vivienne, then Bree, and then I hand one to Kayla.

"To the most beautiful bride," I say, raising my glass up to Kayla. The other three bring their glasses to hers as well.

"Cheers!" we all say together.

We take a sip and Bree says, "You aren't kidding! This is delicious!"

We sip our champagne and talk about the day and how Kayla and Peter's honeymoon to the Bahama's will be the perfect vacation for them. The ride to the venue is quick, we make it there in twenty minutes. As we pull up, we see the groomsmen standing outside.

Freddy parks and comes around, opening the door for me. I slide out and I hear a whistle from one of the guys. I look up and see Peter's older brother, Liam, looking at me with wide eyes.

"Looking good Abby," he says walking up to me. "You've... grown up."

"It's been a while," I say with a small laugh as he bends down to give me a quick hug. "Is your brother inside?"

"Yeah, he's in our waiting room with strict instructions to not come out. The photographer asked us to wait here for all of you and bring you around to where she is. We've already had our pictures with Peter. I guess we're to do them with you girls and Kayla now?" he asks as he steps away.

"Yeah," I say. I lean into the car and tell Kayla that Peter is inside. She nods and starts to scoot on the seat to get out. I step back and let Freddy offer his hand to her. When she steps out, all of the guys let out whistles and place their hands over their hearts, truly blown away by her beauty.

"My brother is a lucky man," Liam says as he takes Kayla from Freddy.

"Thanks, Liam," she says as he walks her towards the venue.

"Hi, Abby right?" a tall blond guy says as he walks towards me. I nod and he says, "I'm Chris, Peter's friend from work."

"Hi Chris, it's nice to meet you," I say as I wait for Brenda and Vivienne to get out of the limo. As Bree gets out, I say, "Have you met Bree? Kayla's cousin?"

"I did, at rehearsal the other day," he says politely. "It's nice to see you again."

"Nice to see you too," Bree says as we walk towards the entrance of the venue.

"I'm sorry I couldn't meet you then," I say, feeling bad once again for missing the rehearsal.

"It's okay. You didn't miss much. You'll be walking with Liam," Chris says with a smile.

We walk into the venue, and I'm shocked at the work that has been done to make Kayla's vision a reality. There's greenery all around with yellow daisy centerpieces on every table, and candles circling the vases. The tablecloths are white and the place settings have white plates with a thin gold ring around the outside. The cutlery is gold and wrapped in a white cloth. The chairs have white seat covers on them and a green ribbon tied around them.

In one corner, the DJ is about done setting up his equipment and diagonal from him, is a mobile bar. She's setting up her cute wine barrels that serve as display tables. Her menu is set out and she's getting her cups and mixers prepped.

We walk through and out the back door to where the ceremony will be held. There are chairs set up with the same white seat covers and green ribbon like inside. The arbor where Peter and Kayla will say their vows is a beautiful dark wood, with greenery wrapped around it and yellow daisies scattered throughout.

Back behind the arbor, is a pond and green trees creating a barrier from the world beyond. The pond is where I see Kayla and the others heading. It's a beautiful setting for pictures.

It doesn't take long for us to finish our pictures and then Kayla is escorted inside while we wait for Peter. He hurries out and skids to a stop in front of us.

"Bree, Kayla, you two look beautiful," he says, giving us both hugs.

"You look pretty good yourself," I say with a smile. He's dressed in a classic black suit with a slim tie, similar to the one Freddy had been wearing. As the photographer is getting us situated, I tell Peter, "Kayla is going to take your breath away."

"I don't doubt it," he says with a big grin.

Our pictures with Peter go quickly and before we know it, we're heading back inside. I grab my clutch, pull my phone out, and check the time, it's 4:50pm. We have ten minutes before Kayla will be walking down the aisle. A lot of people had shown up while we were getting pictures taken so all that needs to happen, is for the wedding party to do their thing, and then it's Kayla's turn.

As I'm putting my phone away, it vibrates in my hand. I look and see I have a message from Kallon.

Kallon: Glad to year dinner went well. Hopefully your plan to hydrate helped with no hangover. But I'm sure you two will be tired. 2am? Watching movies and visiting? You party animals, you. :-D I know the ceremony is about to start so I'll talk to you later.

I'm smiling like an idiot as I put my phone back in my

clutch. I walk over to the wedding party table and find my name written on a teepee folded piece of paper that's sitting on the plate and put my clutch on the chair. I walk through the venue, greeting people as they come in the door, and head out back to take their seats.

I get to our waiting room and find Kayla and Bree, standing by the window, watching the people show up.

"I'm glad we only invited the hundred people," Kayla says nervously.

"You competed in front of more people than that," I say as I walk over to the window.

"Yeah but it wasn't just me they were looking at. I had my entire team around me. These people are here for Peter and me," she says turning to me.

"They're all people you know, family and friends. Just all of them at once," I say rubbing her shoulders. "You'll be okay once we get out there."

There's a knock at the door and Brenda comes in.

"Your dad is here, are you ready?" she asks Kayla.

"Yes," she says with a big smile.

"Let's go!" I say enthusiastically.

We follow Kayla out the door and listen to her dad, Paul, ooh and aww at his baby girl. It's so sweet. Paul offers his arm to Kayla and she takes it. We follow them through the venue to the back doors, which two venue staff will open when it's time for us to start walking.

Liam comes up beside me and offers me his arm.

"Ready?" he asks.

"I'm not the one getting married," I say with a laugh. "Although, I can't imagine a better couple than those two."

"Yeah, they're meant for each other," he says, looking back at Kayla. He looks down at me and adds quieter, "So I heard about you and Jason. What a dick."

"Yeah," is all I say. Liam and Jason used to be just as close as Jason and Peter.

He's about to say something but the doors in front of Chris and Bree open. They start walking at the sound of the music and then it's our turn.

I keep my eyes ahead of us, but I lean into Liam and whisper with a smile on my face, "Don't let me fall."

"I won't," he says as he places his hand on mine.

We get to the front and Peter smiles at us. I'm watching his face as he's looking back down the aisle and I know the moment he sees Kayla. I see him hold his breath, put his hand to his heart, and then he lets his breath out slowly. I see tears well up in his eyes as the biggest smile spreads across his face.

The ceremony goes quickly. Short and sweet just like Kayla said it would. Pictures with the entire wedding party go smoothly. Kayla told the guys they were on a strict no drinking rule until after the ceremony. She said she wasn't paying the photographer to babysit us... them... or for crappy pictures. Luckily, Peter, Chris, and Liam know when to listen and know that Kayla is not one to be disobeyed, especially on her wedding day.

A big, brass, analog clock says it's almost 6 when we're walking back into the venue. We find our seats and wait for the DJ to announce Peter and Kayla as the new Mr. and Mrs. Jacobs. Dinner is served and the DJ plays some soothing music while we eat.

"Do you want something to drink?" I ask Kayla as I stand,

to go get myself a drink.

“Sure, I’ll take whatever you’re having,” she says.

“Peter?” Liam asks as he stands as well.

“Same as you, bro,” Peter says, he hasn’t taken his eyes off of Kayla all evening.

“I’ll walk with you,” Liam says as he offers me his arm.

I take it and walk with him over to the bar to get in line.

He clears his throat and as his grip squeezes on my hand that he’s holding to his bicep again, he asks, “So, are you seeing anyone new?”

“Yeah, I kind of am,” I say shyly. I’d always had a crush on Liam in high school. After all, he was the hot older brother of my friend. But Peter and Kayla have told me that he’s turned into a womanizer, and the appeal he had in high school is gone. He’s still good looking but I’m over the womanizer kind. Plus, what Kallon and I have started, is definitely something I want to pursue.

“That’s too bad,” he says and when I look up at him, he winks. “We could have had some fun tonight.”

I burst out laughing and say, “Liam, I’ve known you too long. It would have been weird to do anything with you.”

“You think so?” he asks with a laugh of his own. I’m grateful he doesn’t take my words offensively.

“I’m best friends with your brother and new sister-in-law. I was at your house as much as I was at mine and Kayla’s. Yes it would have been weird,” I say with another laugh.

“A guy can ask, right?” he asks. He doesn’t wait for my response before he says, “I wasn’t lying earlier, you’re a knockout Abby. Jason was a fool to lose you and the guy who has you now, is damn lucky.”

"Oh Liam, don't lie to the poor girl," a nasally voice comes from behind us.

Liam and I turn and see Veronica standing right behind us.

"Veronica," Liam says with annoyance. "I wasn't lying to her. Abby is beautiful."

"Sure," she says with a sneer at me. She looks around dramatically and asks, "So, where's Jason?"

"Not here," Liam says, his grip on my hand is a little tighter.

"Oh, why is that?" she asks, looking at me like I'm something she stepped in with her shoe.

"You know why," Liam answers for me.

"Oh, that's right. You two broke up," she says with fake sadness in her tone. "That's too bad."

"Hi Veronica, it's nice to see you," I say sweetly. I give her a smile and turn back around in line.

"Next," the bartender says. Liam steps up and starts talking to her.

I feel breath on my neck and then Veronica's voice is low in my ear.

"Did Jason ever confess to you that we used to fuck in his car when you weren't around?" she whispers.

I flinch away from her words and turn to look at her.

"Are you kidding me?" I ask, instantly angry she would say that.

She shrugs and quietly says, "I'm guessing not. You know all those nights he was supposed to be working out for football? Yeah, he was working out, but not in the gym."

I shake my head and say, "Way to keep it classy, Roni."

I use her nickname that she hates. I turn back towards the bar, taking deep breaths to calm myself, and see Liam step away. I step up quickly and ask for a bottle of champagne. The bartender hands me a bottle that's exactly from the hotel.

"What the...?" I ask.

She shrugs and says, "Someone bought all the stuff I brought and then brought in cases of this."

I look to the side where she's pointing and see a couple cases of the stuff stacked up.

"Who?" I ask.

"I don't know who he was," she says with a shrug. "You still want it?"

"Yes please," I say. I grab the bottle and when I turn, Veronica is in my face again.

"So, since you and Jason are over, you won't mind if I have him, will ya?" she asks, looking me up and down,

"He's all yours," I say. I step around her and Liam takes my arm.

"What was that about?" Liam asks.

"Your cousin is one classy girl," I say between clenched teeth.

"What did she say?"

"Don't worry about it," I say shaking my head.

"If she bothers you again, let me know," Liam says but he stops me and makes me look at him. "Abby, I'm serious."

"Okay, I will," I say giving him a smile. He and Peter have always been protective of me, so it's nice to see that hasn't gone away with his womanizing ways.

We get back to the table and Kayla asks what was going on with Veronica. She saw that she'd said something to me that bothered me. I tell her quickly and tell her not to worry about it and that I'm not going to let Veronica rile me up.

"Just let me know if she says anything again, okay?" Kayla says.

"It's really not that big of a deal," I say taking a drink of the champagne I brought to the table. To change the subject, I say, "Do you know who brought this?"

"No," Kayla says after a drink. "Do you think Kallon somehow sent it?"

"Or had Freddy bring it," I suggest. "Who else would have known we were liking it so much?"

We shrug and then the DJ plays a new song and Kayla jumps from her seat.

"We have to dance!" she says excitedly.

I had promised her I'd dance with her until my feet started to hurt, and unfortunately, they haven't started to hurt yet. I let her take my hand as she grabs Peter's hand, and she leads us out to the floor. We start dancing and laughing, just enjoying the moment.

Soon, Veronica walks up and bumps into me, almost spilling her drink on me but I jump out of the way quickly. Luckily, I haven't drank enough that my reflexes are affected yet.

"Ooops, sorry," she says over the music, except the look on her face doesn't match what she says.

"Quit it, Veronica," Kayla says. "If you keep acting like a bitch, you'll be escorted out of here."

"What? It was an accident," she says with a pout.

"Then don't let it happen again," Kayla says with a snarl.

Liam walks up and he's got his tie tied around his head

and his shirt unbuttoned down to his chest. He starts dancing around us and then ends up behind me. He holds a cup of something around my shoulder and offers it to me.

"What's this?" I ask, dancing away from him, to give us a little space. He was starting to dance up on me.

"A drink the bartender said she thought you'd like," he says. "Pink lemonade something or other."

I take a sip and it's good. I smile and say, "Thanks!"

"Where's mine?" Veronica says, crossing her arms over her chest.

"On the floor," Peter says, pointing to where she spilled her drink.

Veronica is about to say something, but her face turns to shock. Her mouth drops open and her eyes practically pop out of her head.

"No... fucking... way," she finally says.

The guys turn and look but Kayla and I are staring at Veronica and her strange behavior.

"What?" We ask at the same time.

Veronica doesn't say anything but points back behind us. I turn and my heart stops and then picks up double time.

Walking towards us, dressed in black dress slacks, a white button-down shirt, black tie, and a black dress jacket to match his slacks, is Kallon freaking Keller. All heads have turned and are staring as he walks straight towards us.

"What the hell?" I say under my breath. I look at Kayla and she's beaming. I turn to her and asks, "What is he doing here?"

"Surprise!" she says excitedly.

"What do you mean?" I ask hurriedly, before Kallon

reaches us.

"He was my last-minute wedding thing yesterday," she says with a laugh. "I texted your parents and Betty to get his phone number so I could invite him to come to the wedding."

"Why would you do that?" I ask, I can't help the smile that's spreading across my face.

"Because you deserve to have a date! And why not have it be who you last kissed," she says with a wiggle to her eyebrows.

I can't say anything else to her because Kallon is just a couple feet away. But before he can say anything to me, or me to him, Veronica steps in front of him.

"You're… you're Kallon Keller," she says loud enough for everyone in the area to hear.

"I am," Kallon says with a light laugh.

"What are you doing here?" she asks, flipping her hair over her shoulder. She looks around and I can see she's got her best smile plastered on her face. I can also see she's sticking her chest out. She's pulling out all the moves, but who wouldn't. My eyes only stay on her for a couple of seconds before their back on Kallon. He's staring at me. I smile.

"I'm here for my date," he says, smiling back at me.

"Lucky you, I'm right here," she says as she reaches out and touches his arm.

A red-hot flame of jealousy rises inside me. *How dare she touch Kallon!* I scream in my head. I'm about to take a step forward but I watch Kallon take her hand off his arm and put it gently down at her side.

"Actually," he says and side steps around Veronica. "She's right here."

Out of the corner of my eye, I see Veronica's mouth open and close like a fish out of water. I don't take my eyes off Kallon as he steps up in front of me.

"Hi," he says with a smile.

"Hi," I smile back with disbelief in my voice. "What are you doing here?"

"When the bride tells you to come to her wedding to be her maid-of-honors date, you do as you're told," Kallon says. He looks over to Kayla and Peter and says, "You look beautiful, Mrs. Jacobs. Congratulations to you both."

Kayla smiles and says, "Thank you."

I turn and say, "Well, let me introduce you officially. This is Peter—" Peter and Kallon shake hands "—and this is Kayla."

Kallon takes Kayla's hand and says, "It's nice to officially meet you both."

"You as well, man," Peter says, shell shocked. He blinks and looks at Kayla, "Maybe we should let them talk. You want to dance, Mrs. Jacobs?"

"Good thinking," she says. Peter pulls her away and they start dancing.

Liam steps up and tries to puff out his chest. He used to be the tallest person I knew, that was until I met Kallon. He's a good two to three inches taller than Liam.

"Hey man, I'm Liam," he says sticking his hand out. When Kallon grasps it, I can see Liam squeezing hard, but Kallon doesn't flinch. Liam asks, "How do you know my girl Abby here?"

"Your girl?" Kallon asks. I see his hand tighten around Liam's a little more which makes Liam wince slightly.

"I've known Liam as long as I've known Peter," I say with an easy smile. "Liam is just as protective as his brother."

Kallon nods his head at me and then turns back to Liam, "I know Abby from her bakery."

"Oh, okay," Liam says. When Kallon lets go of his hand, Liam mindlessly rubs his hand. He looks from me to Kallon and says, "You two have a good night."

"How are you here?" I ask as Kallon steps up to me.

"I got on a plane and flew here," he says with a smile.

"Captain Sterling came and got you?" I ask, shocked.

"He did," he says with a chuckle. He turns and looks around, which has me looking around as well. All eyes are on him and by proximity, me as well.

"Do you want to get a drink and go sit and talk or..." I leave my question open.

"A drink sounds great," he says. He offers me his arm and I take it. His bicep flexing as I hold on to it. My heart jumps every time his muscle moves.

We walk up to the bartender, Kallon puts in his order and then turns to me, "Would you like some more champagne or do you want something else?"

"How do you know I've had champagne?" I ask, surprised.

"Oh..." he says and then looks at the bartender.

"You brought in all the champagne, didn't you?" I ask.

"Well, technically, Freddy brought it in," he says with a chuckle.

"Kallon..." I start to say but he cuts me off.

"I knew you girls liked it so I called the hotel and had them set out a couple cases so Freddy could bring them here," he says dipping his head in a shy manner. He looks up at me with a boyish smile. “Don’t be mad.”

“I’m not mad,” I say, trying to fight a smile. “You just do too much.”

“Do I?” he asks as the bartender hands him his drink. He looks at me expectantly.

I look at the bartender and say, “I’ll take a vodka cranberry, please.”

Kallon smiles and looks back at the bartender with a smile. Once I have my drink I turn and lead us back to my table. On the way, we’re stopped about every five feet for someone to say hi to Kallon. Soon, Dax and Freddy are standing beside us and helping us make it to the table.

“Is it always like that?” I ask when we finally sit down. We’re far enough from the DJ and the speakers that I feel like I can hear myself think properly again.

“Yes, and no,” he says as he takes his jacket off and puts it on the back of his chair. His shirt strains across his wide, muscular chest. I force myself not to lick or bite my lips. I’ve seen him in all his movies, when he’s been shirtless and dang near naked, but seeing him in just a towel on, proved that the camera doesn’t do him justice. He grabs his drink which has me mentally shaking myself out of memories. “People get excited. Usually having Dax and Trevor, or in this case, Freddy around, deters people from coming up frequently.”

“Does it bother you?” I ask, taking a big sip of my drink. *Whew, it’s strong!*

“It used to but now I just take it as part of the job,” he says. “They just want to say hi, maybe get an autograph. And for the most part it’s quick and fairly painless.”

"Fairly?"

"Not in the actual physical form of pain. I still get embarrassed about it all but in small settings, it's okay," he says with a chuckle.

"Have you ever been actually hurt?"

"Not on purpose."

"How do you mean?"

"I was in a crowd, and they were all pushing in, trying to get to me. A woman was pushed so hard she fell at my feet. I bent down to help her and my hand got stepped on. I was able to get her up but then I had Dax and Trevor get me out of there. My hand didn't get broken, but it was bruised pretty bad for a good two weeks."

"Oh my gosh," I say.

"Enough about me," he says as he leans back. He looks at me, his gaze going from my hair down to my feet hidden below my dress. "You look absolutely stunning."

My cheeks heat and I dip my head down. I mutter out, "Thanks."

I see his hand come into view and then his finger is under my chin, lifting my head up.

"I'm serious, Abby. You are the most beautiful woman here. That color—" he takes a deep breath "—compliments you very, very well."

I watch as his eyes linger on my cleavage, and I see his Adam's apple dip down as he gulps.

"Thank you," I say again, louder this time. "You look pretty dang good yourself."

A slow song starts to play, and Kallon puts down his drink and stands. He offers me his hand and asks, "Would you like to dance?"

"Sure," I say. I put my drink down and take his outstretched hand. He doesn't let go of my hand as he leads me out to the floor. He twirls me around and after I finish laughing, I say, "I haven't danced in a long time. I'm apologizing now for the amount of times I'm bound to step on your feet."

"I've got you," he says as he pulls me close. His big hand envelopes my right, as his other hand slides up my back. He takes a deep breath and says, "You smell good."

"So do you," I say, after taking in my own deep breath. His cologne makes my insides flutter. I've always been one affected by smell, scents. And when it comes to men's cologne, it can make or break the attraction. His cologne is making me feel all sorts of turned on. That could also be credited to his hand splayed across my back, his hand holding on to mine gently, but firmly, and having me pressed up against his body.

And so, this is how the evening goes. Dancing with Kallon and joining Kayla and Peter on the floor every so often. And then we'd go sit at our table to visit and drink.

CHAPTER 15

We're sitting at the table and Peter is talking to Kallon about what it's like being a celebrity. I pull out my phone from my dress pocket and see it's after 10pm. We have to be at the airport by 7am, our flight leaves at 10am. If we leave now, I can be to my room around 10:30 and if I go right to sleep, I could get 7 hours of sleep before I have to be up and ready to go.

"Do you have somewhere else you need to be?" Peter asks.

I look up quickly from my phone and say, "Nowhere important, just in bed."

Out of the corner of my eye, I see a look cross Kallon's face that I've never seen before. When I turn my head to look at him, the look is gone, and he just smiles at me.

"Your friend is meticulous about airport rules," Kallon says with a laugh.

I mock glare at him, but Peter asks, "Aren't you flying home in your jet?"

I see Kallon's face turn a little pink. He's always a little embarrassed when people state how obviously wealthy he is, but he just shrugs and says, "She says, and I quote, 'It doesn't matter, things can happen, and we need to be there ready to go if we need to leave sooner rather than on time.' So, we'll end up hanging out on the plane or private lounge for three hours before it's time to leave."

The guys laugh but thankfully Kayla steps in to back me up and says, "If she gets used to flying private but ends up having to fly commercial like the rest of us, —" she winks at me "—then she'll be out of the habit of having to arrive at the airport at a respectable time. Baggage could get misplaced. She could miss her flight. Chaos would ensue. No, I'm with Abby on this one."

"Exactly," I say picking up my drink and holding it across the table for Kayla to tap my cup with hers. When I lean over to her, my leg accidently leans up against Kallon's. I turn towards Kallon, making an 'I told you so' face as Peter and Kayla turn toward each other to discuss when I'll ever have to fly commercial again. Kallon reaches under the table and puts his hand on the inside of my knee, the slit in my dress exposing my leg, and squeezes gently, playfully.

The effect that touch does to me, has me squirming in my seat. I try to pull my leg away, but Kallon holds on to it firmly. I pick my drink back up to hide my smile and I look at him with my eyebrows raised. He looks back at me the same way, his touch turning light as a feather, giving me the chance to pull my leg back. I don't know if it's all the vodka cranberries I've been drinking but I think to myself, *What the hell, a little flirting won't hurt, right?* I press my leg into his and put my foot over his and rub it up his shin just a touch. I sip my drink as I do it and tilt my head down in a 'what about that' type of way.

He licks his lips— which also does something else

entirely to me— looks down at his drink and smiles. His hand trails up the inside of my thigh, my dress rising with his movement. His thumb is rubbing small, soft circles as his hand slowly makes its way up. He stops when his pinky finger makes contact with my underwear.

I see him physically gulp. He looks at me with something like need but also fright in his eyes. His hand slowly works its way back down to my knee. I take a steady breath, remembering to breathe normally, when his hand starts to make its trek back up my thigh. To hide a moan in my throat, I pick up my drink and down it. I cough, covering the moan, and squeeze my legs together.

"You okay, Abs?" Kayla asks, my cough pulling her away from her discussion with Peter.

"Oh yeah, I'm fine," I say. Kallon chuckles from beside me but he gently squeezes my thigh and then removes his hand from my leg. I instantly miss the heat from it. I clear my throat again and say, "I just think it's time for me to go to bed."

Kayla looks at her phone that's on the table and says, "I think we've stayed long enough. I'm ready for our wedding night aloneness time."

"Yeah, alright," Peter says enthusiastically, downing his drink.

Kallon finishes his drink as well and then stands.

"Thanks for the invite," Kallon says, sticking his hand out for Peter to shake it.

"No, thank you, Kallon," Peter says, shaking Kallon's hand. "Thank you for joining us on our special day."

"Have a good night and let us know when you guys make it home tomorrow, okay?" Kayla says with a quick hug.

"I will," I say hugging her back.

As they turn to walk over to their parents, who are still here, I turn slowly to Kallon and look up at him. He smiles down at me as he steps into my space. He looks into my eyes, down to my lips where he lingers for a minute, and then back up to my eyes.

"Can I give you a ride back to your hotel, Miss Rose?" he asks as he half bows to me.

I laugh and push his shoulder. But then I curtsey and say, "Why, Mr. Keller, I would be delighted if you would?"

I grab my clutch off the table and as we start walking, Kallon offers me his arm. I laugh and put my arm through his, my hand resting on his massive bicep. I don't mean to, but I give it a gentle squeeze. I don't let go, holding on like my life depends on it. We make it outside where Dax is waiting with Kallon's car. *When did he let Dax know we were leaving?*

"What about Freddy?" I ask. I look around and see the limo parked a little ways away.

"He's going to drive the newlyweds back to the hotel," Kallon says as we step up to the car.

"Good evening, Miss Rose," Dax says with a smile as he opens the door. It's the first time he's said anything all night.

"Hi Dax," I say with a big smile.

I slide in and scoot over to the far side, like I always do. I'm buckling my seatbelt as Kallon gets in. This car is a little smaller than the one he has in New York, so our legs touch when he's situated.

I bite my lip and look out the window. I feel like I'm 14 years old again, when just the touch from the boy I like sends my heart pounding in my chest.

"You okay?" Kallon asks after a minute and as Dax pulls away from the venue.

"Mmmm," I say and look over at him. "I'm great."

He smiles his devastating smile and asks, "Did you have fun tonight?"

"I did," I say happily. "It was a great celebration for those two."

"They definitely know how to throw one heck of a party," Kallon says with a chuckle.

"Thank you for coming," I say, shyly. I look down at my hands and then back up at him. "I'm really happy that Kayla invited you."

"Me too," Kallon says. His eyes dip to my lips and then back to my eyes. He hasn't made a move to kiss me all night. The most that has happened is dancing really close and his hand on my thigh. He clears his throat and says nervously, "I've been meaning to ask you... I started to yesterday, but got sidetracked."

"Okaaay," I prompt.

"Do you want to go to the premiere of 'Along Came You' with me?" he asks. He's got such a hopeful look on his face, I can't help but smile.

I take his hand and say, "I'd love to go! It's Saturday right?"

Relief floods his face, and he leans back and relaxes, "It is... This one is in Seattle."

"Oh, wow," I say. "I figured it would have been in New York."

"That one is at the beginning of next month," he says. His eyebrows contort and he asks, "Will it be a problem to go to

Seattle?"

"No, I don't think so. I'll have to check with Betty and Royce, to see if they can cover again," I say.

"Not only do I want you to come with me, but—" he smiles "—I thought we could invite Spencer and Mary to come along."

My eyes pop wide and my mouth drops open even wider. I reach out and grab his arm and ask excitedly, "Really?"

"Of course," he says with a laugh. "Do you think they'd want to come?"

"To a movie premiere?" I ask sarcastically. I laugh and answer my own question, "Of course!"

"Then it's settled. You ask them and I'll make sure my manager gets the tickets for us," he says with a smile. He puts his hand on mine and he squeezes gently.

"Thank you," I say, smiling hugely at him. "They'll be so excited."

The rest of the ride to the hotel is a quiet one. I can't stop smiling. It doesn't take long before we're pulling up to the front of the hotel. Dax gets out and opens my door first. Kallon gets out and walks to me, offering me his arm again. My heart rate flares as I take his arm. I look up at him and smile. He bends and for the first time tonight, he kisses me softly on the lips. He pulls back slowly, desire flashing in his eyes.

A horn honks, causing us to jump. We look behind the car we arrived in and see a van waiting to pull in. My face heats from embarrassment and then Kallon is pulling me along with him into the lobby of the hotel. I turn to see Dax getting in the car to move it.

We get to the elevator and while we wait for it to arrive,

Kallon moves his arm from around my shoulders and rests his hand on the middle of my back. I can feel the sexual tension between us rising. My mind goes back to his hand on my thigh at the table just before we left. Heat floods me and I start to think that being alone in an elevator with him might not be a good idea. The building desire in me roars to a demanding flame.

We only have to wait for a minute before the doors ding open. As we step in and turn to face the doors, Kallon lowers his hand slowly down my back. So low, an inch lower and his hand will be on my ass. I bite my lip as I smile but I keep looking forward.

He reaches forward to hit the number 14 for our floor. He'd told me early tonight that the fourteenth floor was his and he only allowed certain people to stay in the suite that Kayla and I stayed in last night. When he stands back up, I can see him out of the corner of my eye looking down at me, smiling. Just as the doors are about to slide shut, a hand comes into view and the doors reopen. A man holds the door and turns and waves to a group of about nine other guys, who look to be hurrying to catch the elevator. Two at a time they step in, nodding at Kallon and then looking at me with sudden drunken desire.

As we make room for each guy that invades our space, Kallon turns to me and moves me to the corner of the elevator. I smile up at him and he smiles back down. He turns so his back is facing me. I put my hands out on his back as he steps back into me, just to let him know I'm literally right behind him. The guys keep pushing in and one gets close to my side. Kallon turns back to face me and puts his arm up to bar the guy from getting any closer and turns his body just a little more, so I'm more secluded from them.

One of the guys at Kallon's back accidently bumps into him. The guy apologizes profusely, and Kallon tells him it's okay. But it's made Kallon take a step closer to me. On instinct, I put my hands out to keep him from completely bumping into me, they land on his chest. I feel him take in a sharp breath and he holds it.

I look up to see Kallon bending his head down towards me, blocking the view from the guys. I keep my hands on his pecs and slowly run my hands over the massive muscles. The feel of his button-down shirt over his hard muscles makes my hands tingle.

I slide my hands down his pecs and when it becomes uncomfortable for my hands to be palms out, I turn them over so the back of my hands are now rubbing Kallon's abs. Even using the back of my hands, I can feel how truly rock hard they are as well. I lick my lips and bite my bottom lip as I look back up at Kallon.

His eyes are burning with need, he leans down, his lips on my ear and whispers for only me to hear, "I want to kiss you so bad."

I turn my face towards his and whisper back, "Then kiss me."

Kallon pulls back a little to stare at me. The elevator stops and I can hear the guys all talking about meeting back downstairs at the bar for a couple of drinks before it closes for the night. A couple guys get off. The door closes and we continue up.

"Are you sure?" Kallon whispers when he's back down to

my ear.

"Kiss me," I say, making my lips touch his ear lobe.

I hear a soft groan escape Kallon's mouth before his mouth is on mine. It's a gentle kiss at first. He's giving me the opportunity to change my mind. I pull his bottom lip in between my lips and let the tip of my tongue touch it. He steps closer to me, his left hand going to my hip but he's so gentle with me I can barely feel his touch. My hands go to his hips, and I squeeze, hopefully showing him, I want him to hold me the same way. He understands. His grip tightens, I can now feel his huge hand on my ass while his thumb rubs against my hipbone.

I feel like Kallon has handed over the reins for this kiss, so I turn my head the other way, letting my tongue slip between his lips just a little. He mirrors me. It's a little more than a gentle kiss but not a full on make-out Frencher.

I hear the door ding a couple more times. I've lost count how many times I've heard it. It dings one more time and last of the guys are getting off. He could have been the only one, I don't know, I don't look and neither does Kallon. But the guy getting off says with a chuckle, "Elevator is all yours, you love birds."

As soon as the elevator door shuts, Kallon takes complete control of the kissing. I was wrong in thinking he was holding back just for me, letting me be in charge. No, he was holding back so he didn't give the drunk guys a show.

He lowers his hand from the wall of the elevator and puts it to my face. He drags his hand that's on my hip, up my body, skimming the side of my breast, caressing my neck, until it's on the other side of my face. He deepens the kiss into such a passionate one, I stop breathing.

He steps into me, pressing me up against the elevator wall. I run my hands around his back, absentmindedly marveling at the muscles back there too. I run my hands back around his arm and up his chest until they're around the back of his neck. I pull him closer to me.

Kallon's hands slide from my face to my shoulders, to the side of my breasts, where they linger just a second, before they slide down and cup my ass. I pull my mouth away and gasp in surprise as he lifts me up and I instinctually wrap my legs around his waist. And then he's devouring my mouth again, pressing me into the wall.

I pull up and into him, trying to get as close as humanly possible to him. I snake my fingers into his hair and pull his head closer to mine. I know we can't get our mouths or our tongues any closer, but I want more... need more of him.

One of his hands is holding me up and he's using the wall as support, while he slides his other hand under the back of my dress, so his palm is touching my ass. Then he does it with his other hand. I moan and press my middle closer to him. He clenches his hands hard onto my ass and squeezes, not unpleasantly. I wasn't expecting this when I decided to wear a thong tonight.

The elevator dings, I look over at the numbers to indicate which floor it is and see it's our floor.

"This is us," I say before I go back to kissing him.

Kallon pulls away and starts to ask, "Do you—" I kiss him. He chuckles and kisses me back. He pulls back again and finishes his question in a hurry. "—want to come to my place?"

"Yes," I say before I overtake his mouth again.

I'm not sure how Kallon manages to pull his card out to open the door and carry me out of the elevator without dropping me, but soon I'm pressed back up against a wall. I pull away and watch as he uses his right hand to insert his key at his door. I kiss down his neck, then back up again until I find his ear. I pull his earlobe into my mouth and suck on it. Kallon draws in a sharp breath again and then he pushes me into the wall with his body. I lean my head back and moan. His weight on me is what I need but being horizontal would be preferable.

He swings the door open and steps inside, kicking the door shut fast with his foot. He pins me to the door, now kissing me on the neck. He works his way down to my collarbones and then his mouth is on my cleavage. I lean my head back and enjoy the feel of his lips and tongue running across the little bit of skin that's exposed.

I can't stand it, I need more. I need to be on my back or on top of him.

I breathlessly whisper out, "Beh... bedroom."

I start to pull my dress over my head before he's moved us away from the door.

"Yesss," Kallon hisses, and then kisses me deeply again.

When he pulls away, I pull on my dress but it's going to have to be taken off from the zipper.

"I need help with my dress," I say breathlessly.

Kallon reaches behind me and feels my back. He starts kissing me again while he blindly finds the zipper and pulls it down. Once it's down as far as it'll go, I pull it up and over my head, our lips parting just long enough for the fabric to be pulled away from me.

I toss my dress over my head, back towards the door. I'm

now just in my black bra and thong. I pull at his shirt between us and manage to get it untucked. He's carrying me further into his suite as I unbutton each of his buttons. When I've gotten most of them undone, I push the shirt open. I run my hands over his bare skin, marveling at how soft he is but also how hard his muscles are underneath.

A small moan escapes me as Kallon starts to kiss my neck again.

He lets out a groan and says as a question, "Can't make the bedroom... Couch?"

"I don't care, just get us horizontal," I plead. I resume our kissing, letting Kallon figure out where we're going.

I feel myself being laid down but then a cold surface hits my back and I let out a sharp cry of surprise.

"What's wrong?" Kallon pulls back in a startled panic. "Did I hurt you?"

I laugh and say, "No, the couch is cold."

"Shit, sorry, hang on," Kallon says as he disappears for a second.

I look around for a quick second and see that he's got a leather sectional with huge leather ottomans that make it look like one ginormous couch... bed... it's a comfy monstrosity. While Kallon disappears somewhere, I take my shoes off and scoot my body back onto the ottomans a little more, so I'm more in the middle of the thing.

I watch Kallon walk out of a room and he's carrying a blanket. He shakes it out and then lays it down beside me. I slide over. I'm on my back but I get on my elbows and look up at him. He slowly takes his shirt and pants off.

"We can stop anytime you want," Kallon says with desire

thick in his voice. I watch as his pants hit the floor and his erection is straining to get out of his boxer briefs. I lick my bottom lip and bit it softly. He says, "But if we do stop, you have got to stop licking and biting your lip. It'll drive me crazy."

I do it again and try to do a sexy eyebrow thing. I feel like I look silly but the look on Kallon's face tells me he thinks it's sexy as hell and then he crawls to me quickly. I lie down and he's over my body in a second.

"I'm serious, Abs, if you want to stop, just tell me and we'll stop," he says sincerely.

I reach up with my hands and run them through his hair. I intertwine them behind his head and pull him down to me and kiss him softly.

"I want this," I say into his lips. It feels so good to say it out loud and it feels even better to let myself truly accept how I feel about him. "I want you."

That's all he needs to hear and now he's back to kissing me deeply again. He leans into me, pushing me down into the comfy cushions. My bra covered breasts are smashing into his bare pecs. He has his left thigh between my legs, and I can't help but rub up against him. *I need more.*

I bend my right leg, that's not being deliciously sandwiched between his strong thighs, up and then I rub my foot from his ass, down his long leg. Kallon's arms are on either side of my face but now he leans to the side and runs his left hand down my shoulder, and over my breast. I arch my back at the contact, but he doesn't linger there as much as I want him to. His hand goes to the side of ribs where he rubs his thumb up and down, and then it's under my bra.

I gasp and arch my back again. His thumb moves over

my nipple and plays with it for a second. Kallon stops kissing me to kiss down my neck to my chest. He pulls the bottom of my bra down just enough that he makes my nipple pop out of the top. His hot, wet mouth engulfs it immediately. My back arches even more. I grind into his thigh as my right leg swings over his hip and presses down on the left side of his ass, pushing him down into me.

His hard erection presses into my left upper thigh. I groan because it's not where I want it. I then suck in a sharp breath as Kallon nips my nipple with his teeth and then sucks it back into his mouth. His tongues twirling around it, bringing it to its full erect size.

Kallon's hand moves from just under my breast and goes down to my hipbone. His hand covers my hip, but he slips his thumb under my thin panty waistband and teases his way over to my pubic area. He pulls on my nipple with his lips as he leans back a little and lets his thumb brush against my hot, wet, middle. I try to grind closer to his hand.

"Mmmmm," I moan out loudly. *Yes, this is what I was wanting*! But as soon as the moan is out, Kallon slips his thumb out and slides his hand down my thigh and behind my knee. I let a whimper escape my lips and I feel him chuckle against my breast.

"Soon, Abby, soon," his hot breath against my skin makes goosebumps popup on my arms. I arch my back, willing him to take my nipple in his mouth again.

He holds onto my knee and then rolls us so I'm on top. He runs his hands quickly to my back and unclasps my bra quicker than I know what's happening because before I have time to realize what he did, he rolls back over so I'm underneath him.

"What the—" I start to ask but he just kisses me deeply.

He then reaches between my breasts and pulls my bra up. I lift my arms and let him slide it off me. He looks down at me and I hear his breath catch. He quickly takes my right nipple in his mouth and sucks not so gently.

"Oh my god," I cry out in pleasure.

Kallon's hand is still behind my knee. After he adjusts himself so he's fully between my legs, I wrap them around his waist to interlock my feet above his ass. He thrusts his erection down into me gently, but our underwear prevents any penetration. His length hits me just where I need some friction.

I let out another moan, but this time Kallon does the same. It's the first sound I've heard him make and it sends shivers over my overheated skin, straight to my overheated middle. I lift my hips and grind into his long, hard shaft, finding just the right spot.

"Oooh," I let slip. I bite my lip just as Kallon takes my left breast into his hand and squeezes it gently. He then moves his fingers to my nipple and rubs it between his thumb and forefinger. All while he's sucking and playing with my right nipple with his tongue. I lean my head back and moan out again. He changes sides, his mouth finally devouring my left breast while his hand goes to work on my right. I grind into him again.

"Mmmmy god," Kallon groans into my soft skin. He runs his right hand that was massaging my left breast, down my stomach until he reaches my thong. In one quick pull, he has them off and is back to kissing me. My sore but erect nipples are pressing into his hard pecs.

Kallon's hand is doing small circles on my stomach as he teases me. It moves slower and slower down to where I need him. His fingers finally touch my patch of hair and his breath catches. He slowly runs his hand down until his cupping me, his palm pressing into my sensitive spot.

"Kallon," I plead.

"Say it again," he says, breathless.

"Mmmm," I say as he presses his hand down, but he doesn't enter me.

"Say my name again, please," he pleads this time.

"Kallllllon," I moan out. As soon as I start to say his name he slips a finger inside me. A moan and a sharp breath in, are all the sounds I can make, "Ugggh ahhh."

He moves his finger in and out in a rhythmic motion that almost has me coming apart already. He adds another finger and pulls my nipple into him mouth at the same time.

"Kallon!" I scream because I'm so close, but not quite there. He can sense that I'm close. He starts rubbing my most sensitive spot with his thumb, with the right amount of pressure and speed that has me arching my back and squeezing around his fingers. An explosion rocks through me! The sensation I feel has me screaming, "Yesss, Kallon! Yes!!"

"Damn your sexy," Kallon says into my chest. He lets me ride my wave of ecstasy. When I'm finished with that first wave, he kisses me and says, "I need you now."

He leans up and back behind himself at a weird angle, reaching over the edge of the cushions. He comes up with his pants and pulls a condom out of his pocket. He lets the pants fall to the ground and then he's ripping the condom open with his teeth. He reaches down with his right hand, pulls his boxer briefs off, and I can feel him slipping the condom over his erect member. He leans back down and kisses me softly when he's finished putting it on.

"It's still not too late, we can stop right now," he says, kissing me sweetly. "We can just keep doing hand stuff if you want."

I put my heels into each of his butt cheeks and push him down into me slightly. I kiss him deeply, letting my tongue do the tango with his tongue before I pull away slowly and say, "I told you, I want this. I want you. All of it, all of you."

Kallon goes back to kissing me and then his lips are kissing trails down to my breasts again. He massages each one and then takes each nipple in his mouth before rolling it with his fingers. He comes back to kissing me while his hand finds its way back down to my hot and ready middle. His index and middle finger start to rub my now over sensitive bud.

"Awww," I cry out in pure pleasure. He keeps rubbing my spot and sucking on my nipples, nipping them occasionally. I feel another wave of ecstasy about to roll through me. Before it hits, I yell, "Kallon, now, I need you inside me!"

Kallon doesn't have to be told twice. He quickly positions his hardness at my opening without the use of a hand— they are too busy holding himself up and bringing me to another climax— and as he removes his fingers, he slides into me just as I'm pushed into my orgasm.

"Oh shit," Kallon moans. He moves his face to my neck and kisses me softly. He slides in some more. He moans out again, "Oh shit. So... sooo tight."

I can barely hear him over the loud rushing sound in my ears.

"Kallon," I beg. I need him to thrust, this climax is hanging on and I know what I need. I need him in deeper. With his name on my lips, I hear Kallon grunt in my ear, and in one hard thrust, he's the rest of the way inside me. I let out a long guttural moan, "Uuuggggnah."

"Shiiiiit," Kallon groans out in ecstasy. He pulls out a little, not all the way and then pushes in quickly. He seems to be holding his breath. He does it again and this time when he pushes in, he lets out his breath in one long exhale as he says, "Fuuuuck me, Abby."

I don't say anything, because I'm fighting a battle between my mouth and my brain. My mouth wants to scream but I know I shouldn't. If I open my mouth, a scream of pure pleasure is going to explode out of me. But I can feel myself starting to lose that battle as Kallon picks up speed. He moves his arms to both sides of my head to give himself better leverage. His moaning and groaning only fuels the fire inside me. I reach down and start rubbing myself. I start rubbing where Kallon had brought me over the edge twice in a short amount of time.

Kallon can feel me tightening around him, he breaths in a sharp breath and exhales a moan. He lowers his mouth to my nipple and as he sucks it in with a hard pull, I lose myself.

"OH!!!!" I scream. My third and hardest orgasm rips through me. I squeeze so tightly around Kallon that he stills, and my nipple audibly pops out of his mouth. I scream again, "OH!!!"

"Abby!" Kallon yells my name in ecstasy as I feel his erection pulsing inside me. I try to relax my inner walls, but it only lasts for a second before I'm constricting around him again. His moan this time is from deep down inside him. It's such a deep, throaty sound when he says, "Oh my god! Abby!"

I finally take a breath and scream his name, "Kallon!"

I, at last, release him and he pumps in quickly. Three, four, five times and then he thrusts deeply one more time. He holds here for what would have been a couple breaths, but we are both holding the air we have left in our lungs.

He slowly lays down on me and lets his breath out and says, "Shit, Abby."

I let my breath out too and a small giggle escapes me. I say, "That was... that was..."

And then I start to cry.

CHAPTER 16

"Abby?" Kallon asks as he pulls away from me. In a more shocked voice he asks, "Abby? Are you crying?"

"Nooo," I say but it's a total lie.

"Oh, shit... Abby," Kallon says hearing the lie in my answer and the hitch in my voice. He now sounds totally freaked out which makes me cry even harder. He slips out of me— which also makes cry even harder than I had been, if that's possible —and moves to the side but pulls me to him. He asks hurriedly in a worried voice, "Abby, what's wrong? Did I... Did I do something wrong? Did I hurt you?"

"You... you..." I can't catch my breath. It's all too much.

"What? What did I do? Tell me so I never do it again," he says, trying to lean away from me so he can see my face. He rolls me off him for just a second, just so he can wrap me up in the blanket we had been laying on. He cradles me to him and begs, "Please, please tell me."

"You... didn't... do... anything... wrong," I say through my hysterics. "I don't... know why... I'm crying."

"You don't know why your crying?" he asks kindly.

"No," I say. I take a breath to calm down and then

another. Then I amend my answer, “Well, I think so. But it’s nothing you did. It’s stupid. I shouldn’t be crying like this.”

“Tell me,” he pleads.

“I’ve never…” I don’t know why I feel so embarrassed to say it.

Kallon stills for a second and then leans away so he can really see me, “You weren’t a virgin were you? I thought you and—”

“Oh no, I’m not a virgin but I’ve never…” *Guh just say it!* I shouldn’t be embarrassed. I take another calming breath and say, “I’ve never orgasmed before and to have three in a short amount of time… I think it’s just a lot for my mind and body to experience all at once.”

Kallon looks at me unblinking. Then he tilts his head and blinks quickly and looks over my head and then back to me. He clears his throat and says, “You’ve never had an orgasm? Like never?”

“I thought I had but nothing has ever felt like that, not even when I’ve—” I shake my head from the embarrassment creeping in but continue anyways “—when I’ve tried to take care of myself. If I couldn’t get myself there and it never happened any other way, I thought I was broken or just someone who couldn’t… have one.”

“Jason never…” Kallon trails off without finishing what he was going to say but I answer him.

“No, he was very single minded. Get his release and move on to something else, like going back to work or whatever else he had going on.”

Kallon pulls me into him some more and hugs me tight, “Well, you are definitely not broken. That was the absolute best sex I've ever had."

"It was by far the best for me, but you don't have to say that just to make me feel better," I say laughing. I don't need him to start lying about how he feels just to make me feel better.

Kallon pulls away and looks me dead in the eyes. I've never seen him look so serious, "I'm not just saying it, Abby. I truly mean it. I've never lied to you, and I won't start lying to you now, especially now. I have never felt anything like that before. That was... mind blowing."

"I want to believe you, but you know how much Jason has messed with my head. I don't want my trust issues he's built inside me to transfer to you but it's hard," I say. He looks like he wants to say something, but I keep talking. "I know you have never lied to me, and you've never given me a reason to believe you have lied or will lie. It's just something I have to work through. I hope you'll understand and not take it personally when I get... I don't know, antsy about things. I've just been lied to and manipulated so much these last 10 plus years by someone who I thought loved me, I just have some insecurities about it now."

Kallon pulls me back to him and says, "I know, and I won't ever make you feel bad for feeling any certain way. However, I will never put you in a situation where you feel like I'm lying."

"I believe you," I say, snuggling into him.

We sit like this for a minute until Kallon tries to adjust the way he's sitting and I hear him groan.

"Are you okay?" I ask, I go to slide off his lap, but he holds me to him.

"I'm great," he says. "It's just... I'm sitting on the crack between the two ottomans and they're starting to shift. I'm afraid we might slip down into them if I don't move my ass over to one side or the other."

I laugh and push off him. The blanket falls off my shoulder and my right breast falls out.

"Damn, Abby..." Kallon says with so much affection in his voice I have to look up into his eyes. "If you don't want round two, I suggest we make sure you stay covered because—" he bites his bottom lips and shakes his head "—I won't be able to keep my hands off of you if you're gorgeous nakedness is out in the open."

I blush and then laugh while I pull the blanket back around me. I scoot until my back is against the back of the couch and lie down. I smile over at Kallon and say, "I think my mind and body need a couple more minutes to recuperate before round two can start."

"As long as you're thinking about round two, I'm okay with a break," he laughs. He crawls over to me and kisses me before he lays down. He sits up quick and says, "I need to take care of something real fast."

"Okay," I say, confused.

He scoots to the end of the cushion, grabs something off the floor, fiddles around his feet, and then stands up. His bare ass on display. My eyes stare at it for a minute before they travel up his back, taking in his muscles, but soon I'm looking back down at his ass. All too soon he's pulling his boxer briefs up. He pauses for a second and does something around his groin area.

"Be right back," he says. I can see he has something in his hand.

Oh, the condom! I'd forgotten about it.

Kallon walks away and I lie back down and think about how crazy this night turned out to be. I can feel my smile on my face and if I'm not careful, it might strain my facial muscles. I roll to my side and giggle a little. I can't remember the last time I've ever felt this good… this happy. Genuinely happy.

I hear Kallon's steps coming back and see he's holding something.

"I thought some refreshments were needed to help restore some energy," he says with a chuckle. He hands me a bottle of water, a single serve container of some apples and caramel sauce, and some turkey pepperoni sticks. He reaches down by his feet and picks up his phone. He taps on the screen and then a light behind us, in a corner, turns on dimly.

"Ooh, that's handy," I say, laughing. "And thanks for these, I'm starving."

We both grab our waters first and down about half of the contents. Kallon grabs the bag of the turkey pepperoni sticks and rips it open, grabbing a couple before handing the bag over to me. I grab a couple too and all but inhale them. I open my apple and caramel package and take my time with them.

A thought comes to me, and I teasingly ask, "So, did you have this planned all night?"

He looks genuinely shocked, and he says, "No, why would you think that?"

"Well, you had a condom in your pocket."

He smirks at me and says, "No, I grabbed it when I got the blanket. Tonight was not planned. It was a very happy turn of events. I've wanted this for a long time, Abby, but I would never be presumptuous enough to think that it would happen.

Especially after our talk. When I grabbed your leg tonight, it was just to be playful. But then I saw the reaction you had when I squeezed. When you pulled away, my reflex to keep you close kicked in which is why I held on. I decided I needed to put the ball in your court, to see what you wanted without words being exchanged or to draw attention to us, which is why I loosened my hold. When I felt you press closer to me and your foot rubbed up my lower leg, I knew it was game on. Maybe not full game on but maybe we were going to move our friendship into whatever next step was coming up. Which is why I—" he gulps at the memory "—ran my hand up your thigh. When my pinky touched you, I thought I'd gone too far. On my way back down, when you choked on your drink, your face turned a little red, so I thought I had embarrassed you. But your small smile told me otherwise."

I laugh, finish my water, and say, "I didn't choke on my drink. I coughed to cover my moan. You were driving me crazy. I've never felt anything like that before."

"Good to know," Kallon says with a wink as he takes a bite of his own apple slice.

After hearing Kallon talk about what happened at the end of dinner, makes my insides all warm and fuzzy again. I stare into Kallon's eyes as I bite into my apple slice and juice runs down my lips. I slowly lick it up with my tongue, Kallon's eyes follow it across my lip and back into my mouth. He swallow's the apple in his mouth and leans forward and kisses me softly, his tongue coming out and sweeping across my bottom lip.

"God you taste good," he says with a groan.

I swallow my apple and lean into him and kiss him.

Wanting more, I push the stuff off my lap to the side and turn more towards Kallon. I slide my leg over his lap and push myself up on top of him. He lets out a groan and pushes the turkey pepperoni stick bag and water bottle off his lap. He grabs my ass in both hands and pulls me closer to him.

I deepen our kiss, pushing my tongue against his lips, he opens willingly. Our tongues mesh together and start their dance that is becoming my most favorite things. I can feel my heart start to pound again. The heat inside me rising. I run my hands softly over the sides of his face, up to his forehead and through his hair until they're at the nape of his neck.

Kallon slows our kissing and then kisses the side of my lips, my cheek, and then over to my ear. He nibbles on my earlobe before sucking it into his mouth. He then kisses slowly down my neck until he's reached my collarbone. He kisses across to my other collarbone and then works his way up to my other ear. A shiver runs through me.

He pulls back and asks, "Cold?"

"Ha!" I laugh out. I kiss him and then in a breathy tone I say, "No, the opposite. I'm so hot right now."

Kallon growls and then rolls us until he's on top of me. He presses his body weight down into me and kisses me passionately. My legs are pinned beneath him since I'm still wrapped in the blanket, but I put my hands on his back and pull him closer.

And then I feel nature calling.

I pull away slowly which causes Kallon to pull away and look down at me. I smile and say, "I'm sorry, I need to use the restroom before we get too carried away."

Kallon laughs, kisses me one more time, and then slides

off me.

"No need to apologize. When nature calls, you better answer," he laughs as he scoots to the end of the couch, holding out his hand to help me. I maneuver myself over to him without the blanket completely coming off me and then he holds my hand as he walks me to a bathroom. He turns the light on and sweeps his hand to gesture me inside.

I do my business quickly and wash my hands. I wrap myself in the blanket and when I open the door, Kallon is leaning against the wall. He smiles his breathtaking smile when he sees me.

"Do you want to move to my bed?" he asks as he steps up to me and runs his hands through my hair on the side of my head and holds me close to his face. He kisses me softly and pulls back, waiting for my answer.

"Yes, please," I whisper out. I let the blanket fall as I pull his mouth back to mine.

He lifts me like he did in the elevator and carries me away, with his hands holding me up by my ass. Kallon doesn't walk long before he's lying me down on a super soft bed. I open my eyes and see he didn't even turn on any lights. I scoot back until I find pillows and lie my head down on one.

I hear the soft sound of fabric hitting the floor and then a drawer being open to my left. Then I hear the sound of paper or foil or something and then the drawer closes. I feel the weight of Kallon as he gets on the bed and crawls over to me. I see his shadowy figure as he leans over me.

"I'm going to turn on a light, is that okay?" he asks.

"Mmmhmm," I say.

Kallon grabs something from his headboard and in a

second a light across the room turns on but is just dim enough I can see him. I see he's holding a little remote in one hand and another condom in the other. He puts both of them on the headboard and bends down and starts to kiss me gain.

He kisses me deeply and then starts to kiss my neck as one of his hands slides down to my breast and palms it gently. He kisses down and replaces his mouth where his palm was, which causes my back to arch again.

"Kallon," I whisper out. That familiar feeling of needs starts to build down between my thighs.

"I've got you Abs," he says into my breast. He pulls my nipple into his mouth and sucks it just hard enough to cause me to gasp.

As he sucks and nips at my nipple, his hand slides down my stomach until he's touching my throbbing bud. He doesn't make me wait like last time before he slides a finger inside me.

I put my hand over my mouth and say into, "Oh shit…"

"Move your hand, Abby, I want to hear you," he mumbles into my breast again.

"Mmm," I moan out as he adds another finger into me. All too soon, his fingers leave me, and his mouth is off my breasts. My eyes fly open, wondering what's happened but I watch in fascination as he puts his fingers that were inside me, into him mouth.

His eyes close and when he pulls his fingers out, he says, "You taste so sweet. I need to taste you again."

He kisses quickly down my stomach until his hot breath is on my now engorged bud. Before I can say anything, his lips envelope it and he pulls it into his mouth.

"Kallon!" I scream. I've never, ever, felt anything like this before.

"Mmm," he moans into me. He slips his fingers back inside me, two this time, not waiting to start with one and bless him for that! My hips buck on their own and I feel myself grinding into his mouth and hands.

"Oh my god!" I scream. "Kallon!"

He sucks on my bud and thrusts his fingers in, in such a rhythmic fashion, I feel myself about to fall apart again. But the release doesn't come, it just keeps building, and building.

"Kall...on... I... Oh... shiiit," I pant out. Just when I think I can't handle it anymore, Kallon presses his tongue down on my bud and then sucks it just hard enough, I explode and scream in ecstasy. The feeling that comes over me can't be described. It's not anything I've ever felt. It last longer than the last three orgasms put together.

When I finally come down from it, Kallon's tongue on my bud is too much. It's too sensitive.

"Mmm, Kallon... I need you... inside me... please," I pant out.

Kallon keeps his fingers inside me, keeping the rhythm he was using, and kisses his way back up to me. When he kisses me, I taste myself on his lips. It's not something I've ever experienced either. Jason never had time for this part of love making, only for me to go down on him. *PRICK!*

Kallon's fingers leave me but they're replaced with his hard erection. In one fluid motion, Kallon is sheathed inside me to the hilt.

"Shit!" I exclaim.

"I'm sorry, did that hurt?" Kallon asks, stilling.

"No... it felt so good," I say running my hands over his

back. "Don't stop, please."

Kallon starts to thrust in and out of me, pulling out almost all the way and then going back in. I feel the need for more. I hook my leg over his and push with my left hand, pushing him to his right, and onto his back.

"Oh, okay," Kallon says with surprise and a smile.

His hands slide up to both of my breasts and starts to massage both of them as I sink down on to him. I gasp as he hits spots he hasn't touched yet.

His hands still on my breasts and they tighten slightly, he groans and closes his eyes, "Shit, Abby."

"Does that hurt?" I ask, the look on his face could pass as pain.

"The opposite, you feel way to fucking good," he says with a moan.

I smile and start to move again. He opens his eyes and leans up and kisses me, rolling my nipples between his fingers.

"Mmm," I moan and press my chest into his hands harder. I put my hands back behind me, onto his thighs, and use them to give me something to support myself with. I start to rock and rotate my hips. My head rolls back, and another moan escapes me, "Mmmmm."

Kallon's hands slide to my back and then we're rolling again.

"I'm sorry but that was way too hot... You're way to hot... I was going to lose it if we stayed like that for too much longer," he says sheepishly.

I laugh a little and reach for him, pulling him down to kiss me, which he does without hesitation. His hand finds my nipple again and starts to play with it while we kiss. He pulls out and thrusts back into me.

"Damn it," Kallon says between clinched teeth. "You're just so damn tight. I don't think any position will keep me from losing it."

"Hold on," I say. I want to come apart with him. He slows his thrusts as I reach down between us, and I start to rub my bud that's not as sensitive anymore but throbbing with need again. Kallon doesn't stop thrusting, so I put my free hand on his chest and ask, "Please, stop for just a second. I want to... I want to..."

I can't finish the sentence.

"Want to what, Abby?" he asks between clenched teeth. When I don't answer, he lets out a moan and says, "You have to tell me what you want, Abs."

"I want to come over the edge with you, let me get there. I'm close but not there yet," I say, embarrassed. Anytime I'd tell Jason to stop and wait, he'd ignore me and plow on through to get his release.

Kallon stills and stops thrusting, and says, "What do you need me to do?"

I smile and ignoring my embarrassment, *If he wants to know, I'll tell him.* I say "Suck on my nipples. I'll tell you when to start going."

"I can do that," he says happily and then pulls a nipple into his mouth as his free hand that's not holding himself up, goes to my other nipple and starts to pinch and roll it just hard enough it feels so fucking good.

With every flick of Kallon's tongue, I feel like I can feel it in my bud. Like the nerve connects from my nipple to it. I start rubbing it, soft and slow at first but as he picks up his sucking and flicking, I add pressure and speed. I close my eyes and imagine his mouth back down there and the feeling builds.

Ecstasy builds even more and when I feel like I'm almost to the edge, I whisper, "Go."

Kallon doesn't move, so I say a little louder, "Go Kallon, please!"

"Uuuuh," he grunts as he pushes in slowly.

"Kallon, please, fuck me, I'm close! I'm so close! FUCK ME!" I scream. I put my hand over my mouth, stopping myself from screaming again.

Kallon lets go of my breast and uses his other hand to get better stability as he pounds into me. With each thrust, I moan out.

"Oh shit," Kallon says through clinched teeth. "Abby... Abby... I'm going to..."

"Me too," I pant. "Don't. Stop. Please."

One thrust. Two thrusts. Three thrusts. Kallon all but pulls out and then thrust into me deep and hard and we both fall into it.

"FUCK ME! ABBY!" Kallon yells into my ear.

At the same time, I scream, "KALLLLLLOOOOOON!"

Kallon stills for a couple thundering heart beats and then he thrusts a couple short times and then he collapses on top of me, breathing hard.

"I... was... wrong," he says between breaths. He takes two deep breaths and smiles down at me.

"About?" I ask breathless.

"THAT was the absolute best sex I've ever had," he says, kissing my cheek, then my neck, then my collar bones, and then he's kissing me sweetly. He pulls away and says, "That was unbelievable."

"Yes, yes it was," I say with a smile of my own. I don't think I have ever felt so... satisfied. My body feels deliciously disjointed, almost like jelly. My fingers and toes are tingly in the best possible way. A current of happiness is buzzing through me.

Kallon kisses me one more time and then rolls off and out of me.

"I'll be right back," he says and gets off the bed. I watch him walk across his room to a door and turns on a light. I see it's his bathroom. The sound of the faucet turns on and then a minute later he's walking back into his room, bare ass naked.

Even after everything we just did, my heart rate picks up at the sight of him. Knowing what he can do with not only his body, but his hands and mouth, I involuntarily squeeze my thighs together. As much as my body wants round three, my mind is telling me it needs sleep, it needs a break.

As Kallon gets to the bed, I sit up and scoot to the edge.

"Do you mind if I use your bathroom?" I ask.

"Go right ahead," he says as he bends down and grabs his boxer briefs. I grab the blanket at the foot of the bed and wrap it around myself and head to the bathroom.

I do my business and then wash my hands. I splash some cold water on my face and neck, to calm my once again over heated body. I look at my reflection and see my eyes look both dazed and full of renewed energy. *How is that possible?*

I walk back out and see Kallon lounging on the bed. There's a dark blue t-shirt sitting at the foot of the bed.

As I get closer, Kallon says, "I wasn't sure if you'd be more comfortable sleeping in something or not, so I grabbed one of my t-shirts for you."

"Thank you," I say, picking it up. I drop the blanket and reach for the shirt.

"If my opinion matters, I say sleep without," Kallon says. I look up at him, just before I slip the shirt over my head and I see his eyes perusing my entire body, desire the main emotion on his face.

"As much as I'd really enjoy another round, I don't think my mind will make it. I feel so wonderfully good right now, I think I could sleep for an entire day," I say with a little giggle and slip the shirt on and then crawl onto the bed. For a split second I don't know where to lie down, but he pulls the blanket, revealing he put on the boxer briefs, and opens his arms and then pats his chest. I go to him and lay my head on his chest, instantly hearing his frantically pounding heart. "Are you okay?"

"Better than okay, why do you ask?"

"Your heart is beating so fast," I say as I put my hand under my head, spreading my fingers out across his pec.

"If you were me and saw the most beautiful woman naked in your room, your heart would be beating just as fast," he says and then he kisses the top of my head.

My cheeks heat at his compliment and snuggle down into him. I kiss his chest and say sleepily, "Good night, Kallon."

He kisses my head again and says, "Sweet dreams, Abby."

CHAPTER 17

Kallon's body glistens with the water from the shower, his muscles ripple with every movement he makes. My eyes follow a droplet from his abs down to his V, and still, it trickles down until hit comes to a stop in the patch of hai—

"Are you alright, Abby?" Betty asks.

I startle out of my memories. It's Thursday afternoon and I've just gotten back from the movie set. I haven't been able to stop daydreaming about Saturday night and Sunday morning in Kansas. Kallon and I had another round of mind-blowing, body tingling sex early Sunday morning before we showered and left for the airport together. The flight home was full of making out like we were teenagers, but we kept it PG-13 for the sake of Louie and Captain Sterling. Dax and Freddy decided to hangout in a room in the back.

My cheeks heat and I smile at Betty before I reply with, "Yes, I'm fine."

"You've been a little out of it since you got back from Kayla's wedding, is everything alright?" she asks as she helps me put things away.

"Yes, all good," I say with a giggle.

She laughs and asks, “Are you going to tell me how the wedding was with Kallon there?”

I turn quickly towards her, my eyes flaring wide.

“How did you know he came?”

“Well, one, Kayla couldn’t get ahold of your parents, so she texted me and asked for Kallon’s number. I asked Dax to ask Kallon if I could give her his number, and obviously he said yes. And two, Dax told me he was going with Kallon to Kansas.”

“Oh, right,” I say with an embarrassed laugh. My cheeks turn even more red but all I say is, “Ummm, it was good.”

“Mmmmmhmmm, just good?” Betty asks with a laugh.

“Okay, really, really good,” I say with a dreamy sigh.

“What happened?” she asks as she wipes her hands on a towel.

“We danced, talked, drank,” I say. Kallon and I had decided to keep ‘us’ just us for a little while. He had said he tries to keep his personal life as private as possible. He did say that if I wanted to talk to my girlfriends about it, I should. But I told him I agreed, no one needed to know about us yet. Even though I don’t really know what ‘us’ means.

“Aaaand?” Betty asks with excitement in her eyes.

She’s not going to believe we didn’t do anything, so I’ll give her a small truth.

“We kissed,” I say as my cheeks heat again.

“Oh my gosh!” Betty squeals.

I put my finger to my mouth and say, “Shh! We aren’t going public, even though I don’t know what we are, so just keep that information to yourself, please.”

She mimics zipping her lips and throwing something over her shoulder, “Your secret is safe with me.”

"Thanks, Betty," I say as I put the last of my stuff away. "I'm going to run up and change and then I'm going to head to Rose's."

"Sounds good," Betty says as she grabs a tray of cookies she was working on when I came in and heads to the front.

"Hey," I say, stopping her before she heads through the door. "Are you sure you're okay with me taking off for another weekend?"

"Abby, we've been over this... You are my boss. You don't have to clear anything with me. But I appreciate you asking, and yes, I'm absolutely fine with it. It sounds like you'll have a great time," she winks and walks out the door.

"Thank you!" I holler and then head to the stairs to go to my apartment.

It doesn't take me long to change and then I'm heading back down the stairs to the kitchen. I open the door and wave to Betty as she helps a customer at the register. On my way to the door, I greet a couple customer's already sitting with their drinks and food. I look out the front door and see Dax standing by the car door, ready to take me to Rose's.

As soon as I'm walking through the door, Dax opens the back passenger door for me and smiles.

"Thanks Dax," I say stepping to the car and sliding in.

He just nods and shuts the door. The drive to Rose's is a quiet one, which has me thinking over the last couple of days. I was a little worried to see Kallon. Would he pretend nothing happened? Would he regret what happened even though he said it was the best time he's ever had? We texted and talked on the phone Monday but I didn't see him until Tuesday, on set.

At first I thought the answer to all of my questions

where yes, he regrated it, because he was acting like he did before the weekend. He was friendly and nice as usual. He helped unload the van and set things up as usual. I had gone to his dressing room, as I've been doing since last year, and he came in a few minutes after me. I was standing by his bookshelf, looking for a book to read. He didn't say a single word but came straight to me and kissed me like I was the breath he needed to fill his lungs. When he stepped back he had told me he'd been wanting to do that since the moment I got to the studio. All thoughts of him regretting anything were obliterated. We stood there kissing like two kids skipping class until a voice came over the speaker in his room, telling him he was needed back on set. Every free moment he had, he was with me in his dressing room.

"We're here, Miss Abby," Dax says. Once again pulling me out of my thoughts. I look around and see he's parked in the back parking lot.

"Thanks, Dax," I say. I smile at him through the rearview mirror and ask, "Are you coming in today or are you going back to Rose Bud's?"

"I thought I might go back to Rose Bud's and have lunch with Betty, if that's okay," Dax says, his cheeks turning a little red.

"Totally fine," I say with a laugh. "It gets a little boring around here just sitting around."

"I don't mind at all," he says before he gets out and opens the door for me. "I'll be back shortly.

"No worries, take your time," I say with a wink.

He shakes his head, but I see a smile spread across his face as he walks me to the back door of Rose's. I enter my code into the door and he opens it for me.

I turn and say, "Go back to Rose Bud's, I'll be fine here."

"I'll be back in an hour," he says with a stern look. He looks around the parking lot, which has me looking around too.

"What are you worried about?" I ask.

"Nothing," he says. "I just don't like leaving you."

"I'll be fine," I say with an eye roll.

"One hour," he says. He turns and walks away.

I go into the kitchen of Rose's and start my routine. I check the main floor and the second floor. We don't have an event, but I still check the third floor and suite and find it's all clean. When I get down to my office, I see Royce.

"Hiya, Abby," he says with a smile when I walk in the room.

"Hey, Royce," I say, returning the smile.

"You excited for your weekend in Seattle?" Royce asks, leaning back in the chair he's sitting in, in front of my desk.

"Yeah, it should be a pretty good time. I'm excited to see Spencer, Mary, and the kids," I say with a smile. I go to my desk and turn on my computer. "Are you sure you're okay with me leaving for yet another weekend?"

"For sure," he says with a grin as he puts his hands behind his head. He looks at me and asks, "Have you fully adjusted to being manager here?"

I shrug and sit at my desk.

"Abby?" he says my name, making me look at him. "It's me, you can be honest."

I sigh and say, "I've accepted it. I miss cooking but I know I can't do it all. Someone needed to step in as full-time manager, to deal with ordering, and customers. I know Bridgette was taking care of inventory for the bars and had started to do it for the kitchen too, but I didn't want her to get burnt out and leave us. I couldn't be in the middle of cooking and be called out to deal with a disgruntled customer. Even if it sucks I'm not cooking in here anymore, it's what's best for Rose's."

"You know you can jump on the line any time you want, it's your restaurant, your kitchen," Royce says, letting his chair settle back down on all fours.

"I know and on busy nights, I will, but I trust you guys to do your jobs and you've proven over and over again that you are capable of running the kitchen. I just don't want you to get burnt out either."

"I won't," he says with a smile. "This is my dream."

"You'll tell me if you need a break?" I ask.

"You'll be the first to know," he says as he stands and goes to the door.

"Hey Royce," I say, stopping him before he goes through the door. When he turns, I say, "Thanks."

"Anytime," he says with a smile. Just as he leaves my office, my phone rings.

I look and see that it's Mary.

"Hello?"

"What are you wearing to the premiere?" she says in a rush. I hear metal on metal. She must be in her closet going through her clothes.

"I hadn't really thought about it," I say. "I was just going to go to a store there and pick something out."

"Abby... it's a movie premiere, it can't be just any old dress."

"Why not?"

"It's... a... movie... premiere," she says it slowly, like I don't understand her words. *"There's going to be cameras all over the place and you're... we're going with the lead male actor. Our photos are going to be all over the internet and papers and magazines... shit, even on TV."*

"I hadn't thought about that," I say, suddenly nervous.

"I'll do some research and see if I can find somewhere here in town that might have something," Mary says hurriedly. *"Any chance Kallon would know of somewhere with premiere appropriate dresses? Spencer has a tux, so it's just us girls that need something."*

"I'll call him. If he doesn't, I bet Randy, his assistant might have an idea. I could also look around here," I say, drumming my fingers on my desk nervously.

"You fly out tomorrow morning, when do you have time for that?"

She's right again. I hate that I didn't think or comprehend the magnitude of going to this premiere with Kallon.

"I'll call Kallon. Don't worry, it'll be fine," I say, trying to sound more confident than I actually feel.

"Let me know what he says."

"I will, thanks for the reality check, Mary," I say with love and really mean it.

"I'm sorry for stressing you out," she says with a small laugh. *"Talk to you soon."*

"Bye," I say and then the call ends.

I scroll down to Kallon's name and tap on it. It rings before Randy's familiar voice answers.

"Hello, Miss Rose," he says happily.

"Hi Randy, is Kallon available?"

"He's changing, so he should be in a couple minutes. Do you want to stay on the line, or do you want me to have him call you back?" he asks.

"If he has a free minute to call me back, that'd be great."

"Sounds good, Miss Rose. I'll tell him."

"Thanks, Randy."

"My pleasure."

The call ends and I put my phone down, just to pick it up again. I open my internet browser and enter a search for stores with ball gowns or prom dresses. Quite a few stores pop up, but they all show that they close at 5 o'clock, that's in two hours. Mary's right, I won't have time to look here in New York before we fly out in the morning.

"Shit," I whisper.

"What's up?" a voice comes from the doorway. I look and see Bridgette standing there with her folder she carries when she's doing inventory.

"Oh, nothing," I say with a shake of my head. "What's up?"

"We got a shipment of champagne in that I don't remember ordering," she says as she walks up to my desk. She hands me a slip of paper and I grab it. I look at the name of the champagne and grin.

"Sorry, I meant to tell you," I smile up at her. "While I was in Kansas, I had some of the best champagne I've ever tasted. Mr. Webb and I decided to order a couple cases to try them out here. I really think they'll be a hit."

"Oh okay," she says with relief in her voice. "I was

worried I had accidently ordered something I shouldn't have. Do you want us to push the last case of champagne we have left of the old stuff or push the new to see how it does?"

"Let's intermix it," I say, looking at the invoice in my hand. "I know the new stuff will fly off the shelves, so I don't want to have that case of old bottles going to waste. Maybe use the older bottles to give to people if they're celebrating a birthday, anniversary, or something like that. And if people ask for a bottle, ask them if they'd like to try the new stuff. Once the old case is used up, we'll let people know we have a new champagne when they order a bottle."

"Okay, sounds good. Thanks, Abby," Bridgette says with a smile. She turns and leaves.

I go back to my computer, entering the inventory into a new invoice to send off to our vendors. I check my email and see that someone has requested to rent our event floor a couple months from now. I click into my calendar and see that the days are open, so I respond back confirming the days are open and send them our contract and the fee it costs to hold the dates.

****RING-RING**RING-RING****
****RING-RING**RING-RING****

My phone ringing startles me out of my concentration the emails have drawn me into. I look down and see Kallon is calling. My heart sputters and then picks up speed double time.

"Hi," I say happily into my phone once I've hit the green accept option.

"Hi," he says back, just as happily.

"How did the rest of the shoot go?"

"Not nearly as fun, once you left," he says with a laugh.

I shake my head but have a huge grin on my face.

"It was fun, but I have a feeling you were distracted from you're work," I say with a little laugh. "Maybe I should stay out at the tables from now on."

"Nope, that's a terrible idea," he says with a chuckle. *"I'm more distracted when I don't get to see you. My mind plays over everything that happened while we were in Wichita. At least when I have you in my arms, even for fifteen to twenty minutes, I can concentrate on work easier."*

"Kallon," I say in an exasperated tone. A thought comes to mind, so I ask, "Why do you talk like that now?"

"Like what?" he asks, confusion think in his tone.

"I noticed it at the park on my birthday. You seem to be expressing your feelings more freely," I say, worrying my bottom lip with my teeth.

"After that first kiss—" he sighs *"—After that first kiss, my mental walls were obliterated. I couldn't hold in how I truly feel about you anymore. I decided I wasn't going to hold back anymore. I'm all in Abby, from the moment our lips touched, I've been all in. I talk freely about my feelings because I never want you to doubt me, to doubt us."*

"What exactly are we?" I ask. I hold my breath, waiting for his answer.

He chuckles and says, *"I don't know about you, but I think boyfriend, girlfriend, is a good place to start."*

"I'm your girlfriend?" I ask, slightly shocked.

"As long as you want to be?" he says, now sounding doubtful. *"If you don't want that, we can go back to being friends*

and business partners."

"NO!" I shout. Royce pokes his head into the office quickly, but I wave him off and motion for him to shut the door. After he does, I say to Kallon, "I want that. I told you in Wichita, I wanted you. I didn't just mean then and there. I just..."

"Just what, Abby?"

"I don't think I can live up to what's expected of Kallon Keller's girlfriend," I say, my cheeks heating as I say the last word.

"And what's that?"

"Your girlfriend is supposed to know the expectations of going to a movie premiere. I had to be reminded by my sister-in-law how big of a deal it is. Which is why I called you. I don't have a dress to wear," I say shyly. "A woman dating a celebrity should know to take things like this seriously. Don't get me wrong, I take it seriously but I'm a woman who lives in jeans, t-shirts, and, or a cooking uniform, or at least I did until I hung that up to be the manager. I don't have dresses in my closet just hanging around to be worn to fancy parties. I don't even think I own a single dress. I had to search for stores that would have the type of dresses I've seen women wear to premiers like the one this weekend because I had no idea where to even begin to look. I—"

"Abby," Kallon interrupts me. *"Breathe. I don't give a shit what the public's expectations are of me, so why would I care what their expectations are of you? All the reasons you just listed, are reasons why I like you so much. You are real. And because I feel like I know you so well, I've taken into consideration that you wouldn't have a dress and I have it under control. I've been in your closet—"*

I interrupt him this time and say shocked, "You have?"

"I got clothes for you last year, remember?" he asks. He doesn't wait for me to respond before he says, *"So unless you've gone on a shopping spree you haven't told me about, I think I know what's in your closet."*

"Okay but what do you mean by you have the dress thing under control?"

"It's a surprise for you and Mary."

"Kallon..." I say.

"Do you trust me?"

"Of course I do."

"Then trust that I have this. I would never do something to make you feel lesser than or uncomfortable or embarrassed." I'm quiet for a minute so he says, *"Abby?"*

"You won't tell me anything?" I ask.

He laughs and says with a sigh, *"All I'll tell you is that you need to have Mary to our hotel room by 10am Saturday morning."*

"Our hotel room?" I ask, my blood pressure rising at the thought of us having a room together again. The fun we had last time makes my heart rate skyrocket.

"Don't worry, it's a suite. It's similar to the one in Kansas, so there's two rooms. So, if you aren't comfortable sharing a bed with me, you have the option of your own room."

"I think the morning before we left for the airport should tell you I'm more than comfortable sharing a room with you," I say and then cover my mouth. My filter clearly isn't working this afternoon.

He lets out a ragged breath and says, *"That's what I like to hear but I don't want to ever assume anything with you. You'll always have a choice with me."*

"I choose you," I whisper.

His quiet laugh lets me know he heard me. He says, *"And I choose you."*

"Abby?" Royce's voice sounds from the other side of the door.

"Hey, I probably better go," I say to Kallon.

"Were your dress worries all that you needed?" Kallon asks quickly.

"At this moment, yes," I say. "Mary had me freaked out."

"I've got a few errands to run but after I'm finished, I can swing by Rose's, if that's okay," Kallon says.

"You don't have to ask permission to come here or to come see me," I say with a smile on my face.

"Abby?" Royce says a little louder and his knock sounds impatient.

Kallon must hear it because he says, *"Sounds like you're needed. I'll talk to you later."*

"Bye," I say.

"See you soon," he says.

I end our call and get up and walk to the door. I open it and see Royce standing with his back to the door, in a defensive stance.

"What's wrong?" I ask, putting my hand on his arm, turning him towards me. When he turns and looks at me, he looks royally pissed off. I step back and ask, "What?"

He answers with one word, "Jason."

CHAPTER 18

My heart goes to my throat and I stare at Royce.

"What about Jason?" I ask in a whisper. I think I know the answer, why else would Royce look so pissed?

"He's out front," Royce snarls. "He's refusing to leave until he talks to you."

I walk back to my desk, grab my phone, and send a message to the group text I have with Kallon and Dax.

Me: Jason is here.

I don't have to wait long for their replies.

Kallon: Stay in your office, Dax do not let that asshat near her. Trevor is going to bring me straight there.

Dax: Coming in now.

I'm a little shocked at Dax's answer. I look at the time and see that I've been here for two hours now. I hear the beep of the security camera detecting someone at the back door, so I look and see Dax punching in his code. A few seconds later, he's standing in front of Royce.

"Where is he?" Dax asks.

"He's out front," Royce says. "He's refusing to leave until he talks to Abby."

"Fuck that," Dax says.

I cross my arms and say, "I'm not afraid of him. I'll talk to him."

"No, you won't," Dax says as he steps beside Royce, after he moves out of the way.

"Yes, I will," I say, my stubborn side coming forward. "I don't want him causing a scene with the customers that are here. He won't hurt me."

"I bet you thought he never would, but he almost killed you, Abby. And I'll be damned if he gets a chance at it again," Dax says, coming to stand in front of me.

"Do you honestly think he's going to do something with you near?" I ask.

The look on his face makes me want to laugh, like he just realized he will be there.

"Okay, but you don't go anywhere alone with him," he says.

"No kidding," I say, slightly offended he feels the need to voice that. "I'll never be alone with Jason again and that's my choice, no one else's."

I put my headset on and tell Sherry that I'm coming up.

"No, Abby. Don't come up here. Jason is here," Patty says in my ear, worry and stress coating her tone.

"Don't worry, Patty. I'll be okay," I say as I walk to the door that leads through the bar.

As I open the door, Dax and Royce are at my back. I stop and turn around.

"Royce, get back into the kitchen. Finish getting things ready for our dinner rush," I say sternly. He looks like he's going to argue so I pull the boss card, one I hardly ever pull, and say, "That's an order."

He looks hurt and pissed, but he turns around and goes back into the kitchen. I turn towards Dax and cross my arms.

"What?" he asks.

"Not a word out of you unless absolutely necessary," I warn.

He puts his hands up and nods. Then he motions with one of his hands towards the front of the restaurant.

I turn and walk through the bar seating area. I look behind the bar and see Cammy standing as close to the side as she can where she can see the hostess booth while also being in her area. Joel and Brent are nowhere to be seen.

"Hey," I say, making her jump. "Where are the guys?"

"Making sure Jason doesn't come any further into the restaurant," she says, walking over to me.

"You all act like he's going to attack me out here in public," I say walking towards the front.

"Who's to say he won't?" she says, her eyebrow raised, as I walk by her.

"Me," I say. I try to sound more confident in my answer than I feel.

I brace myself. This is the first time I'll have seen him since the 'incident', his attack. I take a deep breath and recite in my head, *He will not hold power over me. He does not hold power over me. I do not give him that power.*

I step around the corner and see Jason walled off by six of my employees. Brent, Joel, Pam, Sherry, Joe, and Amanda all form a barrier coming into the restaurant. My sister is standing behind them, behind the hostess bar, looking scared out of her mind. I go to her first.

"Hey Sis," I say as I step up to her and put my hand on her shoulder. She looks at me with terror in her eyes. "Royce needs your help in the kitchen. He's trying out a new sauce and he knows you'll give him an honest answer."

"Are you sure?" she asks with a shaky voice.

"I am," I say. I turn and say to Amanda, one of our servers. "Hey, Amanda, will you take Patty to the kitchen? Royce needs her help."

When Amanda looks at me, she looks like she's about to argue but I give a look that tells her this is not up for discussion. I then tilt my head towards Patty and when Amanda registers how scared she looks, she says, "Sure, come on Patty. Let's go see what the Chef needs."

Before they walk away, I grab the headset on Patty's head and put it down on the counter. When they've gotten out of hearing range, I tap my headset and tell Royce, "Amanda is bringing Patty back. Ask her opinion on a sauce you have on the stove. I told her it's a new one and that you wanted her to tell you what she thought. She's pretty freaked out."

"Got it," he replies.

I take a deep breath and turn to face Jason. He looks at me with relief in his eyes. I take a minute to really look at him. He looks healthy. Healthier than I've seen him in a long time. Before I thought it was just the stress of work and not enough sleep and drinking too much. I know those things had a huge factor in it, but I also know the drugs didn't help either. I step around the booth and stand next to Brent.

As I tap Brent on the shoulder, I say, "You all can get back to work now, I've got this. Thanks."

"Abby—" Brent is about to protest but I cut him off.

"Back to work," I say sternly. "We've got some reservations coming in—" I look at my watch to check the time "—in 30 minutes. Go make sure you have everything ready for your section and for any of those reservations."

They grumble but turn and head off into their designated areas, except for Pam. She walks behind the hostess desk and stands with her arms crossed.

I turn back to Jason and stare at him. When he doesn't say anything I say, "What do you want, Jason?"

He smiles when I say his name. For a split second I see the boy from high school, but oddly enough, the feeling of recognition doesn't stir the feelings of love like I thought it would. I remember the last ten years and last year and that flare of recognition disappears.

He says, "I just want to talk."

"I don't want to talk to you," I say, putting my hands on my hips.

"I got the hint when you didn't respond to my emails," he says with a hint of frustration.

"It wasn't a hint," I say. *How dare he get frustrated with me.*

"I have some things I need to say," he says, taking a step towards me.

I don't move but Dax steps in front of me, and says in a low menacing voice, "One more step and you'll wish you stuck to emailing her."

I put my hand on Dax's arm and pull him back. Jason

puts his hands up and steps back.

"I'm not going to hurt her," he says to Dax. He looks at me, pleading with his eyes, "I'm not going to hurt you."

"I don't care," I say. I shake my head and start to turn and add, "I've got work to get back to."

"Please, Abby," Jason says, really pleading now. "I have to get this off my chest. I have to apologize for everything. Please, give me a chance, hear me out."

I turn and glare at him.

"Jason, I gave you too many chances. You don't get anymore. I. Am. Done," I say through clinched teeth.

He reaches into his back pocket and pulls out an envelope. He reaches his arm out, but Dax is the one to reach out and grab it. Jason almost doesn't let go but when he sees I'm not budging, he lets Dax take it.

"Just read it please," he begs. "You don't have to call me or write me back, just read it okay. If I know you're going to read it, that's good enough for me. I need you to forgive me."

"Jason, if and when I forgive you, it won't be for your benefit, it will be for mine," I say.

He puts his hands up and says, "I know, I know. Just please, read it."

I look at him for a long moment before I nod. He relaxes and takes a step back towards the door leading outside.

"Thank you, Abby," he says as he reaches for the door.

Before he can go through, I say, "Jason?"

He stops and looks at me, "Yeah?"

"Don't come back here," I say sternly.

He stands dumbfounded for a minute but finally nods his head. I turn away from him and walk back through the bar. When I get back into the kitchen, I find Patty standing by Royce with her hands on her hips. The look on her face makes me want to laugh, but I'm not quite in the mood for laughing yet.

"What's going on?" I ask as I walk up beside her. I put Jason out of my mind, for a second.

"He's telling me this is new, but it tastes just like the old sauce," Patty says pointing to the pan on the stove.

I walk over, my back towards my sister, and wink at Royce. He rubs his hand over his mouth to hide his smile. I take a spoon from the drawer and put some sauce on it and put it in my mouth.

"Hmmm," I say. I walk back to Patty and stand next to her and look at Royce. "She's right, Royce. It tastes exactly like the original recipe."

"Shoot, I really thought I had changed something in it," he says acting shocked.

"I told you," Patty says with a big smile.

"Yes, you did," he says bowing his head.

"Patty, why don't you and Amanda head back up to the front," I say, nodding towards the door.

"Is HE gone?" she asks.

"Yes and he won't be coming back," I say, patting her shoulder.

"Okay," she says. She starts to walk away and then turns and points to Royce, "If you need my help again, make sure that sauce is better."

"Yes, ma'am," Royce says laughing a little.

When Patty and Amanda walk through the doors, I turn to Royce and hug him.

"Thank you," I say.

"Is she why you wanted me to stay in here?" Royce asks, stepping out of my embrace. I step back and to the side of his cooking station.

"Yes, and partly because I didn't want you to take Jason's head off," I say with a raised eyebrow.

"I would have," Royce says stirring the sauce.

I pat his arm as I walk by, back to my office. I don't have to say anything to Dax, I know he's following me. I step to the side to let him walk through the door and then I shut it. I walk to my desk and sit. Dax takes the seat in front of me. He offers me the letter.

"Do you think I should read it?" I ask, turning it over and over in my hand.

"The only person who can answer that is you," he says.

I nod. I take a breath and then open the envelope.

"I'm going to step out and call Mr. Keller to let him know everything is okay here," Dax says as he stands back up from his seat.

"Thanks Dax," I say.

I don't wait for him to leave before I pull out the very long letter and start reading.

◆ ◆ ◆

KNOCK-KNOCK

The sound of someone knocking at my office door

makes me jump. I wipe a tear from my face and say, "Who is it?"

"Kallon."

I wipe my face again and take a drink of the water bottle I pulled from my mini fridge and take a sip.

"Come on in," I say.

He walks in and sees me at my desk. Kallon looks at my face and sighs. He shuts the door and walks towards me. He comes and takes the seat that Dax had been sitting in twenty minutes ago.

"Are you okay?" he asks. He looks at my desk and sees the papers from Jason's letter sitting on top of everything.

"Yeah," I say. "Jason gave me a letter."

"Oh," Kallon says nervously. "How do you feel about it?"

I pick up the papers and as I hand them to him, I say, "Pissed off."

His nervous expression turns to shock, "What?"

"He told me about every single time he'd cheated on me. Do you want to know when it started?" I ask.

"Ummm," Kallon says as he takes the papers from me, since I'm still offering them to him. He stacks them neatly and puts them on his side of the desk.

"In fucking high school," I say with a trimmer in my voice. "I honestly don't care because I have you now, but it still pisses me off that the ten years we were together, were a total lie and he didn't have the balls to break up with me because, and I quote—" I grab the papers and flip through them until I find the right paper "—'Abby you were end game. I knew I wanted to marry you at some point, but I just had it in my head that I needed to get as many women as possible out of my system before we got married so I would stop cheating the moment I put a ring on your finger.' He goes on to say that the drugs and alcohol didn't help but he doesn't blame his decisions on them, he's taking responsibility for it all. Can you believe that shit? Can you believe I was actually in love with that asshole?"

"Abby," Kallon says as he stands and walks around the desk. He squats down beside me and turns me in my chair until I'm facing him. "You fell in love with him in high school and he changed. It's okay that you held out hope that he would turn back into the man you fell in love with."

"You sound like Kayla," I say with a laugh.

He laughs and leans up and kisses me softly. When he pulls back, he asks., "How are you now that you've seen him for the first time?"

"I'm fine. It was oddly weird. I didn't have any feelings when I saw him. He looks healthier than he has in a long time, so that's good, I'm happy for him in that regard. But when it comes to him and me, there's nothing."

"I'm proud of you for facing him but I wish you would have waited until I got here," he says with a smirk.

"I don't think he would have waited 20 minutes. I went to go see what he wanted so he would get out of our restaurant," I say with shrug. "Plus, I had Dax."

"Dax told me you told Jason to not come back?" Kallon asks.

"Yeah, I thought that would be best. He agreed," I say, resting my hands on his shoulders.

"Do you want me to get my attorney to get him trespassed so it's official that he can't come back here?" Kallon asks as he runs his hands up the outside of my thighs. A thrum in my veins starts to beat fast.

"Let's see if the verbal warning is enough," I say. Another thought crosses my mind. "Why wasn't I told he got out of rehab?"

"I don't think they tell people that. Only when an offender gets out of jail," Kallon says. He runs his hands down my thighs and then back up again, until their resting on the side of my hips. He looks into my eyes and asks, "Are you sure you don't want an official trespass on him?"

"Yes," I say, a little too breathy. Even with the serious conversation we're having, I can't help but look at his lips and lick my bottom one. I feel my eyes wanting him.

Kallon's eyes flare with his own desire and then he's kissing me deeply. I wrap my arms around his back and pull him in, spreading my legs so he can scoot between them and press our top halves together.

"Abby, the Rickerson's are here," Sherry says into my ear, making me jump.

"What?" Kallon asks, pulling away and glancing over my face.

I point to my ear and say to Sherry, "I'll be right out."

Kallon chuckles and says, "Duty calls?"

"Duty calls," I say with a sigh. "Are you going to stick around or go finish your errands?"

"Now that I know you're okay, I should probably go finish my errands," he says as he stands up.

"Probably a good idea," I say standing when he gives me a little space to do so, even though I step up to him and put my hands around his neck. "I don't think I could concentrate with you here and I definitely wouldn't get any work done."

"Mmmm," he says as he gives me a quick kiss.

I step out of his embrace and walk him towards the door. I squeeze his hand once before I drop it and open the door. We walk out into the kitchen and stop.

"I'll see you tomorrow," I say to him as I step towards the door to the bar.

"See you tomorrow," he says as he walks backwards towards the back door.

I smile and wave and use my butt to push the door open and walk through it. *Guh, that man...* I swallow a sigh and smile at the handful of customers sitting in the bar area. I walk to the front and greet the Rickerson's, one of our weekly reservations.

CHAPTER 19

"Good morning, Miss Rose," a man I don't recognize says as I walk up to Kallon's private jet. Kallon is at my side, holding my hand.

"Good morning," I say. I look at Kallon and raise my eyebrows.

"Abby, this is Captain Craig Zeels. He and Captain Sterling alternate weeks. As does Louie Warrington and Brody Welch," he motions with his hand at a man walking down the stairs of the jet. I recognize him from in the lounge. He'd came in and grabbed our luggage, but it didn't compute that he was our flight attendant.

"Nice to meet you, Captain Zeels, Mr. Welch," I say offering my hand to both of them.

"Pleasure is ours," Captain Zeels says.

Kallon motions for me to head up the stairs so I do. When I get into the jet, I see that it looks exactly like the one I took to Kansas.

"Is this the same one as last weekend?" I ask.

"No, but it's similar," Kallon says as he takes his jacket off and lays in across a chair. I sit down across from it and buckle myself in.

"Can I get you a refreshment before we take off?" Mr. Welch asks.

"I'm good for now, thank you Mr. Welch," I say with a smile.

"Just Brody is fine, Miss Rose," Mr. Welch… Brody says with a smile. He turns to Kallon and asks, "Mr. Keller?"

"Nothing for me for now, thanks," he says and then looks at me with a smile.

"We'll be taking off shortly," the Captain says from the cockpit.

"Sounds good," Kallon says over his shoulder.

"How long did it take to get used to flying like this?" I ask, waving my hand around the jet.

"I'm still not used to it," he says with a chuckle.

"Do you ever fly commercial anymore?"

"Not after the last time," he says with a grimace.

"What happened?"

"I was almost late for the flight because it took so long to get through security and I was stopped every so many feet to take pictures with people. After that, I decided I needed my own jets. I bought two so they could be swapped out to be checked. It also took a while to find pilots and attendants that were a good fit. That was three years ago," he says shyly.

"Only three years ago?" I ask, shocked.

"Yes," he laughs. And then he asks, "Why do you sound so shocked?"

"I don't know, I guess I would have figured it would have been one of the first things you bought," I say with a shrug. "I can see the appeal in having your own space but how much quicker it is to get from one place to another is definitely the best perk."

"Mmm, I don't know," he says as he stands and sits next to me. And puts his hands on the side of my face, pulling me into a passionate kiss. He gives a soft kiss on my lips and then my nose before he says, "This is a pretty good perk."

"Yes, yes it is," I say breathless.

"We're clear for take-off," Captain Zeels says.

Kallon removes one hand from my face and without taking his eyes off of mine, he buckles himself in, and says back to the captain, "We're all good here."

He goes back to kissing me and that's how we start the next five hours. We make out and have a drink, talk a little, and make out some more in our own little flying cocoon of happiness.

◆ ◆ ◆

"Abby?" Kallon's voice wakes me from sleep. I open my eyes and see that I'm lying on his lap. He must have lifted my head at some point and put his jacket under my head. I sit up and rub my eyes. "We're here."

"When did I fall asleep?" I ask.

"After your third glass of champagne," he says with a chuckle. He unbuckles his belt, so I do the same.

"Uh," I say as my head starts to pound a little. Now I remember. We were about two hours into our flight when Brody had popped a bottle of champagne. It was the good stuff from the hotel in Kansas, so it was going down too easily. I grimace and say, “Oops.”

“Are you feeling alright?” Kallon asks as he stands but bends down in front of me.

“Definitely drank too much, too fast,” I say, closing my eyes. I lean my head forward and put it in my hands.

“Let’s get to the hotel so you can take a better nap,” Kallon says as he pulls me up by my arms.

“Okay,” I say and let him walk us to the door.

Brody is holding my bag and I reach in and pull my sunglasses out. I look outside the door to the sky and see that I don’t need them. It’s gray and raining, as per usual for Seattle. As I step out, I feel an unseasonable chill in the air. I look down onto the tarmac and see a car waiting for us.

When I get to the bottom of the stairs, I turn to Kallon and jokingly say, “What, no Dax and Trevor waiting for us? Were they not hiding on the plane somewhere?”

“Normally, yes. There’s a separate seating area they prefer to relax in during long flights, no matter how many times I ask them to sit with me,” Kallon says with a laugh as he walks to the car. I hear Brody walking behind us, rolling our luggage. “But I gave them the weekend off. The agency that I hire my guys through have two here in Seattle that are meeting us at the hotel.”

“Oh,” is all I say as we get to the car. Kallon opens the front passenger door for me and I slide into the seat. Kallon says something to Brody at the back of the car and once the trunk is closed, he walks around to the driver side and gets in. I lean my head back and close my eyes, my head starting to pound a little bit more.

“You okay?” Kallon asks again.

"Just my reward for drinking too much," I say with a grimace.

"Rest. We'll be at the hotel in about twenty minutes," he says as he reaches over and puts the back of his hand on my face and then brushes my hair away.

"We're still planning to meet Spencer and Mary for dinner, right?" I ask, turning my head towards him. I open my eyes and watch as he drives us away from the airport.

"Yeah, as long as that's what you want to do," he answers.

"I do," I say. I smile wide and add, "I can't believe we're here. I haven't seen them since Christmas."

"That was a pretty good party," Kallon says.

For Christmas Eve, this last year, we had a party at Rose's and invited all of our employees and our families. It was Spencer and Mary's turn to come to New York, so Kallon was able to meet them. His parents were in town, so I in turn, got to meet them. Spencer and Kallon hit it off and spent most of the night talking. My parents and the Keller's also hit it off. So well in fact, that they have plans to vacation together later this fall. I was happy that my parents had made friends with the Keller's, it's been a long time since they had friends they could do anything with. Granted, they live on opposite sides of the country but both couples are retired, so free time is bountiful for them.

"How are your parents, by the way?" I ask.

"They're doing well," Kallon says with a smile as he pulls into traffic. "They ask about you all the time."

"Do they?" I ask, surprised. I sit up a little straighter and turn to look at him fully. "Why?"

"Because they could see then, what neither of us were willing to admit," he says with a chuckle.

"Which was?" I ask, wanting to hear him say the words.

"The feelings we had... have for each other," he says, giving me a look that makes my heart want to explode.

"They could see it from one meeting?" I ask, dumbfounded.

"I guess so," he says, turning to look if he's clear to get into the passing lane. "Every time we talk on the phone, Mom asks how things are between us. The night they left to fly home, she told me I needed to quit hiding my feelings for you and make a move. She said a girl like you wouldn't be single forever and if I lost my chance with you, I'd never get it back and it would be my biggest regret."

"She did not say that," I say with an embarrassed laugh.

"She absolutely did," Kallon says seriously but then he chuckles again. "I didn't admit anything to her. I just told her what I'd been telling myself since the moment I met you. Which was that we were friends and business partners. You had just gotten out of a long, serious relationship and even though it ended horrifyingly awful, you needed time to heal and move on from it."

"I did need time," I say a little quieter. "I have moved on. Seeing Jason yesterday proves that."

"I know," Kallon says, reaching for my hand and gives it a squeeze. "I wanted to be there for you, while you healed. I hated seeing you hurt and in pain, but you willing to let me help you, made me fall for you even more. To trust me as much as you did, it meant the world to me."

"I trusted you... trust you, because you are you. I know

you'd never hurt me or let anyone hurt me. I don't know it in the way I thought Jason would never hurt me, that was blind hope. You... I can feel deep down to my bones that you would never, ever, lay a hand on me to hurt me, in any way."

"Not just my hands, Abby. I will never hurt you emotionally or mentally," he says, pulling my hand to his mouth and kissing it softly. "Your wellbeing is my top priority."

I smile and lean my head back. *Is this what total contentment feels like?*

"How's your head?" he asks as he takes an exit.

"Still pounding," I say with a sigh.

"Deep conversations probably aren't helping?" he asks.

"Not my head, but it helps my heart," I say, pulling our interlocked hands to my lap and overlapping his with my free hand. "I truly appreciate you being this open with me."

"And I, you," he says with a smile.

"I'm trying," I say in a whisper.

"I know," he says with a laugh. "Just promise me you won't clam up and hide your feelings from me, whether their good or bad. If I do something that makes you angry, you have to tell me. I know I promised I'd never hurt you in anyway, but I am human, and I might do something unknowingly to hurt your feelings and you have to tell me if, or when, I do. I think I have a pretty good idea on what not to do, not that I would do it intentionally. But like I said, I'm still human and I make mistakes just like everyone else."

"I do too," I say, turning my head towards him. "I think as long as we are completely honest and open with each other, we'll be good."

"Better than good," he says with smile.

"Is this what an adult relationship feels like?" I ask with a chuckle.

"I think so," he says with a smile that induces heart palpitations. He squeezes my hand and turns back to the road.

I lean my head back and watch him drive, letting him concentrate on the road. The drive north to Seattle can be intense, just with traffic alone, but add the torrential downpour of rain that's happening right now, it can be downright terrifying. The drivers here are different from those in New York but in both cities, I try to keep my eyes away from the road, so I don't completely freak out.

I must have closed my eyes at some point because I feel the feather soft touch of Kallon's hand on my face and when I open my eyes, he's leaning towards me. My glasses are off my face and he's holding them in his hand that isn't touching me.

"Hi, Sleeping Beauty," he says in a voice that makes my toes want to curl. "Want to go up to our room and sleep?"

"Mmm, that sounds good," I say as I stretch, my head still pounds away. "But first maybe we can ask the front desk if they have any Tylenol."

"I figured you'd want Midol. I had one of the guys run by the store and pick up a bottle and some Gatorade."

"Oh, that's even better, thank you," I say in awe. It's going to take some time to get used to someone thinking ahead to take care of me.

"Shall we?" he asks, pointing behind my head. I turn and see the hotel a few feet away.

I nod and turn to open the door, but it opens, and a man dressed as Dax and Trevor are always dressed, and also looks just as terrifying as them, offers me his hand. I take it with a smile.

"Thank you," I say shyly.

"Miss Rose," he says with a deep voice.

Kallon walks around the car, with another man, similar to the other, on his heels. He extends his hand to me and says, "Abby, this is Allen and Thomas. They'll be tagging along with us this weekend."

"It's nice to meet you both," I say, nodding to them individually.

"Nice to meet you as well," the one at my door says. "I'm Allen and will be with you should you be without Mr. Keller."

"Oh, okay, thanks Allen," I say with a smile.

"I'll grab your luggage sir, if you and Miss Rose would like to head inside," Thomas says, motioning towards the doors.

"Thanks," Kallon says as he gently pulls us towards the door.

As we get to the check-in counter. The guy at the computer looks up with a smile but it faulters and then returns to look a little more forced, or nervous.

"Mr. Keller," he says with a definite shake to his voice. "Your suite is ready, as instructed. These gentlemen have already been up to the rooms. Your lunch is being prepared as we speak."

"Thanks Collin," Kallon says with a smile. Collin hands him two keys. "This is Miss Rose. If she calls down for anything, anything at all, you make sure she gets it, alright?"

"Yes, sir," Collin says with a smile to me. He looks at his computer screen and types a note. He looks up and asks, "Is there anything I can send up now?"

"No, just lunch for now, thanks," Kallon says as he puts a hand to my back and directs me away from the counter.

"Thanks, Collin," I say kindly.

"My pleasure, Miss Rose," he says with surprise in his voice.

I walk with Kallon around the corner where I see elevator doors. I try not to think of the last time we rode up to a room in an elevator but it's too late. I can feel my face flushing and my pulse quickening. But with my pulsing heart, my head pounds even harder. I don't think I've ever welcomed a headache more. I can't let my erratic hormones for this man take hold in the elevator again. It's daytime, who knows who'd see us if we got caught in the positions we were in last time.

The doors open and we step in, Allen steps in after us and faces the door. *Good, a babysitter. We'll have to behave.* I feel Kallon's hand slide from the middle of my back down to rest just above my ass. I glance up at him and when he looks down, I see in his eyes he's also thinking of our elevator ride last weekend. My cheeks heat again so I turn away from him. I smile and shake my head. I hear him chuckle quietly and then his hand moves from my lower back and then he grabs hold of my hand, interlocking our fingers. He's behaving.

I watch the number at the top tick by. I look over at the wall of numbers and see we're going to the 23rd floor, the top floor.

I look up at Kallon and ask, "Top floor?"

"I had the whole floor renovated to make three large suites. Mine, all of one side, and two to split the other side. Mine has two large master bedrooms, a theater room, living room, kitchen, dining room, game room, and sauna. Also, its own lap pool and hot tub on a private, covered balcony. While the other two have three rooms, one of which is a master. They have the typical living rooms, kitchens, and dining rooms. As well as their own hot tubs and private balconies."

"Wow," I say in complete awe. "No reason to go out if you have all of that in your suite."

"I like my privacy," he says with a chuckle. "If I don't have to go out, I like to have options to entertain friends and family at home."

"Is this your home while you're in Seattle?" I ask.

"It is," he says with a smile. "My only real houses are in Montana and Hawaii."

"So, when you're in L.A., it's a suite like this?"

"Yes," he says as he looks down at me. "My condo in New York was renovated to be similar but it's not attached to a hotel. It's an actual condo building."

"I can't believe I've never been to your place back home," I say with a chuckle.

"We can rectify that when we get back," he says, squeezing my hand. "I'd love for you to come over, anytime you'd like. I'll cook for you."

"I'd really like that," I say, my smile threatening to split my face.

The elevator stops it's ascent. Kallon pulls a key from his pocket and swipes it over a red dot. It turns green and the door dings opens. As we step out, I look down the short hallway and see that the hall that would have been long if it were a normal floor, is blocked off with a wall a little further than halfway down. There are two doors on the right and a little further down the hall, one on the left. We walk past the two on the right and stop at the one on the left.

Kallon uses the same key from the elevator and swipes it across the key reader. The lock audibly clicks, he grabs the handle, and opens the door. He steps to the side to let me walk in first.

I hear him say to Allen, “We’re good for now. Go ahead and leave the luggage just inside the door once Thomas gets up here. We’ll be heading out for dinner at 5:30.”

“Yes, sir,” Allen says as I turn around, my attention on the amazing view of the living room.

The layout is similar to the suite back in Kansas, only bigger. I look down where I think a bedroom is and see a couple more doors. I walk into the kitchen and put my bag down on the counter.

I turn towards Kallon and say, “This is amazing!”

“Do you like it?”

“It’s gorgeous,” I say smiling at him. I look on the other side of the counter and see bottles of Gatorade and a small bottle sitting next to them. I walk over and grab the bottle of Midol and open it. After I have the safety film off, I dump two out into my hand. I grab a purple Gatorade and take the lid off. I pop the pills into my mouth and drink half of the purple liquid before I put the lid back on.

I turn and see Kallon watching me with a smile.

“Let’s turn something on the TV, lunch will be here shortly and then you can rest. Hopefully that headache will be gone shortly,” he says, extending his hand out to me. I walk to him and take his hand.

“Sounds good to me,” I say, letting him walk us to the living room. The TV in here is huge. “If this is the living room

TV, what does your theater room TV look like?"

"A movie screen," he says with a chuckle. When I look at him with big eyes, he laughs a little louder and adds, "Not a huge screen but definitely bigger than this TV."

I shake my head and sit down on the couch. He grabs a blanket and shakes it out before he lays it over me. He sits and reaches for the remote on the coffee table in front of us. He clicks the power button and the TV turns on quietly.

"Any requests?" he asks.

"Whatever you want," I say as I lean my head back onto the couch.

As he's picking something to watch, I close my eyes. My eyes aren't closed for long when I hear one of my favorite TV show's theme song plays over the speakers. The American version of The Office. As a smile spreads across my face, I feel myself slip into blissful sleep.

For the third time today, I hear Kallon's sweet voice waking me up.

"Abby," he says and then I feel his lips on my cheek.

"Mmm," I say as I turn my face towards him. I don't open my eyes, but I find his lips with mine. The kiss is soft and sweet, but that doesn't last long. Soon it's full of need and passion. I push towards him, making him lean back against the couch. I crawl over his lap and straddle him.

"Abby," Kallon moans into my mouth. I pull my mouth from his but kiss down to his neck. "As much as I would love to continue this train of thought of yours, I was actually waking you up because it's time to go to dinner. I'm all for whatever you want to do. We can cancel with your brother and sister-in-law and order room service, but I know how much you were looking forward to seeing them tonight."

My kissing slows and when I pull away, I see desire in Kallon's eyes. I look at the clock on the wall and see we have thirty minutes before we're supposed to be meeting at the restaurant.

I sigh and say, "No, we should probably go."

"Are you sure?" Kallon asks, his hands on my hips grip a little tighter.

I laugh and say, "Yes. If it was just us, I'd say cancel the reservation. But Spencer and Mary had to get a babysitter, it wouldn't be fair to them."

"Alright," Kallon says as he stands with me still straddling him and then he slowly lowers me to the ground. A giggle escapes my lips, but I step back from him.

I look down at what I'm wearing, a comfy hoodie and jogger sweats for traveling, and say, "Give me 5 minutes to change and then we can go."

"Sounds good," Kallon says. I take another step back and see that he's changed from his travel clothes into blue jeans and a black hoodie. My mouth waters at how good he looks in such casual clothes. He points down the hall to the left of the front door and says, "Our room is that way. Your suitcase is in there."

"Thanks," I say as I walk away. If I continue looking at him with my desire for him rising, I don't think I'll be able to stop myself from jumping him. I slightly laugh at myself as I walk down to the bedroom.

I open the door and step into a room similar to the one he has in Kansas. I'm starting to realize all his suites will be the same. I walk to the ottoman that has my suitcase sitting on top of it and open it. I pull out a pair of jeans and trade out my hoodie for a softer, nicer one.

I hurry from the room and as I get to the kitchen, my stomach growls. I look to the counter and see our lunch sitting on a tray.

"Crap, I slept through lunch, didn't I?" I ask as I walk into the living room and sit next to Kallon and put my shoes on.

"I tried to wake you, but you were out," Kallon says with a laugh. "I figured if you got hungry enough, you'd wake up."

"I'm starving," I say. After tying my shoes, I walk into the kitchen and lift a lid from a plate. It's empty. I lift another and see a grilled cheese with fries. "You ate?"

"Yeah, sorry," he says sheepishly from behind me.

I turn and say, "Don't be. I'd feel bad if you hadn't."

I grab a couple fries and walk towards Kallon. He smiles as he watches me eat them, even though they're cold and a couple hours old. He grabs a ballcap from the little table on the wall leading to the front door and puts it on. I grab his hand and we walk towards the door. As expected, Allen and Thomas are waiting for us.

"Hi Allen, hi Thomas," I say as we step out into the hall.

"Miss Rose," Allen says as Thomas just nods at me. "The car is pulled around front, Mr. Keller."

"Thanks," Kallon says as he leads us to the elevator. We have to wait a couple minutes before the doors finally open and we step inside. The ride down isn't as electrifying as the ride up, probably because I know there isn't a bed waiting down in the lobby.

Pull yourself together, woman! Not every thought needs to be about being naked and under... or on top of Kallon. I chastise myself but just the thought of telling myself to stop thinking of Kallon like that, has me thinking of Kallon like that. I hide the laugh that escapes me with a cough.

"You okay?" Kallon asks, rubbing my back.

"Yeah, I'm fine," I say. *Liar, get your head out of the gutter.* I shake my head, trying to get my thoughts away from where they want to go. Just because Kallon and I are in a relationship now, doesn't mean we... I have to be thinking of us doing it all the time. Even if IT is the best thing I've ever experienced.

"Abby?" Kallon says, I look up from the floor and see he's holding the doors open. Allen and Thomas already standing with their back towards us.

"Sorry," I say and my face heats. "I was lost in thought."

"About?" Kallon asks as I step out of the elevator and take his hand again.

"Nothing," I say, my cheeks turning redder.

"I don't believe you," he says with a chuckle.

I sigh and say loud enough for him to hear, "I need to stop thinking about... us. I feel like it's all I think about."

"Oh," Kallon says with an audible gulp. "Then I need to do the same because it's all I can think about too."

"How do we go back to thinking about what we used to before... last weekend happened?" I whisper as we get to the lobby.

Kallon lets go of my hand, to put it on my lower back as

he guides us through the people.

"I think it's all we can think about because it's so new, you know?" Kallon says, his thumb on my back rubbing a small circle. In a low, deep voice, he adds, "And because it's so fucking good."

I stifle a laugh with my hand and lean into him, so he hears me when I say, "It really, really is, isn't it?"

"Mmm," is all he says in agreement when we get out to the car. Allen opens the door for me and I get in. I look behind me and see that Kallon has walked around to the other side. So, I stay put and start to buckle my seatbelt, I won't have to slide over today.

Thomas gets into the driver seat and waits for Allen to get in and once they're buckled, Thomas pulls away from the hotel. He looks in the rearview mirror and asks, "To the Crab Pot, right, sir?"

"Yes, please," Kallon says. He reaches over and grabs my hand. It seems like he can't go more than a couple minutes without touching me. I know how he feels. I can't keep my hands off him either. We just have to behave until we can get back to our room later tonight. I bite my bottom lip and look out the window.

We go two blocks before the car is pulling into a parking lot.

"We're here already?" I ask, looking around.

"Yes," Kallon says with a laugh.

"We could have walked," I say laughing as I unbuckle my belt.

"We can walk back after dinner, if you want," Kallon suggests as he unbuckles himself.

"I think a walk after dinner would be great," I say with a smile.

CHAPTER 20

"Abby!" I hear someone shout as soon as I step out of the car. I turn and see Mary waving at me from the entrance of the restaurant. A second later, Spencer is standing behind her, smiling and waving.

I wave back and wait for Kallon to come around the side of the car.

"I'll park and then I'll be right in," Thomas says to Kallon. Kallon nods at him and as I grab his hand, he looks down at me and the smile on his face widens.

I pull us towards Spencer and Mary and when we get closer, I see when they notice our hands interlocked. Their eyes widen with shock and then they're smiling from ear to ear.

Kallon lets go of my hand to shake hands with Spencer and so I can wrap my arms around Mary and give her a hug. Once we've finished that greeting, I let her go and hug my brother.

"Hi Sis," he says as he hugs me tight.

"Hi Spence," I say squeezing him back.

"It's nice to see you again, Kallon," Mary says as she steps out of the quick hug she and Kallon give each other.

"It's nice to see you as well, Mary," he says.

I step away from Spencer and point to the restaurant, "I'm starving, let's go in."

"She slept through lunch," Kallon says with a laugh because Mary and Spencer are looking at me funny.

"Are you feeling well?" Mary asks as she loops her arm through mine and walks in with me to the restaurant.

"I just had too much champagne on the flight," I say with embarrassment flooding my tone. She looks at me shocked, so I add with a small laugh, "It's really good."

We get to the hostess table and tell the girl standing there the reservation, which it's under Rose. Kallon didn't want to give his name and since there were three out of the four of us with the last name Rose, I didn't argue.

"Here we go," the hostess says. Her name tag says Annie. She's sat us by a window. "Your server will be here shortly but in the meantime, can I get you something to drink?"

"I'll take whatever IPA you have on draft," Spencer says.

"I'll have a vodka tonic," Kallon says nodding at Annie. She does a double take but then looks away. She must decide that maybe he just looks like who she thinks he is, even though he is exactly who she thinks he is.

I swallow the laugh about to burst from me as Mary says, "I'll take a mojito, please."

Annie looks at me expectantly, "Just water for now."

"Sounds good. I'll get those started for you," Annie says with a smile.

"Just water?" Spencer asks with disappointment in his tone.

"I need to hydrate before I start drinking again. I've

already had one headache today from drinking too much too fast, I'm not looking to have another one," I say rolling my eyes at him.

"So…" Mary starts to say. She points between Kallon and me, and asks, "Is this finally a thing?"

"What do you mean finally?" I ask. I look at Kallon and then back to Spencer and Mary.

"We could see how you guys looked at each other at the Christmas party," Spencer says with a chuckle.

"We didn't look at each other in any way other than a friendly, business partner way," I say, my face turning a little red.

"I think everyone could see through it," Kallon says with a laugh. When Spencer and Mary look at him, he adds, "My parents said something similar."

"So, you guys are a thing?" Spencer asks, looking between us and then settles on Kallon with a serious look. *Oh goodness, he's pulling the big brother nonsense.*

I'm about to say something but Kallon reaches for my hand and puts it on the table, Spencer and Mary's eyes go wide as Kallon says, "Yes, we're in a relationship."

"For real?" Mary says, she starts to quietly clap her hands.

"Yes," I say, smiling up at Kallon. "For real."

"Eeek, I'm so happy for you," Mary says.

"I'm pretty happy too," I say as I smile over at her.

Another woman shows up and has our drinks on a tray. She smiles as she says, "I'm Trina, your server for the evening. I've got your drinks here. Who had the mojito?"

As she hands us our drinks, she also does a double take

at Kallon. She swallows and says, "I'm sorry, but are you... are you Kallon Keller?"

"I get that a lot," he says with a shrug, but I see him dip his head a little lower.

"Oh, right, sorry," Trina says with an embarrassed laugh. She grabs menus from under her arm and says, "Umm here are some menus I'll be back in a few to take your orders."

"Why didn't you tell her you are you?" Mary asks and then takes a sip of her drink.

"Because tonight isn't about me," he says with a shrug. He then smiles and adds, "It's about us having a nice dinner together."

"He didn't lie to her though," I say with a laugh. "He does get that a lot, she just chose to take it like she was mistaken."

Spencer and Mary laugh at that and then we look at the menu.

"It all looks so good," I say. I look at Mary and ask, "What do you guys get when you come here?"

We'd chosen this place because it's their favorite restaurant to go to but thet only come on their anniversary.

"I usually get the seafood brochette and Spencer usually gets the crab combo of snow crab and Dungeness and then we share," she says with a smile.

"Have you guys ever tried one of the SeaFeasts?" Kallon asks.

"We haven't," Spencer says. He laughs and adds, "It's a lot of food. It says it's for two or more, but it's always looked more like for four or more to us when we've seen people get it. You either would have to be starving to get it with one other person or be brave enough to take the leftovers home."

"Should we get one?" Kallon asks, looking around the table at us.

"I'm done," I say, looking at the options. "The Alaskan one looks yummy."

"Spencer? Mary? Does that sound good?" Kallon asks. He looks over their head, which makes me look too and I see Trina walking back towards us.

"Yeah, why not," Spencer says. "I'm down to test how much we can eat tonight."

"Sounds good to me," Mary says as she puts her menu away.

Trina steps up to the table and asks, "Have we decided?"

Kallon looks at me and nods so I say, "Yeah, can we do the Alaskan SeaFeast, please. And maybe a sourdough loaf as well."

"Sure thing," she says with a smile.

Before she can go I ask, "Can I get a vodka cranberry too, please?"

"Sure, honey. I'll bring that right out," Trina says with a smile.

When she leaves I look at Mary and ask, "So how are my nephew and niece doing?"

"They're great," she says with a laugh.

"I'm sad I don't get to see them until Sunday morning for breakfast," I say drinking the rest of my water.

"They were disappointed too but getting to hang out with their favorite babysitter made them feel better," Spencer says and then he takes a drink of his beer.

"Awesome babysitters will always trump aunties," I say with a laugh.

"I'm so excited to get to go out twice in one weekend. And to your movie premiere?" Mary says with a laugh. She fans herself and acts like she's fainting. She stops and looks up seriously and asks Kallon, "Abby said you had our dress situation under control?"

"I do," Kallon says calmly.

"Any more details than that?" Mary asks, putting her forearms onto the table.

"Nope, just be ready to be picked up at your house by 9:30 to be brought to the hotel by 10 tomorrow morning, both of you," Kallon says as he looks at Mary and then at Spencer. He puts his hand on my thigh and squeezes. "Everything you'll need will be there."

"That's all? Just be at the hotel by 10?" Mary asks, skeptical. "Wait, picked up?"

"He's sending a car for you. We'll also have to shower tonight," I say with a laugh at their expressions. When I said shower, Kallon's hand on my thigh tightened again. "I have a feeling he's got a team of people coming to beautify us."

"You gorgeous ladies don't need a team of anything to make you beautiful," Kallon says as he leans over and kisses my head. "They're just going to enhance what God gave you."

"Ha! So, there is a team of people coming over?" Mary asks. Kallon takes a drink of his vodka tonic but winks at Mary as confirmation. She claps her hands and says, "Oh my gosh, I can't believe it!"

The rest of the evening we talk about what to expect at the premiere and who Spencer and Mary are excited to see. When our food comes, it's the only time they stop talking so they can eat.

◆ ◆ ◆

We've been finished eating for about twenty minutes now, we're waiting for Trina to bring us the check.

"I'm not ready to go home yet," Mary says excitedly. "I'm having too much fun."

"Would you guys like to come back to the bar at the hotel and have a couple drinks with us there?" Kallon asks.

"Oh man, would that be alright?" Spencer asks. He gives me a sheepish smile and says, "You know we hardly get out, but we never get to go out with another couple."

"I know and yeah, it'll be fun," I say with a laugh.

Trina brings the check, but I hand my card to her before Kallon can. I smile and wave her away before he can notice she's standing there. She smiles and slips away. Kallon looks and sees her walking away. He looks at the table to look for the check.

"Where'd it go?" he asks.

"It's taken care of," I say as I finish the rest of my second vodka cranberry.

"Abby," he growls quietly at me. Spencer and Mary don't hear, they're too busy checking in with their babysitter. "That's not how this goes."

"Yes it is," I say, turning to look at him. I put my hand to his face and add, "This 'paying for things'—" I use air quotes "—thing, goes both ways. Get used to it, buddy."

"Buddy?" he asks, raising an eyebrow at me. His looks down at my lips and then back to my eyes.

I lean forward so that our lips are barely touching and say, "Yup."

When I pop the 'P' I push my lips into his and kiss him.

"I'm happy you two are finally together, but that doesn't mean I want to see this," Spencer says with disgust as he waves a hand at us.

I smile and as I lean away and look towards Spencer, I see Mary elbow him.

"They can kiss all they want," Marry says and then she winks at me.

Trina comes back with my card and receipt.

"What the hell, Abby?" Spencer asks.

"Beat you to it this time, big brother," I say with a laugh.

"If I knew you were going to be sneaky about it, I would have gone up front and paid when I went to the bathroom," Spencer says as he stands and pulls the chair out for Mary. Kallon stands and does the same for me.

"I wasn't being sneaky," I say as I put my card away. "You guys were just busy talking, so I kindly gave my card to Trina so she wouldn't have to wait."

"Yeah, I'm sure that's ALL you did," Spencer says, rolling his eyes.

"Is this something you guys do all the time?" Kallon asks.

"Neither one likes when the other pays, so it's turned into a kind of game to see who can pay for the meal the quickest," Mary says with a laugh. "This is a new one, I didn't even notice Trina come back and leave again."

"It was pretty quick," I say with pride.

"Hmmm," Kallon says. "I guess I'll have to be quicker next time."

"No," I say turning and pointing at him. "You don't get to play."

"The heck I don't," he says, grabbing my finger and pulling me towards him. "If I'm sitting at the table, it's game on."

"Oh man," Mary says. I look at her and she's trying to hide a laugh.

"You don't understand," I say to her. "He's super stealthy sneaky."

"Looks like you need to up your game," Spencer says.

I smile and say with a sigh, "I got tonight, didn't I?"

"That's because I didn't know I needed to be on my game," Kallon says with a smile of his own.

"You need to be on your game all the time with this one," Mary says as she points to me and walks up to me and nudges me with her shoulder.

"Boy do I know it," Kallon says. When I look up at him, he winks at me. *Oh, okay!*

As we step away from the table I say, "That was really good food. Thanks for picking the place."

"We haven't been disappointed yet," Spencer says, from behind Kallon and me. I look over my shoulder and see Spencer sling his arm over Mary's shoulders.

"Neither have I," I whisper up to Kallon. He looks down at me quickly and I wink at him. His eyes go wide momentarily and then the smile that makes my heart want to fly out of my chest, spreads across his face.

He leans down and kisses the top of my head and whispers back, "Game on."

When I say a shiver of anticipation shoots down my body, that's an understatement. I look up at him and the desire in his eyes makes me want to find a closet nearby and hideaway with him.

Two hours, I'm going to give Spencer and Mary two hours and then I'm taking this man, who is now mine, up to our room and—

"Did you still want to walk?" Kallon asks, drawing my attention back to reality instead of in my fantasy.

I look around and see that we're outside. I really need to pay attention to my surroundings and not lose myself in my thoughts.

"Oh, yeah," I say quickly as I realize he's waiting for me to answer. "As long as you all are good with a walk."

"How far is the hotel?" Mary asks.

"Just two blocks," Kallon says, pointing up the road.

"A walk sounds good," Spencer says.

"Did you guys drive here?" Kallon asks.

"No, we got an Uber," Mary says as she steps up beside me. Kallon is on the outside, closest to the road, then me, then Mary, and then Spencer.

"My driver can take you home from the hotel," Kallon says. On que, Allen steps up behind us. "Isn't that right, Allen?"

"Yes, sir," he says.

"Oh, that's okay," Spencer says, looking back at Allen.

"He'll need to know where you live anyways, for when he comes to get you in the morning," Kallon says. "It's really no problem."

"Well, okay, that's true," Spencer says. He reaches behind me and Mary, and pats Kallon on the shoulder and adds, "Thanks, man."

"Don't mention it," Kallon responds with a smile.

We walk in silence for a minute and then a breeze picks up and a chill runs through me.

"What's with the weather?" I ask, looking beside me at Spence and Mary.

"I know, it's abnormally cold," Mary says.

"Forecast says we could get snow, can you believe that?" Spencer asks in disgust.

"It's June," I say, surprised.

"I know," Spencer says. "It's all the over the news stations and online. It's some late winter storm system but after this weekend, we should be back into the early-summer weather."

"Have you heard if we're supposed to get anything back home?" I ask Kallon.

"No, I haven't heard anything," he says pulling me closer to him as I shiver again.

"I should have brought a coat," I say with a laugh.

"I don't mind keeping you warm," he says.

"I don't mind either," I say as I wrap my arms around his waist. He squeezes me tighter to him. I almost trip over my feet but he catches me.

We all pick up our pace and walk quicker towards the hotel. I can see the pull-in area now. We have to wait a ridiculous amount of time at the intersection waiting for the little white man to appear, or maybe it feels like that because we're so cold, but the light changes and we hurry across. When we get to the doors, Thomas is there to open the door for us.

"Thhhhank… you," I say between chattering teeth.

He just nods and holds the door for us and then follows us inside. We head straight to the bar where a fire is blazing against the wall. The guys go to the bar and orders us some drinks, while Mary and I get warm by the fire.

"So, tell me, how are things going with Kallon? How long have you guys been together?" Mary asks in a hurry. She glances behind me, which has me looking too. The guys are still waiting for our drinks. She turns to me with a huge grin on her face.

"Things are good and it's all really new," I say with a big smile of my own. "Like last week new, my birthday new."

"It happened on your birthday?" she asks with quietly contained excitement.

"Yeah, I guess we could say that," I say as I rub my hands against the heat of the fire. "It's when we first kissed."

"I'm sorry what?" Mary says, reaching for my arms and pulling me towards her. "He kissed you for the first time on your birthday?"

I laugh and say, "Yes. But we're wanting our relationship to stay us, even though I don't know how he'll explain me tomorrow at the premiere, unless he doesn't plan on getting pictures with me."

A rock of doubt plummets into my stomach. I look over my shoulder and see the guys still at the bar.

"I'm sure he will," Mary says, patting my arm reassuringly.

"Not that I want to have our pictures plastered all over the news, magazines, or whatever… but I don't want him to feel like he has to ignore me to keep us from becoming worldwide known," I say, turning back to the fire. "Does that make sense?"

"Absolutely," she says turning her back to the fire to warm that side of her. "I get it. You don't want the world to know you guys are together, but you don't want him to treat you like a nobody at the same time."

"I honestly don't think he'll do that, but... he is the one who said he wanted our relationship to stay private for as long as possible," I say a little sadly.

"Maybe he meant just until the premiere," she says, turning back to warm her front. "Maybe to him, the week of you guys having just to yourself, is the longest he's ever had a relationship stay quiet for. Those other girls he's dated, I'm sure they bragged about it to any and all people they came into contact with. You aren't like that."

"No, you're right. I'm sure the week of having our privacy has been the longest he's had to enjoy the relationship without paparazzi in his face asking if the rumors are true," I say. I look at Mary and say, "How does he handle living like that?"

"I think he's learned that it's just a part of the job. I guess you have to ask yourself if it's worth dating him to have your private life plastered all over the place. Your privacy not so private after your relationship is made public," she says as she looks back towards the bar. Her eyes go wide, and she says, "In coming."

I turn and see the guys walking back.

Is dating Kallon worth all that she just said? Having my personal life in public view? My answer is yes, Kallon is worth it.

And honestly, we only let the public know what we want them to know. They can't know what goes on behind closed doors unless we tell them.

I'm smiling again by the time Kallon walks up and hands me my drink.

"Here you go, Abs," he says with a smile of his own.

"Thank you," I say and take a drink. I pull the glass away and look down at it. "This is a good vodka cran."

"Is it?" he asks as he takes a drink of beer.

"Yeah," I say taking another sip.

"Do you guys want to find a table?" Spencer asks, looking around the room. "Or do you need to warm up a little longer?"

"I'm good," I say, looking at Mary.

"I'm good too," she says.

"There's a booth over there," Kallon says, pointing towards the far corner.

"Lead the way," Spencer says, gesturing with the hand holding his drink.

Kallon takes my free hand into his and leads us over to the booth. He steps to the side to let me slide in before him and then he sits beside me, not giving me any space. I lean my head against his shoulder and sigh in contentment. I watch as Spencer has Mary slide in so she's sitting closest to me and then Spencer sits on the outside.

"So, Abby, how's Rose Bud's?" Marry asks, turning towards me.

"It's great, still busy," I say and then take a drink. "We're catering another one of Kallon's movies, so that's been a lot of fun."

"The studio manager really enjoyed having Abby cater breakfast, so she invited her back for another movie," Kallon says as he slides his hand on to my thigh again. "I can't complain, I really like seeing her every day."

Mary awes at that and then asks, "Do you think you'll do another movie after this one is over?"

"Maybe," I say. "I really do enjoy catering the set, but it would be nice to take a break to focus back on the bakery for a little while. I'd have to talk to Steph about it and see if she'd want me back after a break."

"I'm sure she would," Kallon says as he squeezes my leg gently. "She loves you."

I smile up at him and then turn back to Spencer and Mary.

"So, Spence, how work?" I ask.

"Good, busy. I just closed on one of the new buildings going in over by the airport. The company I was brokering for is really happy with the deal, so that makes it easy," he says with a smile.

"He was working so hard on it, there were a lot of late nights," Mary says, looking up at Spencer with so much love and admiration in her eyes, it makes me smile. I've really missed my brother and his wife.

We spend the next couple of hours talking about family and work.

CHAPTER 21

I wake up and hear the shower running in Kallon's attached bathroom. I roll over, taking the sheet with me, and look at the clock on the nightstand. It's 8am. I sigh, realizing I have two hours before I have to be ready. Kallon still hasn't said what he's got planned for Mary and me.

I stretch and feel the delicious pull of my muscles. Last night was another toe curling, Jell-O muscle making night of sex with Kallon, but the feelings that are building inside me FOR Kallon, are on a whole different level. I don't want to say I'm falling in love with him because it would be too soon for that, right? But the feelings I am having are different than what I felt for Jason. That must mean something.

My stomach rumbles so I get out of bed. I wrap the sheet around me and head to the kitchen to see if I can find anything to eat. If there's nothing to eat, then maybe some water will hold me over until Kallon is out of the shower and then we can order breakfast. But when I get to the kitchen, I see a cart has been brought in that has a few dishes with lids on them.

I walk to the cart and lift the first lid and find scrambled eggs, bacon, and hashbrowns. I replace the lid and take the lid off the second dish and see it's a plate of fruit, and the third plate has toast, biscuits, and English muffins. The last plate has the same as the first, except it has over easy eggs.

"Hungry?" I hear from behind me. I turn my head and see Kallon walking towards me in sweatpants and a t-shirt. Thank the heavens because if he was in just a towel, I don't think we'd be eating breakfast any time soon. I can't seem to get enough of this man.

"Famished," I say, and I can't help but bite my bottom lip. Thinking of why I'm so hungry makes my insides tingle.

"Me too," Kallon says as he walks up behind me. He wraps his arms around me and pulls me back against him. I lean my head against his chest, and he bends down and kisses my neck sweetly. "Good morning."

"Good morning," I say as a sigh.

"Sleep well?"

"Mmm, yes," I say as he kisses down my neck to my shoulder. "You?"

"Yes," he breaths into my skin.

A delightful shiver shimmers down my arm on the side he's kissing. Kallon pulls me tighter into him and when I turn my head a little more towards him, he runs a hand up my side, up my arm, to my neck and then strokes his thumb slowly up and down. He moves his lips from my shoulder to my mouth and kisses my lips softly.

"Grrrrrrr," my stomach growls.

Kallon chuckles and reluctantly pulls his lips from mine.

"Let's eat," he says.

"I'm okay with waiting," I say as I turn towards him and

wrap my arms around his neck.

"You might be, but your stomach isn't," he says with another chuckle. "It's going to be a long day of preparations. You need sustenance to make it through."

With a sigh of slight disappointment, I pull away from him, and say, "I know, you're right. I just..."

Kallon waits for me to continue but when I don't, he asks, "You just, what?"

"Can't get enough of you," I say, my face reddening at the admission.

"I'm not going anywhere," he says before he gives me a sweet peck on the nose. "And we have tonight, and any other day or night in the future you want."

"All of them," I say in a slight whisper. Again, astonished at my bravery to tell him exactly what I'm thinking.

"I want them all, too," he says in a deep, sensual tone. He kisses me and then pulls away slowly. He clears his throat and says with a chuckle, "We should eat."

"Alright," I say as I step away from him. I turn to the plates as he wraps his arms around me again. I take the lids off and look down at the food. "When did you order all of this? I didn't hear you get up."

"I ordered it just before I got in the shower. I was starving so I guessed you would be too. I wanted to have food waiting for you when you woke up," he says and then softly kisses my neck again.

"Why are you so thoughtful?" I ask in wonderment.

"Abby," he says and turns my face so I'm looking at him. "I really wish you wouldn't be so surprised at someone wanting to take care of your needs, any needs you might have.

I'm going to do my damnedest to erase all the negative things that Jason has made you believe are normal."

"Which is yours?" I ask, pointing to the plates.

"The one with scrambled eggs. I remembered you like them over easy."

I don't know what to say to that, so I just give him a kiss on the cheek and turn back to the food. I'm willing myself not to cry. *I will not crier. I can't believe he remembered.* I pick up the plate with scrambled eggs, bacon, and hashbrowns and hand it back to Kallon. He steps to the side and adds an English muffin to his plate. I grab a spoon and dish some fruit onto mine and add a piece of toast.

"Table?" I ask.

"Lead the way," he says with a smile.

He grabs the pitcher of orange juice and two glasses with his free hand and follows me to the table. We sit and eat in silence for a few minutes, just enjoying each other's company and the delicious food.

After I take a drink of juice, I ask, "Are you going to tell me what's planned for me and Mary?"

"Just some pampering and in-house shopping," he says with a chuckle.

"In-house shopping?" I ask unsure of what that means.

"You'll see," he says. He looks at the clock on the stove in the kitchen and says, "They'll be here in an hour and fifteen minutes. Do you want me to run you a bath after we're finished eating?"

"No, that's ok. I'll take a shower," I say, smiling. We'd taken a bath together last night after we'd gotten home, so the tub will seem exceptionally large and empty without him in it.

I put a piece of bacon to my lips but before I bite into it, I say, "I'll leave baths as an us thing."

Kallon must have just swallowed something because he starts to cough and splutter, like he'd inhaled sharply at the same time as swallowing. His eyes are wide, and his pupils are dilated, a sign I've realized means he's turned on. I love how responsive he is to just the thought or suggestion of us.

I reach over and pat his back, and chuckle when I ask, "Are you alright?"

He takes a sip of his juice and says between another little cough, "Fine, I'm fine."

I smile up at him and go back to eating. It doesn't take long before my plate is cleared of all food. I drink the last of my juice and go to stand to take my plate back to the kitchen, but Kallon stops me.

"I'll take care of this, you go shower," he suggests as he stands and stacks our plates together.

"It's too bad you've already showered," I say. I can't help but tease a little, my need… want for him taking over. As I walk away, I let the sheet fall down my back slowly, and when it hits my ass, I drop it all together. I stop at the door and turn slightly to the side and stare at him.

"Woman, if you don't want all those people to have to wait outside our hotel door, I suggest you hustle into the bathroom and lock the door," he says with that deep sensual voice again. "Because the next time I have you in my arms, dressed like that—" he points to me "—I'm taking my time with you."

My heart stutters and my cheeks heat at his promise. He leans against the counter, his arms crossed casually over his chest. My eyes catch the site of his hard-on pushing out from his sweats.

"I'd hate for them to wait," I say as I lick my bottom lip and bite it gently. My eyes peruse up his body, back up to his face.

As I walk through the bedroom door, I give him a wink. I see him take a deep breath in and then drops his head down until his chin is resting on his chest. I snicker to myself. I'm glad I'm not the only one that's easily affected by the other person.

I'm smiling when I walk into the bathroom and turn on the water. The room is still steamy from Kallon's earlier shower. I step into the hot stream of water and get myself clean for the big day. The water feels too good on my muscles, it's hard to turn the water off, but when I finally do, I look out to where the towels should be and find none.

"Crap," I say to myself. I raise my voice and holler for Kallon, "Kallon!"

I stand in the shower, dripping wet, and naked, waiting for him. I don't have to wait long before I see the bathroom door open and Kallon pokes his head in.

"Yeah?" he asks. When he finds me in the shower, his eyes all but bulge from his head. He shakes his head and says, "You're really testing my restraint."

I laugh and say, "I'm not trying too, I don't have a towel."

Kallon looks around the room and says, "Shit, I thought there were more in here. Hang on, I'll go get some from the guest bathroom."

As he leaves, I turn the water back on, to keep myself warm. Kallon's back in less time than I thought it would take for him to go all the way across the suite, he must have ran. He sets the stack of towels down but keeps one and walks over to me. I turn the water off and open the shower door. I step up to him, looking him in the eyes, and have to give him credit, his eyes don't stray from mine as he wraps me in the big fluffy towel.

"Better?" he asks.

"Yes, thank you."

He holds me in the towel for a couple heart beats, and then sighs, and steps away from me.

He smiles and says, "I left you something on the bed."

Kallon moves me so I'm facing the door and gently pushes me to start walking. I lead us out into the bedroom and see a small clothing box on the bed.

"What is it?" I ask.

"Open it and find out," he chuckles.

I wrap the towel under my arms and secure it, so it doesn't fall. I'm not totally trying to drive the man crazy, that wouldn't be nice. *Hehehe,* I inwardly laugh to myself. I lift the box and take the lid off. I find pretty blue, silk fabric inside. I lift it up and let the material flutter down.

"It's a robe," I say in astonishment.

"I thought you could wear it while you're getting ready. Instead of the hotel's big clunky kind," he says with a laugh.

"It's beautiful. Thank you," I say and turn to him and give him a kiss. I step away and have a teasing smile on my face when I say, "Now, unless you want to watch me dry off and put my underthings on and help me with this robe, I suggest you turn around or leave the room."

I watch him visibly gulp and his cheeks turn a cute shade

of pink. He licks his lips and his eyes run down my towel covered body.

"As tempting as that is," he says with lust in his tone. "I should probably leave you to it. My will power is dwindling. I need to go pull myself together."

"Really?" I ask, astonished I have this much effect on him.

"You don't understand the power you have over me, Abby," he says, his pupils dilating as they roam over me again. "It's all I can do to keep my hands off of you."

Now it's my turn to swallow hard. I smile up at him and say, "Tonight. The wait will be worth it tonight."

"Tonight is a long time to wait," he says with a chuckle as he backs away from me.

"It feels that way, doesn't it?" I say, knowing all too well how he feels.

He smiles and winks at me as he gets to the door.

"I'll see you out here in a few," he says as he shuts the door behind him.

I let out a sigh and get to drying myself off. After I've wrapped the towel around my head, I grab the new matching bra and underwear I bought just for today. As I put them on, I realize I should have gone with a natural color instead of black. I don't know what color of dress I'll be wearing but I'll need to make sure it's dark, so these things don't show through. I put my arms through the silk robe arm holes and feel the fabric fall against my skin.

"This is heavenly," I say quietly.

I go into bathroom and dig my brush out of my toiletry bag and brush it out. Not knowing what to do with my hair, I grab a clip and twist my hair into a coil and clasp it to my head. I use a makeup remover wipe and take off the residual eye makeup left that the shower didn't remove. Once I'm satisfied it's all off, I put on a little moisturizing lotion and head out to find Kallon.

I find him sitting in the living room, reading a book. I stop and stare at him, mesmerized at how at ease and good he looks doing nothing but reading. He must sense me because he looks up from his book and smiles. His eyes look me up and down and then he closes his eyes as he puts his head back against the couch.

"What?" I ask.

"That robe looks excellent on you," he says with a sigh. He rolls his head towards me and opens his eyes. He chuckles and says, "I need to keep my mind out of the bedroom, but it's so hard not to have these thoughts when you look that good in a thin piece of material."

"You're ridiculous," I say with a laugh and walk over to him. I sit and grab the book in his hands. To distract him and if I'm honest, myself too, I ask, "Is this any good?"

He sits up and looks at the book.

"Yeah, it's about dragons and a bad guy, and the good guys trying to fight their way back to freedom," he says as he reaches up and grabs a stray hair I must not have got twisted into the clip.

"Sounds interesting," I say, looking up into his eyes.

"It is," he says. His eyes look down at my lips and then back up to my eyes. When he looks back down at them, I involuntarily stick the tip of my tongue out and run it across my bottom lip and out of habit, pull my bottom lip into my mouth and hold the side of it with my teeth. He swallows hard and grits his teeth for a second before he says, "It's really hard to not kiss you when you do that. Stop biting your lip."

"Then kiss me," I say, leaning into him. "It doesn't always have to lead to sex, does it? We can enjoy a little make-out time while we wait for whomever it is you've invited over, can't we?"

"I used to think I could handle it but with you—" he takes a shaky breath in "—it's proving to be difficult. But I'm more than willing to practice my control, if you are?"

I put my hand to his chest and lean into him as I answer with, "Practice makes perfect."

"Mmm," he says as he leans down and meets his lips to mine.

As per usual, the kiss starts out soft and sweet but with no time at all, it turns into a passionate lip embrace. Our lip's part at the same time, allowing our tongues to reach each other and start the familiar dance they so desperately need.

Kallon grabs the book from my hands and toss it away. He puts a hand on my knee and slides it up my thigh just as I slide my hands up his chest, behind his neck and pull him to me. He puts his other hand behind my back and urges me closer. I pull him with me as I lean away from him, lying my back down on the couch. Without breaking our kiss, he adjusts himself so he now has one leg between my thighs, while the other is on the outside of the couch.

I run my hands into the back of his hair, feeling the silky softness of it. His hand moves to the outside of my thigh, and he runs it up the side of my waist, to the side of my breast, and then to my neck. I feel him lower his body down to mine, pressing me into the couch cushions. I'll never get tired of how wonderful his weight on me feels.

After a couple minutes of kissing like this, I run my hands down the back of his neck, to his back and pull at the bottom of his shirt. Urging him to take it off. He obliges and reaches back with one hand and pulls it up and over his head. Our kiss breaks for a split second but then his lips are blessedly back on mine.

Kallon drops his shirt to the floor and then puts his hand under my knee that's between him and the back of the couch. He slides his hand softly down my thigh, making the bottom of the robe fall to my hip. When his thumb brushes against my panty waist band, he sucks in a breath, but doesn't stop kissing me. His thumb rubs softly against the thin band before he moves his hand up the side of my hip, up the side of my ribs. The fabric is bunching up weirdly, so I reach in front of us and untie the sash, letting the robe open.

Kallon's thumb starts its soft circles over my ribs as it inches up higher, closer to my breast. As much as I said practice makes perfect, this is starting to feel like practice is going to be over. The need I have right now to have this man inside me is all but consuming me. I push the need down and focus on enjoying what we're doing and tell myself the wait will be worth it.

But when Kallon's hand finds my bra covered breast and palms it, I all but come apart. My back arches into his hand, pressing myself into him harder.

"Mmmm," I moan out into Kallon's lips. Kallon's hand squeezes a little harder, massaging and gripping just right. I can't help the curse that whispers out, "Shit."

"Maybe we should slow—"

I interrupt him and say, "No, we shouldn't. This is fine. We can handle this."

He kisses down my neck and says, "Are you sure?"

"No but it feels too good to stop," I say in a breathy whisper.

"Fuck, Abby," he groans into my neck. I feel him gently press his hips into me and I feel how hard he is.

He's ready just like I am, one word and we could be making each other feel so much better. The thought crosses my mind. *No, we don't always have to have sex. Even if we're grown adults, we can handle a little uncomfortable tension.*

"If you need us to stop, we can," I say, running my hands through his hair as he kisses across my collarbones and nips me on the shoulder playfully.

"I don't need to," he says as he kisses down to my cleavage at the same time he presses into my center again.

"Are you sure?" I ask with a deep breath in.

"I'm sure," he says huskily.

Kallon kisses back up to my mouth and hungerly overtakes me. His tongue moving mine with his, his lips pressing into mine deliciously hard. I rock my hips into his, causing him to press down into me harder. His hand goes back to my breast, and he slips his thump under my bra cup and rubs my nipple.

"Ahhh, Kallon," I moan against his lips.

"Abby," he moans back just as he rotates his hips in a circle, pushing into me.

****RING-RING**RING-RING****

It doesn't register for couple of seconds that a phone is ringing but then both Kallon and I pause our kissing and listen.

****RING-RING**RING-RING****

"That's mine," Kallon says. He reaches over to the coffee table and grabs it without moving himself off me. "It's Allen."

He looks at me and tilts the phone, a silent question on if he should answer, so I nod at him.

"Hello," Kallon says, his voice going to his business tone I've learned he uses with just about everyone but me, my friends, and family. He pauses and says, "Good. See you shortly."

He hangs up and goes back to kissing me. I lean back and ask, "What was that about?"

"Oh," Kallon says as he kisses down my neck. "He was just calling to say he's got Spencer and Mary. They'll be here in about twenty minutes."

"Oh, okay, in that case," I say as I pull his mouth back to mine.

We spend the next few minutes finishing our make-out session. We're both breathing hard when I gently push him back a little from me.

"I might self-combust if we don't take a break," I say, but my legs holding him to me contradict my words.

He pulls away but kisses my nose before he sits all the way up. He pulls me up and adjusts us so that I'm tucked under his arm.

"Better?" he asks.

"No," I say with a little pout as I adjust my robe to cover me up again. "I liked it better when you were on top of me."

He laughs and says, "That doesn't help the self-combustion situation."

"I know, I'm a walking, talking contradiction," I say with a laugh.

"I have to say, I haven't just made-out in a really long time. I feel like I'm in high school again," Kallon says with a deep throaty laugh. "I kind of like it. The anticipation for later feels… nice. Instant gratification is awesome, but the waiting… I haven't felt like this in a long time."

"I know what you mean," I say. "Like, by building up the feelings, could make it even better when it happens."

Just as he says, "Exactly," there's a knock at the door.

"Good thing we didn't get caught making-out or it definitely would have felt like high school," I say with a laugh as Kallon stands up.

He grabs his shirt and puts it back on before he walks to the door and opens it. Spencer and Mary are standing there with Allen.

"I'll go wait downstairs with Thomas and we'll bring the others up when they arrive," Allen says at the door.

"Thanks Allen," Kallon says as he steps aside and lets my brother and his wife in. When Allen turns and heads back to the elevator, Kallon shuts the door, and follows Spencer and Mary into the living room.

"Nice place," Spencer says with a smile as he lays his garment bag on the table. "Morning, Sis."

"Morning," I say as I pull the blanket on the couch onto my lap. The robe is nice but sitting down makes it's a little short. I have more leg showing than my brother needs to see. "Hi, Mary."

"Hi, Abs," she says as she sits on the oversized chair, Spencer squeezes in beside her.

Just as Kallon is sitting down, there's a knock at the door again. He laughs and heads back to the door.

"Mr. Keller!" a woman's voice says eagerly from the door.

"Hello, Bernie," Kallon says happily. I turn to see a woman standing in front of him holding a big black bag over her shoulder and she's got three other people standing behind her holding similar bags.

"Where should we set up?" the woman, Bernie asks.

"I'll show you but let me introduce you first," Kallon says as he steps aside and waves for the four people to walk in.

Spencer, Mary, and I stand, I hastily adjust the robe to make sure it's covering me completely. Bernie is a tall blonde and she's wearing a tight, form fitting black dress. The two guys and a girl standing behind her are wearing black shirts and black pants. The guys are twins and have long dark hair pulled back into low ponytails. The girl is shorter than Bernie but still taller than me. She has red curly hair that's in a high ponytail.

"Bernie, this is Abbigail Rose, my girlfriend—" at the word, Bernie's eyes tighten a little and they do a quick assessment of me "—and her sister-in-law, Mary and her brother, Spencer."

I reach out a hand to shake Bernie's which she sticks out slowly. As she daintily shakes my hand, she says in a forced friendly tone, "How nice to meet you."

Mary and Spencer reach out and shake her hand as well. When Mary turns to stand next to me, her eyebrows raise and she mouths, *Wow.* I keep my facial expressions in place and smile up to Bernie.

"These are my assistants, Matilda and Joe and Jesse," Bernie says as she gestures to the trio behind her.

"Nice to meet you," I say, waving at them. They look shocked at my greeting, so they just nod in response.

"Shall we set up, we've got a lot of work ahead of us," Bernie says with a chuckle. Then looks at me and says, "No offense."

I force a smile and say, "None taken."

She gives me a half smile and then turns back to Kallon and beams, "Lead the way, handsome."

Kallon gestures towards the guest room and as Bernie and her assistants turn to walk, he turns towards me and mouths, *I'm sorry.* I shrug and wave him away.

When they're away from us, Mary says, "What the hell was that?"

"Probably just another one of Kallon's many admirers. She's probably wondering what the hell he's doing with someone like me."

"Don't start that," Spencer says. "We can all see that you are far more beautiful than she is. She's just jealous."

"Whatever," I say. Before either one can argue with me, I say to Mary, "Well we know at least one thing about today. Hair and makeup."

"You think so?" she asks.

"Yeah, they had the same type of bags as the people that spruced up Kayla and me for her wedding," I say as I walk into the kitchen. I open the fridge and find a bottle of water. I hold it up and ask, "Do you guys want one?"

"Sure," they both say.

I hand them one. I open mine and take a drink.

"We might need something strong if that snarky bitch is going to be giving you side eye all day," Mary says.

"Just do me a favor?" I ask.

"If it's to keep my mouth shut if she says anything about you, the answer is absolutely not," Mary says, and I can see she's got her hackles up.

I laugh and say, "Don't leave me alone with her."

"Oh, I definitely won't," she says. She takes a drink and adds, "She's pretty ballsy to talk to you like that with Kallon in the room."

"I've found people that look like her, tend to think they can say whatever they want," I say with a little laugh.

"Put her in her place if she says anything, Sis," Spencer says. "Don't let her treat you like shit and make you feel lesser than."

"I'll try," I say, shaking my head.

Kallon hurries into the room and pulls me to him.

"I'm sorry about her," he says hugging me. "That was totally uncalled for. I've talked to her. She's been warned to treat you with utmost respect, or I'll never call on her services again."

"And what services are those?" Mary asks, crossing her arms over her chest angerly.

"Hair and makeup," Kallon says in a hurry. "I swear, Abby. There has never been anything between Bernie and me. She's never acted like this before."

"When have you used her services before?" I ask.

"She's helped my mom and Kara when they came to my last movie premiere," he states.

"You fly her and her assistants where you need them?" I ask.

"Kind of, it's added into their fee. They fly commercial," Kallon says as he steps away from me. "Are you angry?"

"No, should I be?" I ask with a laugh.

"She was exceptionally rude to you," he says raising his brows at me.

I shrug and say, "That's her issue, not mine."

He pulls me into him and hugs me tightly, "You are amazing.—" he looks at Spencer "—Your sister is amazing."

"Don't you forget it," Spencer says with a little edge in his voice.

"Spencer," I warn.

But Kallon says with a nod, "I won't."

"Oookay, let's go sit in the living room and relax," I say with a laugh. "It's getting a little too tense in here."

"Should we order something to drink?" Mary asks.

"I can have a bottle of the champagne you like brought up," Kallon says as he sits beside me and puts a hand on my knee after I've put the blanket over my lap again.

"Ooooh it's here too?" I ask.

He laughs and says, "Yes, I have it in all of my hotels."

"Yes, please," Mary and I say at the same time which makes us all laugh. Kallon reaches over to the side table and picks up the phone and orders a couple bottles of champagne and some strawberries.

"Two bottles?" I ask.

"I know how much you like it," he says with a chuckle.

"But two?"

"We don't have to drink it all right now," Spencer says with a laugh of his own.

"You just wait," I say to Spencer. "Once you try it, you'll want your own bottle."

"I'm not a big fan of champagne," he states.

"You will be after you try this kind," I laugh.

****KNOCK-KNOCK****

"That was quick," Spencer says.

"When the boss man calls, you run," Mary says with a wink at me.

Kallon chuckles as he gets up and walks to the door.

"Mr. Johnston," Kallon says with a truly happy tone.

I turn and see an older man, with gray hair and who is hunched over a little, standing at the door.

"Mr. Keller, a pleasure to see you this morning," the man, Mr. Johnston, says happily.

"Come on inside," Kallon says.

I watch as Mr. Johnston walks in and he's pulling a rack of black garment bags. Following him are two more men pulling even larger racks full of the bags.

"Our dresses?" Mary asks in an excited whisper.

"I think so," I whisper back.

We stand and walk over to Kallon and the three men.

"Mr. Johnston, this is my girlfriend, Abbigail Rose. And her brother, Spencer and sister-in-law, Mary," Kallon says as he takes my hand and gestures to the other two. "This is the amazing Mr. Johnston. He always knows how to dress people."

Mr. Johnston shakes Spencer's hand and then very gentlemanly kisses Mary's hand and says, "It's a pleasure to meet you both."

He turns to me and takes my hands in his and turns me to the right and to the left. He looks at Kallon and says, "You told me she was beautiful, but you didn't tell me she was this beautiful."

Kallon beams and says, "My apologies, sir."

"You, my dear Miss Rose, are stunning," Mr. Johnston says with a small nod. "You are as naturally exquisite as your surname."

With my cheeks turning red, I say, "Thank you, Mr. Johnston."

"And humble to boot?" Mr. Johnston asks, noticing the change in my cheeks.

"One of the many reasons I like her so much," Kallon says, beaming at me.

Mr. Johnston kisses my right hand and then lets go of both of them. He claps his hands together and says, "Where are we setting up?"

"In the guest room. Bernie and her assistants are setting up now," Kallon says, gesturing towards the room. He lets go of my hand and takes a step in that direction.

"That insipid girl again?" Mr. Johnston says with a sour look on his face.

"She's the best in the business," Kallon says as he tries to suppress his laughter.

"Might be time to try the second best in the business," Mr. Johnston says but he waves Kallon on to walk. He pulls his cart behind him, not bothering to motion for the men to follow with their carts.

"I looove him," Mary says with quiet glee. "He needs to stay in the room with us. No doubt he'll put Snotty Nose Bernie in her place if she's disrespectful to you again."

"I'm disappointed I won't be in the room to hear it," Spencer says with a laugh.

I laugh and start to walk back to the couch when there's another knock at the door. I walk over to it and open it. The room service guy looks to be about my age and when he sees me, his eyes travel up and down my body, pausing at my bare legs from above mid-thigh and then again at the little bit of, like barely any, cleavage that's showing. I pull my robe together to close off any chest skin and look at the guy.

"Uh, room ser-vice," he stutters out. He goes to take a step into the room, but I put my hand on the tray to stop him.

"I can take it in," I say. I put a smile on my face, it's not his fault I'm in the silk robe. "Thank you."

"My pleasure," he says. He winks and then looks me up and down again. I roll my eyes and shut the door on him.

"Champagne is here!" I holler to Mary and Spencer.

"Eeee," Mary shouts happily. "I can't wait to try this 'amazing'—" she uses air quotes "—champagne that you keep going on about."

I put the tray down and Spencer grabs a bottle and expertly pops the cork. He pours four glasses. I hand one to Mary and grab one for each me and Kallon. I'm about to say we should wait for Kallon when he walks into the kitchen.

"Got him all set up," he says. He sees that we have glasses and adds happily, "Ah, it's here."

I hand him his glass and hold up mine. I say, "To a fun day and a fun night. And congratulations to Kallon for another superb movie."

"Cheers to that," Mary says.

"Cheers," my brother says.

"Cheers," Kallon says. After we take a sip he leans in and says, "I was cheers'ing to the fun night part."

He kisses just below my ear and when I look up at him, he gives me a wink.

I wink back and say, "Me too."

He laughs and stands up straight.

"Miss Rose, Mrs. Rose," Bernie says from the side of the kitchen. We all turn and see her standing with her hands behind her back. "We're ready whenever you are."

"Okay, thank you," I say to her. She nods, turns around and walks quickly from the room. I look at Kallon and raise my eyebrows at him.

"I told her to behave," he says with a shrug.

I laugh and grab the open bottle of champagne.

"You boys can have that one, Mary and I get this one," I say with a laugh.

"Take it easy," Spencer warns Mary. "This stuff IS really good."

"I told you!" I say and point at him. He sticks his hand up in defeat and laughs.

"Go have fun," Kallon says.

"What time do we need to leave by?" I ask, looking at the

clock on the wall. I see my phone on the charger on the counter, so I grab it to take with me.

"2 o'clock," Kallon says.

"You think we need four hours to get ready?" Mary asks as she walks over to me.

"No, but it's better to have too much time than not enough," Kallon says. "We can always show up early to the premiere."

"True," she concedes.

"I'd rather not be late," I say as I pull her back with me to head to the guest room.

"Of course you wouldn't," Spencer and Kallon say together. They look at each other and burst out laughing.

I shake my head and turn away from them. Mary and I walk back to our very own makeover room.

"Miss Rose," Bernie says as we walk into the room. "First I want to apologize for any rudeness I had earlier. I'm sorry for acting that way. Second, if you'll allow me, I'd like to do your hair and makeup, with the help of Jesse."

"Thank you," I say, accepting her apology. "And I'm okay with you doing it."

"Thank you," she says. She pats a chair she moved over in front of the mirror in the room and motions for me to sit. "Mrs. Rose, Matilda and Joe will be with you."

"Okie dokie," Mary says. She walks into the bathroom where they have another chair set up.

We're not too far away that we can't talk but we're far enough we can't see each other. I kind of like it, I want to be surprised when they're finished with her. This is a super big thing for Mary. She, like me, never gets dressed up. I'm excited to see how they amplify her natural beauty.

CHAPTER 22

"So, Miss Rose, what are we thinking?" Bernie asks as she puts an apron cape around me and secures it around my neck.

"For my makeup or are you wanting to cut my hair?" I ask.

"Sorry, Miss Rose," she says. She has a smile on her face, but she also looks a little annoyed. "Just your makeup. Unless you'd like a quick trim or something."

"No, no trim. I think just a natural look would be good," I say. I then add so I don't seem rude, "What do you think?"

"Natural is a good way to go," she says. She reaches behind her and grabs her palette of make-up and some brushes and sets them on the table in front of me. She looks at Jesse and says, "Will you re-brush her hair and resecure it in the clip so all of her hair is out of the way?"

I look in the mirror and I'm surprised to see that my hair is a little messy. My mind goes back to Kallon and I making-out on the couch and my face heats. I smile at Jesse as he gently brushes my hair and professionally clips it back up.

"Thanks," I say to him.

His eyes dart to mine and he smiles when he sees me

smiling. He nods in response. I close my eyes as Bernie steps up and she starts putting some lotion type stuff on my face. The next 30-45 minutes are spent in silence. I keep my eyes shut so I don't have to look at her and make the silence seem awkward.

"Alright," she says. "What about your hair?"

"Can you curl it and then do a loose bun at the nape of my neck?" I ask. I pull my phone from under the cape and say, "I have a picture."

I open my phone and pull up my photos and show her the picture I'd found that I thought would be nice. It's not super fancy but I'm hoping it'll be just enough that it looks good.

"Sure," she says with a smile. "I can do that."

A little on edge on her quick agreement, I nod. She takes my hair out of the clip and starts to brush it out as she blow-dries it. As I put my phone away, I feel it vibrate and I pull it back out. It's a text from Kallon. My face breaks into a huge grin.

Kallon: How's it going in there?
Me: Fine. How's it going out there?
Kallon: Great. We're watching a baseball game drinking champagne.
Me: haha That's a unique combination. :-D
Kallon: Definitely new to us.
Me: You guys aren't getting ready yet?
Kallon: No, we've got some time. It won't take us as long. ;-)
Me: Fair enough. :-D

"I'm going to spray your hair, you might want to close your eyes," Bernie says grabbing a can of spray off the table.

"Okay," I say. I put my phone under the cape and close my eyes.

Bernie sprays my hair and moves it around, getting it well covered. I keep my eyes closed as she starts to curl. I almost fall asleep from the feel of her grabbing strands and curling them. I feel her start to twist and pin my hair at the nape of my neck. Her fingers skim my temples and pulls a couple strands and then curls them.

"Alright, have a look," Bernie says.

I open my eyes and see her stepping out of in front of me so I can see the mirror. I look and see a stranger looking back at me. She looks like me but enhanced in the best possible way. My eyes look bigger and brighter. My lips somehow look fuller and are a pretty light pink. My skin looks so smooth and flawless. My hair looks exactly like the picture I showed her.

"Wow," I say in awe. "You... are amazing."

"It's easy when we have someone so beautiful to work with," Jesse says. It's the first time he has said anything. I look at him in the mirror and smile. I don't miss the glare Bernie shoots him but when I look at her directly, she smiles at me and goes to put her stuff away.

"My turn," Mr. Johnston says, walking up behind me. He offers me his hand and says, "Come with me, my dear."

I take his hand and we wait for Jesse to take the apron cape off me before Mr. Johnston pulls me towards the racks of dresses.

"Now, Mr. Keller said he favored you in the wine-colored dress you wore last week but he wanted you to have options. This wrack—" he points to the one he pushed in "—has all wine-colored dresses. Those over there against the wall are all other colors I had in your size and Mrs. Rose's size."

"How did you know our sizes?" I ask, unzipping one of

the ones on the wine-colored wrack.

"Mr. Keller sent them to me," Mr. Johnston says matter-of-factly.

"Oh," is all I can think to say.

I finish unzipping the first bag and pull the dress out. It's the same beautiful wine color that I wore to Kayla's wedding, but it looks as if it would barely cover my chest and nether regions. I shake my head and start to put it back in the bag.

"Don't you worry about putting it back. Just have a gander at them and see which ones you like," Mr. Johnston says as he steps forward and takes the dress and bag out of my hands.

Instead of arguing with him, I nod and go to the next dress. I open it and I see that it's floor length and is held up with spaghetti straps. *This one could be nice.* I smile and pull it out more.

"I like this one," I say.

"We'll hang it here. Keep looking, you might find one you like better," Mr. Johnston says as he takes the dress and pulls it completely from the bag and hangs it on the back of the bedroom door.

I keep looking and the only other dress that I like the cut and design of, is a black floor length but it might be too Prom dress looking. I decide to try it on anyways.

"I think I'll start with these two," I say, pointing at the wine and black colored dresses.

"Sounds good," Mr. Johnston says. "Since you're already holding the black one, why don't we try that one on first."

"Okay," I say.

He takes the dress off the hanger and holds it. I tell

myself my bra and undies are no different from a bathing suit, even though I haven't warn a two piece in years, I slide the robe off and step into the dress. I look over and see his assistants dutifully looking in the opposite direction of me. *Good men.* He pulls it up and helps me get my arms through the straps and then starts to button up the back.

The dress flares out like a bell at the bottom and fits nicely around my waist and chest. The straps feel a little loose on my shoulders but not so bad that it would be an issue. Once Mr. Johnston is done buttoning the back, which takes some time, I pick up the front of the skirt and walk over to the mirror. I don't look horrible but it's not the jaw dropping addition to my beautifully done makeup and hair.

I look at Bernie and Jesse and ask, "What do you think?"

Bernie says, "You look great."

She has a gleam in her eye that makes me think she's not being one hundred percent honest. I look at Jesse, he doesn't say anything but looks at Bernie and then back at me. His head nods ever slightly to the other dress hanging on the door.

"I'll try on the wine one before I make my final decision," I say as I walk back to Mr. Johnston.

"Wise choice," he says as he starts to unbutton the back. "We have plenty of time. No reason to rush picking out a dress."

I look at the clock on the bedside table and see that it's 1:15pm. We don't have SO much time that I can take my time choosing but we have enough that I can at least try on a couple more if neither of my first choices are what I'm looking for.

Once he's finally gotten the buttons undone, he slides it back down, and I step out of it. He grabs the dress off the door and holds it for me as I step into it. The feel of the fabric is like soft butter on my skin as he slides it up. Even though this one has spaghetti straps, they already feel like they're made for my shoulders. The back is a zipper which Mr. Johnston expertly zips up quickly, it stops just below the middle of my back. I can feel the majority of my back is showing. The bottom half of the dress doesn't flare out like a bell but is flowy enough that it's not form fitting. My hands slide down the side and I find, *POCKETS!* I shout excitedly in my head. *Extra points for this dress!*

I walk over to the mirror and my eyes pop wide. It's beautiful! Except, I'm not going to be able to wear a bra. The neckline cuts down in a V shape right around the bottom of my sternum. I turn to see what I can of the back and see that the V goes down to the same point as the front.

"I love this dress but… I don't think I can go braless, I'm not that brave," I say out loud, my cheeks burning with embarrassment.

"We have bra tape and tape that will secure the dress in place against your skin," Mr. Johnston says. "If you want to wear that dress, then we can get you taped up and confined. Those things won't go anywhere once they're taped."

"You seem like a nice guy, Mr. Johnston, but I'm not comfortable having a man help me tape my breasts," I say, my cheeks heating even more.

"I'll help you," I hear Mary holler from the bathroom. I look in the mirror just in time to see Bernie roll her eyes. I look at Jesse and see him smiling at me, he gives me a nod of encouragement.

"Okay," I say to both Mr. Johnston and Mary.

Mr. Johnston snaps his fingers and one of his assistants

grabs a bag from the bottom of his cart and brings it over. Mr. Johnston opens it and pulls out multiple rolls of tape.

He hands them to me and says, "Tape them up and then put your dress on. There's plenty, so if you have to do it over, that's okay. We want you secure and comfortable."

"Thank you, Mr. Johnston," I say, holding my hands out so he can dump the rolls of tape into them.

I walk into the bathroom and catch my breath. Half of Mary's red hair is twisted into a loose bun on the crown of her head. The rest has been loosely curled to flow down her back. Her makeup showcases her high cheek bones and beautiful green eyes.

"Wow, Mare, you look amazing," I say, putting my hands full of tape to my chest. She looks up and her facial expression goes from shocked, stunned, to something like awe.

"Abby?" she asks.

"Yes?" I answer as a question.

"You look like you but not, holy shit!" she says as she stands. Matilda steps back, as she has just finished with her hair, and lets Mary step up to me. "You are fucking stunning!"

"Stop," I say, feeling my face heat again.

"I'm serious," she says as she comes to stand in front of me. "You are a natural beauty and that... Bernie pulled it all together with that makeup and your choice in hairdo makes it... You're just... Wow!"

"Have you seen yourself?" I ask. I turn her towards the mirror and see us standing side by side.

"I have," she says with a smile, understanding I want the attention off of me.

"Have you thought of what color of dress you want to

wear?" I ask as I open a roll of tape.

"Did you see any forest green?" she asks.

"I did!" I say. "Oh, you'll look beautiful in that color."

I look around the room and see Joe standing by the door. When he sees me holding the tape in my hand, he nods and leaves the room. I look over at Matilda and she smiles sweetly at me.

"I can stay and help if you'd like," she says. "That stuff can be a pain in the butt."

"Sure," I say. Then I ask, "Can you rip and hold strips for us?"

"I can," she says as she walks over and shuts the door. She then comes back to us and takes the roll from me after I've ripped a couple strips off.

"Okay, I have no idea what I'm doing," I say as I slide my straps down to expose my bra covered chest. I elbow Mary and say, "And just a heads up, you're about to see a lot of boob that you probably thought you'd never see before."

Mary and Matilda both laugh.

"That's okay," Mary says. "Once you've seen your own, other boobs just don't really seem much different."

I laugh and unclasp my bra and take it off.

"Put the top part back on and so we can see where the tape can't be," Matilda suggests.

"Oh, that's a good idea," I say. I slip the straps back up. Matilda rummages in her makeup back and comes over with a foundation stick that looks dang near exactly like the color of my skin.

"Here, we'll make a mark and then you can rub that in so it's not just a dot on your chest," Matilda says with a laugh.

"You are all sorts of good ideas," Mary says as she makes a mark on me while I stand still.

"I've been doing this for a while, you pick up on tricks like this," Matilda says with a laugh.

"Can I ask why you work with Bernie?" I ask.

"She's the best," Matilda says.

I look at Mary and point at her, "You did an amazing job with Mary, I think you could do really well on your own."

"You think so?" Matilda asks quietly, like she doesn't want Bernie to hear her.

"You're nice, easy to talk to, encouraging, helpful," Mary says, holding up her hand. And then she holds up all ten fingers when she says, "And you know what you're doing with makeup and hair. I agree with Abby, you should definitely break away from her and do your own thing."

"I wouldn't know where to begin and... she's not very helpful or encouraging on that side of things," Matilda says.

"I'd use you again," I say. "If Kallon ever has another event that he wants me to go to with him, I'll use you for it."

"Would you really?" she asks excitedly.

"Absolutely," I say with a smile. "I'll even suggest to Kallon to use you for anything else he might need."

"Oh, I don't want to take Mr. Keller from Bernie. He's her top client," Matilda says hurriedly.

"Yeah well, Bernie isn't very nice to people that Mr. Keller finds important. You'd be surprised what that man will do for her," Mary says, pointing at me. I shake my head as I take my straps back off and lower the top part down now that we have a line to guide us to keep tape away from.

"Alright, now what?" I ask, holding my breasts in my

hands.

"Keep doing that and we'll tape them, so you've got great cleavage but also, so they stay put," Matilda says.

I nod and let them tape me up like my boobs are going to try to escape at any moment. It takes some retaping a couple of times but soon my boobs are secure and feel like they'll stay in this position forever. I pull the straps back up and adjust the dress. I look in the mirror and grin.

"It's looks awesome!" I explain.

"Here, use this tape on the dress and it'll keep the fabric in place," Matilda says as she rips some strips off. I attach it to the inside of the dress and then to my skin, pressing down and then work my way out to the V shape. I twist side to side and the dress doesn't move away from my chest.

"This stuff is magical," I say with a big smile.

"You look fantastic," Matilda says as she hands me a sponge to blend in the little bit of foundation on my chest.

"Thank you," I say. I blend the makeup in the best I can and look in the mirror. You can't even tell there was anything on me. But then a thought comes to mind, "Will that get on my dress?"

"No, it's smudge proof. It's only coming off with soap and water," Matilda says with a smile. She takes the sponge back and starts to pack up her stuff.

"Thank you for your help," I say to her. And then I ask, "Do you have a card?"

"I do," she says excitedly. She goes to her big makeup bag and pulls out a little card case and hands me a card.

"Thank you," I say.

"Yeah, thanks Matilda," Mary says giving her a big smile

of her own.

"My pleasure, ladies," she says happily.

As Matilda starts to put all her stuff away, Mary and I walk to the door. When we walk out, all the guys gasp. I look behind me but don't see anyone. I look at them and they're all staring at me.

"Miss Rose, you are a sight for these old eyes," Mr. Johnston says happily.

"Your dress is amazing," I say with a big smile.

"You make it so," he says. "The dress is just material. You my beautiful child, make it into something more than amazing."

I look around the room and see all the guys smiling at me. I look at Bernie and she has a look of absolute surprise on her face.

"You look... stunning," she says, and it actually sounds like she means it.

"Thank you," I say with a startled laugh. Not liking all the attention, I turn to Mr. Johnston and say, "Mary would like to look at the forest green dress, please."

"Right this way, Mrs. Rose," he says with a big wave of his hand. We follow him over to the rack and she starts to look through them. She pulls one out and she squeals in glee.

"This one!" she exclaims. She pulls it out of the bag and goes into the bathroom. While we wait for her to come back out, I grab my phone off the table and slip it into the pocket of my dress. She emerges a couple minutes later, and her dress is gorgeous on her.

The dress is very long, even with her heels it drags on the floor behind her as she walks. Where my slit goes dang near up to my hip bone, her slit goes just above her knee. I'm a little envious of the slit, I kind of wish mine wasn't so high. Her dress has long sleeves, and the neckline goes down mid-chest so that she's able to wear a bra. Another fact of the dress that I'm jealous of, even though the tape feels like it's going to do the job just fine.

"Wow!" I say, my mouth hanging open. "Gorgeous!"

"I know, right?" she says happily.

"My brother is going to lose his mind when he sees you," I say with a laugh.

"You think this dress can convince him of another baby?" she asks in a slight whisper.

"Mary, that dress can get you anything you want," I laugh out.

"Shall we go show the boys?" she asks excitedly.

"Let me go see if they're ready," Mr. Johnston says. He walks by his cart and grabs a box and continues out the door.

"You two look amazing," Matilda says, coming to stand by us.

"Thank you," we say at the same time.

"You and Bernie did a great job! Joe and Jesse, too," I say smiling toward the guys by the door. They're not paying attention to us anymore. They are too busy talking to the guys that Mr. Johnston brought with him.

"It's our job," Bernie says snarkily. But, she then forces a smile.

I turn from her and put her attitude out of my head. *Whatever her problem is, is her problem, not mine.*

Mr. Johnston comes in a few minutes later and says, "The guys are ready."

He holds the door open and says out to them, "Gentlemen... your beautiful ladies."

Mary walks out first and I hear their gasps. Then my brother's voice says, "Wow, Mare, you look... just... hot damn!"

"Thanks babe," she says in response, with a laugh.

I take a deep breath and walk out of the room. Kallon is smiling at Spencer and Mary, but he must catch movement out of the corner of his eye because he glances my way quickly and then back to my brother and Mary. But then he does a double take, his mouth falls open and his eyebrows raise.

Mary notices Kallon's reaction and turns toward me with a big smile. Spencer looks at her and then Kallon, and then follows their line of sight and his facial expression turns into one similar to Kallon's. Spencer's is a mixture of disbelieve and surprise. Kallon's is surprise, awestruck, and something else.

I look Kallon up and down. He's wearing a black suit with a black shirt and a tie that matches my dress exactly. I look at my brother, who's wearing a black suit and a white shirt and has a pocket square the same color as Mary's dress. *Oh, that's what Mr. Johnston must have had in that box that he brought out.*

I look back at Kallon and smile at him. When I do, his awestruck look intensifies.

"So," I say as I walk towards him. "Will this work for your premiere?"

He swallows hard but has to clear his throat before he can speak. He says, "Umm... yeah... You uh—" he clears his throat again "—you look lovely... sensational... dazzling... devastatingly beautiful... I honestly can't find a word that describes you well enough. Abby, just... wow!"

He puts his hand on his heart and kind of melts down and steps back. He gives me the smile I love the most. The one that makes my knees weak and my heart stutter to a stop and then pick up speed.

"Thank you," I say when I get to him. "You look pretty damn handsome yourself."

He takes my hand in his, bends his head down and brings it up to meet his lips, and gives it a soft kiss. When he straightens, he's smiling at me, and his eyes are shinning with desire.

"Shall we go?" he asks.

"Let me grab my I.D.," I say as I walk over to where I put my bag. I grab my wallet and pull the driver's license out. I go to put it in my pocket and then decide not to. "Shoot, I don't have a clutch or anything to put this in."

"I can put it in my wallet, if you'd like," Kallon says, walking over to me.

"You wouldn't mind?" I ask.

"That's a good idea," Mary says, going over to her bag and pulling her card out. "Spencer, put it in your wallet too, please."

"I don't mind," Kallon says as he holds out his hand for it. I watch as my brother takes Mary's card and slides it behind his.

"Okay," I say with a smile and hand it over to Kallon. He pulls his wallet out of his back pocket, puts mine in, and then takes my hand and turns towards Spencer and Mary.

"Ready?" he asks.

"Ready," they say at the same time.

"Mr. Johnston, will you make sure everyone gets out

okay?" Kallon asks as we walk towards the door.

"Yes, sir, I can do that. Enjoy your evening," Mr. Johnston says with a nod and a smile.

"We will," Kallon says with a smile of his own.

We walk to the door, and I'm not surprised to see Allen and Thomas standing on either side of the door.

"Car is out front and ready, sir," Allen says. He looks at us and then does a double take at me before his attention is back to Kallon.

"Sounds good," Kallon says with a stern look and a nod.

We make our way to the elevator. Kallon gestures for me to get in and then he lets Mary and Spencer in next. He follows behind and comes to stand next to me. His hand goes to my back and he stiffens when he feels that it's bare. His hand slides down until it finds where the V ends. He looks down at me and raises an eyebrow, I mimic the expression. He smiles and slides his hand gently up and down my back.

Allen and Thomas load and press the button for the lobby. As we wait, I notice they have earpieces in and when we're two floors away, I see Thomas whisper something into his shirt cuff. He must have a microphone in there somewhere. When the doors open, I see two more guys that look like Allen and Thomas.

"Brad and Victor are joining us this evening," Kallon says when he notices me looking at the new guys.

I don't ask any questions and just nod. If Kallon thinks it's necessary to add two more bodyguards, who am I to say otherwise. This is my first movie premiere. We make our way to the front, Brad and Victor falling instep behind us, Allen and Thomas leading the way.

We get outside and a limo is parked, waiting for us. Allen opens the door and Kallon nods for me to get in. I slide in and move so that Mary, who follows me has room to sit and find a spot before Spencer and then Kallon follows us in. Kallon comes and sits beside me and must just now notice the slit in my dress because his hand goes to it and his thumb rubs slow circles on my knee.

He leans in, kisses my cheek, and then whispers, "Remind me to give Mr. Johnston a raise."

I laugh and nod at him. It doesn't take long before the car is pulling away from the hotel. I look on the clock to the left of where were sitting and I see that it's 3:48pm.

"Are we going to be late?" I ask anxiously.

"They suggest we get there at 4 but that's only so the photographers have time to take pictures, everything won't start until around 5," Kallon says soothingly.

"Pictures, right," I say. I had momentarily forgotten about that side of the event.

"Don't worry, it'll be fast and painless," he says with a smile. "I've gotten pretty good at making it through the mess of photographers in record time."

"Okay," I say in a small voice.

"So, how long will this event be?" Spencer asks as he looks in all the nooks and crannies of the car.

"There's about an hour of meet and greet. Then mingling with the cast and crew and the creative minds behind the movie, which takes another hour or so. We'll watch the first screening of the movie, which will take about two hours, and then we can either stay for an after party or go home. So about four hours or longer if we choose to stay,"

Kallon says thoughtfully.

"I don't know if we'll be able to stay for long," Mary says disappointment thick in her tone. "Our babysitter said she'd like to be home by 9 o'clock if possible."

"That's okay," Kallon says reassuringly. "I've learned the best time to talk and meet people is before the screening anyways. By the end, some people are three sheets to the wind and aren't too fun to talk to. Or they want to dissect why a scene was cut or how their acting was. I don't usually stay after the movie watching anyways."

I look up at him and say, "Yeah, after all the excitement of the day, early to bed sounds good to me."

He looks down at me and I wink. He winks and squeezes my knee gently. It doesn't take long before we're pulling up in front of a huge building that's lined with photographers and a red carpet. A man is standing on the driver's side of the car and when we come to a stop, Allen gets out and takes a piece of paper from the guy.

"Are they parking the limo?" I ask.

"Yeah, they do that so if a bodyguard doubles as a driver, he or she, can stay with their person," Kallon says as we wait for Thomas, Allen, Brad, and Victor to stand next to the car.

"That's nice," I say, my nerves starting to get to me.

Kallon must hear it in my voice because he puts his finger under my chin and pulls my face towards him. He kisses me softly and says, "There's nothing to be nervous or scared about. We're here to watch the movie based on one of our favorite books, everything else is background noise, okay?"

"Okay," I say, but my voice quivers a little.

"Just hold my hand and you'll be okay," he says as he

squeezes my hand.

I squeeze it back and try to smile.

He looks over at Spencer and Mary and asks, "You guys ready?"

"Hell yeah," Mary says. She looks more excited than nervous.

Spencer just nods, he looks how I feel. I smile at him encouragingly.

Kallon taps on the window and then Allen is opening the door. When Kallon steps out the photographers go crazy. He fixes his suit jacket and then holds his hand out for me to take. I grab it and use it as a lifeline. When I emerge, the photographers all start yelling over one another.

"Mr. Keller, over here!"

"Mr. Keller, here, here! One shot!"

"Who's your date?"

"Who are you wearing, Mr. Keller?"

"Mr. Keller, over here!"

I step up next to Kallon and will myself to relax and smile. I don't need Kallon to have bad press pictures because his girlfriend can't handle a few pictures. I think about all the times Kallon has done or said something to make me feel good. I feel a genuine smile fall into place.

"She's gorgeous Mr. Keller, what's her name?" I hear someone shout.

I look over and see Spencer and then Mary getting out of the car. I look up at Kallon and see him smiling and waving friendly at people. He looks over and when he sees the other two are out of the car, he smiles down at me. So many flashes go off at once.

"Let's go," he says and then starts to walk us to the beginning of the red carpet. About halfway down, someone hollers for Kallon to stop for a picture. He obliges and pulls me to his side, wrapping his arm around my back.

"Who's your date?" someone in the crowd shouts.

"My girlfriend," Kallon says with a proud smile. He looks down at me and beams. I wink up at him and smile back.

"What's her name?" the same voice shouts. Kallon waves and starts walking us again.

Time seems funny on the red carpet. It feels both slow and fast because we stop every ten feet for pictures and then all of a sudden, we're inside, away from all the flashing lights.

"See, not so bad," Kallon says as he pulls us into the crowd of people. I reach back with my free hand and take Mary's hand, wanting us all to stay together. "You did amazing."

"Thanks," I say with a small laugh.

We spend the next hour visiting with the crew of the movie. A lot of them remembering me from my catering business and telling me how they've been having their assistants bring them breakfast from Rose Bud's. Mary and Spencer are thrilled to meet everyone and I'm happy to say they were all very nice to them.

Soon, we're finding our seats and getting comfy to watch 'Along Came You'. But watching this movie is a different experience. They're serving us dinner and drinks throughout the whole thing. I'm too busy watching to really eat but I sip on my drink as the movie goes on.

When the movie is over, the crowd goes into a standing ovation and some people whistle.

"That was so good," Mary says from beside me.

"Did you read the book I gave you at Christmas?" I ask.

She looks sheepishly at me as she continues to clap and says, "I haven't gotten around to it."

"They did a good job of making it into a movie, but the book is always better," I say with a laugh.

"I'm going to start it tonight," she says over the loud noise of the crowd. She taps Kallon on the shoulder and says, "You were amazing!"

"Thanks, Mary," Kallon says with a grin.

After Kallon makes his rounds, congratulating the director and producer, we make our way back out to the party area. Kallon motions Allen over and whispers something into his ear. Allen nods and then leaves quickly.

As we make our way to the front doors, where I see the flashing lights from cameras. Kallon notices me looking at him questioningly, and he says, "I sent him to get the cars. He and Victor are going to take Spencer and Mary home, while Thomas and Brad take us back to the hotel."

"Oh?" I ask.

"Yeah, I think we've waited long enough, don't you?" Kallon asks as his eyes travel hungrily down me and back up to meet my gaze.

"Most definitely," I say as I place my hand on his chest and reach up and give him a quick kiss.

I step away and tell Spencer and Mary the plan.

"Thanks for a great day," Mary says, giving Kallon a hug.

"Yeah, man, thanks," Spencer says, shaking Kallon's hand.

Mary gives me a hug and then Spencer does too.

"We're still meeting for breakfast, right?" I ask.

"Yeah, where should we go?" Mary asks over the noise as more people come into the room.

"Why not the hotel restaurant?" I suggest. "They have really good breakfast."

"Sounds good to us," Spencer says with a shrug.

"See you in the morning," I say, giving them another hug each.

Thomas opens the door and we step out into the craziness outside. The walk back down the carpet doesn't take nearly as long, Kallon doesn't stop for pictures. He just waves and smiles as we walk. When we get to the curb, the limo is waiting for us, and a black SUV is parked behind it with Allen waiting by the door for Mary and Spencer.

"Bye guys," I holler.

"Bye," they say back.

I hurry and get in and slide over so Kallon can get in. Brad shuts the door and Kallon slides over to me.

He's instantly kissing me, which I am all for. My hands slide into his hair and pull him to me. We kiss frantically and then Kallon slowly pulls away and leans over to the side of the car and pushes a button.

"Thomas, go the long way back to the hotel and it's no contact until we get there," he says.

He lets go of the button and as he comes back down to me, Thomas' voice comes on through the speaker and he says, "Yes, sir."

"I've been wanting to do this from the moment we were interrupted this morning," he says and lays me down on the long seat of the limo. He kisses me hard with his lips and then kisses down to my exposed cleavage. He pulls my dress up and runs his hand along my leg until he reaches my undies. He pulls them down and off.

"Kallon?" I ask, breathless.

"Trust me?" he asks.

I look down at him and then nod. He smiles and then kisses my sternum before he goes down below my dress. My back arches and I bite my hand to keep from screaming his name. I shove my dress into my mouth to keep me quiet all the way back to the hotel. The ride back was gloriously long.

CHAPTER 23

I'm lying on my side, just starting to wake up, well aware my alarm hasn't gone off yet. I feel the sheet covering me being pulled down my body, the silky fabric smooth against my skin. When it gets down to my mid-calf, I feel a finger skim up my leg, to my hip, to my ribs and then back down to my leg. It's so feather soft I almost think it's not real, until it starts its way back up. Once it gets to my ribs, it moves to my back and makes lazy circles.

"Mmm," I say, smiling sleepily. "That feels nice."

"Good morning," Kallon says, his breath tickling my face.

I open my eyes and see him mere inches from me. I don't have to stretch for my lips to find his.

"Good morning," I mumble against his lips. "What time is it?"

"7:30," Kallon says as his fingers continue to tickle my back.

"Mmm," I say as I lean into him, forcing him to his back. I kiss him deeply as I swing my leg over his legs and straddle him. I pull away and look him deeply in the eyes, "We're meeting my family for breakfast in an hour, right?"

His pupils dilate and he says, "Yes."

I bend down and kiss him again, pulling his bottom lip into my mouth gently. I feel a moan vibrate up his throat, which makes me smile. I let go of his lip and kiss down his neck, down to his collar bone, down to his pec. I flick my tongue across his nipple, causing him to suck in a sharp breath. I kiss over to his other nipple and again, flick my tongue across it.

"Shit, Abby," he says with a growl.

As I kiss back up his neck, I rotate my hips and feel his hard erection press against my ass cheek.

"Do you have another condom?" I ask, kissing to his ear and pulling his earlobe into my mouth.

"Yesss," he hisses out.

I continue kissing his neck and playing with his ear as he fumbles with something on the nightstand. Soon I hear ripping and then his hands are behind me. Once his hands are back to my hips, I reach down and take his erection firmly in one hand and guide it to where I need it.

As I slide down him in one fluid motion, Kallon sucks in a quick breath through his teeth and then moans out, "Abbbby... Shhhhit.... Fuuuuck..."

"Mmm," I say as I take possession of his mouth.

As I start to rock my hips, causing his erection to slip out just to the tip, I take him all the way to the hilt in one movement again. My inner walls clench at the heavenly feeling of him being so deep and filling.

"Fuuuck," I say with my own moan.

Kallon's hands on my hips, hold me as I speed up my

rocking. After a minute or two, his hands slide deliciously up to my waist and then they're palming my breasts. His thumbs roll my nipples between his forefingers and pinches just to the line between pain and pleasure. The sensation has me rocking faster.

"Kalllll," I say in a plea and a warning. My hands have been on his chest, using him as leverage but now I slide one hand down where I can rub myself into oblivion.

"Abby, shit... I'm... I'm..." Kallon says while gritting his teeth. I can feel he's fighting to not let loose.

"I'm almost there," I say, rubbing myself harder and faster, to match my rocking. "Pinch my nipples again, I liked that."

"Fuck me," Kallon growls but he hasn't gone over the edge yet. He stills and does as I ask. He rolls my nipples just a little harder.

"Yes!" I exclaim. "Just like that... YES!"

It doesn't take but one or two more rolls of each nipple before that exquisite sensation I've come to realize is the precursor to my orgasm flows to all my extremities. I apply more pressure to my little bundle of nerves and clinch Kallon and then I'm falling into ecstasy.

"Oh, fucking shit," I moan. "Now Kal, I'm... I'm..."

With one hand still holding a nipple in between his fingers, he takes his other hand and grabs my waist. He holds me to him as he lifts his hips up to meet me and thrusts deeper inside of me.

"Abby," Kallon moans my name. And with one hard thrust, he groans out in the deepest voice I've ever heard him use, "Fuuuucking hellllll!"

He moves his hand from my nipple to my waist to help hold me as he thrusts a couple more times and then he stills. I collapse on top of him and put my head to his chest. We're both silent, breathing in deep, calming breaths.

"That was..." Kallon says as he lets loose a deep breath.

"Yeah," I say, panting slightly.

"It just keeps getting better," he says as he runs his hands from my hips up to my back and starts his sweet circles again.

"Yeah it does," I say with a giggle and give his chest a kiss. I turn my head and see the clock on the nightstand says it's 7:50am. We need to be down in the restaurant in 40 minutes. I groan as I slide off Kallon, onto my back. "I don't think there's enough hours in the day to satiate my need for you."

My face goes red. I didn't mean to say that out loud. I roll my lips into my mouth and gently bite down. *I'll be damned if I say anything else as embarrassing right now.* Kallon must have felt me stiffen because he rolls to face me.

"I'm sorry, I didn't mean to say that," I blurt out. "I just meant... I really enjoy sex with you."

Kallon chuckles and says, "I really enjoy sex with you too and I also agree with you. There definitely is not enough hours in a day to do all the things we need to do, when what we want to do is so, so much better."

I laugh and turn my head to look at him.

"We need to get up and get ready," I say as my eyes travel from his face to his chest, to his abs, to his— *He's still hard?* My eyes dart to his eyes and I raise my eyebrows at him.

"I told you I agreed that there weren't enough hours," he

says as he looks down at himself. He shrugs and says, "I'll have to learn to live with it."

I bite my lip and try to do the math on if we have enough time for round two but decide against it. My nephew and niece are cute, but they turn into little monsters when they get hungry.

"We'll have to wait until we get home," I say with a sigh. "Let's hurry and get ready so we can go get some food."

"I think I can speak for both of us when I say that the waiting yesterday led to some pretty amazing pleasure later on in the evening," Kallon says, as he lazily runs a hand down my hip to my knee.

"Mmm," I say as my memory brings back last night.

Kallon had stayed down on me, bringing me over the edge multiple times before we got back to the hotel. He tucked my undies into his coat jacket and helped me pull my dress down. I let my hair down before we got out of the car, I could tell I'd made a mess of it rolling my head side to side. It was difficult to keep quiet so Thomas and Brad didn't hear me losing my mind.

Once we got to the elevator, Kallon made Brad wait for Thomas in the lobby. We had the elevator to ourselves all the way up to our floor. To say we were ready to ditch our clothes by the time we made it to the living room in the suite is an understatement. With Kallon's help, we made quick work of removing my boob tape. We made it as far as the couch before I had Kallon's pants down around his thighs and his incredible erection inside me.

Round one was a quick one, just to take the edge off. With my legs still wrapped around his waist, Kallon carried me into the bedroom and round two and three lasted much, much longer.

"Abby?" Kallon says my name, drawing me out of my reverie. I look at him and he asks with a soft laugh, "Where did you just go?"

"To last night," I say, putting my hand on his chest. I lean in and give him a kiss.

"Mmm," he says against my mouth before he pulls away. He says, "I haven't been able to stop thinking about last night either."

"If we start talking about it, we're not going to make it to breakfast," I say sadly.

Kallon pulls me to him and kisses me deeply.

"Then that will have to hold us over until we get home," he says as he pulls away.

"Let's hurry then," I say, rolling away from him. I stand, not bothering to take the sheet with me and say as I head to the bathroom, "We probably shouldn't shower together?"

Kallon doesn't say anything right away, so I look over my shoulder at him. He's staring at me like he can't get enough of me. I pause and turn to look at him, his eyes widen, and I watch as they travel from my legs up to my face.

"Sorry, did you say something?" he sounds honestly confused as to why I'm just standing here.

"You staring at me like that answered my question," I say with a laugh.

"Which was what?"

"That we shouldn't shower together."

"If you're set on having breakfast with your family... No, no we should not shower together," Kallon says with a chuckle. He leans back and puts his hands behind his head. The movement makes all of his muscles constrict and flex.

I shake my head and turn around and walk towards the bathroom. I say without looking, "You are evil."

He hollers at me with a laugh, "Why do you say that?"

"You know exactly why," I say as I turn to shut the door. I stick my tongue out at him and then smile.

Since we now only have about 30 minutes, I take a quick shower. I wash my hair, it still has all the hairspray in it, and wash all my lady bits. I get out and holler at Kallon.

"I'm all done, you can come get in now."

I wrap the towel around my back that I used to dry myself off with and tuck it in by my chest. I grab one of the smaller towels and wrap my hair into it to dry it a little more. I open my toiletry bag and pull my brush and makeup remover out. As I start to remove the makeup the shower didn't remove, the bathroom door opens, and Kallon walks in with a smile. And that smile is all he has on.

I smile back at him and say, "Shower is all yours."

"Thanks," he says as he walks by. As he does, he reaches his hand out and rubs it across my ass.

"Hey, hands to yourself, sir."

He puts his hands up, palms facing me, and says, "I can't help it, you're irresistible."

I roll my eyes and laugh at him.

"You should make your shower a cold one," I say as I point my brush at his still hard member.

"That's probably a good idea," he says as he looks down at himself.

I force myself to focus on my face, and not watch him

shower. I brush my hair and decide to just put it in a messy bun. I add a little eye mascara and eyeliner.

I walk out into the bedroom and dig through my suitcase and find my jeans and the light hoodie I had packed for today. I throw on a bra and undies, then socks, and then put my clothes on. I'm putting all of my other clothes into my suitcase when I hear the water turn off and then Kallon walks out of the bathroom with a towel around his waist. I don't think I'll ever get used to seeing him like this, he takes my breath away each time.

"You look nice," he says as he walks over to his suitcase. He pulls out his own pair of jeans, a black t-shirt, boxer briefs, and a fresh pair of socks. I dutifully ignore him when I hear his towel hit the floor. I finish packing and turn towards, him. He's got his bottom stuff on and is pulling on his shirt. His muscles ripple as he pulls the shirt over his head.

"You look good too," I say with a smile when he catches me looking at him. I pick up the dress and ask, "What do I do with this?"

He'd ripped it in his haste to get it off me last night, the zipper had gotten stuck.

"Just leave it here. I'll have Mr. Johnston come back and see if he can fix it," he says with a chuckle, but I see his cheeks flush a light pink.

"Okay," I say with a smile and lay it on the bed. I go into the bathroom and grab my bathroom bag and then add it to my suitcase.

Kallon is putting his dress shoes into his bag and then he's waiting at the door for me.

"You aren't taking your suit with you?" I ask, pointing to

it. He had left it on a chair last night after he'd gathered it from the floor in the other room.

"Mr. Johnston takes care of it for me," he says with a shrug. "He keeps track of all my suits and tuxes."

"Oh, that's nice," I say. I can't imagine having enough money that I could pay someone to take care of my fancy clothes. But then again, it would be really convenient to not have to worry about packing them while traveling.

"Ready?" Kallon asks as I walk up to him.

"Yup," I say. I kiss him quickly on the cheek and add, "I just have to grab the couple of things in the living room."

"Me too. I think my phone ended up somewhere out there," he says with a laugh.

"Mine too," I laugh with him.

We walk into the living room and find our phones on the floor next to the couch. Kallon's wallet is lying next to them. He hands me my phone and pockets his stuff. I look and see that I have about twenty-five percent left of my battery. *I'll charge it on the plane.* I walk into the kitchen and grab our chargers off the counter. I hand him his and put mine in my bag. I glance at the clock on the wall and see that it's a little after 8.

"All set?" Kallon asks as he reaches out for my suitcase.

"Yup," I say but instead of giving him my bag, I take his hand. "I'd rather hold your hand."

"Fair trade," he says with a wink. Before Kallon opens the door, he puts on his baseball hat. When he opens the door, we find Allen and Thomas standing outside.

"Morning Mr. Keller, Miss Rose," Allen says with a nod.

"Morning," I say, smiling warmly at them both.

"Morning," Kallon says. "We'll be having breakfast

downstairs but will need to be leaving a little after 9."

"Sounds good, sir. We'll have the car ready for you," Allen says as he takes Kallon's suitcase. Thomas reaches for mine, so I roll it over to him.

"Thank you, Thomas," I say as he takes it. He once again just nods in acknowledgement.

We walk to the elevator and have to wait a couple minutes before the door opens. Flash backs from last night race through my mind, heating my cheeks and my belly. I look up at Kallon and smile at him.

"Elevators are dangerous," he says for only me to hear.

I giggle and whisper back, "Dangerous in the most phenomenal way."

He laughs and nods his head. He pulls me to his side and drapes his arm around my shoulders. I wrap my arm around his back and rest my head on his chest.

The ride down doesn't take long. Once we get to the lobby, Allen and Thomas leave us as we enter the restaurant. Spencer and Mary wave at us as we scan the room. My niece and nephew, Annie and Max, turn and when they see us, wave ecstatically.

We walk quickly over to them and before we can sit down, the kids jump out of their seats and jump into my arms. I catch them both, hugging them tightly.

"Oh, I've missed you guys," I say, bending down so they can stand in front of me.

"Miss you too," Max says with a huge smile. I look at Annie and she hides behind my leg, being shy in front of Kallon.

"Annie, do you remember Kallon?" I ask her but she

shakes her head. "He's my friend."

She looks at him and then hides again. We laugh as we walk the short distance to the table.

"She might be the first girl to shy away from you," Spencer says with a chuckle as he shakes Kallon's hand.

"Atta girl, Annie," Kallon says as he smiles at her. She ducks behind me as I sit next to her in the booth.

Conversation between Kallon, Spencer, and Mary picks up from where it left off last night at the premiere. I enter in and out of the conversation, answering Max's questions and coloring with Annie. All too soon, we're walking to the front doors, saying our goodbyes again.

"When will we get to see you again?" Mary asks as she pulls away from our embrace.

"I'm not sure," I answer sadly. "Can you guys come to New York any time soon?"

"Maybe during summer?" Mary asks Spencer after he's done shaking Kallon's hand.

"Yeah, I think we could make that work," he says with a smile down at her.

"We'll have to plan something," I say. "Let me know."

"We will," Spencer says as he hugs me. "Tell Dad, Mom, and Patty we said hi and give them hugs for us."

"I will," I say as I step back to Kallon.

"Let us know when you land," Mary says as she's being pulled down the sidewalk by Max. He'd had enough sitting around, I'm actually surprised he lasted as long as he had.

"Will do," I say.

"Bye," Mary and Spencer say at the same time and wave at us.

"Bye," I say and wave back.

Kallon raises a hand and says, "See you later."

Kallon puts his hand on my lower back and turns me to him. I smile up at him and kiss him softly on the lips. I can't let myself get carried away, there isn't anywhere for us to have decent alone time. I can behave until we get back to New York.

A shiver runs down my spine as the wind blows into us. The air is especially cold today. I look out at the sky and see some angry gray clouds in the distance. *It's June for crying out loud.*

A car pulls up and Thomas gets out of the front passenger side. He opens the back door and Kallon gestures for me to get in. I slide in and buckle while Kallon gets in. I slide my hand over to his and hold on to it, it's fast becoming a habit.

"What time—" I yawn "—are we supposed to take off?"

"Any time after 10," Kallon says with a smile. "Do you need a nap?"

"After last night and this morning, yes," I say quietly so that Allen and Thomas can't hear me.

"Rest up, I plan on making you even more tired tonight," Kallon says in his deep, sexy voice.

"Sounds like a plan to me," I say, leaning my head against his shoulder and closing my eyes. The overwhelming need for sleep takes me under.

◆ ◆ ◆

"Abby," Kallon says my name softly. I feel his hand caress my cheek and then my neck. "We're at the airport."

"That was quick," I say, opening my eyes and looking around.

"Traffic was light," Kallon says with a chuckle. "Let's get onboard and you can go back to sleep."

"Okay," I say. Allen opens my door and I'm greeted with a burst of frigid air. I suck in my breath and hiss out, "What the crap?"

"They've got the jet nice and warm for us," Kallon says as he starts to get out of the car. He hurries around and tucks me under his arm to protect me from the icy wind.

"This is ridiculous," I say as we hurry to the stairs leading up to the jet.

"Morning, Miss Rose, Mr. Keller," Brody says as he holds out a blanket for me. "I thought you'd like to wrap up. It's a little chilly today."

"Oh, bless you Brody," I say as I turn and let him put the blanket on my shoulders. Kallon pulls it tight in front of me and then rubs my shoulders. I turn and head up the stairs quickly, not wanting Kallon to freeze. I look behind me and see Brody carrying our suitcases and the car pulls away.

We get onboard and see Captain Zeels in the cockpit. He turns and smiles at us.

"Welcome aboard, Miss Rose," he says. He nods at Kallon and adds, "We're clear for takeoff as soon as you've taken your seats, sir."

"Thank you, Zeels," Kallon says.

I walk to about mid jet and grab a seat facing the front of the jet this time. I can feel the warm hair blowing in from the vent. I take the blanket from around my shoulders, buckle my belt, and then pull the blanket up to my chin,

"You'll warm up soon," Kallon says as he sits down next to me. "If there was a sleeper in the back, I know of a way I could warm you up quicker."

I elbow him in the side and laugh, but then I see Brody walking towards us. I whisper hiss to Kallon, "Shh, you can't talk like that."

"Why not?" Kallon asks in his regular volume.

"It's not nice," I say, giving him a look but then bust out laughing,

He laughs too but stops when Brody steps up beside him.

"Can I get you two a drink before we take off?"

Kallon looks at me, but I shake my head and say, "I'm good for now. Thanks, though."

"We're okay, thanks," Kallon says. He turns to me and pats his shoulder. "Rest, we'll be home before you know it."

A yawn escapes me which makes me laugh a little, but I lean my head onto Kallon's arm. I wrap my arm touching him, under and around his, so I can hold his hand. I close my eyes and listen to the sound of the engines, and once again, I doze off to dreamland.

I'm jolted awake by the feel of the jet going up and then down really fast. I sit up fast, my eyes flying wide. I look around and see Kallon looking towards the cockpit.

"What's going on?" I ask, rubbing the sleep out of my eyes. My heart pounding fast at the unexpected jolt.

"We've gotten into a winter storm," Kallon says. "The turbulence is being nasty."

"Do we need to land somewhere and wait it out?" I ask anxiously.

"Unfortunately, there's nowhere to land," Kallon says sounding upset. "We're too far away to turn back. The closest place is ahead of us, so the best plan is to keep on our flight plan."

The jet bounces up and down again and again. I reach out and grab Kallon's arm and my other hand goes to the armrest.

"It's okay," Kallon says as he puts his hand over mine. "I won't let anything happen to you."

I'm too scared to tell him there's not a lot he can do if we crash, but I keep that thought to myself. The next bout of turbulence makes some things back by Brody topple over. He unbuckles and starts to pick the stuff up quickly.

I open my mouth to tell him to buckle back up, but I feel like I'm going to puke. I take calming breaths, telling myself turbulence is normal and that we'll be fine. But the next jump the jet does makes my heart fall to my stomach and then when the jet falls back down, my ass leaves the seat until the lap buckle presses into me and keeps me from completely flying up to the ceiling. When the jet bounces back up, my ass hits the seat, and my heart feels like it falls all the way to my feet this time.

I hear beeping coming from the cockpit. And then the jet starts to vibrate roughly.

"Shit," I hear Captain Zeels shout.

Kallon looks like he's about to unbuckle his belt but then

another bump makes him reach out and grab his armrest.

"Do not take that thing off," I say through gritted teeth. I let go of my armrest and put that hand on his, keeping him put.

"I was just going to tighten it," he says as he reaches down and tightens his belt and then does the same to me.

More beeping sounds from the cockpit and then the vibrating turns into full on shaking. The front of the jet dips and if I wasn't belted in, I would have a front row seat next to the captain.

"What's happening?" I shout over the beeping and now a loud alarm is going off.

"I think..." Kallon says and then pauses. He looks at me with the most horrified look on his face. "I think we're going down."

"What?" I cry out. Tears start to pour down my face.

Kallon turns and covers his body over mine, holding me so tightly it's almost painful. I reach out and hold him just as tight.

"Brace for impact!" we hear Captain Zeels yell.

"I've got you... I've got you... I've got you," Kallon repeats over and over until the jet hits somethin suddenly hard. From clenching my teething together tightly, I feel like they could shatter from the jarring impact.

The plane turns to the side, and I hit my head on the window and then blackness instantly takes me.

CHAPTER 24

I feel myself starting to wake up and I feel a heavy weight on my lap. *Kallon must have fallen asleep on me.* When I feel more awake, I'm greeted with a ringing in my ears and a pounding headache. *I must have drank way too much last night,* I think to myself as I try to open my eyes. But reality hits me hard when I get my eyes open.

Kallon is in fact lying on my lap but we're on the jet. Memory of the crash rushes through me. I look down at Kallon and touch his back.

"Kallon?" I say in a shaky voice. He doesn't respond. Panic coats my voice as I say louder, "Kal?"

He still doesn't respond. Hysteria threatens to take over as I turn him so I can see his face better and I see a massive gash on his forehead. I gasp and then hold my breath as I reach a hand to his neck and pray to find a pulse. I find one and let out my breath and start to bawling.

"Kal?" I cry, giving him a gentle shake. He still doesn't respond. I look up to the cockpit and see Captain Zeels is hunched over and part of the windshield is gone. I look beyond the windshield and see nothing but white. I look to where

Brody should be sitting but don't see him. I look to the floor and see his feet sticking out from beneath what looks like a toppled over cart and countless other things.

"Kallon?" I shout, hoping this time he'll answer me, but he doesn't.

I grab his shoulders and using all my strength, push him so he's leaning back against his seat. The blood from his head wound has left a huge patch on my pants. I unbuckle my seat belt and stand. I'm greeted with dizziness. I put my hand to my head and feel wetness. When I pull it away I find blood. *I must be bleeding too.* I take calming breaths and check myself for any other injuries, but I don't find any. I then unbuckle Kallon's seatbelt and as carefully as I can, I ease him down to the floor and do a quick check of him. I don't find any other injuries, at least no visible ones.

I stumble to Brody and move all the random stuff off him and then push the cart away. I gasp as I see his arm behind his back in an unnatural position. I carefully roll him away from his injured arm and then gently pull it out from behind him. I lay it across his chest and then use a towel lying nearby as a sling to secure it to him.

I grit my teeth and head to the Captain. I have to check him, but I'm really scared he might be dead. I step next to him and breathe deeply as I look around at his face. He's bleeding from his head worse than Kallon. I reach for his neck and find a pulse. *Thank the heavens!*

I turn his chair as far around as I can and unbuckle him from his seat. The cold air coming in from the broken windshield is going to make this situation so much worse. Pushing that thought from my head, I try with all my might to be gentle with Craig, as I lower him to the floor. I slide my arms under his armpits until he's in the crook of my arms. I pull him out and lay him next to Brody. It's as far as I can get him. He's a big guy.

I step around Brody and Craig and look in the cupboards for a first aid kit. I don't find one. I remember Kallon saying there was a place to sit in the back, so I make way to the back of the plane, stopping to check on Kallon. He's still bleeding profusely but he still has a pulse.

Once I get to the back room, I find a closet full of blankets and finally an EMT size first aid kit. I open it and find just about anything I could need. I grab a couple towels from a cupboard and head back out to the front. But I spot something in the corner. I walk over to it and find a large mat. I pick it up and start to drag it to the front.

"This might work to block the open windshield," I say to myself. "It could keep the cold air out, at least a little bit."

I kneel down next to Kallon and put a towel to his head. I'm about to pull it away when I feel something trickle down my face. I reach up and I'm reminded that I'm bleeding as well. I think adrenaline is keeping the pain away, for the time being.

Deciding I should probably at least put a bandage on my head so I stop bleeding all over the place, I dig through the bag to see what I can find. I see a couple foam neck braces and pull them out and set them beside me. I grab a shiny can in the bag and use it as a mirror. I see a huge goose egg that has a large gash down the middle of it. I find a gauze that looks to be big enough and set it on my leg. I grab the med tape and rip off a couple strips, using the bag to hold them. I put the gauze to my forehead and then tape it in place. Once I'm satisfied that it won't go anywhere, I turn my attention back to Kallon.

Before I move the towel from his head, I place one of the neck braces around his neck as carefully as I can. When I move the towel I see where the bleeding is coming from. He has a large cut on the side of his head, above his ear, not on his forehead like I thought. I put the towel back and then dig in the bag to see if there's anything I can use to stop the bleeding. I find some bigger gauze pads and pull them out. I also find some adhesive bandage wraps and decide that'll work to keep the pads in place.

I open one of the gauze packets and roll out a good amount of the wrap before I remove the towel again. I quickly put the gauze on and apply pressure, it starts to look soaked instantly. I put the wrap down and reach for another gauze packet and open it with my teeth. I pull the gauze out and put it on top of the one that's on his head. When I see that it stays white, I grab the wrap and wrap it around the front of Kallon's head. When I get to the back of his head, I make sure the gauze won't fall off before I reach back and gently lift his head up off the floor. I go around his head three times before I'm satisfied that the bandage won't go anywhere.

I check his arms and legs the best I can to see if I can feel any indication that he might have any broken bones, but I don't find anything. I grab the med bag and the towels and head back to Brody and Craig. I check Brody over again for any blood and luckily I don't find any. I turn to Craig and see he looks a little pale.

"Shit," I say out loud. *He must be losing more blood than I thought.*

I hurry and put a neck brace on him as well and then

put a towel where I think he's bleeding from, the right side of his forehead. I rip open three gauze packets and l get some more wrap unrolled. I remove the towel and see that I guessed correctly. He has a gaping wound just below his hairline on his forehead. I hurry and apply all three gauze pads and then wrap his head three times. I sit and watch to make sure he doesn't bleed through the bandage. While I wait, I check him for any noticeable broken bones but again, I don't find any. Once I see that he's not bleeding through the bandage, I hurry to the back of the plane and grab blankets for the three unconscious men.

I lay one on top of Kallon and check his bandage, it still looks good. I go back to the other two men. I tuck a blanket around Brody and then the other around Craig. When I stand, my head pounds so hard, it about drops me back to my knees. I dig through the med bag that's still next to Craig and find Tylenol. I pop three and choke them down, I don't have time to look for something to drink.

Satisfied with doing what I can for the guys, I look around for mine and Kallon's cellphones, but I can't find them anywhere. I look for my bag, but it could be anywhere in this mess. I see the mat lying on the floor, and I'm reminded I was going to try to block the broken windshield. I pick it up and walk back to the front and climb into the cockpit. It takes a minute, but I figure out how to maneuver the mat so it covers about ninety-five percent of the broken window. I smile and sit back in the captain's chair. I look around and try to find what switch works the radio to use it to call for help. It takes me a minute, but I finally find it. I start on Channel 1.

"Anyone there? Mayday. Mayday. Is anyone there?" I say and then wait a couple minutes. "Mayday. Mayday. Is anyone there?"

I wait a couple more minutes and then change the channel to 2 and try again.

"Mayday, Mayday. Is anyone there?" I ask again. When I don't get a reply, I go to Channel 3 and try again. Once I get to 4 with no reply, I decide to check on the guys.

I find Craig starting to bleed through his bandage, so I add two more gauze to his head and secure it with new med tape. I walk over to Kallon and see he's still good. I stand and look around. I lean over and look out the window and see we're in the middle of a blizzard.

"Great," I say annoyed. "Just what we need."

I look around our seats for our cellphones, but I don't find them. I walk around the other sitting areas, and I still can't find my bag. Shaking my head, I head to the area Brody usually sits and pull out the food I find in the cupboards, and I find some small notebooks.

"Hmmm," I say. "It might be good to keep track of when I check these guys. So, if... no when, when we're rescued the paramedics will know what I did if I'm not conscious to tell them.

I put some food down next to Craig and Brody and then grab three notepads. I rummage around in the drawers until I find a pen. I write Brody's name on the first page of the one I'll use for him and write what I found and what I did to hopefully help him. I go to look at my wrist for the time, but I'm reminded that I didn't bring my watch with me. I look to Craig and Brody's wrists and see that Craig is wearing one. I gently take it off his arm and put it on mine. When I look at the time, I'm shocked.

Craig's watch tells me it's 12:18. I would have figured we'd been here —wherever here is— longer than an hour or two. Unless the watch is broken, it does in fact show it's 12:18.

I grab Brody's notepad and guestimate how long it's been since I woke up and guess about what time I started working on them all. After I've written in all the guys' books, I put the two by Craig and Brody and then walk back to Kallon and put his beside him. I walk back to the back room and pull out some more blankets and add one to each of the guys.

I go back to the food and start separating it into piles to figure out what we have to work with, as well as all the drinks that were in the little fridge. Once I have it all organized, I go and check Kallon again. He's still good. I walk to the front to check on Craig again. He needs another gauze added. I add two more and tape them to him. This bleed through wasn't nearly as bad as the last, so hopefully he stops bleeding soon. I make a note in his book and then go to the cockpit.

I start with Channel 5 and work my way through all the channels with no response on any of them. Just as I'm about to start over and try Channel 1 again, I feel something trickle down my neck. I reach up and find blood.

"Shit," I say. I walk back out of the cockpit and stop at the med bag and grab a couple gauzes and the med tap. I head to the back where the bathroom is and use the mirror this time. When I look at myself, I see that I've completely soaked through the bandage. I apply two gauzes with pressure and tape them securely in place.

On my way back to the front, I check Kallon who is doing the same, as are Brody and Craig. I grab a couple more Tylenol's, hoping the right amount will make my head stop hurting. I sit and eat some crackers and drink some water, maybe that'll help the pain meds take effect.

I go to the cockpit and start over on the Channels. I still get no response. I walk back out to where Kallon and I were sitting and dig down into the seats to see if maybe our phones fell into the crack. My hand comes in contact with something and when I pull it out, it's my phone. I dig around some more and find Kallon's phone.

"YES!" I exclaim. I tap the screens and my heart plummets. We have no service. I turn to my Emergency settings and send out an SOS message, in hopes that if at some point, I get at least one bar, the message will be sent. I also notice that it says it's Monday and the time is 1:27pm. I look at the watch on my wrist and see that it also says 1:27.

"How long was I knocked out for? It's Monday afternoon? Was I really unconscious for 24 hours? How can that be, wouldn't our head injuries have bled us out?"

I know head injuries can bleed like crazy, but we don't just have a cut on our heads. Not wanting to focus too much on the why's, I count our blessings and go check on the guys.

After I record no changes, I check the phones and find no service still. I go back to the cockpit and try the radio again. I'm not surprised when I don't get a response. I walk to the back and grab the rest of the blankets and a pillow. I cover the guys with another blanket each and then go and sit next to Kallon.

I feel exhausted and cold. I grab my blanket off the floor near where I was sitting and put it over Kallon. I then lift all four blankets and snuggle in next to him, careful not to move him. I put the pillow under my head and decide to take a nap.

CHAPTER 25

I wake with a start and look around, remembering instantly where I am and what happened. I scramble to my knees and check Kallon. He's breathing evenly and his bandage hasn't bled through. I grab my phone from the floor and check the time. It's 7:09pm, still Monday. I write in Kallon's book and then stand and stretch quickly.

I hurry to Brody and Craig and check them. Thankfully Craig hasn't bled through his bandages in the hours that I was asleep.

"Maybe the worst for them is over," I say, feeling that overwhelming exhaustion hit me like a ton of bricks again. I push it down and away as I write in their books and then go and sit in the cockpit.

I try to send another SOS from my phone and then I use the camera to check my bandage and see that I need another gauze. I grab two from the med bag with the tape again and go sit in the cockpit. I use my camera to put the new gauzes to my bandage. When I'm finished, I turn the chair towards the control panel. I start my Channel surfing on the radio, putting the headset on.

"Mayday. Mayday. Is anyone there?" I ask unenthusiastically.

"Yes, we're here! My name is Elliot Jones, I'm an FAA agent. Who is this?"

My heart flies to my throat.

"My name is Abbigail Rose. I'm a passenger on Kallon Keller's private jet. I don't know the number or any of that."

"Oh, thank goodness. We've been trying to reach you. Where is your pilot, Miss Rose? A Mr. Craig Zeels?"

"He's unconscious. Kallon and Brody, Brody Welch, the flight attendant, are also unconscious."

"Is there anyone else on board?"

"No, just the four of us."

"Okay, can you help us by flipping the location toggle. It will send out a signal every five seconds so we can pinpoint your location."

"Yes! What does it look like? Where do I look?"

"It's a big red switch, in the middle of the controls. Down to the right of the steering column, do you see it?"

I look around and see two large red switches.

"There are two," I say, pointing at the switches like I think if I don't they'll disappear. There's no response from Elliot, so I ask, "Hello? Are you still there?"

"Switch them both. One is for the signal and the other is for the emergency lights on the outside."

I turn on both switches.

"Okay, done."

"Okay, while we wait a minute to see if we catch your signal, can you tell us what happened and what injuries there are?"

"We left Seattle around 10 am Sunday morning. I'm not

sure where we are but we flew through a massive snowstorm. Then the plane started shaking and bouncing really bad. It was the worst turbulence I've ever experienced. Craig yelled for us to brace for impact and then Kallon wrapped himself around me. I remember bumping into him and then my head hit something really hard. I woke up and realized we had crashed. I checked on everyone. Kallon has a gash on his head, but I was able to get it to stop bleeding. I don't think he has any other injuries, at least not visibly. Brody has a broken arm but nothing else as far as I can tell. Craig has a gash on his forehead, and it seems the worst. I had to add quite a few new gauze pads to his bandage before it would stop seeping through. But, I don't think he has any other injuries either."

"And yourself?" Elliott asks as I take a breath.

"I have a large goose egg on my head with a pretty good size gash as well. I had to add two gauzes not too long ago. I took a nap and woke up to it soaked through. I don't have any other injuries. I have a bad headache that I can't seem to get rid of. Oh, I also put neck braces on Kallon and Craig, just to be safe."

"It sounds like you've done amazingly well. Do you have EMT training?"

"None. Just basic CPR and First Aid," I say. I hear him say something away from the microphone.

"Good news Miss Rose, we have your location... what's that —" he says that away from the microphone again *"—Miss Rose, have you been sending SOS messages from your cellphone?"*

"Yes," I say. I'm filled with so much relief, I start to cry.

"Okay, sit tight, help is on the way. I'm going to sign off for now, but we'll make sure this Channel is clear just for you in case

you need something, okay?"

"Okay."

"Don't hesitate to reach out if you need anything. If you hit the button to the right of where your headset is plugged in, you can hear us over the speakers in case we need to get ahold of you."

"Okay."

I take the headset off and push the button that Elliot told me to push. I check on Craig and Brody and find no changes, although Craig still looks pale. I walk to Kallon and check on him and happily find no changes as well. I walk back to the med bag and grab the bottle of Tylenol and dump out four this time. I take the bottle with me as I stop and grab a bag of chips and a water and go sit down next to Kallon.

I eat a couple chips and drink some water before I take the pain reliever. *I wish my head would stop hurting.* I drink the rest of the water and eat the rest of my chips. I feel my eyelids getting heavy, so I lie back down next to Kallon like I had before and close my eyes.

I'm startled awake by my name being called loudly.

"Miss Rose, are you still with us?"

I scramble to my feet, ignoring the dizziness and nausea that swims through me, and I hurry to the cockpit. I put on the head set quickly.

"Yes, I'm here."

"I have some good news. The local law enforcement and their search and rescue rallied and got set up when they received

your SOS messages so when we told them your location, they said it would take them about three hours to get to you. That was two hours ago. They should be getting to you in about an hour. Can you look out any of the windows and see anything?"

I look out and says, "No, it's too dark."

"Okay, that's alright. You've crashed in the Rockies, Northwest of Denver, CO."

"Is there anything I can do to help them find us quicker?"

"No, just sit tight they'll be—" crackle noise *"—soon."*

"Hello?"

No response.

"Hello? Elliot?"

No response.

"Don't panic, help is on the way."

I check my phone and see that it's almost 9:30pm but then my screen blinks black and when I push the side button, it shows a dead battery. I chuck my phone as I go and check Craig and Brody and make a note in their books that they seem to be stable. I go and lie back down next to Kallon, but I can't relax.

I go to the back room and rummage through the drawers and find an air horn. I hurry to the side door and open it as much as possible, which is just barely enough for my hand to reach outside. I blow the horn, and it hurts my ears and head. I grit my teeth and blow it again. I shut the door and lean over to the window closest to the door and I look outside. I see this side of the jet is up against a bunch of trees.

"Ugh... mmmm... ugh..." I hear pained moans from behind me. I turn and see Kallon reaching a hand up to his neck and then to his head.

"Kallon!" I shout and race over to him. "Try not to move."

"Abby?" he says as he opens his eyes. "What happened?"

"We crashed," I say. Kallon tries to sit up, but I gently push him back down.

"What?" he exclaims. "Are you okay?"

"Stay down, please. I'm okay."

"My head," he groans out.

"Yeah, you have a gnarly gash. Does anything else hurt?"

He moves his arms and legs and then tries to move his head to the side but can't because of the neck brace.

"No, everything else feels fine," he winces and touches his head.

"Do you want to try some Tylenol. There is nothing stronger."

"Yes, please."

I grab the bottle from my pocket and dump out a couple pills. I walk over to the pile of food and grab some crackers and a water. I help Kallon eat and drink and then pop the pills into his mouth.

"Why do I have this on?" he asks as he touches the brace.

"Precaution, leave it on. I didn't know if you'd hurt your spine while you were—" I take a shaky breath "—while you were protecting me as we crashed."

"Didn't do a very good job, did I?" he asks, reaching up and touching my bandage on my head.

"Are you kidding?" I say as I take his hand. "This is all I have to show for being in a plane crash. You have a similar injury and possibly something else."

"Nothing else hurts," he states as he takes another drink of water. Then he eats another cracker. Worry crosses his face and his eyes dart around all that he can see and asks, "Brody?

Craig? Are they? Are they okay?"

"Yes, well no but yes. Both are still unconscious like you were. Craig has a bad head gash but no broken bones that I can see. Brody has a broken arm, as far as I can tell."

"Is anyone coming to get us?"

"Yes, they should be here within the hour. I lost radio connection with the FAA agent, but before that, he assured me they'd be getting to us soon."

"What time is it?"

I look at the watch and say, "It's after 9:40pm, Monday night."

"Monday?" he chokes out the water he just tried to drink.

"Yeah, you guys have been out for minute."

"And you? You've done all of this alone?" he points at his neck, his head, and then at me.

"Well yeah, what else could I have done? I wasn't going to let you all bleed to death."

Kallon tries to take his neck brace off.

"What are you doing? Leave that on," I say again as I sit in front of him and stop his hands from removing it.

"I don't need it, my neck is fine," he says, holding my hands. "I want to kiss you."

I lean towards him and say, "I'll give you a kiss if you leave that thing on. Just until a paramedic can say it's okay for you to take it off."

"Deal," he says, pulling me towards him by my hands.

I laugh and bend the rest of the way down to him and kiss him. I ignore the throbbing this angle has on my head.

"Abby," he says against my lips. I pull back and stare at him. "I really, really like you."

I laugh and kiss him softly and then mumble against his lips, "I really, really like you too, Kal."

"Have I told you how much I love it when you call me that?" he says and then kisses me sweetly.

I smile into his lips and pull away so I can lie down next to him, placing my head on his chest. He wraps his arm around me and holds me tightly to him. I'm about to fall back asleep when we're started by Elliot's voice over the speaker.

"Miss Rose, are you there?"

"I'll be right back, that's the FAA agent, Elliot. Stay put, please," I say to Kallon as I roll away from him.

Kallon nods and rests his hands on his chest. I hurry to the cockpit and put the headset on again.

"I'm here."

"Did you blow a horn of some type recently?"

"I did, yes!"

"Do it again. The search party heard it and were able to redirect themselves towards you. They were close but the blizzard was proving to be difficult."

"Okay!" I exclaim. I put the headset down and rush back out.

"They're close," I say to Kallon as I go to the door. I grab the air horn and stick my hand back out as far as I can reach and give it three long, loud blows. I count to ten and do it again. And wait another count of ten and blow it again, three more times.

My hand is starting to freeze so I pull it back inside.

"I'm going to go check on Craig and Brody," I say to Kallon as I set the horn down next to him. "I'll be right back."

"Okay."

Brody still looks the same, but Craig looks even paler. I bend down and look at his bandage closer, but I don't see any more blood. I run my hand over his shirt and behind his back, but it comes away clean. *I don't understand why he keeps getting paler.*

I walk back to Kallon and say, "Brody still looks the same, but Craig looks paler. I sure hope the search team is as close as Elliott says. I don't think he'll last another day out here. He must have some internal injuries."

"Do you hear that?" Kallon asks.

I stop before I say no and listen.

"That sounds like a snowmobile," I say excitedly once I hear the sound Kallon had heard.

"Yeah, it does," Kallon agrees with a huge smile.

I run back to the door and start blowing the horn with a vengeance. I don't stop even when I can see the headlights of our rescuers pulling up beside us.

"It's okay, we're here!" one of them shouts as he jumps off his snowmobile. I stop blowing the air horn and feel myself shaking.

Four large side by sides pull up behind the five or six snowmobiles.

"Are you Miss Rose?" a man asks.

"I… am…" I say through chattering teeth.

"How's everyone doing in there?" he asks as I watch as the other start to unload things from the snowmobiles and the back of the side by sides.

"Kallon.. woke… up—" shiver "—Brody… is sttttill… out.. bbbbut hasn't… chhhhanged... Craig… seems… worse… He nnnneeds… tttttaken ffffirst."

"How are you doing?"

"I'mmm okkkay… I th-th-think my… adrenalin… is ffffading… and shhhock is… setting in… I ddddon't feel… too cccold… but I'm… shhhhaking… unnncccconnnntrrrrolllllabbbbbly nnnnow," I finally get out.

"Okay, we'll get you guys out of here," he looks at the tree that's keeping the door from opening all the way. He turns and shouts, "We're going to have to cut this tree down!"

Without needing to be told, I go back over to sit next to Kallon. He tries to wrap a blanket around me.

"Breathe Abs, you did great. Just breathe and we'll be going home soon," he says as he wraps his arm around the front of my waist. His arm is wonderfully warm.

It doesn't take long for them to get the tree out of the way. When the first person comes in the plane, I start to cry.

"It's okay, Abs," Kallon says, pulling me closer to his side.

"I know… I'm… jjjusssst so… happpppy they'rrrre… here… I wwwas… so… scccared," I say through chattering teeth while trying to not burst into hysterics.

"I know and you did so good," he says, squeezing me.

A lady first responder comes up to me and says, "Miss Rose, my name is Kami."

I wave her off and point back to the front and say, "Craig first… He's… innn… bbbbad shhhhape."

"Shock isn't something to mess with, "Kami says.

"Th-th-th-ank you… but I… wwwwant Crrrraig taken… first," I chatter.

"Abby maybe—" Kallon starts to say but I cut him off.

"Nnnno Kkkkkal," I take a steading breath. "You gggguys ffffirst."

"Not a chance, you're going out before me," he says sternly.

I ignore him as I watch Kami and another EMT go to Brody and Craig. Kami runs to the door and yells that they need stretchers before she runs back to the guys. Soon three more guys come in and two are carrying stretchers.

Another EMT guy comes on the plane and I point at Kallon. He starts looking him over. We hear Kami yell, "One coming out."

I was watching Kallon get checked so I didn't see her go to the door. She stands off to the side as two guys haul Craig out the door on one of the stretchers. I look back at Kallon and see the EMT helping Kallon sit up. When I look back at the door, another EMT is coming in after Craig is long out of sight.

He comes to me and says, "Can I have a look at you?"

I nod and sit patiently while he prods around my head, I wince every time he applies any type of pressure. The throbbing picks up and the ringing starts again. He turns my head to the side so I can't see the front of the plane, but I hear Kami says, "We're ready with the second."

I turn my head and watch them take Brody out. When he's out the door and gone, I feel my body sag, so I lean into Kallon for support.

"Abby?" Kallon says as he tries to lean around me. "Hey, stay awake!"

"It's okay, Mr. Keller, we've got her," I hear someone say beside me.

I try to turn my head to the voice, but it feels so heavy. I try to look over at Kallon, but I'm overwhelmed with the need to shut my eyes and go to sleep. The outside of my vision starts to get hazy and dark. I close my eyes and blink hard, trying to clear out the fuzz but when I open my eyes, it's all dark.

It's all dark. Pitch black. I feel myself sigh and let the darkness take me under.

CHAPTER 26

BEEP——**BEEP**——**BEEP**——**BEEP**

It takes me a minute to figure out what that sound is, but I realize it's a heart monitor. I turn my head and feel something pull on my nose. I reach up to feel what's in it and I'm greeted with a sharp pinch on the top of my hand.

"Easy there," I hear a familiar voice say. I open my eyes and see Jason sitting in a chair next to my bed, the opposite side of the hand that got pinched. He's holding my free hand. I look down at my pinched hand and see I have an IV stuck into it. He reaches up and pushes a button on a cord.

"Jason?" I ask confused, looking around the room. "Where am I?"

"You're at Presbyterian," he says with a smile.

"In New York?" I ask.

"Yes," he says with a nod.

I close my eyes tight and think hard about how I got here and come up with nothing. I look down at my hands and reach up with my free IV hand and touch my head. I feel it wrapped in a bandage. I touch my nose and find that I have nasal oxygen.

"What happened?" I ask.

"You don't remember?" he asks.

I gently shake my head no.

"You were in an accident," he says.

I blink and look up at him and ask, "I was?"

"Yes, you got here a couple of days ago," Jason says, squeezing my hand. "Your parents are out of state, and you still have me as your emergency contact, so they called me."

"Still have you..." I start to say confused, but then my memory comes back. Jason attacking me. The year since then. Kayla's wedding. This past weekend. I pull my hand out of Jason's and say, "What are you doing here?"

"I came to be with you," he says.

"No," I say. "I remember everything now."

"I'm sorry," he says, reaching for my hand again. "If I could take everything back I would. You wouldn't be lying here in a hospital bed if we had still been together."

"Jason, you put me in a bed similar to this a year ago," I say through clenched teeth.

"I know and I'll spend the rest of my life making that up to you," he says and then he pulls a small box out of his pocket and opens the lid. There's a huge diamond ring inside it. "Marry me."

He doesn't ask, he says it as a demand.

"No, Jason. I don't want to be with you," I say, panic starting to rise inside of me. I reach my hand back and push the button again and again.

"Please, Abby," he pleads. "Let me show you how much I love you."

"NO!" I shout. "Get out of my room!"

"Abby," he says, stunned.

A nurse comes in and stops at the door.

"Is everything okay?" she asks.

"No, I don't want him here," I state as I pull my blanket up to my chest. "He's not supposed to be near me."

"Abby, that—" Jason starts to say but I cut him off.

"I have a restraining order against you, you know that," I say. "Jason, we're over. We've been over the second you put your hands on me a year ago. Get. Out!"

My head starts to throb harder.

"Sir, I think you should leave," the nurse says.

"But I'm going to marry her," Jason says.

"You are not," I say exasperatedly.

"Sir," the nurse says, coming to stand next to him. "It's time to go."

"But—"

"Out," she says, pointing towards the door. Another nurse shows up at the door. "Leah, please escort him to the front doors. He's not to be allowed back into Miss Rose's room."

The nurse, Leah, nods and steps out of the way as Jason stumbles to her.

"Have you been drinking?" I ask in shock.

"I've been worried about you," he says as he gets to the door. "I love you."

"And that right there is another reason why we are over," I say as I lean my head back against my pillow.

I watch as Leah gestures for him to continue walking. He gets out of sight when I hear him say, "I'm going to marry you, Abbigail Rose!"

"You might want to get that restraining order tightened up," the nurse says from beside me. I nod my head and then wince. "How are you feeling?"

"My head hurts," I say and then panic hits me. I blurt out, "Kallon?"

"He's alright," she says patting my shoulder as she looks at the monitor.

"Craig and Brody?" I ask trying to sit up.

"It's okay, they're all fine. Just calm down," she says. "I'm your nurse, Jill."

"Where are they?" I ask.

"Mr. Zeels is in ICU, he's improving but hasn't woken up yet. Mr. Welch is down the hall and woke up this morning. Mr. Keller is across the hall," she says as she turns and points.

We see a nurse trying to keep him in his bed, but he's determined to get up. She gestures for him to wait so he sits on his bed, his eyes not leaving me. Once she has his IV pole ready, he stands and gathers his gown behind his back and walks over to my room.

"Abby?" he says hurriedly. Jill moves to the other side of my bed, looking over my own IV pole. When he gets to my side he says with so much relief in his voice, it makes my heart squeeze. "Abby..."

"Kallon," I say reaching out my hand to him.

"You scared me! Don't do that to me ever again," he says with worry.

"What did I do?" I ask, confused.

"You passed out on us and have been asleep for more than 24 hours," he says, sitting beside my bed, taking the chair Jason had been occupying.

"What? Really?" I ask, shocked.

Jill steps up and says, "You had been through something extremely traumatic. You suffered a head injury, luckily not a severe one but you still received a nasty gash and a decent concussion. You've been unconscious for 36 hours. Your mind and body went into survival mode which included taking care of the other three people on the jet with you. Once the rescue team got to you, your body and mind relaxed, which caused your shock to hit you hard. You were sleep deprived, stressed, hungry, hurt, and cold... add shock to that and it's a recipe for disaster. Some people die from shock alone, Miss Rose, but if it hadn't been for you, those three would have died."

"They would have been okay," I say sheepishly.

"No, ma'am," Kallon's nurse says. "Mr. Keller here and Mr. Zeels would have bled to death from their head injuries and Mr. Zeels had some internal bleeding, as did Mr. Welch. They would have been dead well before the rescue team got there, if you hadn't done what you did. You couldn't see their internal injuries but how you took care of them, you saved their lives. By applying multiple bandages to their head wounds, you stopped them from bleeding out, you saved them."

"Don't head wounds bleed worse than anywhere else?" I ask. I can't imagine they wouldn't have stopped bleeding on their own.

"Yes, that's correct. Head wounds do bleed heavily but Mr. Keller and Mr. Zeels' head wounds were deep and wide. They needed pressure and something to stop the bleeding for it to actually stop," Jill says.

"You really did save our lives," Kallon says.

"You saved mine," I say back.

"Hardly," he says with a wave of his hand.

"You wrapped yourself around me when we were going down. I would have been hurt far worse than I was had you not done that, so because of you—" I pat his arm "—we're all alive."

He shakes his head.

"I knew you'd find a way to shrug off being called the hero," he laughs.

"I am not a hero," I say. To the change the subject, I ask, "How is Craig? How bad is he?"

"He's not great but he'll be okay," Jill says.

"And Brody?" I ask.

"I'm okay," Brody's voice says from my doorway. I look and see him standing with his arm in a sling and he's holding his IV pole with his other hand.

"Mr. Welch!" Jill exclaims. "What have we said about leaving your room without Niki with you?"

"Not to, but I wanted to check on Miss Rose," he says sheepishly. "I feel fine."

"We've been over that too," a nurse says from behind him, I assume it's Niki.

He ignores her and looks at me, "How are you, hon?"

"I'm good… I'll be okay," I amend. My head is starting to hurt really bad again.

"They told me what you did for us," he says. He nods to me and says, "Thank you!"

"Any of you would have done the same," I say.

"How are you, Abby?" he asks. "I'm glad your awake."

I look at Kallon and the nurses and say, "I'm okay. I'll be good to go soon."

"They told me what you did for us," he says again. He

also nods again and adds, "Thanks for that."

"Okay, Mr. Welch, why don't we go back to your room?" Niki suggests.

"Am I repeating myself again?" he asks, confused.

"You are, but that's okay, hon. Your brain just needs to rest so it can heal," Niki says, turning him gently towards the door.

"Explain to her what's wrong, won't you?" he asks her as they walk back through the door.

"Maybe Jill can, I'll take you back to your room," Niki says, nodding at Jill.

"I sure will, go get some rest, Mr. Welch," Jill says as Niki walks Brody down the hall.

"What was that about?" I ask.

"He's having some memory issues because he has a concussion, a pretty severe one. He didn't have a gash or cut to show he had a head wound, the injury went inward, which is far worse. The doctors are certain he'll fully recover but he needs to rest. He'll probably listen to Niki now that he has seen you're okay. He was pretty persistent on checking on you," Jill says. "Both of them were."

She eyes Kallon with a look.

"I'm not going to feel bad about wanting to check on her. You guys wouldn't tell me anything," he says a little angrily.

"Mr. Keller, we've told you we aren't allowed to, it's against the law," his nurse says.

"Mel is right," Jill says. *Bless her for finally saying her name.*

I wince a little as the pounding in my head starts to get

worse.

"You okay?" Kallon asks.

"My head is starting to hurt again," I say.

"I'll get your next dose of pain meds," Jill says.

"You're probably due for your next dose too," Mel says to Kallon.

Both nurses leave.

"So, how did we get from the plane back to New York?" I ask.

"We were loaded up into the side by sides and they drove us down to a road that had ambulances waiting for us. They air lifted Craig and Brody from a field about twenty miles away from where they loaded us into the ambulances. Once we got to the Denver hospital and we were stable, I requested we all get sent to Presbyterian. At first they argued but I told them I'd be covering the hospital bills and I wanted us all here. So, they got a medic plane to fly us from Colorado to here. I had them knock me out for the flight, I was a little... anxious," he admits, embarrassment showing on his face.

"I would have been too," I say, squeezing his hand.

"Abby," Kallon says my name in an unsure way. He looks from my hand up to my face. He takes a deep breath and asks, "Why was Jason here? I tried to tell the hospital staff he wasn't allowed near you, but they wouldn't listen. They said they'd put a call into the detective I told them to call but I don't know if they actually did."

"Apparently I still have him as one of my emergency contacts. When they couldn't reach my parents, they called him."

"And did I hear him say you're... you're going to marry

him?" he looks down at my hands but looks up quickly when he doesn't see a ring on my finger.

"No!" I exclaim. "Absolutely not! He brought in a ring and told me to marry him. I immediately told him no and asked him to leave. The nurses all but had to haul him out of here."

"I'll call Dax and Trevor and have them come to the hospital. I should have done that before," Kallon says, holding my hand gently but firmly.

"I don't think he'll come back," I say.

"We aren't going to underestimate him and what he'll do to get you," Kallon says.

Remembering that Jason had been drinking, I say, "Okay."

"Okay?" Kallon asks seeming to deflate. "I thought I was going to have to try harder to convince you."

"Jason's drinking again and he's unpredictable when he's under the influence."

"Alright," Kallon says as he picks up my hand and kisses it. "If I can borrow your room phone, I'll call Dax. They're both downstairs."

"You can use it," I say as I lean my head back and close my eyes. The pain in my head is getting so severe, I feel like I might puke.

Kallon lets go of my hand and I hear the legs of his chair scrape across the floor, the sound sending daggers into my head. His soft footsteps walk to the other side of the room and I hear him start to whisper after a few minutes. My ears start to ring so I can't hear what he's saying. Soon, his hand slides into mine. I open my eyes and see him sitting beside me again.

"Are you okay?" he asks with concern.

"My head just really, really hurts," I groan out. I close my eyes tightly and I feel tears stream down my face.

"Do you want me to go find Jill?"

"No, I'll be okay. I can wait for her to get back."

"Are you sure? If you're hurting—"

"I don't want you to leave me," I say as my voice breaks. I still can't fully believe that we made it out of that crash, not unscathed but alive.

"Okay," he says, squeezing my hand. "Okay, I'll stay here."

I must have fallen asleep because the next thing I know, I'm being gently shaken awake.

"Abby," Kallon's voice says softly.

I open my eyes and find him leaning in towards me.

"Mmm," I moan out.

"Jill is back with your medicine," he says. I look over his shoulder and see Jill standing by the door with a tray.

"I brought something for you to eat as well," she says as she walks into the room. "It's lunch time. We thought you two would like to eat together."

I see Mel walk in behind her.

"Sure," I say. My head feeling like it's about to burst in half. Food doesn't sound nearly as good as pain meds, but I know if I don't eat, they won't work as good and will upset my stomach even more than it already is feeling.

Jill sets my tray on the portable table and brings it over to me. I see some soup and my favorite hospital food, warm Jell-O. Mel puts Kallon's tray on another rolling table that I hadn't noticed just inside the door.

"You have a couple choices for pain meds," Jill says. "Mr. Keller said you prefer to not have hard pain killers, so I brought Tylenol and Ibuprofen if you would rather take them."

I smile at Kallon and then look at Jill, "I do prefer Tylenol and Ibuprofen over anything else, thank you."

She hands me one of the little plastic cups on the tray and I see pills inside of it. I pick up the cup of apple juice and take all four in one go. The juice taste really good so I finish it before I put the cup down.

"Thank you," I say again, as I reach for the Jell-O. "I think I'm hungrier than I thought but I feel nauseated from my head hurting."

"Sometimes when you haven't eaten a decent meal in a long time and have trauma, both physical and mental, feeling nauseated is common," Jill says as she checks my vitals quickly.

"Mr. Keller, here are your pain meds as well," Mel says, handing Kallon a similar plastic cup. He dumps them in his mouth and then takes a drink from his cup of water.

I see that Kallon's lunch consists of a sandwich, fruit, and a cookie. He's probably had a couple meals now and his body can handle something more than liquid. I learned from last year, they won't feed you anything of substance until your body has proven to keep liquids down.

"Push the button if you guys need anything else," Mel says as she walks to the door.

"Thanks," Kallon and I say at the same time. I look over at him and he winks at me.

"Don't forget to get some rest," Jill says as she walks to the door too.

"We will," I say, reaching for my bowl of chicken noodle

soup. I take a bite and the taste makes me sigh. "This is good."

"I thought so too when we got here," Kallon says as he takes a bite of his sandwich.

"Have they said how long we have to stay?"

"We can probably leave tomorrow. There's not a lot they can do for us and now that you've switched to over the counter meds, they don't need to keep you."

"Good, I'm ready to be home."

"Me too," Kallon says, reaching out and taking my hand. He puts his sandwich down and looks at me with a shadow of fear in his eyes. "When the plane was going down, I honestly thought we weren't going to make it home. When you passed out, I thought that I was losing you in the absolute final way. I've never been so scared."

"I know the feeling," I say as I put my bowl of soup down. "When I woke up and found you slumped over my lap and you weren't responding to me calling your name? And I rolled you so I could see your face and I saw how bloody you were and how it was gushing out of you? I thought I had lost you. Finding your pulse was such a relief, it about knocked the wind out of me."

"That must have been terrifying," Kallon says, reaching his hand out and grabbing mine, pulling it to his mouth and kissing it.

"It was but, I'm so thankful we're both… we're all okay," I say, taking a steading breath and willing myself not to cry. *I will not cry for what could have happened but will be happy for how it all turned out.*

There's a knock at the door and Mel comes in, she's got a smile on her face and looks at Kallon.

“Good news, Mr. Keller, the doctor has cleared you to leave. You’ve been discharged,” Mel says as she walks over to the bed. “We can take your IV out since it's just been to get you hydrated.”

"What about Abby?" Kallon asks.

"Seeing as she just woke up, she’ll have to stay today and get some tests done this afternoon,” she says. She looks at me and adds, “If all your tests come back good, you should be discharged tomorrow.”

Kallon looks at me and smiles a half smile and shrugs.

“I’m glad you get to get out of here,” I say. “You’ll get to go home and get some good rest.”

“I don’t have to leave do I?” Kallon asks Mel.

“You can stay until visiting hours are up, but you aren’t a patient here anymore,” she says with a smile.

“I’ll go change and then I’ll spend the rest of the day with you,” Kallon says as he stands.

I look at his tray and see he’s finished his lunch somehow. I look down at my bowl and find it half full. As I pick it up, I nod at Kallon, take a spoonful and eat it.

When Kallon gets to the door, he turns and smiles, “Dax and Trevor are here.”

Kallon nods at someone and then goes across the hall to his room where he shuts the door, probably to change out of his gown. A second later, Dax and Trevor walk through my door. They both look like they haven’t slept.

“Hi,” I say to them both.

“Hi to you,” Dax says. “You two scared the shit out of us.”

“Yeah,” Trevor says.

“Sorry,” I say with a smile.

Dax walks over, leans in and gives me a timid hug.

"It's so good to see you, girl," he says.

"It's good to see you too," I say laughing. I'm surprised at his gesture. I look at Trevor and say, "Both of you."

"So, I hear jackass Jason was here," Dax says going to stand back by Trevor.

"He was," I say, nodding and I'm rewarded with a dull throb.

"He won't bother you again," Dax says as he walks out the door. He's back to big brother Dax.

"No, he won't," Trevor says following Dax out. *Guess I've got two brother bodyguards now.*

They are strange men. So quick to change from friendly to businesslike. I guess with their profession, they have to be. I bet it's also hard for them to show any emotion. I hope Betty can show Dax that it's okay to let loose and show how he feels.

I finish eating before Kallon comes back in, so I lie my head back and close my eyes, deciding to take a nap now that my head isn't pounding. A good rest will make me feel so much better, I'm sure of it.

CHAPTER 27

When I was woken up a few hours ago, I found Kallon sitting in the chair beside me reading a book. I had been asleep for a couple hours when Jill had come in to wake me to take me down for a CT scan. They were concerned about me having such a severe headache.

After I got back from the scan, the doctor came in and did some vision and hearing tests, which I had passed. The only thing to do now was to wait for the results of the CT scan which the doctor said should be on his desk by morning.

A new nurse shift came on and Crystal was assigned to me, she seemed nice but couldn't stop fawning over Kallon. It didn't seem to bother him, so I tried to not let it bother me.

Kallon and I have just finished dinner. I was able to eat an actual meal, grilled chicken breast, roasted veggies, rice, and a slice of chocolate cake. It was the best meal I've ever had. I laughed at that thought because I knew deep down that wasn't the truth but after what I had eaten over the last couple of days, it was the best meal.

Now we're saying our goodbyes since visiting hours are over.

"I'll be back first thing in the morning," Kallon says. "Do you want me to swing by your place and get you some clothes to change into?"

"That would be great," I say. "Could you call my parents when you get your new phone and tell them not to worry about coming back. When I talked to them this morning on the hospital phone, they were trying to make plans to fly home tomorrow or as soon as possible. There's no reason for them to come home, I'm fine."

"I can try," Kallon says with a laugh. "Your mom sounded pretty set on coming back. Patty was also in favor of coming home too."

My parents had taken Patty to Hawaii as a Christmas present, they weren't do back until next week as they had left on Saturday. But our accident had apparently spurred them into wanting to come back.

I shake my head and say, "Have her call me again, maybe I can talk her into staying."

"Sorry, Mr. Keller," Crystal says from the doorway. "Visiting hours are now over. Can I walk you and your friends out?"

"Friends?" Kallon asks, turning towards her.

"These fine gentlemen out here," she says, pointing behind her back.

"Dax will be staying," Kallon says.

"Sorry, Mr. Keller but that's not possible," she says apologetically.

"He's Abby's bodyguard," Kallon says sternly.

"I assure you, Mr. Keller, Miss Rose is safe here," she says with a smile at me but beams at Kallon.

"I'll be fine," I say to Kallon. "Visiting hours are over."

Kallon looks at me and then at Crystal. He lets out a sigh when he realizes he can't pull any strings around here to get his way.

"Fine, but we're going to be here the moment visiting hours start in the morning," Kallon says.

"That's 7am, Mr. Keller," Crystal says helpfully.

"Thanks," he says tersely. "Can we have a minute?"

"Sure," she says sweetly and steps outside, shutting the door.

He leans in and gives me a kiss. I put my hand into his hair on the back of his head, avoiding his bandage that's covering his stitches. I hold him to me, deepening the kiss. My heart rate monitor goes haywire. He looks up at it and then at me, "Hmm, I kind of like hearing how I make you feel."

"You don't need a machine to tell you that," I say with a wink.

He smiles and says, "Get some rest. I'll be back in the morning."

"I will," I say as I watch him walk across the room and open the door.

"Dax, Trevor, you're with me. We'll be back in the morning," Kallon says.

"What?" I hear Dax say in confusion.

"Hospital policy," Kallon says.

I watch as Dax moves from the side of the door and looks in at me. He nods and then follows Kallon in the direction I guess is the elevators. I lean my head back and close my eyes. The sooner I fall asleep for the night, the sooner morning will come, and I can get out of here.

I'm just about to fall asleep when I hear Crystal's voice in the hallway.

"I'm sorry sir, but visiting hours are over. It's time for Miss Rose to get some much-needed rest."

"Can I have just ten minutes with her?" a voice says that makes me instantly on edge. *Jason.* He's using his most persuasive tone with her.

I hope she says no right away but his tone must have worked on her because she tells him, "Ten minutes and then you have to leave."

"That's all I need, thank you," he says sickeningly sweet.

He walks into the room with the swagger I know as his, 'I'm here to impress', walk. I try to look relaxed, but I am anything but that.

"Jason, I'm really tired and my head is starting to hurt really bad, can we not do this?"

"I just want to talk, please," he says. I see he's got a bouquet of roses in a vase in his hands. He holds them up and says, "I got you your favorite."

I sigh, and says, "Umm thanks. But Jason, you aren't listening to me."

He walks over to the counter and puts the flowers down. And then, he walks over and takes the seat next to my bed.

"I figured out one of the problems," Jason says as he sits. "I'm sorry I had a drink, it won't happen again. I went to an AA meeting and I'm planning to go twice a week until I get this completely under control."

"That's great Jason, but there's more than just that as a problem between us," I say. "You never listen when I talk."

"Sure, I do," he says. He reaches into his pocket and holds

something in his lap. He grabs my hand and slips the ring on my finger as he asks, "Abbigail Renee Rose, will you marry me?"

Stunned I stare at him.

"Babe?" he asks.

"Are you kidding me?"

"No, I want to spend the rest of my life with you," he says with a big smile like he's expecting a congratulations for finally figuring out that he wants me.

"This is what I'm talking about. You. Don't. Listen. To. Me," I say enunciating each word. "I'm happy that you're getting help for your addictions but not in the way you think I am. I don't wish you any ill will, but I am done with you. You took me for granted for too long, you cheated on me throughout our entire relationship, and you put me in this hospital last year. My middle name is Marie, not Renee. And my favorite flowers are sunflowers, not roses, which I've told you multiple times. We are not getting back together, ever."

"So, is that a no?" he asks looking confused.

"Yes, Jason, that's a no. A big fat no."

He stands and wipes his face off. He looks pissed but then he bends down faster than I can think and kisses me. I push him away and slap him.

"Stop it, Jason!"

"Take the night to think about it," he says as he saunters over to the door. "I'll be back in the morning, and you can tell me your real answer."

"No is my real answer," I snarl. I wipe my mouth. He tastes like whisky.

"Sleep well, baby," Jason says at the door. "Love you."

He walks away before I can tell him to stop staying that.

Crystal comes in the room a minute later and has a big smile on her face.

"Well, he seems nice," Crystal says sweetly. "It was nice of him to bring you your favorite flowers."

"They aren't my favorite," I state.

"Huh... I would have thought with your last name as Rose, they'd be your favorite," she says as she smells one of them.

"So does everyone else," I say with a roll of my eyes.

"Mr. Keller brought you sunflowers," she says, pointing to the vase full of my actual favorite flowers sitting close to the window.

"He's the only one who listens," I say giving her a genuine smile now.

"How nice," Crystal says. I can't tell if she's being snarky or sincere. She looks at my hand and her eyes go wide. I follow where she's looking and see the ring on my finger.

I quickly cover my hand and ask, "Is it okay if I go to sleep now?"

"Absolutely," she says beaming.

She leaves the room and I try to take the ring off, but it's stuck. I put my finger in my mouth and try harder to pull it off but all it does is make my finger turn red and swell up a little.

"Shit," I whisper to myself. I'll have to figure out how to get it off tomorrow. I'm too tired to deal with it now.

I roll onto my side, away from the injury on my head. After I calm down from this last interaction with Jason, I fall asleep.

Crystal only woke me up once throughout the night. She took my IV out and said that I had had enough IV antibiotics that I could take them orally, now that I was taking my pain meds orally as well. She also gave me another couple of pain meds to get me through the rest of the night.

I wake up to the sound of whispered voices. I peek out from one of my eyes and see Dax and Kallon standing against the wall, over by the window. I turn to my back, look at them, and smile.

"Morning," I say. I raise my hand and wave.

Kallon's smile falls from his face as he catches the glint off something on my hand. I look and I remember last night's conversation with Jason. Kallon's happy expression turns from happy to extremely angry to hurt in a second, and he turns to leave the room.

"Wait," I yell, sitting up in my bed and throwing my legs over the edge. I stumble as I try to catch him. He turns just in time to catch me.

"Fuck, Abby," he snarls. "Are you trying to hurt yourself more?"

"No," I say as I try to force the sob in my throat back down. "I'm trying to stop you from leaving so I can explain this shit."

I raise my left hand to show the ring.

"I don't need an explanation," he says.

"Yes, you do," I say. I hurry and tell him what happened last night. Just as I'm finishing, Crystal and Sue walk in, it must be shift change again.

"Oh, Mr. Keller, you proposed?" Jill asks excitedly.

"What?" Crystal asks with a laugh. "No, last night her boyfriend came in and proposed. It was so sweet. My heart about flew into the air when she said yes."

Kallon looks down at me and his nostrils flare.

"I didn't say yes," I say to him. I look at the nurses and say, "I didn't say yes."

Crystal looks confused and says, "I heard you say 'Yes, Jason'."

Kallon steps away from me.

"NO! No, I wasn't saying yes to him," I say, holding on to the front of his shirt to keep him from leaving. "I told him 'Yes, Jason, that's a no. A big fat no.' He wouldn't believe me that I was saying no. He said he'd be back this morning for my real answer, Kallon. You can ask him yourself."

"Jason, the one we put down to not be allowed in here?" Jill asks.

"I thought you had but he was here last night. Just after Kallon, Dax, and Trevor left," I say.

Kallon's eyes shoot to mine. He looks at Dax and then back down to me.

"Crystal, did you not look at the list of people to not allow in here?" Jill asks sternly.

"He didn't tell me his name," she answers timidly. "He was so sweet and nice."

"Come with me," Jill says as she grabs the other girl's elbow and pulls her from the room.

"Please, Kallon," I plead. "You can't honestly believe I'd lie to you about how I feel about him and how I feel about you.

I told him no. He wouldn't believe me."

Kallon steps away and leaves the room. I feel like I've been punched in the gut.

"Hang on, Miss Abby," Dax says but before he can take a step to follow Kallon, we hear shouting in the hall.

"What the fuck are you doing here?" I hear Jason yell.

"I can ask you the same question," Kallon yells back.

"I'm here to see my fiancé," Jason hells back.

"Dax," I say panic coating my tone. Dax nods and hurries from the room. I follow, but I'm so much slower. When I get to the hall, I see Kallon and Jason standing in front of the nurse's station. It's completely empty at the moment.

"From what I heard, you don't have a fiancé," Kallon snarls.

"She doesn't know what she wants," Jason screams.

"I think she does and it's not you," Kallon says with steely calm.

Jason steps up to Kallon and gets in his face, "You don't know what the FUCK you're talking about!"

"Stop it!" I shout as I shuffle down the hall. Having not walked in a couple days is proving to be making this difficult. "Jason, stop it!"

"Aww there she is," Jason says as he steps around Kallon but Dax steps in front of him, making him come to an abrupt halt. "Excuse me, I'd like to talk to my fiancé."

"I am not your fiancé!" I shout. "I told you that last night."

"Then why are you still wearing my ring?" he asks, gloating.

"Because I can't get the damn thing off," I say, half

crying. I try pulling it off again, but it feels like my finger will come off before this stupid thing. "It's too small and you forced it on my finger like you forced your kiss on me, too."

Kallon's eyes fly to mine, I might have left that detail out. He takes a few steps towards Jason but stops when he's about a foot away.

"Baby, you're hopped up on morphine, you don't know what you're saying," Jason says with a forced laugh.

"She doesn't take morphine, dumb ass," Kallon snarls behind him which makes Jason jump and step to the side, so Kallon isn't at his back.

"You know I only take over the counter pain meds," I say and then I think maybe he doesn't. "Don't you?"

"How would I know that?" he scoffs.

"Because you were with her for about nine years," Kallon says, his face turning red. I can see he's getting mad. I step between him and Jason.

"Jason you need to leave, and you need to leave me alone. We are through. I'll get the restraining order redone so it's more severe if I need to, but I need you to leave me alone," I say the last part slowly, so he understands me.

I go to walk away but Jason grabs my arm and swings me back to him.

"Fuck that," he snarls.

Before I can collide with Jason's chest, chaos ensues. Kallon pulls me quickly away and I don't think Jason was expecting it to happen because his grip on me slips away and I'm swung away from him and into Dax's arms. Kallon turns and punches Jason so hard that I hear cracks.

"Awww!" Jason bellows. "You broke my fucking nose!"

"Good thing you're in the hospital then!" Kallon roars. "Don't fucking touch Abby again!"

"I'm going to sue the shit out of you," Jason says and then he laughs like a lunatic. "You're so fucked!"

"You broke a restraining order three times, dick head, and you put your hands on Abby again," Kallon seethes "I'd say you're the one who's fucked."

Realization hits Jason and he looks at me with dread, "Abby, I... Please, I can't go back to jail."

"Not my problem," I say. I turn out of Dax's arms and start to walk back to my room. I can feel him behind me.

"Abby, please!" Jason shouts.

"What in all that is holey is going on out here?" I hear Jill say. "What has happened to your nose?"

I go into my room and hear Dax shut the door as I walk over to the bed. I sit down and put my head in my hands.

"Are you alright?" Dax asks.

I look up and I can feel my face looks completely devasted. I look down at my hand and see the ring on my finger.

I start to cry and say, "I just want this thing to come off."

Dax walks over to the sink and gets some soap on his hand. He walks over to me and puts his hand out, asking for mine. I put it in his big soapy hands, and he rubs the soap all over my ring finger.

"You know, Kallon believed you when you told him what happened," Dax says, talking to me as he works the soap onto my finger.

"Sure, it didn't look like it when he left the room," I say. Now that everything is calmed down, I can feel how hurt I am about that.

"Put yourself in his shoes," Dax says. "If you saw him in a similar situation after seeing the person you love wearing another person's symbol of affection on his finger or something like that, and then you were told how it was forced upon him once again, wouldn't you need a minute to calm down?"

"Wait," I say, putting my right hand up in a stop position. "He loves me?"

"Abby," Dax says exasperatedly as he massages the soap in some more. "Of course he does."

"He hasn't said it yet," I stammer out.

"Just because he hasn't said it, doesn't mean he doesn't feel it. Guys tend to show it before they say it, especially when they truly, wholeheartedly fall in love with someone," Dax says and then he slides the ring off my finger. He holds it up and turns my hand over, so it's palm up and puts it in my hand.

I walk over to the counter, put it down, and wash my hands. When I get back to my bed, there's a knock at the door. Dax looks at me and when I finally nod at him, he walks to the door and opens it. It's Kallon.

"Can I come in?" he asks.

I nod as I situate myself on my bed. I pull the covers up and hug them to me.

"Are you alright?" he asks, his voice heavy with emotion.

I nod again.

"Are you mad at me?" I just stare at him. *Am I?* I see he's holding ice to his hand. He asks, "Are you mad at me for punching him?"

That I know the answer too, "No, not for punching him. But for hurting yourself again, yes."

I reach my hand out, wanting him to come to me.

Dax clears his throat and says, "I'll be outside."

"Let me see your hand," I say when Kallon gets to the side of my bed. He sits by my leg and gives me his hand. I take the ice off and look at it. "Do they think it's broken?"

"No, just a little sore," he says. He smiles a cute half smile and says, "It's the first time I've ever thrown a punch over a girl."

I look up at him with raised eyebrows.

"I saw red when he put his hands on you," he says as an explanation. He raises his uninjured hand and runs his thumb against my cheek. "I didn't like it."

"I didn't either," I say in a quiet voice. The feel of Kallon's hand on me is the total opposite of how I felt when Jason touched me.

"I'm sorry for earlier," Kallon says as he cups my face and pulls it up so I'm looking into his eyes. "I also didn't like seeing another man's ring on your finger."

"I tried to get it off last—" I start to say but he puts a finger softly to my mouth to stop me.

"I know," he says. "It was just a shock to see it and then to hear how it all happened. Also, you left out the kissing part."

"It wasn't something I wanted to relive," I say.

"I understand that but if something happens, I need to know everything," he says, cupping my face again.

I hold his hurt hand in mine and look him in the eyes when I say sincerely, "Okay."

Our eyes lock for a minute and then we both look down

at each other lips. It's been too long since I've felt them on mine. He leans in slowly and I lean to meet him. The moment our lips touch, the familiar zap of electricity flares inside me.

He pulls back just enough that our lips are barely touching, and he says, "I love you, Abby. I've loved you for a while now, I'm sorry it's taken me so long to tell you."

My heart races and I can't help the tear the falls down my cheek.

"I love you too, Kal," I say softly.

I press my lips back into his and feel myself melt into him. He wraps his arms around me and pulls me close to him. In his arms, is where I will spend the rest of my days.

A special thank you to my Beta readers. I really appreciate all the time and support you all have given me through the process of writing "Rose's" and "Rose Bud's". It's been another long road, but with your encouragement and enthusiasm throughout it all, I was able to keep moving forward. Thank you, THANK YOU, THANK YOU for once again being in my corner and coming along this journey with me!

Logan Nedrow
Jane Wisdom
Stephanie Mays
Lacey Warner
Nina Stephens
Danielle Martin
Melissa Kendall

www.ingramcontent.com/pod-product-compliance
Lightning Source LLC
LaVergne TN
LVHW041055080826
845145LV00007B/1580

* 9 7 8 1 9 4 6 3 5 3 1 3 9 *